"The cube has sustained damage, Captain," Kim reported.

"Their shields are failing and I'm detecting overloads in several systems. The unregistered vessel's shields are at eighty percent of maximum."

Paris was torn between admiring B'Elanna's success and getting her the hell out of danger as soon as possible. The shuttle maneuvered easily around the larger ship, avoiding direct fire. Still, the situation could change in seconds.

"Open a channel," Paris ordered.

"Channel open," Lasren confirmed.

Before Eden could object, Tom said, "This is the Federation *Starship Voyager* to the pilot of the unregistered vessel. Do you require assistance?"

A garbled response came over the comm.

"Lasren, can you clean that up?" Paris demanded.

"Commander," Eden said angrily.

Paris turned directly to Eden and said softly, "Captain, my wife and my daughter are aboard that ship."

Eden's eyes widened in surprise but she replied just as softly, "Your recently deceased wife and daughter?"

"Yes, Captain," Tom confirmed.

"You're sure?"

"Yes."

STAR TREK VOYAGER®
UNWORTHY

KIRSTEN BEYER

Based on *Star Trek®*
created by Gene Roddenberry
and
Star Trek: Voyager
created by Rick Berman & Michael Piller & Jeri Taylor

POCKET BOOKS
New York London Toronto Sydney Boreth

Pocket Books
A Division of Simon & Schuster, Inc.
1230 Avenue of the Americas
New York, NY 10020

This book is a work of fiction. Names, characters, places, and incidents either are products of the author's imagination or are used fictitiously. Any resemblance to actual events or locales or persons, living or dead, is entirely coincidental.

This book is published by Pocket Books, a division of Simon & Schuster, Inc., under exclusive license from CBS Studios Inc.

First Pocket Books paperback edition October 2009

POCKET and colophon are registered trademarks of Simon & Schuster, Inc.

For information about special discounts for bulk purchases, please contact Simon & Schuster Special Sales at 1-866-506-1949 or business@simonandschuster.com.

The Simon & Schuster Speakers Bureau can bring authors to your live event. For more information or to book an event, contact the Simon & Schuster Speakers Bureau at 1-866-248-3049 or visit our website at www.simonspeakers.com.

Cover art by Michael Stetson; cover design by Alan Dingman

Manufactured in the United States of America

10   9   8   7   6   5   4   3   2   1

ISBN 978-1-4391-0398-2
ISBN 978-1-4391-2348-5 (ebook)

For Marco Palmieri

"Perfection is terrible, it cannot have children."

—Sylvia Plath,
"The Munich Mannequins"

CHAPTER ONE

Warning. Quantum phase stability at ninety-six point seven five one percent and falling."

"*P'tak!*" Miral said gleefully from the seat designated for a navigator that B'Elanna Torres had modified with a special booster attachment to secure her three-and-a-half-year-old daughter during flight.

"Computer," B'Elanna said as her patience wore dangerously thin, "recalculate phase variance and adjust deflector control." Turning to Miral she added, "We don't use that word, honey."

"*Calculation complete. Modifying deflector telemetry,*" the computer advised.

"Computer, calculate revised phase stability."

"*P'tak!*" Miral said again, a little more ferociously.

"*Phase stability at ninety-nine point nine two five percent.*"

"Thank you," B'Elanna replied. Once upon a time she never would have addressed any ship's computer so politely, but since the computer was one of only a few adult voices B'Elanna heard regularly throughout the past fourteen months, she had come to think of her shuttle's computer as a friend and an ally.

B'Elanna swiveled her chair to face Miral and said with

less congeniality, "Miral Paris, when I tell you that we don't use certain words, what does that mean?"

Miral drooped her head a little and focused her attention on what remained of her cranberry snack bar. It was possible that some of her afternoon treat had made it into her stomach, though judging from the large chunks of pressed grains, nuts, and berries that clung precariously to her sticky cheeks and fingers and dotted her overalls, she had spent most of the last hour playing with her food rather than eating it.

"Dunno," Miral said, pouting.

"Look at me," B'Elanna commanded. All the years she had spent in charge of *Voyager*'s engine room had prepared her to face critical systems failures, devastating encounters with hostile alien species, and spatial anomalies, but throughout it all she never had to use the tone she found herself using most often with Miral. Then again, her subordinates in engineering had rarely, if ever, lied to her face.

"Miral Paris, look at me," she said again.

Miral gave her a cursory glance before filling her mouth with all that she could of the remaining snack bar.

"Miral," B'Elanna snapped.

She finally got the child's attention. Tom's blue eyes, wide as saucers and pleading for mercy, met B'Elanna's. Just below them, Miral's full cheeks ballooned to almost their maximum as her baby teeth furiously chewed and strained against her tightly closed lips.

B'Elanna struggled not to smile. She had spent weeks teaching Miral table manners and apparently the only part that had really stuck was the importance of chewing with one's mouth closed.

It's a start, B'Elanna acknowledged to herself even as she fortified her determination to curb Miral's penchant to repeat words B'Elanna often uttered in frustration despite the fact that they were completely inappropriate for a child. She suspected that Miral only did it to elicit a response from her. However, it would never do for her to greet her father in a little more than two weeks, after not having seen him in more than a year, by saying, "Hello, *p'tak*!"

B'Elanna insisted a little more gently, "You do know."

"Are we there yet?" Miral asked, spilling a few crumbs down her front.

"Don't change the subject," B'Elanna said, seeing right through her daughter's pitiful attempt at a diversion. "There are certain words that children should not use, even if adults may use them sometimes. You still have many words to learn, and when you have learned them all, you will get to choose which ones you want to use. Until then, I choose for you. Is that clear?"

"Sorry," Miral said, sighing, clearly terribly put-upon by this regulation.

"I love you, honey."

"Love you, Mommy," Miral tossed back more out of habit than genuine emotion. "Mommy, sing the good night stars song?"

"Don't you want to wait until bedtime?" B'Elanna asked.

"No, you sing. Kula sings bad."

Kula was a holographic nanny B'Elanna created to tend to Miral during their long journey when the shuttle's systems required B'Elanna's complete attention. Miral's criticism suggested that Kula's vocal subroutines might need a little work.

"Okay, honey, you start." B'Elanna nodded.

Star, star, bright in the sky,
The time has come to close your eyes.

B'Elanna felt as if her heart were melting; the little girl's charm kicked into high gear and her voice was thick with happiness.

Star, star, never you fear,
I'll wake tomorrow and you'll be here.

"*Warning,*" the computer's voice interrupted.

Star, star . . .

"Hush, honey," B'Elanna said quickly.

"*Quantum phase stability at ninety-five point nine six nine percent and falling.*"

An unpleasant jolt of adrenaline shot through B'Elanna. This was the last leg of a journey that had begun two and a half years ago. A renegade Klingon sect that believed Miral to be the *Kuvah'magh,* or Klingon savior, had decided the best way to avert the apocalypse Miral's birth signaled was to kill her. Ever since, B'Elanna and her husband, Tom, had sacrificed their own happiness protecting their only daughter; they were to reunite once and for all in just a little more than two weeks.

More surprising was the fact that this long-awaited event would be taking place in the Delta quadrant. B'Elanna assumed she'd seen the last of it long ago when after seven long years of being stranded there *Voyager*'s crew had managed to return home. But just a few days earlier, B'Elanna had received the rendezvous coordinates from Tom confirming that Starfleet was once again sending *Voyager* into the Delta quadrant. Tom was serving as the ship's first officer.

In truth, B'Elanna didn't relish spending the rest of their

lives in one of the worst areas of space she'd ever known. However, her well-founded fears were quelled when she realized the Delta quadrant was as far from the Warriors of Gre'thor—the renegade Klingon sect—as it was possible to get.

B'Elanna was worried that the quantum slipstream drive might need some coaxing to take them the forty-five thousand light-years they needed to go. The *Home Free,* as she had privately christened the shuttle officially known as *Unregistered Vessel 47658* that had been her and Miral's home for more than a year, was a technological marvel. In addition to the slipstream drive, it boasted a prototype benamite recrystallization matrix, a communications array that put larger ships to shame, navigation and scanning systems that were boosted beyond normal capacities by Borg-inspired designs, and the smallest possible holodeck for Miral.

Her previous uses of the slipstream drive had been limited to a few short hops where slipstream velocity had never been maintained for more than thirty seconds. The trip to the Delta quadrant was going to take a little over two hours. In the nod to her belief that the worst-case scenario was often the most likely, B'Elanna had set her course and engaged the new drive in plenty of time for her to make numerous stops along the way.

During the last two hours, she had been forced to contend with updates indicating that the phase integrity of the slipstream corridor was falling. These announcements had come so regularly—every fifteen minutes or so—that B'Elanna had grown accustomed to them. But it had only been minutes since the last warning, which likely meant something was seriously wrong.

"Kula," B'Elanna called, instantaneously activating the

holographic nanny, a grizzled old Klingon warrior based on a dear and now departed friend. When the hologram appeared, B'Elanna nodded to Miral, then headed down a short flight of stairs in the main cabin to the shuttle's engine compartment.

What she found was that the deflector controls—a key component of the slipstream drive—were beyond maximum tolerance levels.

"Son of a—" she began before biting back the end of that statement. Miral didn't need to learn any other new words today.

B'Elanna manually reconfigured the settings as patiently as possible, even as the phase integrity had slipped inexorably below ninety percent. At around eighty-five percent, give or take point two percent, the slipstream corridor would destabilize completely and more than likely the shuttle would be torn to shreds when it emerged.

"Computer, what's our time until we reach the terminal coordinates?"

"*Twenty-five seconds,*" the computer replied dispassionately.

These were going to be the longest twenty-five seconds of her life.

"*Warning,*" the computer advised again.

"Mute all audible warnings," B'Elanna ordered. From her main engineering control panel she could see everything she needed without the computer adding to her elevating anxiety.

She recalculated the phase variance of the corridor using a program she had designed that featured a number of Borg algorithms inspired by Seven of Nine. Compensating for these variances had been the unattainable goal which had forced *Voyager* to abandon slipstream technology. As her shuttle was smaller and infinitely easier to stabilize, thus far her program had worked. But now it seemed to be at its limits.

Ten more seconds and the slipstream drive would automatically power down.

Just hold it together, B'Elanna prayed as she watched the phase integrity reading creep down to eighty-seven percent.

She held her breath as the drive's high-pitched whine shifted downward—then every system on her board spiked into the red as the corridor dispersed, depositing the shuttle at the right coordinates. A series of concussive blasts echoed all around B'Elanna as several critical systems overloaded simultaneously. Out of the corner of her eye she noted a power-rerouting protocol initiated by Kula, undoubtedly to activate a protective forcefield around Miral.

B'Elanna was left with several fried panels, exploded plasma conduits still sparking in protest, and a bitter, tinny odor filling her nostrils. She could have replicated some of what she needed but the replicator was fried. She was forced to confront what had always been her worst nightmare when she had been planning this trip. The repairs were going to take days, and they could only be accomplished at a well-stocked spaceport.

The *Home Free* would hang dead in space until Tom arrived. But *Voyager* might be detained, and rations and water were low.

What I need is a friend, B'Elanna thought morosely. The direness of her predicament threatened to overwhelm her, until she remembered that she actually had a friend not that far from her current location.

I wonder if he's missed me as much as I've missed him,

B'Elanna mused as she quickly set to work on her communications array.

"Seven? Seven, where are you?"

Chakotay's heart still pounded from having forced open the door to Seven's San Francisco town house after she failed to answer his repeated knocks. As he completed a frantic search of the first floor, he tried to imagine what could have gone wrong in the six hours since he'd last seen her.

Much of the previous evening had been devoted to a lengthy visit at the hospice where Seven's beloved Aunt Irene had been placed. Though Seven had fought against this step, Chakotay had finally managed to help her accept that this was both necessary and in Irene's best interests. Seven had been Irene's primary caregiver throughout the past eighteen months as Irumodic syndrome had begun to ravage Irene's mind. However, Seven was no longer in any condition to continue providing constant care for her aunt. Further, the doctors had assured them that Irene's suffering would likely end in a matter of days.

When Seven and Chakotay had parted after the visit, she had insisted she was weary enough to sleep, and he had taken her at her word. Still, he found it hard to believe that she had fallen into so deep a sleep that she would not have heard him pounding on her front door. Panic quickened his breath and his pace as he rushed up the stairs to the second level and continued his search, all the while calling out, "Seven? Seven, where are you?"

Chakotay finally found her seated in a darkened corner of her bedroom. Her hands were clasped tightly around her knees, and her deep blue eyes were wide but vacant.

"Seven!" he said in alarm.

She remained perfectly still, though she blinked lazily in what he hoped might be some kind of response.

Chakotay quickly pulled back the nearest curtain to better evaluate her condition. Her pale skin was a shade lighter than usual, and her forehead, cheeks, and hands were clammy to the touch. Her long, strawberry-blonde hair had been piled loosely atop her head, and several unruly strands were plastered to the back of her neck. She wore a pair of dark black pants and a fitted red tank top. The jacket lying rumpled at the foot of her bed would have completed the casual ensemble. Chakotay didn't begin to relax until he confirmed that her respiration and pulse were slow but strong and steady.

He had feared something like this might happen. Seven had endured so much in the past few months. It would have broken most people long before now. Lifting her gently, he placed Seven in bed and began to survey the room, to see if he could figure out what might have forced her to retreat into her mind.

Seven had begun her life as Annika Hansen, a human girl who had been assimilated by the Borg when she was eight. Years later, she had been assigned by the Borg to interface with their new "allies" aboard *Voyager*. Ultimately, the alliance had served its purpose but to secure their safety, Chakotay and Captain Kathryn Janeway decided to sever Seven from the rest of the Collective. At first, Seven resentfully resisted their decision, but over time she began to appreciate the individuality the Borg had stolen from her and she became a valued member of *Voyager*'s crew.

The ship had managed to complete what should have been a much longer journey from the Delta quadrant to the

Alpha quadrant. Upon her return to Earth, Seven was initially considered a curiosity by all but her aunt, who had welcomed her home with open arms, despite having given up her niece for dead. Ultimately Starfleet had begun to appreciate Seven's brilliance and over the past few years had often called upon her to lend her expertise and to teach at the Academy. Her input had never been more valued than a few months earlier when the Borg had launched an invasion of the Alpha quadrant, intent on destroying the Federation. Seven had stood at the Federation president's side, advising her throughout the conflict. The Caeliar, a powerful and xenophobic species—heretofore unknown to the Federation—had transformed the Borg from members of the Collective to members of the Caeliar gestalt, ending the hostilities.

The transformation had liberated billions of Borg, and had rid Seven of her Borg nature—synthetic implants that regulated many of her critical biological systems. Physically she was still as strong as ever. However, mentally she was now torn between her own thoughts and a voice that constantly repeated, "You are Annika Hansen."

Seven had struggled valiantly against this voice for months, but her control had begun slipping recently as a series of traumatic occurrences overwhelmed her: her aunt's ever-worsening condition and the deaths of her former crewmate and dear friend B'Elanna and her little daughter, Miral Paris. Seven had not questioned her ability to keep the voice in check until she realized that she would be forced to do it alone; all her other friends departed aboard *Voyager* on a dangerous new mission to the Delta quadrant.

When Chakotay learned that Seven was struggling alone, he realized he had to help her through it. They formulated a plan and were now only days away from leaving Earth to begin their new journey.

Clearly in the last few hours something had pushed Seven beyond her formidable endurance.

There was an untouched glass of nutrients by Seven's computer interface, but otherwise the desk's surface was clear. *What the hell happened?* Chakotay thought as he teetered frantically toward panic. Shifting his attention to Seven's computer, he noted that her message center was active on the display and the most recently completed transmission had come from the hospice center. With trembling hands, he activated the playback and one of Irene's nurses appeared on the screen.

"I'm so sorry to tell you this, Professor Hansen, but Irene has passed away. I was certain you would want to know immediately. We will keep her remains in stasis. We know how important it is for you to say good-bye."

Despair and anger welled in Chakotay's heart. He had been fond of Irene and comforted by the eagerness with which she had accepted Seven into her life. She was a bright and compassionate woman, and Seven had bonded with her quickly. Irene was the first real family Seven had ever known. Irene's illness had contributed to Seven's current state and the nurse who had contacted her with the sad news couldn't have known the damage she had done. Still, Chakotay felt the irrational urge to wring the nurse's neck.

He perched on the edge of Seven's bed, taking her clammy hands in his.

"Seven, you have to listen to me. I know this is difficult, but we both knew this day was coming. Irene wouldn't want to see you like this. She loved you and only wanted the best for you. You brought great happiness to her life when you came back and the way you have cared for her during the last few years of her life has been her greatest comfort. Come with me now so we can say good-bye. We'll stay as long as you like. But you have to snap out of this. Seven? Seven, can you hear me?"

The long silence convinced him that Seven was lost. He hurried to the computer and dispatched two urgent messages.

Now, all he could do was wait.

You are Annika.

Seven stood in the open plaza of a magnificent city. Wide moving walkways transected the white marble ground at regular intervals and on several levels. The massive courtyard was surrounded by tall steel-and-glass edifices, and the sky had a faint amber glow. There was a long reflecting pool shallowly filled with dark water directly before her. There were strange statues and well-trimmed trees manicured in absurd shapes scattered about. The city appeared to be completely deserted, and the eerie silence suggested the city was not the bustling metropolis the structures suggested it was.

She approached the pool and examined her reflection.

You are Annika, the voice said again.

Seven refused to be baited into another argument with the intruder in her mind. Surely by now it knew where she stood on the issue.

You are Annika.

"I am Seven of Nine," she murmured automatically.

Suddenly, the water began to tremble. Seven backed away cautiously as a small figure emerged. She was both familiar and completely alien.

A young girl with long strawberry-blonde hair stood on the water. Her face was unmistakably human, but her arms reached almost to her knees, and her wide, large feet each had only two toes and a claw-shaped appendage. She was swathed in diaphanous lavender fabric that reached her ankles.

"Why do you resist?" the girl asked.

"Who are you?" Seven demanded, terrified that she already knew the answer.

"I am Annika/*You are Annika,*" the girl and the voice replied simultaneously.

"I am Seven of Nine," Seven shouted back defiantly.

A sad but wicked smile spread across the girl's face.

"Not anymore," she assured Seven.

Seven suddenly found herself immobilized. Her skin began itching and tightening and felt as if it were solidifying. A gasp caught in her throat, stopping the scream that rose from the core of her being.

Annika began to giggle.

Help me, Seven thought in terror.

But even if her plea had been audible, there was no one left to hear it.

A light knock sent Chakotay hurrying from Seven's side and down the stairs. He opened the front door to find a calm and very self-assured young cadet standing before him.

"Icheb." Chakotay smiled in relief before gathering him into a friendly embrace. "Thanks for coming so promptly."

Icheb returned his affection a little formally before pulling away to ask, "Where is Seven?"

"Upstairs," Chakotay replied evenly.

Worry darted across the young man's face. "Something's wrong, isn't it?"

Chakotay raised a hand to forestall further questions.

"Why don't you have a seat, and I'll explain."

Icheb's chin lifted and his head tilted slightly to the right, as if he were processing a request he found disturbing. It reminded Chakotay of the days when he, like Seven, had been more Borg than not.

Finally Icheb made his way into the living room and perched himself on the end of the sofa, his hands folded compliantly in his lap.

"Before I go any further, Icheb, I need to ask you something," Chakotay began hesitantly.

He nodded slightly for Chakotay to continue.

"How have you been feeling these last few months?"

"Very well, thank you," Icheb replied automatically.

"Are you sure?" Chakotay asked.

"Quite."

As the young man looked healthy enough, Chakotay wasn't inclined to push the point further, though it was still difficult to understand, given Seven's state.

Chakotay swallowed hard before continuing. A deeply ingrained sense of duty made it difficult for him to risk compromising the trust Starfleet had once placed in him, as well as Icheb's future with the organization he had wholeheartedly embraced. Unfortunately, Seven's life might now well depend upon it.

"As I am sure you are aware, several months ago, the Borg invaded Federation space and were only defeated by a race of aliens called the Caeliar."

"I have heard the name, Captain," Icheb replied, "though I have no knowledge of their activities during that battle.

Cadets are under strict orders to not pursue any inquiries regarding the Caeliar at this time, though many of us, as you may imagine, are understandably curious."

"Of course you are," Chakotay said. "And as of now, it's just 'Chakotay.' I resigned my commission a few days ago."

"Why?" Icheb asked defensively, as if he had taken Chakotay's action personally.

"I can't serve Starfleet and help Seven at the same time, and right now, she needs me more than Starfleet does," Chakotay replied.

Icheb drew a breath to ask another question, but Chakotay continued.

"What I'm about to tell you is sensitive information and I am trusting you to keep this between us."

Icheb's cheeks reddened as the implications of this request sank in, but he finally nodded his assent. He had only learned to love and admire Starfleet from the crew of *Voyager,* who had rescued him from the Borg. However, there was no question where his greatest loyalty would always lie.

"We don't know much about the Caeliar," Chakotay said. "But we do know that they didn't so much defeat the Borg as assimilate them."

Color quickly drained from Icheb's face. *Assimilated* was not a word one could just toss around among former Borg.

Chakotay continued. "It is my understanding from Seven that the Borg were actually spawned thousands of years ago by the Caeliar, quite unintentionally. What the Caeliar did at the height of the invasion was to bring those lost souls back into their gestalt. The Borg were transformed into Caeliar and to hear Seven describe this transformation, it was a frightening but ultimately wonderful thing."

Icheb rose in alarm.

"But I've spoken with Seven several times since then. Was she . . . ?" he began.

"No," Chakotay assured him without letting him finish the obvious question. "Seven was transformed. Her Borg implants dissolved. And though she was momentarily able to experience the Caeliar gestalt, she was ultimately severed from the connection. As best we can tell, she is now fully human."

"How is that possible?" Icheb demanded. "Seven could not survive without her implants or the regeneration process. They could not just disappear. Something must have replaced them."

"That's my belief as well," Chakotay said, nodding. "The Caeliar are composed of catoms—engineered particles that can be programmed to take on any form. I believe her implants were replaced by catoms."

"Is that a good thing?" Icheb asked warily.

"Physically, she's fine. Starfleet Medical, and the Doctor, have confirmed it. But ever since the transformation, Seven has been hearing a voice in her head that insists Seven is Annika Hansen."

"But she *is* Annika Hansen," Icheb said, "though I know she does not prefer that designation."

"Annika was assimilated at the age of eight. Seven's memories of that child are few and far between, and many of them are painful. She has always thought of herself as Seven of Nine. She grew and matured as a Borg and is now reluctant to heed the will of the voice which seems to insist she must abandon all that she became as a Borg. Initially, she attempted to adapt, hoping the voice would subside. But over the last few weeks, Seven has experienced a succession of traumatic events: the hospitalization of her aunt, the loss of

B'Elanna and Miral, and the departure of most of her former crewmates aboard the *Voyager* fleet. Since then, Seven has found it more difficult to deal with the voice."

"Seven is losing her battle, isn't she?" Icheb asked.

"I'm afraid so," Chakotay replied. "But I think that together, we can help her."

"How?"

"Before we get into how, I need to know something," Chakotay insisted. "You, too, were once Borg. Did you sense anything at all like what Seven has described?"

"No," Icheb said without hesitation. "But you must remember that shortly after *Voyager* returned to Earth, I was imprisoned, along with Seven and the Doctor, and for several days was denied the ability to regenerate. My Brunali physiology completely reasserted itself during that time and I lost the use of and need for my few remaining implants. They have since been removed from my body."

"Good," Chakotay said, relieved.

"But how . . . ?" Icheb began and was quickly silenced by another knock at the door.

"Hang on," Chakotay instructed before moving briskly to answer it.

As expected, another old friend, Sveta, stood before him, her strong features coldly calculating and her mane of fine white hair pulled into a neat braid that ran down the center of her back almost to her waist. Though she had been responsible for bringing Chakotay into the Maquis more than ten years earlier, she didn't appear to have aged a day since then.

"Thank you for coming," Chakotay said sincerely.

"You said it was urgent," she replied warily.

"It is," he insisted. "Please, come in."

Sveta cast a penetrating glance directly into his eyes. He understood her concern. The last time she'd seen him he'd been mired in his own dark struggle, and she had rebuked him harshly for wallowing in his despair. They had not parted on good terms, but now was not the time to try to mend fences.

Fortunately, Sveta seemed to immediately sense both his urgency and his command of himself and the present situation. "It's good to have you back." She smiled as she crossed the threshold.

"It's good to be back," he agreed.

CHAPTER TWO

The Doctor would never be able to have a biological offspring. He was a hologram, so procreating was an impossibility. Still, he believed the sense of deep pride he experienced while sitting aboard the *U.S.S. Galen*—an experimental medical vessel he and his creator, Doctor Lewis Zimmerman, had designed, with considerable help from their longtime associate, Lieutenant Reginald Barclay— might be like the pride a new parent would feel.

The first sickbay he had ever known—on *Voyager*—had been efficient in its specifications, if a little too utilitarian. Though no one would necessarily enter *Galen*'s evaluation suite and applaud the décor, the Doctor believed that the softer browns and subtle greens of the color scheme made the space welcoming. More important than these superficial changes were the design features he had insisted upon, which made the entire suite more pleasant and useful for both physician and patient.

His private office was situated near the entrance so he could see when anyone entered, even if the computer was not programmed to alert him about new arrivals. The sickbay consisted of three emergency biobeds and a series of private exam rooms, innovations he knew his patients would appreciate. Separate surgical, intensive care, and recovery wards were adjacent to the main sickbay. Two larger wards one deck below could be activated in the event of a fleet-wide catastrophe. The Doctor hoped against hope never to see those wards used, though his many years in Starfleet had convinced him that such hopes might be unrealistically optimistic.

The *Galen*'s primary function was to provide medical support to the Federation fleet that would depart for the Delta quadrant as soon as its diagnostics were complete. As such, the vast majority of the medical vessel's space was the Doctor's domain. However, unlike other medical starships, the vessel was meant to be staffed almost entirely by holographic personnel in times of emergency. Therefore, holographic emitters had been installed throughout the ship. Unlike a holodeck, they did not alter the space into whatever an individual might desire; they activated emergency medical, engineering, or security holograms as required.

While the Doctor had focused his attention on creating the perfect medical facility, Zimmerman and Barclay had focused on the hologram designs. Thus far, those with whom the Doctor had interacted—primarily doctors and nurses—all appeared to be meeting or exceeding expectations. He doubted if anyone required to use *Galen*'s facilities would question who the real staff were versus who the holographic staff might be. The Doctor fervently hoped that one day, such distinctions would be meaningless.

His office chronometer beeped, alerting him that he was due on the bridge. Reg had a request for *Galen*'s commanding officer, and he didn't like facing her alone.

Of course, this had nothing to do with the officer herself. Clarissa Glenn was an intelligent, articulate, and eminently professional officer. She had also completed her medical training and Starfleet's rigorous command track—a rare accomplishment. Though Glenn held the rank of commander, as the ship's lead officer she enjoyed the title of captain. Thus far, the Doctor had been impressed by Glenn and the other organics assigned to the *Galen*. All seemed to respect the significance of the vessel's undertaking and certainly treated him with the deference and respect due any senior Starfleet officer.

But Barclay had been tongue tied in Glenn's presence from the moment they were introduced. The Doctor didn't have to guess why. The captain was young and quite attractive. She was a few inches taller than the Doctor and kept herself in excellent physical condition. Her hair was long and reddish-blonde; she usually kept it neatly braided when on-duty. Her eyes were an unusual shade of light green. In short, Glenn was everything Reg could have wanted in a woman, even without considering her other formidable accomplishments, and this tended to make Reg a nervous wreck.

The Doctor hurried down the short hallway toward the turbolift, which took him up two decks to the bridge. He wondered if Reg would ever grasp the fact that he was a fascinating man, and should feel more than comfortable interacting with Glenn.

Probably not, the Doctor thought, then was cheered by the prospect of beginning a new and challenging project.

Commander Clarissa Glenn sat in the center seat of the *Galen*, a calm expression on her face. Prior to reporting for duty that morning, she had spent an hour in her quarters practicing *dashtenga* yoga, a hybrid that combined ancient *hatha* poses with more rigorous Vulcan breathing and meditation techniques she'd learned years ago during her medical residency on the Tendara Colony. Strengthening her body and clearing her mind were as essential to her as eating and sleeping. Her command duties often made it challenging for her to maintain those rituals. However, the commander understood the benefits far too well, and always made time.

The *Galen*'s bridge might seem small by some standards, but Glenn decided that the three rear stations arranged behind her single seat—tactical, ops, and science—and the single-man flight control panel in front of her created a cozy, minimalist space from which to direct the ship's operations.

Fresh-faced, recent Academy graduate Ensign Ben Lawry sat at the conn looking anxious. She couldn't blame him. Starfleet had just invested countless hours and valuable resources equipping nine vessels, including *Galen,* to travel to the Delta quadrant. Quantum slipstream drives were a relatively new propulsion system, and the critical phase variance calculations required to sustain a slipstream corridor—though calculated by the main computer—were executed by the flight controller. Even the slightest error could produce disastrous results. It was a challenge for a single vessel. Within a few minutes, Lawry and eight fellow helmsmen would be expected to coordinate their efforts so the entire fleet could journey together through a single corridor. Such a task would have unnerved even an experienced pilot with the sternest constitution. Lawry's taut mien suggested he'd forgone both a good night's sleep and breakfast before reporting for this morning's monumental challenge.

The young man's nervousness reminded Glenn of her days as a resident, when she'd had the overwhelming sense that she was an imposter who had been assigned a task for which she was not prepared and who would therefore be exposed at any moment.

Glenn rose and went over to him. "Ensign Lawry," she said, careful to keep her voice low.

"Yes, sir?" Lawry replied. His spine stiffened and his shoulders tensed.

"Do me a favor?" Glenn asked.

He was surprised to hear what sounded like a personal request from his commanding officer. He swiveled his chair to face her and replied, "If I can, sir."

"Breathe," Glenn said intently.

It sounded like an order, so he complied. His attempt was shallower than Glenn would have wished, but it did manage to relax his shoulders a little.

"Is there anything else, sir?" he asked, clearly wondering if he was missing something.

"Again," Glenn commanded, "a little deeper."

Lawry breathed deeply and his face finally lost the aspect of a trapped animal.

"What's our status?" Glenn asked.

"We're awaiting clearance from *Voyager* to begin the first test run, sir."

"Then let us await what will surely come without fear of unforeseen consequences," Glenn said, repeating a personal mantra that often sustained her when she faced daunting situations.

"Yes, sir." Lawry nodded with clear and firmly set eyes as he turned back to his post.

Glenn heard the faint swish of the bridge doors opening but refrained from directing her attention there. It was difficult at times to remember that one could choose which stimuli to respond to and which to ignore, but she approached her command decisions the same way she had been trained to approach her medical ones. Awareness of potential distractions was helpful until it limited your ability to focus on the task at hand. Right now, her task was to make sure all the officers on alpha shift were performing their assigned duties efficiently and with composure. If her attention was required elsewhere, she'd wait until someone requested it.

"Good morning, Captain," the smooth and confident voice of her chief medical officer said congenially.

"Good morning," Glenn replied, turning to address the Doctor. Standing a pace behind him was her engineering and holographic specialist, Lieutenant Reginald Barclay. "To you both," she added quickly.

"Lieutenant Barclay has a request he would like to make, Captain," the Doctor said.

She hadn't known the Doctor or Lieutenant Barclay for very long. Her first impression of the Doctor had been positive. She found it refreshing that his creator had selected to use his own image as a framework for the hologram rather than some idealized physical template. Thus, the incredibly advanced hologram, who contained within his program the medical knowledge of thousands of individual physicians, stood before her in the guise of a medium-height, balding, middle-age human male. The Doctor was a highly skilled physician and his obvious enthusiasm for his current assignment was contagious. Glenn looked forward to having him on board for their upcoming mission, given his previous experience in the Delta quadrant.

Lieutenant Barclay was a little harder to wrap one's mind around. His record was a testament to years of solid service. He had distinguished himself repeatedly aboard *Enterprise*, and he had gone on to do seminal work at Project Pathfinder with the eminent holographic designer Lewis Zimmerman. But Barclay's timid nature belied his accomplishments. Glenn wanted to sit Barclay down and gently assure him that there was less to fear in the universe than he clearly believed there to be. The lieutenant was definitely the oddest confluence of character traits she had ever encountered in a fellow officer.

"And is there some reason the lieutenant isn't making that request himself?" Glenn asked.

She regretted her words as soon as they left her lips. Lieutenant Barclay responded by studiously examining the base of her chair.

"Lieutenant Barclay is more than capable of making the request himself, Captain," the Doctor replied in a way that suggested he hoped rather than believed this to be true. "However, I wanted you to be aware that he has my full support in his request."

"Thank you, Doctor," Glenn replied. "You may consider me so apprised. Lieutenant?"

"Yes, sir, ma'am, I'm sorry, Commander . . . er, Captain," Barclay stammered.

"'Sir' is fine," Glenn said encouragingly.

Barclay took a deep and restorative breath before continuing: "It occurred to me that this test run presents us with an excellent opportunity to evaluate multiple systems with which I'm sure we will all wish to become more comfortable throughout the course of our journey."

Glenn tried to guess what he was getting at but found herself at a loss.

"Such as?" she asked.

"The ESHs," Barclay said with a little more confidence.

"The Emergency Security Holograms?" Glenn asked.

"Yes, sir. Yes, that's exactly, those are precisely . . ." Barclay said, losing a little steam.

"While we have tested these holograms extensively at Jupiter Station, this would be our first opportunity to test them under more stressful and realistic circumstances," the Doctor added on Barclay's behalf without missing a beat.

"Do either of you foresee any likelihood that we will be boarded by hostile aliens during our upcoming test flight?" Glenn asked, biting back a smile.

"Of course not, no," Barclay said, deflating further.

"However," the Doctor interrupted, clearly unwilling to be dissuaded by simple logic, "the few living and breathing officers aboard the *Galen* might be unaccustomed to several of the features of our holographic security contingent, including their appearance; the sooner they become accustomed to seeing the ESHs, the easier it will be for them to adapt to this capability of our magnificent little ship."

The commander felt her brow wrinkling. "Their appearance?" she asked. "They're security officers, aren't they?"

"Yes. However, their matrices were based on templates of some of the more fearsome species Starfleet has encountered throughout the years. They are all, of course, programmed to respond as any Starfleet officer would, though their battle tactics are suited to the strengths of their particular species," Barclay said. "The Gorn, for instance, might utilize their tail in . . ."

"I'm sorry, did you say Gorn?" Glenn asked, taken aback.

"Yes, sir," the Doctor said, smiling proudly. "The ESG Mark-1 has proved to be quite fierce in hand-to-hand combat, though the Pahkwa-thanh and the Hirogen also possess unique capabilities that I'm sure you'll find impressive."

Until that moment, Glenn hadn't really considered the

appearance of her holographic security staff. Somehow she had assumed that like the Doctor and subsequent versions of the Emergency Medical Holograms developed throughout the years, the officers would have been based on humanoid templates. Glenn recognized this as an inappropriate ethnocentric bias the moment it occurred to her. The commander wondered if Ensign Lawry, Ensign Drur at ops, Lieutenant Velth at tactical, and Ensign Selah at science, all humanoids, might also be surprised to find themselves suddenly surrounded by alien officers.

"I see your point," Glenn said. "Thank you for the suggestion, Lieutenant Barclay. Please proceed."

"Thank you, sir," Barclay said and nodded more confidently as the Doctor beamed beside him.

As they departed the bridge, Glenn found herself wondering exactly what she'd gotten herself into when she had accepted command.

Breathe, she reminded herself. *Just breathe.*

Voyager's first officer, Lieutenant Commander Thomas Paris, usually tried to take things in stride. As a veteran of *Voyager's* unprecedented excursion to the Delta quadrant, there weren't many things that could shake his confidence or set his nerves on edge.

But as he followed the captain from her ready room to their seats, surveying the crew on the way, his gut tensed. Every one of *Voyager's* alpha shift bridge posts were currently being manned by their assigned officers—Lasren at ops, Kim at tactical, Patel at science, and Conlon at engineering—with one glaring exception. The helm was still under the control of its gamma shift officer, Ensign Gleez.

Captain Afsarah Eden, an ebony-skinned, lithe woman who looked many years younger than the fifty-plus years Tom estimated her to be, seated herself gracefully in the center chair as Tom took the one to her left. After spending so much time on *Voyager*'s original bridge, Tom still found it a little weird to see the new, extra chair to Eden's right, meant for a mission specialist or the Admiral of the Fleet, should the admiral choose to observe from the bridge. This morning, like most mornings since the fleet had launched, Admiral Batiste had clearly chosen to leave matters in Eden's capable hands. Paris still couldn't believe the two of them had once been married and—despite what had to have been a painful divorce—still managed to serve together cordially.

Though Eden appeared calm, there was no mistaking the mild displeasure in her tone as she leaned toward Tom and asked, "We seem to be one crewman short this morning, don't we?"

Keeping his voice low, Paris replied, "I'm sure she's on her way."

"She knows what time alpha shift begins, right?" Eden asked lightly. Tom thought she was teasing him, but they hadn't served together long enough as captain and first officer for him to be certain.

"If there's any confusion on that point, I'll be certain to clear it up," Paris assured the captain. As *Voyager*'s former flight controller, Tom knew that on a day like today the most dangerous place on the ship would have been between him and his helm. After days of simulations it was time for the first test run of their new slipstream drive. Gwyn should have arrived early just out of a sense of enthusiasm. Further, her terribly conspicuous absence reflected badly on Tom's ability as first officer. Thus far he'd found Gwyn competent, if a little intense.

Finally, the turbolift doors opened and every head on the bridge turned to see Aytar Gwyn bent over, struggling to pull on one of her boots. Only once the task was complete did the young woman realize she was the center of attention. Righting herself quickly, she ran one hand through her short, spiked, deep-blue hair, briefly revealing a series of light brown geometric shapes running along her hairline, lifted her chin defiantly, and hurried to her post.

Paris wasn't impressed but noted a slight smile on Harry's lips as he lowered his head and returned his attention to his station, where it belonged.

Gods help us all if Harry takes a liking to her, Tom thought disdainfully. From the looks of things, Gwyn was shaping up to be a handful. The last thing Tom wanted to hear was his best friend defending clearly inappropriate behavior.

"Good of you to join us, Ensign," Eden said with obvious disapproval.

"Not a problem at all, Captain," Gwyn replied cheerfully as she quickly configured her controls and began her pre-test checklist.

"It will be if you're not at your post on time from this day forward," Paris added.

"Understood, sir," Gwyn replied with a nod.

Paris believed that a certain amount of nerve was essential in a good pilot. Any number of people could master the technical skills of the conn, but it took a special combination of cocky and cool to make a great pilot. You had to live for the risks but also be able to intuit which risks were worth taking. Gwyn was already choosing poorly, and that hardly boded well for her.

"Lieutenant Conlon, what's our status?" Eden asked.

"All vessels are standing by, Captain," Conlon replied.

Tom did not know *Voyager*'s new chief engineer yet. She had just transferred from the *da Vinci* and had quickly come up to speed on the new engine specs and already appeared to treat the slipstream drive with the same proprietary pride that B'Elanna had reserved for the warp engines.

"Mister Lasren, open a channel to the fleet," Eden ordered.

"Channel open, Captain."

"This is Captain Eden to all fleet vessels. Go to yellow alert and stand by to coordinate slipstream flight."

After a moment, Lasren reported, "All fleet vessels signal ready, Captain."

"Very good." Eden nodded. "Maintain open channel, Ensign. Nancy?"

Conlon muttered something too soft for Paris to hear. He guessed it was her wish for the drive to behave itself over the next few minutes. Finally, in a steady voice she called out, "We're ready, Captain."

Eden nodded sharply. If the test run unnerved her in the least, Paris couldn't tell.

"Ensign Gwyn, confirm heading one three six mark two," Eden requested.

"Confirmed."

"All fleet vessels match course and speed, one quarter impulse."

As Tom imagined the eight vessels that composed the fleet lining up like soldiers behind *Voyager,* his heart skipped a beat. He suddenly realized how much he envied Gwyn her job right now.

"Course and speed confirmed," Gwyn reported.

"Increase speed to full impulse," Eden requested.

"Confirmed," Gwyn stated after a brief pause.

"Ensign Gwyn, initiate formation of slipstream corridor on my mark: five, four, three, two, one . . . mark."

Tom felt the same slight lurch he had always imagined during the hundreds of simulations when *Voyager* had tested slipstream technology years earlier. He knew it was an illusory response to the sight of the formation of the violent, pulsing white tunnel that churned around the ship once the slipstream was initiated, rather than a sign that the ship's inertial dampeners were failing.

"*Voyager* has achieved slipstream velocity," Gwyn confirmed from the helm. It was a testament to how far Starfleet had come in perfecting this technology that the ship moved with such grace and ease into a speed that made warp nine point nine look like a casual stroll.

"*Esquiline*, confirm synchronization," Conlon requested.

"*Confirmed*," a male voice crackled over the comm.

Over the next thirty seconds, each successive vessel, the *Quirinal*, *Planck*, *Galen*, *Curie*, *Demeter*, *Achilles*, and *Hawking*, added their confirmation that they had successfully entered the corridor *Voyager* had formed.

Paris proudly announced, "The *Voyager* fleet has entered synchronous velocity." He had to quell the urge to applaud Conlon. By any objective standard she and her fellow fleet engineers had just accomplished an extraordinary achievement.

"Well done," Eden agreed. "Maintain heading."

"Aye, Captain," Gwyn replied.

The fleet would travel approximately three thousand light-years in the next eight minutes. Tom studied the incoming station reports that were constantly updated on the console in his armrest and sighed deeply. He hoped for the best, but experience had taught him that when playing with fire it was best to remain cautiously optimistic.

"Vorik, I'm reading a spike in your stabilization grid. Is there a problem?" Conlon inquired of *Hawking*'s chief engineer. Tom knew that bringing up the rear in this exercise was even more challenging than taking the lead, which was why Vorik's ship had been singled out for this honor. The *Hawking*'s position was the most dangerous, but Tom knew Vorik could pull it off. He had trained under B'Elanna for seven years in the Delta quadrant, and served as *Voyager*'s chief engineer for three years after that. He'd only requested a transfer for this mission to serve under another old mentor, Captain Bal Itak, who commanded *Hawking*.

"*The phase variance modulations are off by a factor of point zero, zero, zero, zero, one eight,*" Vorik reported calmly, "*but they remain within tolerance.*"

"That's got to make for a bumpy ride, though," Paris heard Gwyn mutter to herself.

Suddenly the bridge began to rattle.

Paris cast a quick glance at Conlon who was simultaneously trying to diagnose the problem while monitoring the status of the rest of the fleet.

"Adjusting phase modulation algorithm to compensate and transmitting to the fleet," Patel advised Conlon quickly.

"Thanks, Patel," Conlon replied absently.

Unfortunately the new calculations were still off as *Voyager* continued to quake and shudder.

This had always been the challenge with slipstream propulsion, as Paris knew all too well. Even in the most stable corridor, random phase variances made maintaining course and speed at such incredible velocities difficult. The vast majority of Starfleet's efforts in making the drive viable had been in mastering the processing speed and complicated calculations required of the main computer to adjust to the variances.

"Voyager, *this is the* Achilles," a strained voice echoed over the comm.

"Go ahead, *Achilles*," Eden replied to the ship's pilot, Ensign Mirren.

"Our stabilization field is approaching tolerance."

"Understood," Eden said, her frustration mounting. Turning to Conlon she asked, "Do we need to abort?"

Conlon nodded grimly, clearly sharing the captain's disappointment.

"Eden to the fleet, prepare to return to full impulse on *Voyager*'s mark. Ensign Gwyn . . ."

But before Eden could complete her sentence, *Voyager* was struck by a surge so fierce it almost threw Tom from his seat.

"Slipstream corridor destabilizing," Gwyn reported calmly.

"Prepare for emergency shutdown," Eden began.

"I wouldn't do that," Gwyn shot back.

"It's not your call, Ensign," Eden quickly reminded her.

"Due respect, Captain," Gwyn replied as her hands moved deftly across her panel, "I can compensate for the variances manually and bring the fleet out in synch. Otherwise we're going to scatter."

Eden threw Conlon a questioning look to which the lieutenant responded with a nod that clearly gave Gwyn the go-ahead.

"Lieutenant Patel, route Ensign Gwyn's calculations automatically to the fleet," Eden ordered.

"Everybody, hang on," Gwyn advised.

That's exactly what I want to hear at a time like this, Tom thought bitterly as he clutched his armrests tightly.

Over the next few seconds, Gwyn proved as good as her word. The ship continued to shudder mercilessly, yet Gwyn's manual modifications showed that she was reconfiguring the phase variances on the fly, feeling her way through the task in a way no computer could.

Grudgingly, Paris's respect for the pilot went up by several degrees.

Finally, the tumbling white tunnel dispersed and Paris heard everyone on the bridge simultaneously sigh with relief as the viewscreen once again displayed a vast field of stars.

Eden rose from her seat and placing a gentle hand on Gwyn's shoulder said, "Good work, Ensign." Turning to Conlon she asked, "What happened, Lieutenant?"

"As best I can tell, the coefficient for maintaining synchronization is off. Each individual drive is functioning properly, but there's a drag created by utilizing the same corridor that throws off the calculations enough to make the last few vessels vulnerable to stabilization errors," Conlon replied.

"How fast can you fix it?" Eden asked.

"I need an hour with the other chiefs to verify the readings we got and revise the algorithms," Conlon replied.

"Do it." Eden nodded. "Stand down yellow alert." Turning to Tom she added, "The bridge is yours. I'll be in my ready room. Please ask Admiral Batiste to meet me there."

"Aye, Captain," Tom replied, rising to his feet.

As Eden moved toward the ready room doors, Tom took the measure of the rest of the bridge crew. Once Eden was out of earshot he said, "This is just the universe's way of telling us we can do better, right, everybody?"

He was rewarded by a chorus of grins and a "Yes, sir," from Ensign Lasren, which suggested he had taken the remark too seriously, as was the young Betazoid's wont. After giving Conlon a reassuring smile he moved to Gwyn.

Lowering his voice he said, "That was grace under pressure, Ensign."

"Thank you, sir," she replied, a little too pleased with herself.

"How were you able to adjust so quickly to the phase variances?"

Gwen shrugged. "I did what felt right."

"Felt?" Tom repeated.

"It's what I always do when I fly, though I have to admit, I've never felt anything quite like *Voyager*."

"You're talking about instincts, right?" Tom asked dubiously.

"I guess," Gwyn replied. "I'm half Kriosian. My mom was a pretty strong empath, which sucked for me growing up. I think I got a little of it, but I don't use it—I mean on purpose, if that makes any sense."

Paris nodded, thoughtfully. In a way it did. *Voyager* used bioneural gelpacks, which, while technically not *alive*, might facilitate a connection like the one Gwyn described. He made a mental note to ask Counselor Cambridge about it. "The thing is flying the way you did is only part of the job. Don't ever be late for your shift again. Understood?"

"Understood, sir." Mumbling under her breath, she added, "If you'd ever had sex with a Deltan, you'd have been late for your fair share of shifts too, sir."

"Something you'd like to share?" Paris snapped.

"No, sir."

Tom was instantly aware that she reminded him of someone he hadn't thought of in a long time; himself, when he was her age. This unpleasant revelation was followed immediately by the formation on his lips of the response his father, the admiral, would have undoubtedly made.

"There are a lot of interesting things to see in the Delta quadrant and this is the best seat in the house, but you could easily miss all of them. Have you ever scrubbed a plasma conduit with a microfilament?"

"No, sir," Gwyn replied, paling visibly.

"Take my word for it, you don't want to."

"No, sir."

"As you were."

As Paris returned to his seat to contact Admiral Batiste, Harry leaned over his shoulder and whispered, "What was that all about?"

"I'll tell you later," Tom replied.

"She's something else, isn't she?"

Tom shook his head and staring grimly at Harry said softly, "You should ask Mirren."

Harry paused, first confused, then enlightened, and finally disappointed.

"Damn," he said under his breath. "Hang on, I thought having intimate relations with a Deltan was fatal."

"Dangerous, but definitely not deadly," Tom replied with a knowing smirk. "Personally, I think the Deltans started that rumor just to make themselves more interesting."

Harry heaved a resigned sigh before returning to his post.

One of these days Harry's going to fall for the right girl, Tom assured himself. It was just a pity he wasn't going to be aboard *Voyager* long enough to see it.

CHAPTER THREE

A pair of mismatched shuttles outfitted with imposing phaser cannons towed B'Elanna's ship through the security grid established around the asteroid Neelix and some five hundred of his fellow Talaxians now called home. When she reached Neelix, she had been forced to pull a fussy Miral onto her lap to confirm her identity. To say Neelix had been shocked by her presence in the Delta quadrant would have been gross understatement. However, once he'd confirmed their identities, he had quickly dispatched the shuttles to her location. Three days later, they reached New Talax.

When B'Elanna disembarked in the asteroid's small shuttle hangar, Miral clutching to her tightly, Neelix's roguish grin at the sight of them melted away all the years of distance between them as surely as if they had never existed.

"If you aren't the most beautiful sight." He smiled through glistening eyes as he folded mother and child into his arms. Miral squealed in protest, but Neelix would have none of it, deftly prying her from B'Elanna's grasp and lifting her high overhead to get a good look at her. By the time she had been returned to the deck, she was staring at Neelix in wonder.

"I never did have the chance to meet you in person, little Miral, but you have always had a special place in my heart. My goodness, look how big you've gotten."

A petite Talaxian female with fine, blonde hair stood just behind Neelix throughout their preliminary greetings. A reticent-looking boy standing beside her kept his eyes glued to the deck resolutely.

"Hello, Dexa," B'Elanna greeted Neelix's wife, extending her hand, which was immediately rebuffed in favor of a hug.

"Welcome to New Talax," Dexa said warmly. "It's wonderful to see you again. You remember our son, Brax?"

"I remember the thousand questions he had for me and my engineering staff the day you both toured *Voyager*," B'Elanna said, smiling. "Hello again, Brax."

"Ma'am," he said politely.

"Dexa has prepared a succulent feast for both of you," Neelix added. "Well, maybe *feast* isn't the right word. Our supplies are quite limited, but still . . ."

"I'm sure it will be wonderful. Miral and I are starved," B'Elanna assured him.

Dexa gently coaxed Miral into taking her hand and began to lead the way through the cavernous halls toward their private residence. Neelix bounced along beside B'Elanna, his arm draped over her shoulder as if he feared that releasing her would make her vanish.

"I don't mean to pry," Neelix said softly as they walked, "but where's Tom?"

"He's *Voyager*'s first officer now," B'Elanna replied, suddenly realizing how much ground there was to cover between the two of them.

"Oh, I knew that," Neelix scoffed. "I just assumed that if you were here, he couldn't be far behind."

"He isn't," B'Elanna was relieved to be able to tell him truthfully. "But how did you know that?"

"Admiral Janeway, of course," Neelix answered. "I'm still the Federation's official ambassador to the Delta quadrant and as such receive regular, or fairly regular, reports. Though, to be honest, lately the reports have been few and far between," Neelix trailed off. "Actually, it's been more than a year since the last communiqué arrived from the admiral. Did you by any chance bring a new one or perhaps a message from Samantha or Naomi?"

B'Elanna felt her face fall. She had long ago accepted the harsh reality of Kathryn Janeway's death. She grew suddenly cold as she realized that Neelix would have had no way of knowing.

They reached the entrance to Neelix's quarters, and B'Elanna nodded for Dexa and Brax to enter with Miral as she pulled Neelix aside. Her eyes began to burn with fresh tears as she said, "I don't know how to tell you this, Neelix."

Neelix was no stranger to tragedy. Sensing B'Elanna's pain, he took her gently by both hands and squeezed a little of his strength into them.

"Better get it out quickly, then," he said.

Swallowing hard, B'Elanna said, "Admiral Janeway is dead, Neelix. She died investigating a Borg cube that entered the Alpha quadrant over a year ago."

Neelix's eyes widened briefly, as did his mouth. Finally his head began to move slowly back and forth.

"That's not . . . I mean it doesn't seem," he stammered. As his breath began to come in short, quick bursts, he finished, "It's not possible."

"I'm so sorry, Neelix."

Only then did she see his face begin to contort as he visibly struggled to hold back the tears.

Icheb stood at attention, his default position when in doubt, as Chakotay ushered Sveta inside. She wore a simple brown tunic of light fabric, belted tightly by a dark leather strap at her small waist. Beneath the tunic were a pair of loose trousers and soft, well-worn boots. Her dark eyes scanned the room in a manner which suggested to Icheb that she lived in a constant state of curiosity or alertness. Though the top of her head barely reached his shoulders when she finally came to face him, Icheb sensed a taut, wiry strength in her.

"I'd like you to meet an old friend of mine," Chakotay said by way of introduction. "Sveta, this is Icheb."

Icheb automatically extended his right hand, and Sveta shook it more gently than he expected.

"Hello, Icheb."

"Ma'am," he replied.

"Why am I here?" Sveta asked, turning to face Chakotay.

"I'm going to attempt a *Pacrathar*." was Chakotay's puzzling reply.

Sveta's face quickly transitioned through surprise and concern before settling on reticence.

"A what?" Icheb asked.

"It's a sort of vision quest, but it is unique in that it is not performed by an individual. It is the creation of a joint meditative state," Chakotay explained.

"*Joint* as in, including me?" Icheb asked, dismayed.

"Kaslo was a long time ago," Sveta interjected with an unmistakable hint of warning.

"I know," Chakotay said, "and if you're not up to it, I completely . . ."

"Oh, I didn't say that," Sveta said, cutting him off. "But

I would like to know what would make you willing to risk it, especially considering how things turned out last time."

"A friend needs my help," Chakotay replied. He then went on to share a little of Seven's history with the Borg and the Caeliar. Soon enough, Sveta nodded, apparently satisfied.

"But how is this supposed to help her?" Icheb asked. *And how exactly did things turn out last time?* he wondered.

"Over the last several days, Seven has been lucid most of the time. This morning she received word that her aunt died, and I believe this triggered some sort of psychological break. She's conscious, but she won't talk to me. I don't know any other way to reach her."

"And why aren't you taking her to a doctor?" Sveta asked.

"Seven doesn't trust Starfleet to evaluate her objectively at the moment, and frankly I can hardly blame her. I believe she is now being sustained on some level by Caeliar catoms. Should Starfleet confirm their existence—" he said.

"—they'd never let her go," Icheb finished for him.

"What I have observed leads me to believe that Seven is actually at war within herself. She is battling her human nature, her Borg nature, and her new Caeliar nature, and it's hard to tell right now who's going to win. But if we can reach her and provide her with enough strength to hang on, I believe we can stabilize her condition long enough for me to find her the help she really needs."

"The Caeliar?" Icheb guessed.

Chakotay grimaced. "What they broke they might be able to fix. I'm going to take Seven to find them."

"Do you know where they are?" Icheb demanded.

"No, but I do know where to start looking."

"Why do you need me for this?" Icheb asked. "I have no experience in this sort of thing but you seem to . . ."

"Seven and I only recently reconnected after a long time," Chakotay interjected. "I'm not sure she trusts me, but I know she trusts you. I need you there with me."

Sveta nodded, though Icheb remained unconvinced. Taking Chakotay's hand, she said, "You should prepare yourself. I'll explain the ritual to your young friend here."

"Thank you." Chakotay smiled before retreating upstairs.

Turning to Icheb, Sveta considered him kindly and said, "Don't worry. It's not like anybody died last time."

"If it was your intention to comfort me with that remark, I suggest you try an alternate strategy," Icheb replied seriously.

Icheb entered Seven's bedroom behind Sveta. Something in him rebelled at this intrusion into Seven's privacy, but if what Sveta had described as the rest of their afternoon's activities was accurate, he had barely begun to compromise Seven's personal space.

In all the years Icheb had known Seven, he had rarely given thought to the emotional connection between them or how to best categorize it. When they first met, she had been something of a mother to him and the other young Borg liberated from the Collective. Over time, however, especially after Icheb had the opportunity to meet his biological mother, that description had begun to feel inappropriate. The concern Seven regularly displayed for his well-being was certainly evidence of friendship, though he rarely felt that she was as needful of his presence as he seemed to be of hers. Only when the time had come for him to contemplate the possible loss of Seven, when her cortical node had failed, was he forced to accept that any label he might apply to their relationship was inadequate. Icheb had quickly discovered that he was more than willing to sacrifice his own life for hers, which spoke of a deeper bond. Her adamant refusal of his offer indicated that she shared his feelings. Since then, he had come to think of her as family. Perhaps *sister* came closest to an acceptable term.

Still, Seven had always remained an aloof and terribly private individual, and much as he understood the depth of her need, Icheb could not shake the belief that Seven would not approve of their present course.

Seven lay upon her bed, staring at the ceiling. A strange object—which Icheb supposed was the *akoonah* Sveta had described—rested by her right hand. Chakotay sat near it, his eyes closed. The room's curtains blocked out the early morning sun, and the temperature approached stifling. Sveta had already explained that the ritual in which they were about to engage was traditionally performed in a sealed hut heated by a fire. Icheb was silently grateful that the home's fire-suppression systems made that impossible.

Sveta had Icheb sit on the opposite side of the bed, next to Chakotay. Chakotay's breath was shallow. Icheb understood that Chakotay had already entered a private meditative state.

During the *Pacrathar*, one individual would be the center of the group. In essence, that person, Sveta in this case, became a primitive, biological version of a Borg interlink node. As a disinterested, third party, she would remain firmly grounded in the real world while Icheb and Chakotay journeyed together into what Sveta had described as "the place in between realities." Apparently without Sveta's presence there was a chance that Icheb and Chakotay could become permanently lost in this alternate realm. Nothing in Icheb's studies of quantum, temporal, or spatial mechanics allowed for the existence of such a place, but he accepted the premise for the time being. Icheb attempted to put what he was about to experience into some context to which he could relate—his short life as part of the Collective, or what he knew of Vulcan mind melds—though he believed that the *Pacrathar* owed more to spiritual exploration than physical reality, and this only heightened his reservations.

Chakotay took a deeper breath and, opening his eyes, turned his attention to the *akoonah*. He then carefully positioned Seven's fingertips so that they rested lightly on the interface. Both Chakotay and Icheb joined hands with Sveta and placed their remaining free hands simultaneously on the pad of the *akoonah*.

Icheb was immediately conscious of a faint buzzing sensation in his head, a lightness to which he was unaccustomed, along with a disorienting wave of nausea. He barely registered Chakotay's words as he closed his eyes and inhaled deeply to calm his stomach.

"Akoochimoya. We are far from the lands of our ancestors. We ask the spirits to guide us in our search for the one we know as Seven of Nine."

Icheb felt himself moving through what felt like warm water. He clutched Sveta's icy hand tighter until the movement stilled and he felt solid ground beneath his feet.

Opening his eyes he was awestruck by what he beheld. He stood at the base of a tree with a thick trunk and large, drooping boughs on a small land mass at one end of a long, rectangular pool. Massive buildings rose up from the white marble paved ground of the courtyard. Apart from himself and Chakotay, who he now realized stood beside him, the area appeared to be deserted.

Where are we? he asked Chakotay, who was taking in the scene with wide-eyed wonder.

I believe it's called Erigol, he replied without moving his lips. *It was/is a Caeliar city.* Icheb was struck by the reality that wherever they were, they had access to each other's thoughts. There was something familiar and comforting in the sensation.

Have you been here before? Icheb asked.

No. But Seven described it to me. She saw it during the transformation.

Above them, Icheb heard a faint rustling, followed by a childish giggle. He and Chakotay exchanged a brief, knowing glance.

Seven? Icheb called out in his mind.

Another giggle answered him.

Icheb looked up into the canopy of wide leaves and dark limbs and saw a small shape.

Hello? Who's up there?

Go away, a petulant girl's voice commanded.

We can't do that, Chakotay replied.

I don't want you here, the girl said more forcefully.

I don't doubt that, but we're not leaving, so you may as well come down, Chakotay insisted.

Icheb was struck by the thought that good as Chakotay's intentions might be, he clearly hadn't spent as much time around difficult children as Icheb had.

We don't need her to play with us, he advised Chakotay. *We can have plenty of fun here on our own.* Sensing Chakotay's approval, he searched the ground and quickly found a few loose rocks. He picked them up and began to toss them one at a time high into the air until they fell into the pool at a great distance with a satisfying splash.

I can do better than that, Chakotay said and began to search for his own rocks.

Bet you can't, Icheb challenged, more for the child's benefit than any desire for real competition.

Sure enough, though, Chakotay sent his first rock even higher than Icheb's previous efforts, and both watched as it fell almost to the middle of the pool.

How did you do that? Icheb asked.

Certain rules are easier to break here, Chakotay said, smiling.

Let me try, a small voice insisted.

Icheb turned toward the girl, who somewhat resembled images he had seen of Seven when she was a child, except for certain alien characteristics.

Go ahead, he said, offering her one of his rocks.

Her tosses made Icheb's and Chakotay's look pitiful by comparison.

What's your name? Chakotay asked, as the girl tossed another rock.

Annika, she replied.

Icheb felt irrational fear rising within him. He worried that this strange child might be all that was left of Seven.

Are you all by yourself here, Annika? Chakotay asked.

Most of the time, she replied. *But I like it that way.*

It must get lonely, Icheb suggested.

It's still better, Annika insisted.

Icheb knelt so he could bring his eyes level with hers and said, *Better than what?*

Annika shrugged and began to search the ground for more rocks.

Icheb, Chakotay said, commanding him with his thoughts to look around him more closely. Standing at the far side of the pool was a single statue with a more humanoid shape than the others which he now realized graced the plaza. Icheb moved quickly to study it and confirmed that it was a form of a Borg drone. Beneath the armor and implants he saw a face which was strikingly familiar: the face of Seven of Nine.

This sent a cold chill down Icheb's spine he watched Annika approach the drone fearlessly and clamber up onto its shoulders.

Don't worry, she can't hurt anyone anymore, Annika informed them both.

Do you know who she is? Icheb asked.

One of billions, Annika replied.

Turning, Icheb watched as the other statues in the plaza began to morph and coalesce into drones. Soon they were surrounded by these cold figures. Annika sat atop the shoulders of the Seven drone, caressing her head with her long, powerful arms. Then in a swift movement, Annika pulled hard on the statue's head and with a crack ripped it from its place and sent it rolling onto the ground.

They break too easily, Annika assured him.

You are Annika, a new voice boomed.

I know! Annika shouted back, moving on to another drone and tearing off its arms.

As she destroyed the other Borg statues, Icheb moved to pick up Seven's head and studied it. Suddenly its lips began to twitch. Its single eye opened abruptly, filled with terror as it said, *Assistance is futile.*

Icheb almost dropped the head as the sky darkened all around him. Looking up, he saw the amber glow dimmed by the arrival of dozens of Borg cubes which quickly blotted out the sky, pulsing with angry green light.

Annika paused to stare in horror at the sky.

Now see what you've done? she snarled angrily at Icheb and Chakotay.

You are Annika, the new voice insisted again, shaking the buildings.

Turning to Chakotay, Icheb demanded, *What do we do now?*

We have to reach Seven, Chakotay replied. Taking the head from Icheb's hands, Chakotay placed it back atop the statue where it miraculously sealed itself back in place.

Help me, Chakotay commanded, as he began to tear at the implants and armor which shrouded the drone.

Icheb began to pry loose all that was Borg.

Stop it! Annika shouted, rushing toward them. *You can't do that.*

Yes we can, Chakotay replied.

Piece by piece they began to discover the human figure of Seven buried beneath the stone façade of technology. As Chakotay continued his work, Icheb grasped one of Annika's hands and pulled her toward the statue.

What did you do to her? Icheb demanded fiercely.

I didn't do anything! She's just like the rest of them, Annika shouted. *I hate her! Everybody here does!*

I don't hate her, Chakotay said gently to Annika. *Icheb and I miss her terribly and want to help her. You have to let us do that.*

No! Annika cried out, pulling free from Icheb and retreating to the safety of the tree.

You are Annika! the voice commanded, only this time it was the voice of a billion drones joined as one, causing the ground to shudder.

Seven, Icheb cried out. *Seven, can you hear me?*

We are here, Seven, Chakotay added. *You are not alone in this.*

I'm not giving you up, Seven, Icheb shouted, amazed at

the desperation he heard in his voice. *Say something, please.*

You are Annika, the Borg collective insisted again.

Shut up! Icheb shouted defiantly. *She was Annika. She was also Seven of Nine, Tertiary Adjunct of Unimatrix Zero One. But she is stronger than both of them. She is Seven, my teacher and my friend. She is the only family I have left and I won't let you have her. Do you hear me?*

Chakotay placed his hand on the still shoulders of Seven of Nine. *Seven, listen to me. I know you are frightened, but you can't give in to your fear. It has paralyzed you. It doesn't matter what the Caeliar want or what Annika wants. All that matters is you and what you want.*

The Borg destroy everything they touch, Seven's voice cried out. *They won't even leave me this.*

The Borg are gone, Seven, Icheb shouted in frustration. *They no longer exist.*

I am Borg and I exist, Seven replied.

You are a unique individual, Seven, Chakotay insisted. *You are a human with memory of the Borg who was once touched by the Caeliar. But none of these things can define you. They are only parts of the whole.*

The Caeliar didn't want me. They only wanted Annika.

You don't know what they wanted, Chakotay argued. *And the only way you're going to find out is if you come with us.*

Suddenly, angry green fire began raining down on the city, pulverizing the buildings. Annika screamed shrilly in the distance.

Chakotay turned to see the little girl cowering at the base of the tree, her long arms wrapped around her knees and her head ducked low.

Turning back to Seven's still form, Chakotay said, *We're leaving . . . now!*

Seven stared past them at the child. With a wary nod she placed one hand in Icheb's and the other in Chakotay's.

Icheb felt the ground falling away from him too soon but quickly found himself seated on the bed in a pitch-black room. After a moment someone turned on a small lamp that rested on the table by Seven's bed. Once his eyes had adjusted, Icheb saw Seven sitting up, her face a mask of confusion. Rising on stiff legs, he moved to join Chakotay in helping her to her feet.

"Seven?" he said, searching her face.

She nodded, pulling him into a fierce hug.

"Thank you," she said softly. Turning to include Chakotay and Sveta, she added, "Thank you for coming after me."

"So I guess this time it went a little better?" Sveta asked.

CHAPTER FOUR

B'Elanna and Neelix had lost track of time. In the hours that had passed since Dexa's truly delicious dinner had been cleared, Brax hurried out to meet with friends. Dexa had pulled Miral into her lap to read her a selection of Talaxian folk stories, and the two old friends filled each other in on the few high and many low points of the years that had separated them.

They spent considerable time sharing their favorite memories of Kathryn Janeway. B'Elanna wondered if Neelix found this as comforting as she did. She had been forced by her circumstances to grieve for the captain alone. The daily remembrance of her, along with the many other honored dead, had been a healing balm to B'Elanna's troubled heart. She was amazed that Neelix's favorite recollections, when added to her own, lightened the burden she carried.

Neelix also filled her in on the vast progress made by the community of New Talax, including establishing trade and normalizing diplomatic relations with a number of nearby civilizations, as well as strengthening their offensive and defensive capabilities. Neelix had spent a great deal of his first year in New Talax creating training regimens for the colony's security personnel and outlining the priorities for the engineering staff. He had recently been asked to lead an exploratory group tasked with searching for additional asteroids within the belt that might, in time, be converted to similar life-sustaining areas to minimize the impact of their growing population.

"It's amazing how people thrive when they are at peace," Neelix mused.

"That it is," B'Elanna agreed.

He had then listened with the gentle patience she well remembered as she told him of her encounter with the *qawHaq'hoch*, their kidnapping of Miral to keep her safe from the Warriors of Gre'thor, and the decision she and Tom had reached to eliminate the threat the Warriors posed by faking their deaths. Finally, B'Elanna admitted that she was scheduled to meet up with Tom and *Voyager* in a matter of days, at which point Tom would resign his commission and the three of them would set off to build a life in the Delta quadrant.

Neelix had murmured affirmatives and nodded as her story progressed, but once she was done his eyes seemed to betray misgivings.

After a brief pause B'Elanna filled by draining the dregs of the "coffee" Dexa had served after dinner, she demanded, "What?"

"What? Nothing," Neelix replied too quickly.

With an abrupt sigh, B'Elanna got up, and said, "I should really go check on Miral. I'm sure Dexa's worn out by now."

"Of course," Neelix agreed. "There's just one thing, though."

B'Elanna froze for a moment before resigning herself and sitting back down.

"What?"

"I just don't remember B'Elanna Torres ever accepting

defeat like this. She was always so determined to make the universe do as she wished no matter what. And she certainly never used to run away from a fight," Neelix said in the seemingly innocent manner that left little room for offense or argument.

B'Elanna felt her ire beginning to rise and replied, "The B'Elanna Torres you used to know didn't have a child's welfare to put ahead of her own."

"Of course," Neelix said, nodding. "But still . . ."

"Out with it, Neelix," B'Elanna said more harshly.

Thankfully, Neelix rarely paid attention to tone.

"You and Tom have obviously gone to great lengths in the interests of protecting Miral; but at some point, there are other valuable lessons you are going to have to teach her, especially if there's any chance that her purpose as the *Kuvah'magh* is to be fulfilled."

"Neelix, she's three and a half. We're still working on colors, letters, and numbers."

"Children absorb everything, B'Elanna," Neelix said with more conviction. In this at least, both of them knew he was standing on solid ground. "The only things that have ever really hurt the children in my life, little Naomi and now Brax, were the things I tried to hide from them. Ultimately it didn't serve any of us well. And while I don't doubt that you and Tom might be all Miral could possibly need for now, what happens in a few more years? The day is going to come when her universe will have to get a little bigger. And I'm sorry, but the idea of the three of you constantly on the run in your shuttle or settled on some deserted planet eking out an existence doesn't really sound like something that's going to serve Miral very well. You and Tom found a path together on *Voyager*—a road that led both of you to the best you had to offer. I don't understand why you wouldn't want to share that with Miral. When I think of how Naomi grew and thrived aboard *Voyager,* and how the challenges we face here on New Talax are turning Brax into such a responsible and intellectually curious young man, I couldn't be more proud. Can you honestly tell me that the thought of spending the rest of your lives alone on some uninhabited planet could compare with the other options you should be considering?"

"We've made our decision," B'Elanna said, surprised by the uncertainty she heard in her own voice.

"Well, that's the nice thing about decisions." Neelix smiled. "Every day you have the chance to make a better one."

"I can't ask *Voyager*'s crew to take responsibility for Miral's life. Apart from Tom and Harry, most of those people are strangers to me."

"A stranger is just a friend you haven't met yet," Neelix said, and shrugged.

"I'd be putting them in harm's way."

"Isn't that what they signed up for when they joined Starfleet?"

"This is different. This is my personal problem."

"Since when? For the people who love you, and I count myself among them, your problems are theirs. You are one of the strongest people I've ever known, B'Elanna. But going it alone led you to some pretty dark places in the past. Your family on *Voyager* never let that go on for long. And honestly, I think if you could step outside yourself for a minute and look at this from where I'm sitting, you'd agree with me. At the very least, I'd like you and Tom to consider making your new home here with us."

B'Elanna was incredibly moved by his offer.

"Neelix, if the Warriors of Gre'thor ever found us here . . ." she began.

"I'd make them wish they hadn't," Neelix assured her as his eyes flashed icily, "and so would a certain Klingon warrior I used to know."

Soft footfalls broke the tension between them. They turned in unison to see Dexa hovering over them, worry furrowing her brow.

"I'm sorry, but I think you should check on Miral," she said.

"What is it?" B'Elanna asked, jumping to her feet.

"It's probably nothing, but she seems to be running a slight fever," Dexa replied.

Seven was unaccustomed to the silence in her mind. Nonetheless, she accepted the reprieve her recent encounter with Chakotay and Icheb seemed to have granted her and fervently hoped it would become permanent.

Icheb had repeatedly offered to remain with her until she departed with Chakotay the following afternoon. Her heart wished to reward the courage and deep affection he had shown by entering into the *Pacrathar* with Chakotay, but Seven worried that these feelings were evidence of weakness and not strength. After several moments spent assuring each other of their mutual regard and her promise to keep him apprised of her emotional well-being, Seven had insisted Icheb return to the Academy. In addition to instructing him to maintain his progress in her absence, she also requested that he keep a watchful eye on Naomi Wildman, who was due to enter the Academy in the fall.

"Watchful?" he had asked, needing clarification.

"Do not smother her," Seven suggested. "But make sure she is aware that you are available to counsel her should the need arise."

Once Icheb had departed, Seven had made excellent use of her newfound sense of strength, replying to several urgent communications she had been neglecting, and advising the Academy that she required an indefinite leave of absence for personal reasons.

With her affairs in order, only one task remained, and though she hesitated to complete it, Seven was also aware that to leave it undone was unthinkable.

Chakotay insisted on accompanying her to the hospice. Though Seven's stomach writhed as she approached the entrance, she reminded herself that no one present would have any reason to suspect that she was in less than perfect health.

In a clear effort to deflect any unwarranted attention, Chakotay took the lead in cheerfully greeting the nurses who had attended Irene in her final days and who had subsequently arranged for the disposal of her remains. Seven was presented with an urn containing Irene's ashes, and together, they left the hospice and utilized a nearby public station to transport to a small, secluded beach at the north end of San Francisco Bay.

Seven was struck by the lightness of the urn she held gingerly in her arms. She tried to call up a mental picture of Irene as she had been when Seven first returned to Earth. Instead, Seven could remember only the pale husk of what had once been such a vibrant woman, lying in her hospice bed, surrounded by low, humming machines. Still, Seven found unexpected consolation in the thought that she had been granted this moment, at least, to bid her farewell.

Chakotay seemed to share the heaviness of Seven's spirit. Seven had resented his absence as Irene's condition had worsened. Now she understood that his struggles had blinded him to the suffering of others. She could not condone his behavior, but she had accepted his apology.

"Would you like to say something?" he asked kindly.

Seven paused.

"What is there to say now?" she asked.

Chakotay smiled faintly. "Imagine she were standing here with us. What would you tell her?"

Seven tried to do as he suggested. Staring out over the clear blue water, a color she suddenly realized had been close to that of Irene's eyes, she began.

"I saw Icheb today."

It seemed odd to mention something so trivial at such a moment, but she couldn't help herself. Irene had always shown a lively interest in even the most mundane details of Seven's life.

"He received the highest marks in his class this year, as we suspected he would. I do not yet know what specialties he may pursue in his final year as a cadet. We didn't have time to discuss it. He did, however, express his sadness at your passing. I am certain that when he came to the house he was hoping you might have left a few slices of strawberry pie for him. It remains his favorite."

After a long silence, Seven suddenly found it easier to remember what Irene had looked like in better days, and the memory of her aunt's patient eyes gave her strength to continue.

"I am departing Earth tomorrow," Seven said. "I am not well, and I believe that to restore my health, this journey is necessary. I do not know when I will return."

Seven tried unsuccessfully to swallow the discomfort that was rising in her throat. "I can never truly thank you for all you have given me. You were unexpected."

Tears began to flow down her cheeks, but she didn't bother wiping them away.

"Your home became my favorite place. Your memories of my father brought him back to me more clearly than all his logs ever could. Your support enabled me to adapt to my new life here, and your generosity has shown me my own deficiencies in that regard. I will miss you. But I will adapt. You would expect nothing less of me."

Seven turned her tear-streaked face to Chakotay and saw that his eyes, too, were glistening. He took the urn from her arms so she could loosen the lid in preparation to scatter Irene's ashes.

Seven took the urn and stepped to the edge of the shoreline. Before she emptied it, she whispered, "I do not know if you can hear me, but if you can, I want you to know that I love you, Aunt Irene. I will remember you and all that you have given me."

Seven gently tipped the urn on its side and scattered the ashes into the bay.

She started to turn back to Chakotay when a new and frightening thought formed in her mind. She tried to accept it as part of Irene's greatest gift to her. Annika Hansen had been little more than a blur, an indistinct memory and a semi-familiar face in old family photographs until Irene's remembrance of her brother's only child had been added to Seven's own. Now that little girl was more real to her than she had ever imagined, and though she feared her power and her pain, she could not deny that Irene had brought her back to Seven in a way not even the Caeliar could have managed.

"Annika wishes you peace," Seven finally said.

And so do I, she thought sadly.

CHAPTER FIVE

After more than two weeks of tests and tweaks, the fleet had flawlessly demonstrated to Eden's satisfaction that traveling within the same slipstream corridor was both possible and safe. They were currently grouped not far from what had once been Deneva and was now an ashen shadow of its former beauty, and within hours would travel their first major distance to the terminus between the Beta and Delta quadrants.

Eden entered her ready room and found her ex-husband, Admiral Willem Batiste, sitting at her desk.

And this day started out so well, she mused.

Willem had remained in his quarters during most of the test period. This might be evidence of his confidence in the fleet's commanding officers. But Eden knew his penchant for micromanagement too well to believe it. He wasn't hovering over her shoulder because he was working on something else. Odds were, unless she managed to unintentionally get in his way, she would never know what it was.

He studied her monitor with a scowl, clearly not pleased by what he saw. His rugged face had a taut, almost pale quality this morning, and she believed his short, fine black hair was finally beginning to betray him in small flecks of white and an overall loss of sheen.

You were a lot more handsome when I married you, Willem, she thought. Up until the moment she accepted this command, Eden wouldn't have hesitated voicing such a comment. Once he became her superior officer, everything about their relationship had changed once again. She secretly believed that the only way they would ever survive this mission together was if they both took professionalism to unexplored heights. She didn't know which of them would break first, but she didn't want it to be her.

"What in the blazes has your chief engineer done to the deflector array?" the admiral asked gruffly, without looking up.

Eden bit back the first five replies that came to mind and settled for, "The precise calculations necessary to compensate for the phase variances required a few minor alterations. I can assure you, it's still within regulations."

"And you approved this, Captain?"

Tension knotted the tops of Eden's shoulders as she straightened a little and replied, "I did," with just enough residual tone to dare him to second-guess her. She couldn't resist adding, "I thought it might be nice, since our mission is to explore the Delta quadrant, if we actually all arrived there together and in one piece."

Batiste let her sarcasm slide, asking, "When are we going to depart?"

"Tom tells me we should be under way in the next few hours. It's important we get this right, so I'm willing to give engineering all the time they need."

"Tom?" Batiste echoed with a hint of disdain.

"I'll call my senior officers what I like, Admiral," Eden countered. "I find a more congenial manner instills both trust and respect."

"They're not your friends, Afsarah," Batiste reminded her.

"Neither are you, Admiral."

Eden wished she could have taken those last words back but was spared further self-recrimination by a chirp from her combadge.

"*Ops to the Captain.*"

"Go ahead, Ensign Lasren," Eden replied.

"*We've been hailed by a civilian vessel, the* Alpha Flyer, *Captain. They are requesting permission to come aboard and meet with you.*"

"Who are they?"

"*The request was made by Seven of Nine.*"

Eden's heart actually paused for a moment at this news. She had offered Seven a position with the fleet weeks ago and been rather perfunctorily dismissed. It seemed too much to hope that she had changed her mind, but if there was even a chance, Eden would be more than happy to hear her out.

"Allow the ship to dock, and escort Seven to the conference room," Eden replied as she turned back toward the door. Before she reached it she was conscious of Batiste's presence at her heels.

"I'm sure this is nothing you need to trouble yourself with, Admiral," she said pointedly.

"I'm as curious as you are, Captain," he said, smirking.

Repressing a sigh, Eden made her way across the length of her bridge to the opposite set of conference room doors.

She and Batiste endured only a few moments of silence before the doors slid open. Seven's regal figure entered, followed by the last person in the universe Eden ever expected to see aboard her ship: *Voyager*'s former commanding officer, Captain Chakotay, wearing a casual pair of slacks, a tunic, and a jacket.

"Hello, Seven," Eden said, crossing to extend her hand to hers, which Seven accepted. "It's nice to see you again."

"Thank you, Captain," Seven replied.

Turning to Chakotay, Eden extended her hand to him and said, "You're out of uniform, Captain."

Chakotay smiled with a hint of self-deprecation as he replied, "It's just 'Chakotay,' Captain Eden. I resigned my commission several weeks ago."

The admiral was standing a few paces behind Eden as she took in this startling news. Finally Eden relieved Chakotay's discomfort by adding, "I don't know if either of you have met the admiral of the fleet, Willem Batiste."

As they exchanged polite greetings, Seven said a little harshly, "The admiral and I have met."

She likes him less than I do, Eden realized.

The captain motioned for them to take a seat as she and Batiste situated themselves across the table.

"To what do I owe this unexpected honor?" Eden asked as they were settling themselves.

Without betraying a hint of enthusiasm, Seven said, "You had indicated that my presence would be beneficial to the fleet. I have come to offer my service."

Eden felt her face breaking into a smile until Willem broke in to ask, "Why?"

"Admiral?" Seven said, inclining her head ever so slightly in his direction.

"You refused Captain Eden's offer the first time it was extended," Batiste replied. "I want to know why you've changed your mind."

Something defiant and a little hostile flickered across Seven's alabaster face.

"My circumstances have changed since the last time we

spoke," Seven said evenly. "Initially, one of the most significant obstacles was the health of my aunt. She has since passed away."

"I'm so sorry to hear that, Seven," Eden said with genuine sympathy.

"Thank you, Captain," Seven said. "In addition, it is my understanding that part of this fleet's mission is to confirm that the Caeliar are gone. I believe my assistance in this respect would be valuable to the fleet."

"You think they're still out there, don't you?" the admiral said, as if confirming a long-held suspicion.

"As I said when I was interviewed by Command, I am not certain what I believe," Seven replied. "But I would like to investigate it further and a posting with this fleet is the only way to accomplish it."

Batiste sat back in his seat, considering Seven with obvious skepticism.

Worried that he might actually kill her proposition without even uttering another word, Eden quickly said, "We would be delighted to have you aboard, Seven."

"Before you agree, Captain, I must make you aware of certain matters relating to my personal health, and must advise you of the terms under which I am prepared to accept this assignment."

Batiste had barely inhaled to retort that setting "terms" was not her place when Eden preempted him, saying, "By all means."

Seven paused to collect herself, an odd sight to see as she was one of the most unflappable people Eden had ever encountered. Finally she said, "When the Caeliar transformed the Borg, I was briefly connected to the Caeliar gestalt. It was a unique experience and one that is difficult to describe. I was severed from that link but since that time I have continued to sense a presence in my mind. Please understand that I am in perfect physical health. However, over time, this sense of a lingering connection to the Caeliar has remained and actually grown stronger."

"What is the nature of the connection?" Eden asked.

"I can only describe it as a voice," Seven replied.

"What does it tell you?" Batiste asked warily, beating Eden to the punch.

"It says that 'I am Annika Hansen,' over and over again."

"That is your human name," Eden said.

Seven nodded. "It has been my preference since I separated from the Borg to designate myself as Seven of Nine. I do not understand why the insistence of this voice that I am Annika is so troubling, apart from the fact that Annika essentially ceased to exist at the age of eight. Obviously I am no longer Borg, but I have struggled over the years to establish an individual identity which encompasses the best of what is human and Borg within me. The voice seems to insist that I must disregard a vast part of my life. I have found that most troubling. If we can successfully locate the Caeliar, whom I believe might still be out there, they might be able to help me resolve this issue."

Eden allowed herself to sit in silence as the implications of Seven's words arranged themselves in her mind in a long series of bright red flags.

"So you aren't so much offering your service to the fleet as requesting our assistance," Batiste finally said.

Chakotay had sat in placid silence until now. His eyes flashed briefly as he said, "For many years now, Seven has responded time and again to any and all requests made of her by Starfleet. She has never accepted a commission. She has served diligently and loyally whenever and wherever she was asked, including at the Palais de la Concorde during the Borg Invasion. Never in all that time has she made a personal request of Starfleet. I think it's the least Starfleet can do."

"And what's your interest in this, Chakotay?" Batiste asked with a healthy dollop of condescension. "Are you using your free time to transport wayward civilians around the quadrant?"

"I requested Chakotay's presence," Seven objected, "and the only thing I ask is that you allow him to remain onboard as my advisor."

A veritable bouquet of new flags shot up in Eden's head, but she held her peace. It was clear that Seven *needed* to accompany the fleet, but it was equally evident that her presence, even in a diminished capacity, would be a great asset. The captain questioned Chakotay's motives in accompanying Seven, but did not doubt that if she refused, Seven would change her mind.

"Do you find that arrangement acceptable, Chakotay?" Eden asked.

"I do," he said sincerely. "Seven and I have been friends for a very long time. She saved my life and the lives of *Voyager*'s crew more times than I can count. To assist her now as she works through this difficult issue is the least I can do for her."

"Captain, a moment?" Batiste interrupted.

With a deferential nod, Seven and Chakotay rose and excused themselves, moving to stand outside the door where a security officer stood at attention.

"I think we should refuse their request," Batiste said before the air had settled.

"Admiral, did you ever actually read the full text of the report I prepared for Project Full Circle on *Voyager*'s time in the Delta quadrant?"

"Many times, as you well know."

"May I point out a few salient facts. Seven is an extraordinary individual. Everything Chakotay has said about her service to Starfleet is true. More important, Starfleet wants to confirm that the Borg and Caeliar are nothing but a memory, and it's possible that Seven is now the closest we might come to a living, breathing Caeliar detector. We already know that if the Caeliar don't want to be found, they won't be. They've turned xenophobia into an art. She can help us. And we can help her. It's a win-win from where I sit."

"What about Chakotay?"

Eden shrugged. "As long as he limits his activities to advising Seven, I can accept it. I can also think of a couple hundred ways that another person who's actually been in the Delta quadrant could come in handy."

Batiste considered her words, or more accurately, if Eden still knew him as well as she thought she did, calculated the force requirements in continuing to argue the point. "You actually think the man who used to command this ship is going to be content as a *civilian* advisor to one crew member? I couldn't do it, and I don't think you could, either."

"He's not going to have a choice, Admiral," Eden replied coldly.

"It's your ship, Captain," he finally replied, rising from the table and exiting the room to the bridge.

"Damn straight," she muttered before signaling the security officer to allow Seven and Chakotay to re-enter.

Eden then graciously accepted Seven's terms, asking only that she report at once to sickbay for a full medical evaluation. The captain then ordered that until Seven had successfully resolved her issue with the voice, she would also be expected to meet regularly with the ship's counselor, Lieutenant Hugh Cambridge.

To Eden's surprise, Chakotay agreed that Counselor Cambridge would be most helpful. But he suggested that *Voyager*'s former EMH, with his vast knowledge of Seven's prior medical history, might be better equipped to treat Seven than the new CMO.

Eden agreed and ordered Paris to assign them quarters. The captain then returned to the bridge, where she ordered the *Achilles* to retrieve the shuttle and stow it aboard the fleet's engineering transport. Normally she didn't second-guess her decisions, but Eden found herself wondering how complicated this mission was going to get.

And we're not even in the Delta quadrant yet, she thought, shaking her head.

———

Eleven days after B'Elanna arrived at New Talax, her shuttle was once again in working order. Neelix had assigned a team of eager engineers to assist her. B'Elanna discovered that what they lacked in expertise, they more than made up for in curiosity and enthusiasm.

Unfortunately, the same could not be said for the three doctors and six medical technicians who staffed the asteroid base's infirmary. Dr. Hestax, a wizened, spindly man who looked as if a strong wind might blow him over, had been the first to tend to Miral once B'Elanna confirmed that her temperature was definitely running high. The fever had soon given way to a general lethargy and inability to keep down solid foods. Hestax had initially prescribed rest, liquids, and constant attention. The doctor hesitated to deliver any antiviral therapies as he could not be certain that the hybrid child's physiology would tolerate them. "Best to wait it out," he said sagely the night Miral had arrived in the emergency ward for treatment.

Over the next five days, Miral appeared to rally. She remained confined to liquid nutrients. By the end of the sixth day she actually managed to climb out of her crib twice on a young medic's watch, giving B'Elanna hope that she was on the mend.

However, the seventh night brought those hopes crashing down. The fever returned and an angry rash appeared on her stomach. Miral cried for ten grueling hours as Hestax was still unwilling to risk anything more than a topical cream until he could analyze a skin culture to determine the nature of this new symptom. At B'Elanna's insistence, he did review the medical references in her shuttle's database and finally settled on an antiviral injection he was willing to introduce into Miral's fragile system.

Four days later, Miral had fallen into a terrifying stupor. She was languid and unresponsive; all Hestax could confirm was that her immune system was still fighting off the infectious agent, and he still believed the child would conquer it.

B'Elanna was standing over Miral's crib, gently caressing her clammy forehead, when Neelix arrived.

"All the diagnostics are complete and it appears that the *Home Free* is once again space worthy," he said as cheerfully as possible.

"Thank you, Neelix," B'Elanna murmured.

"How's our little warrior?"

"I've never seen her like this," B'Elanna said softly.

"She's going to be fine," Neelix assured her.

"You don't know that," B'Elanna retorted sharply.

"Yes, I do," Neelix insisted.

B'Elanna tenderly adjusted Miral's blanket, then pulled Neelix to the far side of the infirmary so as not to disturb her.

"This isn't right," B'Elanna whispered hotly, bathing once again in the familiar waters of righteous indignation that had once been so familiar. "She's not getting any better, and there's nothing anybody here can do to help her."

"Doctor Hestax is doing the very best he can," Neelix said without a trace of defensiveness.

"His best isn't good enough!" B'Elanna replied. "Your doctors are so far behind Federation medical technology it's terrifying."

This harsh estimation of his people clearly troubled Neelix, but he had the good grace to accept it stoically. He had spoken at great length for days about the wonderful accomplishments of his people as they struggled to survive in one of the harshest environments imaginable. In every respect but this, B'Elanna could agree they were succeeding admirably. Neelix's obvious chagrin tempered and refocused her rage.

"I'm not blaming you, Neelix," she added. "You and your people have been incredibly generous. This is my fault. She's never suffered from anything more serious than colic or a cold . . . it just never occurred to me . . . I should have made damn sure I had an EMH with me."

"*Voyager* will be here in less than two days," Neelix offered. "You'll depart first thing in the morning and before you know it, Miral will be in the most capable medical hands possible."

"What if they're delayed?" B'Elanna demanded. "What if my slipstream drive gives out again and I never even make it to the rendezvous coordinates. I don't know how much time she has left."

Neelix pulled her into a firm embrace and whispered softly, "Miral is going to survive this, B'Elanna. You'll see."

Much as she wanted to, B'Elanna no longer believed it to be true.

———

Chakotay had never seen anything like the *Galen*. As a prototype vessel, he wasn't certain if it had yet been classified, but structurally at least, it appeared to be a cross between a *Nova*- and *Miranda*-class science vessel. The main section had six decks. It was constructed in a wide triangular shape and the nacelles were mounted on short pylons extending directly from the drive section.

Commander Glenn, the vessel's captain, met Seven and Chakotay in the transporter room. She offered them a brief summary of the ship's unique characteristics as they made their way to sickbay. Seven already knew a great deal about the *Galen* and had described it to Chakotay on their journey to rendezvous with the fleet. Still, Chakotay found the proud captain's guided tour fascinating. It could accommodate a crew of thirty. The emergency wards—which took up the bulk of decks five and six—could easily treat a hundred wounded. More interesting were the holographic systems installed throughout the vessel, including medical, engineering, and security personnel. They were designed to come online only as needed. Since the Doctor had been one of the ship's designers, Chakotay knew he would be keen to see these holograms used frequently. Chakotay found himself thinking that he might be glimpsing a part of Starfleet's future.

Glenn tried to engage Seven in conversation as they walked, but Seven responded with brisk, succinct answers. The commander graciously turned them over to a cheerful, petite young woman with short raven hair whom she introduced as Ensign Meegan McDonnell, one of their medics.

"How may I assist you?" Meegan asked kindly as she gestured Seven toward a biobed.

"I wish to see the Doctor," Seven replied simply.

"Which doctor?" Meegan inquired.

"*The* Doctor," Seven emphasized.

"Are you referring to the Chief Medical Officer?" Meegan went on, unperturbed.

"Yes," Seven said, her frustration clearly mounting.

"Please lie down here and I will perform a few basic scans to gather the pertinent baseline information before we trouble him," Meegan said as she turned to gather her tricorder.

"That won't be necessary," Seven insisted more firmly. "Please advise the Doctor that Seven of Nine wishes to see him."

"As I'm sure you can imagine he is terribly busy, and we do not waste his time," Meegan countered just as sternly.

Chakotay couldn't tell if Meegan had been well-trained or well-programmed. In either case she had to be the assistant of the Doctor's dreams. He was certain the Doctor had never received such deference from his previous assistants, though Kes might have come close. Sensing Seven's growing unease, Chakotay quickly tapped his combadge, saying, "Chakotay to the Doctor."

A familiar and surprised voice replied, "*Captain Chakotay? What are you doing aboard the* Galen?"

"I'll be happy to explain. Could you transfer your program to the main sickbay immediately?" Chakotay replied.

"*Certainly. Is there an emergency?*"

"There's about to be," Chakotay said, as he gently put Meegan out of Seven's reach and quietly thanked her for her efforts.

Within moments the Doctor materialized with a wide smile and a heavy dose of sarcasm saying, "Please state the nature of the . . ." Before he had completed what had once been his standard greeting, however, he noted Seven's presence and, with dozens of questions writ plainly on his brow, moved toward her in concern. At Seven's request, they adjourned to his private office. Chakotay settled himself on a low stool at a diagnostic station to wait as Meegan did her best to look busy.

"I hope you understand, it's nothing personal," Chakotay offered as Meegan brushed past him with a stock of newly replicated hyposprays.

"Of course," Meegan replied, clearly not mollified.

Well-trained, Chakotay decided. *I'm guessing human.* He doubted even the Doctor could have programmed an assistant to be so sensitive.

"Seven and the Doctor have a long history together," Chakotay offered.

"I know," Meegan said a little too testily. "He has spoken of her frequently."

And possibly a little jealous, Chakotay realized with an inward smile.

He knew there had been a time when the Doctor had nursed feelings beyond professional for Seven. They—like Chakotay's—had long since settled into friendship. It was nice to think the Doctor might have other possibilities on the horizon. Chakotay found himself wondering if the Doctor was even aware of the feelings of his medical assistant.

It seemed Chakotay had a lot of catching up to do with his old friends.

CHAPTER SIX

ieutenant Nancy Conlon was almost ready to call this a good day. Five hours earlier, the *Voyager* fleet had begun a synchronous slipstream flight from just outside the Deneva system to the terminus of the Alpha and Beta quadrants. This was not a test. It was the first sustained flight for the fleet since their launch several weeks earlier.

And to Conlon's satisfaction and credit, it had gone off without a hitch. Her team was already celebrating. She couldn't blame them. Most of them had been pulling twenty-hour days since the first test flight and all that effort had finally paid off.

Conlon wasn't ready to join in yet, though. Years spent toiling in the odd confluence of space, technology, and sentient beings kept her enthusiasm on a short leash until the day's work was complete. The celebration would have to wait until she had completed her post-flight evaluation of every last millimeter of her engines.

Every diagnostic so far had shown minor expected stresses. As she filed them away, a low growl from her stomach reminded her that she should eat something. She couldn't honestly remember when she'd last eaten.

Lunch yesterday, maybe?

As Conlon started planning the menu for her congratulatory dinner, Lieutenant Neol appeared to burst her rapidly expanding bubble of happiness.

"You might want to take a look at this, Lieutenant," the portly Bolian sighed, placing a padd in front of her.

"Why do I get the feeling I'm not going to like whatever this is?"

"Because you're not," Neol deadpanned before returning to his station.

Conlon took a moment to drop her head and roll it gingerly left and right, eliciting a few loud and satisfying pops before addressing the bad news. After a quick glance she moved briskly from her small private office in engineering's upper level, a luxury no matter the size, and quickly slid down the utility ladder that led to the heart of her engine room.

Her new hybrid warp-slipstream core now stood where a standard warp core used to be. The upper portion remained a standard warp drive and was filled with pulsing blue plasma. The base of the core, a clear wide tube that flashed intense amber light and within which rested the benamite crystals powering the slipstream drive, was the cause of concern. Conlon quickly logged into the main control panel and ordered a level two diagnostic of the benamite crystals. The results confirmed her worst fears.

"Conlon to Captain Eden," she called, activating her combadge.

"*Go ahead,*" Eden's warm and rich voice replied.

"Do you have a minute to report to engineering?"

"*Not really. I'm on my way to the final command crew briefing with Admiral Batiste. Can it wait?*"

Nancy debated for only half a second.

"I'm sorry, Captain, but I'd like you to see this before the fleet separates."

"*Understood. I'll be there right away. Eden out.*"

Conlon closed her end of the comm before allowing a sigh of frustration to slip past her lips. This *had* been a good day. What she had just learned led her to believe that the fleet's mission might either be much shorter or a whole lot longer than any of them had planned.

Eden wasn't comfortable in engineering. As any Academy grad, she had a working knowledge of her ship's systems, but that knowledge was not deep. Eden liked to think of herself as a big-picture person. She was an avid researcher and analyst, a purposeful leader, an able diplomat, and a steady commanding officer. But whenever conversations turned technical, as they often did in this part of the ship, the captain usually felt like she was reporting for an exam that she had crammed for rather than mastered the subject.

One of the things Eden liked about her chief engineer was that Nancy never seemed to tire of answering her questions.

She found Conlon in her office, staring in dismay out the window that separated her private sanctuary from the hustle and bustle going on below.

"What do you have, Nancy?" she asked, diving in.

Conlon rose to greet her and got right to the point, handing her a padd to examine.

"Thirty percent of *Voyager*'s benamite supply is currently in use. Equivalent percentages are standard throughout the fleet at this time."

"And you're about to tell me why that's a problem?" Eden asked.

"Benamite is incredibly rare. I'm actually surprised we managed to find enough to equip the fleet for this mission in the first place. All our tests indicated that the life of an average crystal in use for slipstream propulsion should be a year or more, obviously depending upon a few critical variables, including duration of sustained slipstream flight. We've just executed our longest flight to date and though the crystals remained stable, I'm now detecting numerous unanticipated microfractures. At this rate, we will have to replace the existing crystals in forty-five days at the most."

Eden did a little math in her head and quickly realized where Conlon was going with this.

"We'll exhaust our supplies in three months? We're supposed to be out here for at least three years," Eden said.

"And unless we can find an alternate source of benamite or find a way to extend the life of our current reserves . . ."

"Have you double-checked these findings with the other fleet vessels? Is there any chance this is a problem unique to *Voyager*?"

"I'm still waiting for confirmation from *Demeter, Curie,* and *Quirinal,* but the other vessels are all reporting similar findings. I'm sorry, Captain."

"Don't be sorry," Eden replied, "get busy and find me another solution."

"Yes, Captain." Conlon nodded. "I've already assigned a team to go over our last flight and look for any anomalies that might explain the fractures. There's a slight chance this is a one-time problem, but I doubt it. I've also spoken with all of the other fleet chief engineers and we're set to meet at the end of this shift and compare notes. I know they're every bit as eager as I am to find a way to fix this."

"Captain Farkas is about to take the *Quirinal, Planck,* and *Demeter* about forty thousand light-years from our present position, so almost twice the distance we just covered, to follow up on a discovery the *Aventine* made several months ago. Is that mission going to be delayed by this?" Eden asked.

"No," Conlon replied.

"*Voyager, Hawking,* and *Galen* are scheduled to hit the Delta quadrant tomorrow. Any reason to delay that?"

"We're not going to be able to fix this overnight," Conlon replied. "We need to monitor it closely and look for alternatives, bearing in mind that if we can't resolve it, or if the crystals start showing more serious fractures under stress, we'll need to consider altering our long-range plans."

"Understood. Thanks, Nancy," Eden said, nodding. "Keep me posted."

"Aye, Captain," Conlon said.

Eden then hurried to join the meeting of the other fleet captains already in progress in the conference room. She assumed they had also probably just heard this news from their respective chief engineers. She didn't think any of them would be pleased, least of all Admiral Batiste.

Lasren said Chakotay wasn't in uniform. What do you think that means?

Harry directed the message to Tom's station below him and waited. A few moments later Tom's reply appeared.

I don't know.

Harry hurriedly entered: *Why are they still on the* Galen? *It's been more than a day since they arrived. Is Seven okay?*

Tom kept neutral and he answered: *I don't know.*

Frustrated, Kim resigned himself to watching the view of the *Achilles* on the viewscreen as it dropped the first of dozens of subspace relays that would be seeded throughout the area and along the route *Voyager* would be traveling shortly to ensure that long-range communications with the Alpha quadrant would be maintained while the fleet was in all but the most distant fringes of the Delta quadrant. The *Esquiline* and *Curie* would shadow them as they worked and regrouped with the rest of the fleet in three weeks.

At ops, Lasren provided intermittent confirmations that the relays were functioning properly while Harry ran continuous scans to ensure that the fleet would not be disturbed by any potentially hostile parties. The predictable regular curves he was reading didn't suggest any danger and for that, Harry was grateful.

Harry Kim had suffered perhaps more than his fair share of doubts about this mission when he'd first been briefed, but after a few weeks settling in with the old and new faces all around him, he was finally starting to enjoy himself again.

Tom remained a little distant whether their communications were surreptitiously written or spoken, but that was due primarily to the incredibly heavy workload he carried as *Voyager*'s first officer. Less than a month ago, Harry had been the one to tell Tom that his wife and daughter had been killed during the Borg Invasion of the Alpha quadrant. Tom and B'Elanna had been formally separated for months, and they hadn't lived as a family for more than three years. Yet, it amazed Harry that Tom was able to continue to perform his duties while the pain he had to be carrying weighed down on him. The few times Harry had pressed his best friend, Tom had refused to discuss it. Privately, Harry worried that Tom might be mired in the denial stage of the grieving process, but he had no idea how to help him move beyond it.

With Captain Eden otherwise occupied, Tom sat in the center seat, constantly monitoring ship-wide reports and activities from the data panel embedded in the arm of the chair. Harry had his own work to do at tactical. As security chief, he was responsible for a staff of fifty and had drilled them mercilessly during the test runs. Prior to the unexpected arrival of Chakotay and Seven, Kim had been dying to get a closer look at the *Galen*. The Doctor's early reports of the progress of the Emergency Security Holograms created for that vessel had made him wonder if he would be augmenting his staff in a similar manner at some point. His experience with a wide variety of holograms made Harry conscious of the weaknesses that went along with their strengths. He was content that the *Galen* be the first to thoroughly test these new holograms but he was considering a proposal to cross-train his staff with Captain Glenn's at the first opportunity.

A discreet blip on his comm panel alerted him to a message from Lasren. He quickly locked down his panel and walked the few paces to the first post he had occupied aboard *Voyager*—ops.

"Problem, Ensign?" he asked under his breath.

"I think it's a glitch," Lasren replied, pointing to his display. "The new comm relays send out a lot of interference while they're synchronizing, but during that last burst I thought I saw an actual carrier wave."

"Show me," Harry instructed. He loved his job at tactical, but he'd never forget the seven years he'd spent in Lasren's current shoes. The young Betazoid was by no means a novice. He'd held his post for almost three years, including during the battle at the Azure Nebula where hundreds of Starfleet vessels had been destroyed in minutes and Harry had sustained critical injuries. To this day Kim believed it had been a miracle *Voyager* had escaped annihilation. Lasren was tough and incredibly conscientious. But like Harry, back in the day, he sometimes missed the forest while engrossed in the study of a particularly interesting tree.

Kim took a moment to scan the reading and much to his alarm found himself agreeing with Lasren. He nodded silently to the ensign and moved to take the seat beside Tom.

"Something wrong, Harry?" Paris asked softly without looking up.

"I don't want to sound paranoid," Harry began.

"Too late," Tom noted with a faint smile.

"Someone on this ship just piggybacked an unauthorized transmission onto one of our new relay signals."

"Why would anyone do that?" Tom wondered aloud.

"I don't know, but given the strength, it looks like whoever did was sending that message pretty far."

"How far?"

"Maybe as far as the Delta quadrant."

Tom's face fell into more serious lines. "I'll check it out."

"You want some help?"

"No." Tom shook his head. "I got it."

"Okay," Harry replied, rising. "Want to grab dinner after our shift?" He'd been making similar offers for days but Tom had continued to distance himself by begging off each time.

Tom shocked Kim by replying, "Sure."

"Oh, great." Harry smiled. "Maybe by then Seven and Chakotay will be free and we can find out what's really going on."

Tom favored Harry with a wry smile.

"I know. You don't know," Harry answered for him.

Paris took a deep breath and did his best to look busy as Harry crossed back to his station. He'd been holding on to that message for B'Elanna—confirming *Voyager*'s arrival at the rendezvous coordinates—for days. He'd decided that the transmission could be most easily masked during the initial deployment of the relays.

But you have to get up pretty early in the morning to get anything past Lasren, Tom reminded himself.

It didn't matter. Lasren would trust Harry and Harry would trust Tom to determine if the transmission was evidence of any threat to the fleet. By the time Harry figured out that he'd been lied to, Tom would no longer be aboard. He'd be with his family. With fewer than twenty-four hours to go he found it almost impossible to think of anything beyond his arms around them.

Paris couldn't believe that his Starfleet career was over. He was surprised by how much it bothered him. At least Tom knew that he was leaving the ship in good hands. Having risen higher than he had ever believed possible within Starfleet, Tom was about to walk away without a backward glance.

"And I was so sure Commander Paris was having a little fun at my expense," Counselor Cambridge said wryly as he stepped into the *Galen*'s sickbay. Chakotay was standing beside the ship's chief medical officer, who for reasons that completely eluded the counselor *still* only called himself "the Doctor." Opposite them, seated upright on a biobed, sat Seven of Nine. As always, the sight of her made Cambridge wonder where he'd left his last breath.

"Hugh," Chakotay said, smiling warmly as he turned to shake his hand. They'd served together for three years, but it was only recently that they had become close.

"You've been with the fleet two days and this is the first I'm hearing of it?" he asked in mock annoyance.

"We were given temporary quarters aboard the *Galen,* though it's my understanding that as soon as the Doctor sees fit to release Seven from observation, we'll be transferring to *Voyager,*" Chakotay replied, smiling.

Cambridge shot an appraising glance at the Doctor, who was completing a tricorder scan of Seven.

"Two full days of observation? Is someone being a little overprotective of their patient?" Cambridge asked Chakotay quietly.

"Not in this case, I'm afraid," Chakotay replied.

Turning to the Doctor, Cambridge extended his hand. "Doctor, I have been summoned. The question remains, to what end?"

The Doctor took the counselor's proffered hand. "I will, of course, forward you my complete analysis for your review, but the concise version is this. A little more than five months ago, Seven underwent a process by which the Borg implants that had once sustained her biological systems were replaced by what I am going to call, for lack of contradictory evidence, Caeliar catoms. She has shown no physical signs of distress as a result of this process; however, Seven has reported a consistent presence, is that fair?" he asked Seven pointedly. When she nodded he continued, "A presence that seems intent upon convincing her that she is no longer Seven of Nine, but rather Annika Hansen."

It was the most remarkable story Hugh Cambridge had heard in a long time. The fact that its subject was a woman he had admired from afar since the first day they had met was enough to pique his interest. Sensing where this was going, he realized that any hope he might once have nurtured of getting to know Seven better had just been dashed. She was about to become his patient.

"That sounds terribly unpleasant," Cambridge said, meeting Seven's eyes.

"I have provided Seven with a neural inhibitor," the Doctor continued, pointing out a small, metallic oval affixed to the base of her skull just below her right ear. "I have monitored her steadily for the last thirty-six hours and it seems to have silenced the voice in her head."

"But it's not a long-term solution, is it?" Cambridge pointed out.

Seven, obviously growing weary of everyone present talking about her rather than to her, said, "Captain Eden has insisted that you monitor me until such time as my condition has been resolved."

Turning to Chakotay and the Doctor, Cambridge asked, "Gentlemen, would you excuse us for a moment?"

Once they had stepped out, the counselor planted himself directly before Seven, crossing his arms at his chest.

"And I'm guessing you find the prospect of my participation in this process utterly distasteful," Cambridge allowed.

"I will abide by the captain's request," Seven acknowledged.

"But not willingly," Cambridge noted, "which is going to be a problem."

Seven's gaze hardened, a feat the counselor hadn't actually suspected was possible until he actually witnessed it.

"I do not know what you require of me, Counselor," she replied. "But if it is in my power, I will do my best to comply."

"Prior to this transformation the Doctor described, do you believe you had fully recovered from the trauma of having once been a Borg drone? Put it this way, is there a reason you never chose to refer to yourself as Annika Hansen *before* this presence began making its troubling demands?"

"I have been referred to as Seven, Annika, and Professor Hansen, depending on the party addressing me," Seven replied, "and though I have found it annoying to correct people over an insignificant matter, what I am experiencing now is different."

"You consider your identity insignificant?" Cambridge asked.

"Until now, I have never had cause to question my identity. I considered my *designation* irrelevant," Seven corrected him.

"Until now?"

Seven paused briefly before asking, "Are you attempting to be helpful?"

"No," the counselor replied. "At this point I'm just trying to figure out how much help you're actually going to need."

"If my concerns are a burden to you—" Seven began.

"Not in the least," Cambridge assured her. "But here's the bottom line. If you don't want my help, then I can't help you. The good Doctor here may be able to address your most troubling symptom. My job will be to address the underlying cause, which I'm not convinced began *only* five months ago. Unless you are willing to explore that possibility, and agree to participate fully in the process, there's really nothing I can do for you."

Seven's face flushed as she bit back the desire to tell him exactly where he could shove his help.

"Very well. I will comply," she finally replied.

"Then we'll begin first thing in the morning," Cambridge said. "Do you know where my office is aboard *Voyager*?"

"I will find it."

"Excellent. Eight hundred hours." Cambridge smiled. "I look forward to it."

Cambridge left her to consider his words, which he had no doubt would disturb Seven sufficiently through the night. Quickly he poked his head into the Doctor's office where he was waiting with Chakotay.

"You never bring me easy problems, do you, Chakotay?" he quipped lightly.

"There wouldn't be any fun in that," Chakotay replied.

"Should I assume that you are going to be with us for a while?" Cambridge asked.

Chakotay nodded.

"I'd have given anything to see the look on Montgomery's face when you told him you were leaving Starfleet," the counselor said, smiling conspiratorially.

"So would I," Chakotay agreed. "Unfortunately, circumstances didn't permit that. I submitted my resignation in writing."

"Pity."

"I must say, Chakotay," the Doctor interrupted, "it seems an extreme measure to take. Even if they weren't prepared to give you command of *Voyager* again, I'm certain Admiral Montgomery would have found another post for you."

"I'm sure he would have gotten around to it eventually. I just couldn't wait, and neither could Seven," Chakotay replied. "If the Caeliar are still out there, this fleet will be the first to find them. Seven needs to know what happened to her."

"But it could take years," the Doctor worried.

"And in the meantime, she will have the most capable support I know of, yours, the counselor's, and mine."

"Of course," the Doctor nodded, "but . . ."

"But what?" Chakotay demanded.

"What if we never find them?" Cambridge finished for him.

"Then we'll adapt," Chakotay suggested.

The stares of concern that flashed among the three of them sealed a silent agreement.

We might, Cambridge thought sadly, *but I have no idea if Seven will.*

Given how much this extraordinary woman had already endured, never mind the invaluable service she had offered the Federation time and again, the counselor was suddenly struck by the enormity of what might be lost if they failed.

"Right," Cambridge muttered. "We'd best get started then."

CHAPTER SEVEN

Voyager was late.

If Tom's last message was accurate, they should have arrived at or near enough B'Elanna's coordinates for her long-range sensors to have detected them by now.

B'Elanna had hung all her hopes for Miral's recovery on the appearance of the ship she had never intended to set foot upon again. She had no idea who their new chief medical officer might be. But as long as the doctor was Starfleet, she assumed he would be a vast improvement on the medical staff from New Talax.

If they ever get here, she worried silently.

Her stomach ached with an unpleasant combination of fear and nausea. Miral rested beside her in her booster seat, her head tipped forward at that sharp angle only babies seemed to manage with ease. B'Elanna had programmed a subscreen of her control panel to display constant readings of Miral's vital signs. B'Elanna subconsciously matched her breath to the slow but steady blip monitoring her child's heart.

The last time B'Elanna had risked Miral's life without informing Tom, three years earlier when she had first learned of the danger posed by the Warriors of Gre'thor, it had almost strained her marriage to the breaking point. She didn't want to make that mistake again, and truly, the likelihood that any transmission she sent would be picked up by the Warriors of Gre'thor was infinitesimal. The problem was she didn't know where *Voyager* was. If they were en route, like they were supposed to be, the slipstream corridor would garble any incoming transmissions. Anything received would be automatically stored in a buffer until the ship emerged from slipstream velocity, so whether she sent a message now or later, they wouldn't receive it until the point had become moot.

Of course if they weren't already on their way that probably meant they wouldn't arrive for hours. Telling Tom to hurry up or his daughter might die wasn't going to help, though it might limit the number of recriminations between them should the unthinkable come to pass in his absence.

B'Elanna needed a plan, or she was going to lose what little patience she still had. The nearest inhabited system her charts showed was twelve light-years away. She would give *Voyager* ten hours. If they didn't appear, she would make the short trip and take her chances with a hopefully friendly alien species.

Running her hand lightly over Miral's forehead ridges, which were uncomfortably warm to the touch, she quickly amended her plan.

Eight hours at the most.

She was spared the need to reconsider again by a blurt from her sensor relay.

Kahless be praised.

A ship was approaching at warp speed and would be within range in minutes.

"It's going to be okay, sweetie," B'Elanna said softly as her heart climbed into her throat. "Daddy's almost here."

"*Warning, unknown vessel approaching,*" the computer advised.

"It's not an unknown vessel," B'Elanna chided. "Why are you reading it wrong?" she asked, wondering how many new bugs she was going to find in her system since the well-intentioned Talaxians had been mucking around it. B'Elanna had supervised their efforts but hadn't focused on them as sharply as was usual, given the amount of time she'd spent in the infirmary with Miral. She'd already been forced to reprogram the replicator that had offered *leola* root stew no matter what she ordered.

Quickly reinitializing her scanners, B'Elanna muttered softly to the computer, "Look again." But before the computer had time to adjust to the baseline parameters, she encountered a sight she had never expected to see again. All too soon it filled her viewscreen.

"That's impossible," B'Elanna said, wishing that her eyes were deceiving her.

A massive cube hung before her in space.

As her heart took several deep, painful pounds, B'Elanna waited for the standard greeting of the Borg, promising assimilation. Her hands flew over the controls, rerouting power to shields, charging phaser banks, and preparing one of the ten precious transphasic torpedoes she'd carried for just such an emergency to launch.

After thirty seconds, she realized that the vessel was not behaving like a Borg ship. Come to think of it, apart from its shape, it didn't look at all like a Borg ship. The surface lacked the intricate black hull that had always appeared to her as something unfinished. In its place was a polished gray alloy her sensors weren't identifying. The ship was also uncharacteristically refraining from scanning or threatening her in any way.

The Caeliar? B'Elanna wondered.

She knew next to nothing about them, apart from the fact

that they had helped the Federation defeat the Borg in the last moments of the invasion. The news feeds B'Elanna had intercepted since then had been filled with outlandish speculations about this incredibly advanced species.

Her Starfleet training reasserted itself. This could be a first-contact situation.

With shaking hands she opened a channel and began transmitting standard friendship greetings.

Ten seconds later, an angry purple burst of phased energy erupted from a corner of the cube and shook her ship from stem to stern, rousing Miral from her slumber. Her alarmed cries intensified with the second volley that B'Elanna had immediately moved to evade.

Apart from the sheer rudeness of the exchange, B'Elanna was confused by what she was seeing. The alien ship's energy weapons were strong, but her shields were holding and could likely sustain such fire indefinitely. She hesitated to shoot back as she didn't want to make a bad situation worse. There was a chance these were warning shots, and hardly the most destructive the aliens had at hand.

They obviously weren't Borg, but B'Elanna had a hard time believing they were the Caeliar. What little she knew suggested that the Caeliar could easily have disabled or destroyed her vessel in one shot.

Against her better judgment, B'Elanna decided to give diplomacy one last try.

"Alien vessel, cease fire. You have engaged a civilian vessel. I have a child on board. I do not mean you any harm and if I have violated your space, I will be happy to depart in peace. Please stand down."

In response, the ship sent forth three quick bursts that B'Elanna also found disarmingly easy to evade.

She was clearly out of safe options and Miral's plaintive wails reminded her that she was risking more than her own life. With one hand she plotted an escape route and powered up her warp drive. She would run as far as was required to lose her combative new friends but hopefully not so far that *Voyager* wouldn't be able to locate her if they ever arrived. A nagging thought snapped into the front of her mind. Neelix's voice reminded her with harsh simplicity that *she never used to run from a fight.* She risked much by standing her ground, but there was no way to know what she might lose if she failed to be here when Tom reached these coordinates.

Neither option was particularly good, but something she hadn't felt in years, something she had buried, rushed through her veins reminding B'Elanna that she was, first and always, a warrior.

She had been pushed to her limits by the Warriors of Gre'thor. She'd lost something to them she hadn't even missed until this moment. She had unconsciously chosen to become a victim, and that had left her frightened and alone. It had made B'Elanna think that she had no control over her destiny. It had separated her and her daughter for far too long from the man she loved.

A Klingon chose how they faced life and death. She didn't plan to die, but suddenly she knew in her bones that she didn't plan to live by anyone else's terms.

B'Elanna shut down the warp drive and pushed her impulse engines to maximum as she came about to face her assailant.

"You'd better have more than that in your torpedo tubes," she said aloud, "because I'm done running."

B'Elanna returned fire.

Captain Eden had sat calmly in her chair on the bridge for the hour it had taken *Voyager*, the *Hawking*, and the *Galen* to cover the twenty-plus thousand light-years between the fleet's first stop at the terminus of the Beta and Delta quadrants to the first location they were going to investigate. The fleet had separated into three groups of three ships. The first group was tasked with investigating a potentially dangerous alien species encountered during the *Aventine*'s prior investigation of a series of subspace corridors that had granted the Borg easy access to the Alpha quadrant. The second group was following slowly on *Voyager*'s heels dropping communication relays along the way.

Paris was looking forward to the end of this particular leg of the trip, mainly because he knew B'Elanna and Miral would be waiting there to greet him. But he was also curious to see what was left of the transwarp hub *Voyager* had destroyed four years earlier. Their rendezvous point was the last stop *Voyager* had made in the Delta quadrant and it was poetic that it would be the first place the fleet would investigate. Tom hadn't spent a lot of time wondering what they might have missed when they left the Delta quadrant behind. Picking up where they had left off just seemed right.

Starfleet Intelligence's reports assumed that they would find nothing. All traces of Borg technology had vanished along with the Caeliar. Whether or not this would include the debris of a vast unicomplex remained to be seen.

Though he was still getting used to seeing the trim, ebony-skinned figure in the command seat, the last several months working to ready the fleet had banished any concerns Paris had felt in serving under her. Eden was sharp and tough. She began every morning with a long list of orders, but Tom took comfort in the fact that her personal list was usually twice as long. She treated her senior officers as trusted comrades, encouraging them to show initiative and rewarding them with heartfelt praise when they managed to exceed her high standards. It was still too soon to tell whether or not she would bond with those who had been with *Voyager* the longest. The sudden death of Admiral Janeway followed too quickly by the chaos of the Borg Invasion during which Chakotay had completely unraveled had left those who had served together for eleven years shell-shocked. It was clear that some of the newer officers, including Conlon and their new CMO, Doctor Sharak, were warming to Eden. Counselor Cambridge, Paris had learned, was an old friend of Eden's. Tom had served for three years with Cambridge aboard *Voyager* without ever developing the casual warm regard for him that Eden obviously felt.

Paris found himself considering the differences between *Voyager*'s female captains. Kathryn Janeway had been ferocious, driven by a passion for exploration. She was protective of her crew, quick to find the brightest spot in any catastrophe, headstrong, and sometimes reckless in battle. Afsarah Eden's power was calmer and deeper. There was a regal quality to her that went beyond her exotic beauty. Her wide, dark eyes set above an aquiline nose punctuated by firmly set, full lips were always hungrily searching, an inquisitiveness borne of a desire beyond exploration. She seemed to be seeking synthesis, whether of a new technology or a character trait of a crewman. She rarely spoke freely. The distance she kept was professional and appropriate to her station, but Tom felt that if he ever needed to cross that line, she would respond with patience and respect.

She was fifteen years older than Janeway had been when

she assumed command of *Voyager*, and with her age had come a sense of both calm restraint and poise. Eden hadn't spent all her years in Starfleet exploring space. Scuttlebutt had it that she had passed on a promotion to join the fleet. Paris wondered if commanding *Voyager* might have meant setting aside her goals.

Her former husband, Admiral Willem Batiste, was less of a mystery. Tom had spent more time on and off duty around this breed of man than he'd cared to. Batiste, like so many of his father's friends, carried himself with an energy that dared anyone to contradict him. Though Tom had never witnessed anything but the utmost in professionalism from either Eden or Batiste, he secretly wondered how Eden was able to serve under him.

He and Harry had managed to catch a quick dinner in the mess the night before, but messages to Chakotay and Seven had gone unanswered. Tom was curious what had brought them to the fleet but this mystery could wait.

Gwyn—who hadn't stepped so much as a hair out of line in the last two weeks—interrupted his reverie as she announced, "Dispersing slipstream corridor."

Paris had finally become so accustomed to the transition during their test runs that he had started to take it for granted. The turbulent white tunnel vanished as the ship's inertial dampeners strained to compensate for the abrupt shift in velocity. After a few seconds, the viewscreen showed a serene starfield.

"Helm, full stop," Eden commanded. Turning her head toward Tom with a faint smile, she added, "How does it feel to be back, Mister Paris?"

"Weird," Paris replied honestly. He read subtle disappointment in her face, so he added, "But in a good way."

The captain asked, "Gwyn, what's our distance to the nebula?"

"One point six light-years, Captain."

"Let's take a look, shall we? Helm, plot a course."

"Aye, Captain," Gwyn replied.

"Bridge to Admiral Batiste," Eden called.

"*Go ahead.*"

"We have arrived at the coordinates and are preparing to investigate the nebula that was the site of the transwarp hub."

"*Keep me informed. Batiste out.*"

"Ensign Lasren, advise *Hawking* and *Galen* to hold position until we return."

Tom wondered if the uncomfortable warm and prickly sensation he was experiencing might have been his blood pressure rising, as there was no report yet of B'Elanna's ship.

"Lasren, are long-range sensors detecting anything unusual in the area?" Paris asked.

"I'm recalibrating our sensors to compensate for the nebula, sir."

"Captain," Kim's troubled voice piped in. "I'm picking up high energy discharges near the nebula."

"Source?" Eden asked.

Paris had to hold tightly to his armrests to avoid coming out of his chair. Harry finally said, "Two ships, an unregistered vessel similar to Federation design and a much larger vessel of unknown origin." He added, "The larger vessel has a cube-shaped configuration."

"Is it the Borg?" Eden asked calmly.

"The readings don't match anything in our database. There are traces of tritanium, but the alloy and weapons signatures don't appear to be Borg."

A small mercy.

"We should investigate," Paris quickly advised Eden. *Please,* he added silently.

"Agreed," Eden replied. "Ensign Gwyn, alter course to intercept. Lieutenant Kim, Yellow Alert."

Within moments the battle in progress appeared on the viewscreen.

"Life signs?" Eden asked.

"Two Klingons aboard the unregistered vessel. No life signs detected aboard the cube. It appears to be fully automated."

"More Klingons in the Delta quadrant?" Eden asked, her brow furrowing.

"The cube has sustained damage, Captain," Kim reported. "Their shields are failing and I'm detecting overloads in several systems. The unregistered vessel's shields are at eighty percent of maximum."

Paris was torn between admiring B'Elanna's success and getting her the hell out of danger as soon as possible. The shuttle maneuvered easily around the larger ship, avoiding direct fire. Still, the situation could change in seconds.

"Open a channel," Paris ordered.

"Channel open," Lasren confirmed.

Before Eden could object, Tom said, "This is the Federation *Starship Voyager* to the pilot of the unregistered vessel. Do you require assistance?"

A garbled response came over the comm.

"Lasren, can you clean that up?" Paris demanded.

"Commander," Eden said angrily.

Paris turned directly to Eden and said softly, "Captain, my wife and my daughter are aboard that ship."

Eden's eyes widened in surprise but she replied just as softly, "Your recently deceased wife and daughter?"

"Yes, Captain," Tom confirmed.

"You're sure?"

"Yes."

Eden's jaw clenched but it was clear she didn't doubt him. It was equally clear that once the confrontation was done, Tom was going to have a lot of explaining to do.

"Red Alert," Eden called out. "Battle stations." Klaxons sounded as the bridge was bathed in a crimson glow.

"Shields at maximum. Charging weapons," Harry said.

"Ensign Gwyn, put us between the shuttle and the cube. Ensign Lasren, as soon as we're in position, advise the pilot of that shuttle to drop shields and prepare for emergency transport."

Voyager moved gracefully into position. The shuttle disengaged. The ship shuddered as the fire intended for B'Elanna was absorbed by *Voyager* instead. Kim's reports indicated that they had sustained no serious damage.

"Return fire?" Kim asked.

"Not unless it becomes absolutely necessary," Eden replied. "Lasren, have we got the crew of that shuttle on board yet?"

Tom's breath caught in his chest until Lasren replied, "Confirmed, Captain. Two individuals transported aboard. They require medical attention and are on their way to sickbay."

With a firm nod and a withering glance at Paris, Eden ordered, "Lock onto the shuttle with a tractor beam and get us out of here. Full impulse."

The helm began to execute the maneuver but the alien ship, which obviously didn't know when it was beaten, pursued and continued to fire.

"What are they doing?" Kim asked. "They couldn't take that shuttle. They don't stand a prayer against us."

"There's no one aboard to reason that out," Lasren reminded him.

Eden addressed the pursuers. "Alien vessel. We mean you no harm. We have just recovered two of our people and do not intend to continue these hostilities. Stand down."

The only response was continued, intermittent phaser fire.

"Lieutenant Kim, can you target their propulsion system?"

"It's hard to say, Captain," Harry replied. "Our sensors show fifteen different configurations that could indicate propulsion."

"Pick the two most likely and fire," Eden ordered. "I want to disable them, not destroy them."

Bright blue beams intersected with the cube and massive explosions bloomed across its scarred hull.

"Brace for impact!" Harry called as the subsequent immolation of the cube sent violent shockwaves spreading through space, tossing *Voyager* about in their wake.

Once the dust had settled, Eden turned a hard gaze toward Paris, but addressed Kim.

"Do we need to look at the definition of *disable*, Lieutenant Kim?" she asked.

"I'm sorry, Captain," Harry replied. "The ship had sustained too much damage. I can confirm that no-life forms were aboard."

"Stand down Red Alert," Eden said cheerlessly. "Begin full analysis of the debris. I want to know where that ship came from and to whom exactly we now owe an apology." To Lasren she added, "Contact *Hawking* and *Galen*. Advise them to regroup at our position to assist in the investigation."

Finally the captain turned on her first officer. "Why is it, Mister Paris, that we couldn't manage five minutes in the Delta quadrant without ticking off the natives?"

"I'm sorry, Captain," Paris said earnestly. "Permission to report to sickbay?"

"With me," Eden replied in a voice that chilled him. Rising from her seat she headed toward her ready room. "Mister Kim, the bridge is yours."

CHAPTER EIGHT

The Doctor considered the hypothetical catom. It was truly a miraculous piece of engineering. He had studied a wide variety of molecular technology, but the catom in its elegance and simplicity put the the the nanoprobe to shame. Of course, it frustrated him to a degree that he wasn't certain he was actually looking at a catom. He had isolated discrete packets of molecules within Seven where once, much cruder machines had been integrated into her organic systems. For now, he labeled these particles catoms. Understanding exactly how they worked was going to take time.

In essence, catoms were programmable matter. They could reconfigure themselves, presumably into any shape or arrangement required by the systems they were sustaining. It seemed likely that since these catoms were keeping Seven alive, their configurations might be more specific than the catoms that reshaped Captain Erika Hernandez, a human woman who had become part of the Caeliar gestalt. Only after Admiral Batiste had cleared the way had the Doctor been able to access Hernandez's classified medical file. He knew that the best minds in Starfleet Medical were trying to understand how the catoms altered her human physiology. The Doctor knew he was at a disadvantage but he had confronted deeper medical mysteries since he had first been activated and did not doubt his ability to rise to this challenge.

An incessant chiming broke his concentration, which he realized was a comm request from *Voyager*'s sickbay. Doctor Sharak, *Voyager*'s CMO, was the first Tamarian the Doctor had met. For years, the universal translator was unable to render the Tamarian language into Standard. Finally, a Tamarian captain, Dathon, had risked his life and that of Captain Jean-Luc Picard in a bid to bridge this gap. It was discovered that the Tamarian grammatical structure was based on metaphor. Several members of Doctor Sharak's species had built upon those first tentative steps by immersing themselves in Federation culture, resulting in new translation protocols.

Sharak was the first Tamarian to enter Starfleet's service. As the principles of science were universal at their most basic levels, the fact that a scientist whose language was based on metaphor could communicate more easily in these realms was understandable. What made Sharak remarkable was that while studying at Starfleet Medical, he mastered Standard.

The Doctor opened the channel, and Sharak's wide, mottled face appeared before him.

"Greetings, Doctor," Sharak said amiably.

"How may I assist you, Doctor Sharak?"

"Do you retain within your personal database baseline analysis of a Miral Paris?" Sharak asked.

"Of course," the Doctor replied, wondering why Sharak might require this information.

"Would you be so generous as to transmit it to me?"

"Immediately," the Doctor said, nodding. "Is there anything else?"

"No."

"You should have the files now," the Doctor replied as he confirmed the upload from his database.

Sharak signed off without further comment and his face was replaced by the standard Starfleet symbol.

Resuming his analysis a troubling, recurring subroutine pestered the Doctor until he realized it would disrupt his concentration if he failed to address it. He quickly reactivated his comm panel to hail Doctor Sharak. Moments later the face of Sharak's nurse, Ensign Eline Bens, appeared.

"May I speak with Doctor Sharak?" he inquired.

"*The doctor is with a patient but I will have him get back to you as soon as possible,*" Bens said.

"I understand. I'm just curious about a request he made to review an old patient file. Can you tell me why he wished to see Miral Paris's records?"

"*Miral Paris is his patient. Could you excuse me, please?*" Bens abruptly terminated the transmission.

The Doctor sat stunned for two point six seconds before contacting Commander Glenn.

"*What can I do for you, Doctor?*" she asked.

"Captain, I have to get to *Voyager* immediately. Are we close enough to transfer my program?"

"*We're en route to meet up with them now,*" Glenn advised. "*We should be in range in the next few minutes. What's going on?*"

"Doctor Sharak's nurse has just advised me that he's treating one of my old patients."

"*I'm sure Doctor Sharak has matters well in hand,*" Glenn noted.

"The patient in question died three months ago."

Glenn immediately replied, "*Understood. Ensign Lawry, increase to maximum warp. Get us within range of* Voyager, *now, and hail Captain Eden for me.*"

The moment her ready room doors closed behind them, Eden turned to Paris, her obvious sense of betrayal plain in her troubled eyes.

"You weren't surprised to find that ship here, were you, Mister Paris?"

"No, Captain," he admitted. "Though I was surprised that they were engaged in battle."

"Explain," Eden ordered.

Tom took a deep breath. "A Klingon sect known as the Warriors of Gre'thor tried to kill my daughter three years ago."

Eden nodded for him to continue.

"The Emperor Kahless, B'Elanna, and I all agreed that the only way to stop them was to make them believe that B'Elanna and Miral were dead. B'Elanna constructed that ship at a civilian facility. During the Borg Invasion she ejected wreckage near one of the battle sites and when it was found, they were declared dead. I provided B'Elanna with our rendezvous coordinates."

"Was it your intention that B'Elanna and Miral would join you here on *Voyager*?"

"No, Captain," Paris replied. "We intended to set off on our own, as far from the Warriors of Gre'thor as possible."

Eden's eyes narrowed. "I'm pleased Starfleet was able to accommodate you, Mister Paris," she said with evident disdain.

"Captain, I'm sorry—" Paris began as Eden moved past him toward the doors.

"For the moment, I'm still your commanding officer," Eden cut him off. "You will report to your quarters while I speak with your wife."

Though it cost Tom dearly, he nodded his assent. The

disappointment flowing from her was palpable. He hadn't known her long enough to feel he owed her anything more. He'd done his duty well. He was surprised then when he felt his face flush in shame as Eden led him back to the bridge.

I did what I had to do, part of his mind insisted.

As Tom was trying to determine how he was going to live with his shame, Eden added to it by saying, "Lieutenant Kim, please secure Mister Paris in his quarters. Lieutenant Patel," she added, nodding to the science officer, "the bridge is yours."

The three entered the turbolift in silence and Paris felt that quiet grow heavier until they reached deck five and Eden exited without a word. The moment the doors had closed Harry blurted out, "It took me a minute to verify my readings and to cross-check them with Lasren's, but I know I'm right. B'Elanna and Miral were on that shuttle, weren't they?" Harry demanded.

"Yes."

"And you knew?"

"Yes."

If Eden's dismay had been palpable, Harry's was like a punch to the gut. Tom couldn't tell if the tears welling up in Harry's eyes were of relief or anger.

"You knew they weren't dead," Harry confirmed though he clearly didn't want to believe it.

"I'm sorry, Harry. It was the only way," Tom attempted.

"No it wasn't," Harry replied, his voice rising. "Since when do you lie to me about something like this? Who are you?"

"Harry, please understand. They were going to hunt Miral down and kill her. I couldn't let that happen."

"I don't care," Kim answered, not mollified in the least. "This isn't how we do things. We're family. When we need help, we ask for it. You let me believe . . ."

"I had to."

Harry shook his head, aghast.

"No. No, you didn't."

Harry led Tom out of the turbolift and down the corridor without uttering another word. He left Tom locked in his quarters, wondering how what was supposed to have been the happiest moment of his life in years had just become so miserable.

Eden entered sickbay to find B'Elanna Torres, *Voyager*'s former chief engineer. She'd read Torres's file numerous times. A headstrong and passionate woman who tended to live in emotional extremes, she was an ingenious officer.

B'Elanna stood watching with consternation as Doctor Sharak and the Doctor tended to the small, still figure who had to be Miral Paris. Clearing her throat slightly, Eden extended her hand. "Ms. Torres, or do you prefer Mrs. Paris?" she asked. "I'm Captain Afsarah Eden."

"'B'Elanna' is fine, Captain Eden," B'Elanna replied tensely as she accepted Eden's hand.

"Was your daughter injured in the battle we just witnessed?"

"No," B'Elanna replied, shaking her head. "She's been sick for two weeks. When we arrived in the Delta quadrant my ship was damaged. I contacted Neelix, an old friend—"

"The Talaxian?" Eden interrupted.

"Yes. His people helped me make repairs. But almost as soon as we arrived, Miral fell ill and they weren't able to help her. If you hadn't arrived when you did, I don't know if she would have survived."

"Doctor Sharak," Eden said, turning to her CMO. "What is your patient's status?"

Sharak was engrossed in his study of Miral's readings. Without looking up he replied, "It appears that the child has been infected by a most hearty virus. She will recover."

"No thanks to her mother," the Doctor said.

"I beg your pardon, Doctor?" Eden asked as B'Elanna flushed with either anger or relief.

The Doctor accepted a hypo from Nurse Bens and dispensed it gently into Miral's limp arm. Then he turned to the captain and B'Elanna.

"Miral was exposed to a simple Talaxian flu. Most children her age who are cleared for interstellar travel receive several vaccinations that Miral appears to have missed. If they are regularly exposed to a variety of species and those species' respective germs, their immune system learns to fight off the simplest infections. Would I be correct in assuming," he asked B'Elanna, "that you have kept Miral secluded over the last three years?"

"Yes," B'Elanna replied.

The Doctor shook his head in frustration and continued, "By doing so you have inhibited the development of her immune system. Even in a preschool setting, where she would have interacted regularly with other children, Miral would have been exposed to common infectious agents. You kept her in a bubble and now her immune system is ill-equipped to fight off exotic pathogens like the one she encountered among the Talaxians."

"I was only—" B'Elanna began.

"Captain," the Doctor said, ignoring B'Elanna's attempt at justification, "it is my opinion that at least for the next several months, this child should be seen regularly by a competent physician."

"I concur," Sharak added from Miral's bedside.

Eden turned to B'Elanna, who was clearly taken aback both by the Doctor's report, and the hostility with which it was delivered. "I spoke briefly with your husband and he indicated that all of you had planned to leave *Voyager* as soon as possible. Even before I heard the Doctor's evaluation, I must admit, I thought that to be an incredibly foolhardy notion. Your service records indicate that you are both quite capable, but you know how dangerous this quadrant of space is. Are you willing to reconsider your plans, or are you going to force me to make this decision for all of you?"

B'Elanna stood in shocked silence. She glanced at the Doctor with a mixture of sadness and reproach. "Please understand, we made the choices we did because we didn't want to add our burdens to yours. The Warriors of Gre'thor should no longer be a threat, unless they learn Miral is still alive."

"With all the resources of Starfleet behind us, I'm sure we can sustain the illusion," Eden assured her.

"I'd be willing to accept any arrangement you would find appropriate, Captain."

"Welcome aboard," Eden said with a tight smile.

"Thank you, Captain."

"If you'll wait here, I'll allow your husband a few minutes' leave to see you."

Once the captain departed, B'Elanna turned back to the Doctor.

"I'm sorry," she offered softly.

"I thought you were both dead."

"I know."

After a moment, his eyes began to glisten. "I can't tell you how relieved I am to find that I was misinformed."

B'Elanna didn't know which of them moved first to close the space between them. Soon, however, she found herself in a tight embrace. After a moment, the Doctor released her and gestured with a nod for her to look over her shoulder where Tom stood in forlorn silence, staring at Miral.

"What's wrong with Miral?" he asked, clearly expecting the worst.

"She's going to be fine," B'Elanna replied as she reached out a hand to pull him close. Tom took her face in his hands and kissed her tenderly. She then threw her arms around his neck, and for a few seconds, her universe was complete.

The Doctor broke the spell. "I have to say I'm surprised by the disregard you have shown me and the rest of your friends, Commander Paris. I didn't realize you had it in you."

"I never meant to hurt you or anyone," Tom said honestly. "I only hope that you can understand why it was necessary and that in time you will be willing to forgive me."

"Oh, you'll have plenty of time to make it up to me," the Doctor smirked.

Tom paused, confusion flashing in his eyes. Turning to B'Elanna he asked, "What's he talking about?"

B'Elanna felt a smile spreading across her face.

"There's been a slight change of plans," she replied.

CHAPTER NINE

Chakotay found Seven in *Voyager*'s astrometrics lab, which she had helped design. Control panels embedded in the walls were linked to an interface station in the center of the room. Beyond a railing that bordered the station, a wide platform gave way to a large screen. Linked into *Voyager*'s sensors, it displayed detailed scans of surrounding space in minute detail.

Seven appeared to be engaged in a sector by sector scan of the ship's immediate area. He didn't have to ask what she was looking for.

"How did your session with Counselor Cambridge go this morning?" he asked cheerily as he stepped to her side at the central station.

Without tearing her eyes from the screen she replied evenly, "The counselor is a difficult individual."

"He grows on you," Chakotay assured her.

"So does fungus," Seven replied without missing a beat.

"Is your combadge malfunctioning?" Chakotay asked gently.

"Not to my knowledge."

"We've been asked to join the senior staff in the conference room. Didn't you get the call?"

Seven's hands froze over the panel and her breath quickened. She tapped her combadge and it chirped as she opened a connection. She quickly tapped it again to close it.

"I've been so focused on this task that I didn't realize . . ."

"It's all right," Chakotay said patiently. "I understand that you're anxious to begin your search for the Caeliar. Perhaps your neural inhibitor is malfunctioning."

Seven nodded warily.

"We'll have the Doctor take a look at it again as soon as the meeting is over," Chakotay suggested. "We shouldn't keep Captain Eden waiting."

"No."

As they headed for the doors Seven asked, "Do you know what this meeting is about?"

"I don't," Chakotay replied, though he was understandably curious. It would be the first senior staff meeting he had ever attended on board without any specific role to play.

Get used to it, his better angels advised as they hurried through the halls toward the conference room.

Paris stood alone in Eden's ready room, shifting his weight from one leg to the other nervously. After his brief reunion with B'Elanna and Miral he had returned to his quarters and awaited further instructions from the captain. He'd been surprised and relieved when they came only a few hours later. He was summoned to meet privately with her and his gut was winding its way into ever-tightening knots as he waited for her to arrive.

The moment she did, he snapped to attention.

"Lieutenant Commander Paris reporting as ordered, Captain."

Eden nodded briskly as she stood before him. He wondered if he might have just said those words for the last time in his career. Now that he knew B'Elanna had agreed to remain on *Voyager* for the foreseeable future, he realized he didn't want to do so as an observer or a crewman. It was hard to imagine another fate, however, so he resolved himself to accept whatever was coming.

"It appears that you and your family are going to remain on board," Eden said briskly.

"Yes, Captain, and I'd like to thank you for allowing it," he said sincerely.

"You're welcome."

After a tense pause, Paris said, "I accept that you are going to reduce me in rank."

"You do?"

"Yes, Captain," Paris replied forcefully. "I realize that my actions were unbecoming of your first officer."

"Unbecoming . . . ?"

Tom swallowed hard.

"Permission to speak freely?" he asked.

Eden nodded. "Granted."

"For better or for worse, *Voyager* gave me back my life. I became a good Starfleet officer and a better man serving her and her captain. I wanted to stay aboard but I couldn't imagine a way to do that and keep my family safe."

"Why didn't you come to me?" Eden asked.

Paris suddenly realized that the idea had never crossed his mind. He was struck by how great the gulf was between them. He wouldn't have hesitated to go to Captain Janeway or Captain Chakotay with such a problem. The disappointment in Eden's face suggested she was well aware of this.

"Are you telling me that if I had come to you, you would have helped us?" he asked.

"You didn't give me the chance," Eden said honestly. "You talked about this ship and her captain. You have done a disservice to both of us. You're *my* first officer. I need to trust you for the good of my ship and my crew." After a long pause, she added, "That trust has been broken."

"I know, and I'm sorry."

"Don't be sorry," Eden said. "Earn it back."

Tom nodded intently. "I will. Thank you, Captain."

Since the days of wooden sailing ships there has been one constant: the fastest form of communication was scuttlebutt. Between the unexpected arrival of Seven of Nine and Chakotay and the morning's battle to recover an unregistered Federation shuttle, the rumors were flying.

Lieutenant Conlon reported to the conference room as ordered to find the captains, first officers, science officers, and chief engineers of *Voyager, Hawking,* and *Galen* assembling around the large triangular table. She'd heard that this room had been all but destroyed during the Borg Invasion and had been rebuilt to allow up to fifteen individuals to meet comfortably. As best as she could tell, the only ones missing were Commander Paris and Admiral Batiste.

She had a quick question to run by Vorik, so she made her way to the side of the table where he stood waiting for Captain Bal Itak of the *Hawking* to finish his remarks. Itak actually looked old even for a Vulcan, which was remarkable. The slight stoop in Itak's shoulders and his fine white hair suggested he might have recently seen his sesquicentennial.

". . . but all four are inhabited," Itak finished as Conlon stood beside Vorik.

"Fascinating," Lieutenant Lern, *Hawking*'s science officer, noted. "Will the subspace instabilities you discovered inhibit our ability to safely approach the system?" she asked Vorik.

"With proper modifications to the shields and deflectors, they should not," Vorik replied.

Conlon tugged as unobtrusively as possible on Vorik's sleeve.

"A moment, Lieutenant?" she asked.

"Of course," Vorik said, stepping away from the others.

"What sort of deflector modifications are we talking about?" she asked.

"Minimal. I will, of course, forward the specifications to you as soon as I have completed them."

"Thanks," Conlon said with a nod. "I'm also curious to know whether or not you've completed your post-flight diagnostic of the slipstream drive and deflector components."

"No, Lieutenant. You would have received them, as you requested, had I done so."

"The thing is, we finished up ours just before I got the call for this meeting and apart from the microfractures . . ." she began, but was cut off by an announcement: "Admiral on deck."

She turned to see everyone else in the room standing at attention. Once the admiral had taken his seat, Conlon settled in beside Vorik, realizing that directly across from her were *Voyager*'s former captain, Chakotay, and a striking woman who had to be Seven of Nine.

"Good afternoon," Batiste said briskly. He hadn't struck Conlon as a particularly warm man on the few occasions she'd heard him speak. Then again, most admirals weren't. She secretly believed that good cheer and compassion were surgically removed prior to one's promotion. What puzzled her was that he had once been married to Captain Eden. In temperament and leadership style, they appeared to be polar opposites. Of course, Conlon preferred Eden's way of doing things. She just wondered what had ever drawn them together.

"We have a lot of ground to cover. Before we proceed, have we made any progress on the issue of sustaining or supplementing our benamite reserves?" the admiral asked flatly.

Eden quickly replied, "Not yet, Admiral. Lieutenant Conlon has a team working on it."

"As does Lieutenant Vorik," Captain Itak added softly with a nod to his chief engineer.

"Lieutenant Benoit," Commander Glenn said, offering her young chief an encouraging smile, "has had our Emergency Engineering Holograms running diagnostics and simulations for the past three days."

"We're going to need a strategy sooner rather than later, people," Batiste barked.

"Understood, Admiral," Eden said.

"What benamite reserve problem?" Seven interjected.

"Lieutenant Conlon?" Eden said, nodding for her to explain.

Clearing her throat lightly, Conlon said, "During our first sustained slipstream flight from the Deneva system to the terminus of the Beta and Delta quadrants, the benamite crystals used suffered unexpected microfractures. If we cannot correct the problem—"

"The fleet will be forced to return to the Alpha quadrant in three months rather than three years," Seven finished for her.

"Yes," Conlon agreed.

"We should begin long-range scans for alternate sources," Seven suggested.

"Already done," Conlon advised her.

Batiste turned to Eden and said, "Perhaps before we continue, Captain Eden, you should brief the others on the additions to *Voyager*'s personnel roster."

"Thank you, Admiral," she acknowledged politely. "I'm sorry to disappoint whomever had 'Captain Chakotay has arrived to assume command of *Voyager*' in the speculations pool," she said lightly, "but as you can see," she went on with a hint of a grin in response to Chakotay's much wider smile, "Seven of Nine and Chakotay have joined the fleet. Seven was invited to participate in this mission before the fleet's launch and I'm sure I speak for all of us when I say that her joining us is appreciated. Seven will be assigned to a special project in *Voyager*'s astrometrics division for the time being and will also serve as an advisor to the fleet. For those of you who have been fortunate enough to serve with her in the past, I'm certain that you greet this news, as I did, with great enthusiasm. Chakotay has chosen to resign his commission from Starfleet but will also accompany the fleet in an advisory role to Seven. On behalf of all of us, I welcome both of them aboard."

This was met with polite applause, which reddened Seven's fair cheeks.

"However, there is a further addition to *Voyager*'s crew. I must advise all of you that what I am about to say is considered classified. You will each be responsible for advising your crews to the sensitivity of the matter."

Eden cleared her throat before continuing. "It was reported that Commander Tom Paris's wife and child were killed during the Borg Invasion." Eden then tapped her combadge and said, "Commander Paris, please report to the conference room."

A collective gasp sounded as moments later, the doors behind Eden opened and Tom and B'Elanna entered.

Conlon watched as both Seven's and Chakotay's faces filled with mingled disbelief and joy.

"A sect of Klingons known as the Warriors of Gre'thor believe that Miral Paris is a fated savior of the Klingon people. She was abducted and nearly killed and since then, Commander Paris and B'Elanna have done what they could to make the Warriors of Gre'thor believe that Miral was dead. We welcome B'Elanna Torres and Miral Paris aboard *Voyager*. We do not anticipate encountering the Warriors, but I have assured the Paris family that if we do, we will not hesitate to defend them. In the interest of avoiding any such unpleasantness, for the duration of our mission they will be entered into the ship's manifest under aliases."

"Be sure and advise your crews that the first person who refers to them in official reports by anything other than their aliases will spend this entire journey scrubbing plasma conduits," Admiral Batiste added. "Are we clear?"

There were nods all around. Paris and B'Elanna quickly took their seats beside Captain Eden. Glancing around the rest of the table, Conlon saw either polite curiosity or genuine happiness. For her part, Conlon felt no small amount of consternation. B'Elanna Torres was a legend among the engineers who had served with her. Living up to her reputation would have been one thing.

Living in her presence?

That was something Nancy Conlon was not at all certain she was up to. Her spirits were buoyed, however, by the thought that at least now she would have a chance to consult and possibly learn a little something from one of the best engineers in Starfleet.

Eden raised her voice to settle the table as she continued, "I have asked B'Elanna to join this meeting in hopes that she might be able to shed a little light on her encounter with the alien vessel." With a nod, she indicated that B'Elanna should begin.

The shy smile that had been B'Elanna's default expression since she walked into the room vanished and Eden watched the transformation between the woman and the Starfleet officer. Technically, B'Elanna still enjoyed the rank of lieutenant commander. She had been on extended leave since the birth of her child. At some point, the issue would have to be resolved, but for now, Eden was content to allow her to reacclimate to the ship and get settled before pressing the issue.

"The vessel approached my position," B'Elanna began. "Given its configuration, I thought that it might be the Borg. I noted the strange alloys present in the hull. When I attempted to hail the vessel, its only response was to open fire. I defended myself, and then *Voyager* showed up."

"You knew we were coming," Paris said a little too pointedly. "Why didn't you just fall back and wait for us?"

"I had no way of knowing exactly when you would arrive," B'Elanna replied. "I worried that if I left the area, I might miss the fleet. And frankly, the alien ship's weapons systems weren't that impressive."

"Is it possible that these were part of the transformed Borg we've heard so much about?" Batiste asked. "Or perhaps, the Caeliar, Seven?"

"No," Seven replied without hesitation. "The Borg are no more. And this could not have been the Caeliar."

"How can you be certain?" Batiste asked.

"Commander Torres's ship survived the encounter, and *Voyager* destroyed it easily. What Starfleet knows of the

Caeliar's technology suggests that if it had been the Caeliar, this would not have been the case."

Batiste seemed to accept Seven's reasoning. "Captain Itak," he said sharply, "I believe you were able to trace the vessel?"

The *Hawking*'s commanding officer replied gravely, "We began by analyzing the ship's warp trail and we believe we have discovered the system of origin. It is located four light-years from our present position and is interesting in at least one critical respect."

At this, Itak tapped a control on the table's edge, activating a small holographic projector embedded in the center of the conference table. A three-dimensional representation of the system appeared for all to examine.

"Fourteen planets orbit a single, Class-F star. The third and fourth are Class-M. Our long-range scans indicate that these two planets, along with the seventh, which is Class-J, and the tenth, a Class-Y, show abundant life-form readings. We are definitely looking at a system that is home to billions of beings."

"A gas giant and a Demon-class planet show life-form readings?" Paris asked.

"Yes," Itak confirmed evenly.

"That is interesting," Paris noted.

"I believe I just said that, Commander."

As Eden considered the reality that these billions might now be their enemy, Itak continued. "Our analysis of the nebula has been completed. There is no sign of the transwarp hub. We are reading a large number of subspace instabilities. This entire sector appears to be filled with similar instabilities that may be the aftereffects of the Borg network's destruction. Further study will be required to confirm this hypothesis."

"Have you detected any other vessels in the system?" Batiste asked.

"Yes, sir," Itak replied. "A small contingent appears to be present in orbit of the third planet."

"Are all their vessels automated?" Eden asked.

"Unknown. They are heavily shielded," Itak replied.

"It is safe to assume that the vessel we encountered was not their best armed or best defended," Batiste interjected. "Captain Eden, I'd like you to take *Voyager* and attempt to establish contact. This fleet cannot start its work in the Delta quadrant by acquiring a reputation of firing first and asking questions never."

Although Eden shared the sentiment, she was equally cognizant of the danger her ship now faced. "Aye, sir. I'd like to request that the *Galen* accompany us," Eden said.

"Very well," Batiste agreed. "I'll join the *Hawking*. I'd like us to get a better look at these subspace instabilities. Will they impede warp drive within the sector?"

"No, sir," Vorik chimed in.

"Then let's get to it," Batiste said, rising from his seat.

As the room emptied, Eden noted Conlon moving swiftly toward her.

"Something wrong, Nancy?" she asked.

"I'm going to take the slipstream drive offline for at least the next twenty-four hours if that's all right with you," Conlon said.

"Why?"

"It's probably nothing, but I'm not taking any chances," Conlon replied, clearly puzzled. "We ran a full diagnostic just after the excitement ended this morning and there's a processing delay somewhere between the drive and deflector controls. We might have burned out a few components.

I need to do a visual inspection to be sure. At any rate, I wouldn't feel comfortable attempting another coordinated slipstream flight until I find the problem."

"Track it down," Eden ordered.

"I will," Conlon replied. "If you could manage to keep us out of any fights for the next couple of days it would be a lot easier," she added semi-seriously.

Eden assured her chief engineer, "That's always my goal."

B'Elanna kept her seat as everyone began to hurry from the room. On their way out, Vorik and Seven paused to express their pleasure in learning that she and Miral were unharmed and B'Elanna assured them that she was delighted to see both of them again. She hoped they would speak again as soon as their respective duties permitted.

As they left she reflected that it had been years since she had participated in a meeting like this one and it was strange to sit there with no real responsibility resting on her shoulders. It was also refreshing to be intrigued by the prospect of encountering a new species. B'Elanna found it puzzling that the billions of life-forms present in the system would have chosen to explore space using only automated vessels.

Unless their primary intent isn't exploration, B'Elanna thought.

A pair of familiar hands settled themselves on her shoulders. Turning, she saw Chakotay smiling down at her.

"Hey," she said, smiling wistfully as Chakotay sank down into the empty seat beside her. The room was all but empty now.

"I still can't believe it," Chakotay said, irrepressible happiness writ large on his face.

"I've missed you too," B'Elanna replied.

"When can I see Miral?"

"I'll take you down to sickbay right now if you like. She's probably sleeping, but you're welcome to come just the same."

Chakotay nodded. B'Elanna felt an uncomfortable weight nestled in her stomach. Raising her defenses she asked, "How come you're not as pissed at me as the Doctor was? Or Harry, for that matter?"

Confusion flashed across Chakotay's face.

"Why would I be pissed at you?"

A new and even more troubling thought entered B'Elanna's mind. "You weren't upset when you heard that I died?"

"I was devastated," Chakotay replied seriously. "I'm sure everyone was."

"Well, I'm sorry we had to put you through that," B'Elanna apologized.

Chakotay took her hands in his.

"Listen to me. In the last few years I've lost too many people who were important to me. I'd give anything to have them back. I respect the choice you made. Truth be told, I probably wouldn't have been much help to you at the time," he admitted, chagrined. "But if I've learned anything, it's this: Life is much too short to waste time wallowing in the past, especially when the future hands you a second chance. I love you, B'Elanna. You and Tom and Miral, you're part of my family. There's not a lot I wouldn't forgive you."

B'Elanna felt fresh tears rising but composed herself as she said, "Thank you. You don't know how much that means to me right now. But I've still got work to do mending fences with everyone else."

"Give them time," Chakotay advised. "It's a lot to take in all at once."

B'Elanna nodded. "I can do that." After a moment she asked, "Why did you resign your commission?"

"Command took *Voyager* from me. They questioned my abilities and my judgment."

"That doesn't make any sense."

Chakotay half-smiled in recollection. "Talk to Tom. It will make more sense. At any rate, they were going to get around to giving me a new assignment at some point, but I couldn't wait for that. Seven needed me."

"Really?" B'Elanna asked, surprised.

"Yes," Chakotay said, nodding. "She's been through a lot, particularly in the last few months. She's more vulnerable now than I've ever known her to be."

"Are you and she . . . ?" B'Elanna trailed off.

It took Chakotay a moment to follow.

"Are she and I what?"

"A couple again?" B'Elanna replied dubiously.

Chakotay shook his head. "No," he said, dismissing the notion out of hand. "We're friends. Good friends. But anything more is completely out of the question."

"Why?"

Chakotay shrugged. "I have some healing to do myself before I even entertain the idea of a new relationship. And that's the last thing she needs right now. Seven and I didn't work out the first time for good reasons. We don't need to go down that road again just to end up in the same place."

"Isn't it hard for you though?" B'Elanna asked, leaning in closer and lowering her voice.

"What?"

"Being here? Being around all of this without being a part of it?"

"I could ask you the same thing," he replied.

B'Elanna shook her head. "I just got here. And right now all I care about is making sure Miral gets better and settling in with Tom. We haven't lived as husband and wife in years."

Chakotay considered her appraisingly.

"Uh-huh."

"What?"

"Nothing."

"What?" she asked again, more insistently.

"I know you, B'Elanna Torres. You're not going to be happy sitting idly by while everyone else around you is busy exploring the Delta quadrant."

B'Elanna struggled to deny his words, despite the fact that she was already toying with the same conclusion.

"Are you?" she asked.

"I made my choice," he said. "I'll figure out how to live with it."

"When you do, let me know," B'Elanna replied.

CHAPTER TEN

Harry sat somberly before an untouched plate of grilled salmon. Right now, Tom and B'Elanna were hosting a private dinner in their quarters for Chakotay, Seven, Barclay, and the Doctor. Harry hadn't felt bad begging off when Vorik had done the same. Miral had been released from sickbay near the end of his duty shift and Tom had been walking around with an annoying spring in his step since. Harry had already told B'Elanna how happy he was to see her, and he'd get around to checking in on Miral later. But he simply couldn't pretend that everything was fine between him and Tom.

No matter how many ways he tried to look at the situation from Tom's point of view, he couldn't see himself making the same choices Tom had. Yes, B'Elanna had insisted. And given all she'd been through the first time she'd faced the Warriors of Gre'thor, Harry got that her fear had made her all but completely irrational on the subject.

Not that she was going to win any Most Rational awards even before those dark days.

And yes, a promise made between a husband and wife was important. Harry had to believe that Tom *wanted* to tell him the truth all along but between B'Elanna and Kahless, he'd been outnumbered and really forced into deception.

But then again . . .

This was the place where Harry's reason hit a solid wall of confusion and anger. At the end of the day, no matter what B'Elanna or Kahless or anyone else might have insisted, had Harry been in Tom's place he never would have been able to bring himself to lie to his best friend. He couldn't have done it, knowing the depth of grief Harry would feel when he learned of their supposed deaths.

He had gone back and forth a hundred times since B'Elanna had asked him to join them all for dinner. Harry still hadn't had a chance to catch up with Seven and Chakotay or to find out what had convinced them to join the fleet. And he really was anxious to see Miral. Harry had wept openly the first time he'd held her in his arms the day she was born, and begun to spin a future in which he would be the cool uncle who she could always turn to when her parents just didn't understand. The thought of B'Elanna's death had been painful, but the thought of Miral's had been something beyond pain. It had been entirely unacceptable.

But Harry knew himself well enough to admit that he would never have made it through dinner without betraying his anger and confusion. His mind understood, but his heart remained completely irrational on the subject. He couldn't shake the thought that somewhere along the line, Tom had begun to define friendship differently from him. As much as he wanted to for B'Elanna and Miral's sake, he didn't think he could play the part that would be expected of him.

He stared again at his salmon. He was hungry. And the thought of taking a bite turned his stomach.

"Lieutenant Kim?" a voice interrupted his thoughts.

Looking up he saw Nancy Conlon standing beside the empty chair opposite him. The rest of the mess was all but deserted. Harry hadn't gotten to know Nancy that well. He had held two tactical drills during which her engineers had performed like engineers, more concerned with their engines and ship's weapons than their own safety. When he'd pointed out to Conlon where improvement was needed, she'd cheerfully agreed and promised to add it to her list of things to do. And she'd said it all with a smile you didn't notice amid her otherwise rather plain features. Conlon wore her dark brown hair in a tight ponytail. When he looked at her, she was all big brown eyes with nothing to soften or frame them. And she had retained her Academy figure, though maybe she was just naturally petite.

"Lieutenant Kim?" she said again, a little more forcefully, pulling Harry into the present.

"Sorry," Harry replied automatically. "What can I do for you, Lieutenant?"

"Is this seat taken?"

"Go ahead," Harry replied.

After a brief, uncomfortable silence she asked, "Something wrong with your salmon?"

"No," he said, shoving the plate a few inches away. "I'm just not all that hungry."

"Okay."

After another short pause, Harry wondered if he was being rude.

"Help yourself, if you like," he offered.

"Why not," Conlon replied, reaching for the plate and his fork. After a few hearty mouthfuls she added, "Thanks."

"No problem," Harry said, moving to rise from his seat.

"Hang on," she said between bites, thrusting a padd across the table at him. "I didn't just come looking for you because I was hungry. Wait, that didn't come out right. I didn't know . . ." she said, flustered.

Despite his dark mood, Harry felt his mouth tilting toward a smile. He resumed his seat. "Slow down. Finish chewing. Swallow."

As he gave these instructions Conlon matched her actions to his words. When she had finished he said, "Speak."

"Yeah, one of these days I'm going to get around to table manners," Conlon said sheepishly. "I've got a problem, and I'd like you to take a look at it."

Harry dutifully picked up the padd and quickly absorbed its contents.

"Microfractures, eh?" he finally said with an air of a seasoned veteran.

Conlon considered him warily as she replied, "Uh-huh. And it's not just *Voyager*'s benamite crystals. Every vessel in the fleet showed the same results after our last slipstream run. Granted, the last one was pretty long. But I'm pretty sure the point of having this nifty new drive is to be able to use it to cover as much distance as we want as often as we need to and unless I can find a way to fix this, that isn't going to happen."

Harry tossed the padd back to her and feeling better than he had all night said, "Problem solved."

Conlon's face betrayed utter incredulity.

"How?" she demanded.

"Are you finished eating?" Harry asked.

Conlon immediately dropped her fork. "If you're serious, I am."

"Let's take a walk," Harry replied.

Nancy followed Harry out of the mess hall and only when they had reached the turbolift and he directed them toward the deck housing the shuttlebay was she able to guess at their destination.

Conlon could tell Kim was enjoying himself at her expense. Every spare moment she'd had—and there hadn't been many since she'd learned of the benamite problem—she'd been fretting over a solution. Thus far, all she had come up with was shortening the fleet's mission.

She'd come to Harry hoping for a little unconventional perspective. When she'd taken over for Vorik, the Vulcan had scrupulously and in mind-numbing detail given her his appraisal of each of her staff members. Harry Kim was on the short list of non-engineering specialists who could provide valuable insight.

Her days on the *da Vinci* had taught her that establishing cohesive working relationships between staff members could be tricky. She was new to *Voyager,* but the engineer understood that she was going to have to make sure Kim understood who was in charge of this little corner of the universe.

Toward this end, she decided to change the subject, as he was clearly not going to tell her more about his miraculous solution until they'd reached the shuttlebay.

"Can I ask you something else?" she said as the turbolift doors slid open.

"Sure."

"Isn't B'Elanna one of your oldest friends? I mean, you served together in the Delta quadrant, didn't you?"

Harry tensed at her side, but kept his voice even as he replied.

"We did. And she is."

Conlon worried that she might be trespassing on too personal ground but was going to feel even dumber than she already did if she let it go at that.

"I thought so. You just don't seem as happy as everyone else was today to learn that she's still alive."

Kim paused his steps and turned to face her.

"I am happy to see her," he said coldly. "I'm thrilled she's still alive."

"Okay."

"Okay," Harry repeated and continued walking.

Nancy would have been content to remain silent for the remainder of their walk. She would have been ecstatic had she thought to construct a time machine before she entered the mess hall so that she could have erased this moment from history now that it had occurred. She lagged a little behind as she tormented herself with these thoughts until Harry stopped again and looked her way.

"I'm sorry," he said.

"No apology necessary," she replied hastily. "It's none of my business."

Both the gloating and the hostility in Harry's face were gone and in their place she caught a glimpse of genuine misery.

"You're right. It isn't. But I don't mind that you asked."

I don't know about that, Nancy mused.

Harry continued, "I love B'Elanna and Miral. I wanted to die when I thought they were dead. Having them back is a miracle and I am grateful. I'm just pissed at Tom."

"I'm sorry to hear that," Nancy said as kindly as possible. "You two are friends. You'll work it out."

"Maybe," Harry said with a shrug.

Realizing that crossing into this personal territory might feel more comfortable if she made an unpleasant confession of her own, Nancy said, "I have to say, though, I probably wasn't as happy to see B'Elanna walk into that room as everyone else was."

"Why not?" Harry asked.

"She's B'Elanna Torres," Nancy replied, as if that should more than explain it. "She's the miracle worker of the Delta quadrant. She's one of the reasons this ship made it home in one piece. To hear her former subordinates talk, she walks on water, leaps Borg cubes with a single bound, and recalibrates magnetic constrictors just by glancing in their direction."

She felt better when Harry grinned at this description.

"I'm sure everyone is assuming, now that she's here, that we'd all be better off if she just took her engine room back right now," Nancy admitted.

"You're wrong," Harry said more seriously. "First of all, that engine room is nothing like the one B'Elanna left when she started her leave more than three years ago. It's yours now. Second, most of the people on this ship haven't been with *Voyager* all that long. You stepped in and so far, you've worked a few miracles of your own. You've kept the mission on schedule and you've solved every problem I've seen thrown your way."

"Until now." She frowned.

After a pause Harry said, "But if you're really that intimidated by B'Elanna, you're not going to be happy at all when I show you what's behind those shuttlebay doors."

"What's behind those doors?"

Harry led her into the shuttlebay and directed her toward the ship they had retrieved that morning.

Yet another Torres masterpiece, Nancy realized, her confidence taking another blow.

Kim unlocked the ship's main door and led her down a few steps into the engine compartment. He allowed Conlon to silently study the slipstream drive B'Elanna had engineered, which was similar, though not identical, to the

Starfleet one. Nancy immediately found herself wondering why B'Elanna had chosen to align the injectors at such an odd angle and whether or not those were actually regenerative circuits she was looking at. These thoughts were relegated to the back of her mind when she discovered a small chamber installed opposite the main drive that housed what looked like benamite crystals.

She moved closer to study it and within moments understood Harry's sublime confidence of a few minutes before.

"Is that a—?"

"A benamite recrystallization matrix," Harry finished for her.

"How did you know about this?"

"My security team gave the shuttle a once-over, per regulations, the moment we brought it on board."

"How did she—?"

"I don't know," Harry cut her off again. "But if I were you, I'd ask her."

Seven of Nine perched on the edge of the chair with her hands clasped tightly in her lap. Until her implants had been replaced by the Caeliar, she had never found 0800 to be an onerously early time of day. With sleep remaining elusive, the position required more concentration than it used to.

"You know it's not actually necessary to sit at attention," Counselor Cambridge said dryly.

Seven noted that he rested in what appeared to be flagrant ease, well into the seat of the soft, black leather chair that was a mirror image of hers. His long legs were crossed at the knees and his right foot twitched occasionally, particularly when she remained silent for any lengthy stretch.

When she refrained from adopting a more relaxed pose, Cambridge continued, "How was last night?"

"Is that relevant to our discussion?" Seven asked.

"Seven, I get that you are most comfortable in an arena when you are able to exert control. You are obviously disciplined, eminently capable, and probably accustomed to being the smartest person in the room."

Cambridge leaned forward, his elbows resting on the tops of his thighs as he set his chin upon his joined hands.

"When you're here in this room with me, that's not going to be the case. We can't both have control right now. You're going to have to cede that to me. The good news is, I am also disciplined, capable, and smarter than you, at least when it comes to the problem that's on the table right now."

After a brief pause, Cambridge asked again, "How was last night?"

"It was enjoyable," Seven replied curtly.

"To you?"

"To everyone present."

"I don't care about them right now," Cambridge clarified. "Was it enjoyable to you?"

"What difference does it make?" Seven demanded.

Cambridge sighed. "For the first time in years, you were able to interact socially with the people who formed your first support system beyond your parents—whom I know you do not remember well—and the Borg. This is complicated by the fact that up until yesterday, you believed that two of those people were dead. Do you see where I'm going with this?"

"You wish to ascertain whether or not I still feel comfortable in their presence," Seven answered. "You wish to know if I harbor any resentment or feelings of inadequacy as a result of the deception perpetrated by Commanders Paris and Torres. You are attempting to determine whether or not this group will effectively help or hinder my efforts to regain my equilibrium."

"Wrong," Cambridge replied flatly.

Seven was momentarily dumbstruck. Finally she asked, "What else could be the point of your question?"

"Glad you asked. I'm trying to determine the levels of emotional response that you are currently capable of experiencing."

"Oh," Seven said, puzzled.

"This is going to go a lot quicker as soon as you decide to trust me a little."

Seven considered the concept.

Trust.

"I do not trust you," she finally realized.

"Obviously. And why should you? You don't know me from Adam."

"Adam?"

"A biblical reference. An archetypal figure that appears under various guises in many creation stories," Cambridge explained, then paused to give the back of his head a vigorous scratch. "The point is, you and I haven't known each other all that long and the only reason you are here is because Captain Eden has ordered you to."

"Chakotay believes you can help me."

"And do you trust Chakotay?"

Seven paused again.

"I used to," she admitted. "We were separated for several months. Prior to that separation he behaved in an uncharacteristically unsympathetic manner, but he has been most helpful of late."

"But do you trust him?"

"As much as I trust anyone," Seven acknowledged.

"Did you trust the Borg?" Cambridge asked.

"When I was part of the Collective, trust was irrelevant. We were joined in a common purpose. We knew each other's thoughts. Deception was impossible."

"And is there a feeling or an emotional response you associate with that state?"

Seven searched her memory. In the silence of her mind it was almost a pleasant activity.

"Peace," she finally said.

"Good." Cambridge nodded. "And was that the last time you knew peace?"

"Yes," Seven admitted.

"You've said that during the transformation, you were momentarily linked with the Caeliar gestalt. Was that also peaceful?"

"No," Seven replied, shaking her head. "It was chaotic. It was powerful. But it went beyond peace."

"In what way?"

"It was completion," Seven replied, a little uncertainly.

"The end of something?"

"Yes," Seven realized. "It was as if every question I had ever known was instantly answered. But still, there were possibilities, questions beyond any I had ever conceived, and a compelling desire to explore those questions."

After a brief silence Cambridge asked, "Do you believe that the Caeliar are a superior species to the Borg and to humanity?"

"They are."

"Really?"

"Their technology has advanced far beyond the Borg and humans. They have achieved harmony of thought and purpose without the need to reduce one another to mindless obedience. They are beyond superior. They are perfection."

Cambridge sat back again and uncrossed his legs, resting his feet flat on the floor.

"Is perfection a good thing?" he finally asked.

"Obviously," Seven retorted sharply.

"Interesting," Cambridge said, tugging gently at his stubbly beard.

"You don't agree?" Seven asked.

"Not at all," he replied. "I can't imagine anything more boring." When Seven didn't immediately contradict him, he went on, "Seriously, what do you do once you're perfect. What's the point of existence after that? It's an extreme. It's the end of the story. You can't be more perfect than perfection. It's a binary state. You are or you aren't."

"Isn't perfection the goal to which all sentient beings aspire?" Seven asked.

"No," Cambridge replied, "because most sentient beings recognize it as unattainable. Humanity aspires to achieve our fullest potential, realizing that for every individual the bar is going to be set according to their capabilities and their opportunities. There is no such thing as perfection in the sense of objective reality."

Seven felt her cheeks growing warm.

"Do you find that concept troubling?" Cambridge asked more gently.

Seven was too quick to shake her head.

"And while the Caeliar gestalt might have felt like the epitome of achievement, at least for the part of you that was once Borg, I submit to you that what little the rest of us understand of the Caeliar paints a very different picture."

"In what way?" Seven demanded, wondering on whose behalf she suddenly felt so insulted.

"They are xenophobic in the extreme. Their compassion, prior to their recent contact with the Federation, did not extend beyond their borders. They possess a superiority based solely upon their technological achievements that many other species will, given time, master and surpass, and I question their ability to recognize the value of unique individuals."

"Why?"

"Isn't it obvious?"

Seven struggled to see beyond the criticisms laid before her. In a blindingly painful moment it hit her.

"They didn't take me with them," she finally offered. "But they must have found me insufficient in some way," she added quickly.

"Or they were too blind to realize what they were missing," Cambridge suggested.

"I do not believe that is the case," Seven objected.

"But do you at least agree that it is possible?"

Seven grabbed the arms of her chair and slid rearward until her spine rested comfortably, supported by the chair's firm back. Though she imagined that the counselor might revel a bit in this little victory, she no longer cared and noted that his expression remained neutral.

"How was last night?" Cambridge asked suddenly.

"It was difficult for me to engage with my friends," she admitted hesitantly. "I realize that they are happy to once again share each other's company, and I experienced great relief when I learned that B'Elanna and Miral were alive. But we have not shared common experiences or pursuits for many years. We no longer seem to know one another as well as we once did."

"So there's distance between you?"

Seven nodded.

"And how does that distance make you feel?"

"It is painful."

"That's good to hear."

"Why?"

"Because you retain your ability to feel human emotions, more deeply than you probably suspect at the moment."

"I have seldom found my emotions to be helpful," Seven warned.

Cambridge smiled.

"You will," he assured her. "Trust me."

Seven eyed the counselor warily. "Annika Hansen was human. As such, she was at the mercy of her emotions."

"Is that why you resist the voice?"

"I do not believe so," Seven admitted. "I cannot accept the notion that I am only Annika Hansen. I do not even know who she would be, had she never been assimilated."

"And you may never know," Cambridge offered. "Annika is an insufficient designation. It cannot begin to contain all that you are."

"Then why would this voice, assuming that it was left by the Caeliar, wish to reduce me to less than I am?"

"I don't know," Cambridge replied. "In your years with the Borg you experienced something quite unique and you gained the collected wisdom of billions of beings."

"You believe it was a good thing that I was assimilated?" Seven said in disbelief.

"That is something only you can decide. Because you value what the Borg gave you, you are reluctant to part with it, even to bow to the will of those you believe their superiors. But you can't have it both ways. Either the Caeliar are right, and you should purge yourself of your past, or the Caeliar are wrong."

Seven sat in stunned silence.

"I'd like to suggest that you are now faced with a unique choice, one that most of us will never have the opportunity to experience. You are not only human or Borg or Caeliar, but also all three. But only if you are willing to embrace that reality."

"The voice will not allow it."

"Let's find out," Cambridge suggested.

"How?"

"Disengage your neural inhibitor."

Her hand shaking, Seven did so.

Within seconds, the voice once again began to encroach upon the silence. Seven felt her chest begin to tighten.

"You hear it again, don't you?"

"Yes."

"You are more powerful than the voice, Seven. You are something of which the voice cannot conceive. Silence it."

Seven repeated these words in her mind as the voice grew louder.

"I . . . cannot . . ."

Cambridge leaned forward, taking Seven's hands in his.

"You can."

Seven closed her eyes and attempted to force the voice to do her will. When the sound was all she was conscious of, she abruptly reached up and switched the inhibitor on again. She opened her eyes, realizing that her breath was coming in great heaves, expecting to find disappointment on the counselor's face.

Instead, she saw respect.

"Well done," Cambridge said with a smile.

"I failed," Seven insisted.

"You tried," Cambridge corrected her. "You are one of the bravest individuals I have ever known."

Seven was suddenly conscious of his hands, holding hers tightly. She pulled them back quickly.

"I'll see you tomorrow, Seven."

With a nod, Seven rose and left the office.

CHAPTER ELEVEN

"Don't move," B'Elanna whispered.

Tom lay opposite her, staring into her eyes with an intensity that suggested a desire to lose himself in them forever. Although they had begun the previous night nestled securely in each other's arms, at some point while they slept, Miral had forced her way between them and now lay sprawled with one arm across B'Elanna's abdomen, a leg atop Tom's.

Tom reached toward his wife and gently brushed back a tangle of long hair until his hand came to rest on B'Elanna's cheek.

"You know I don't want to," Tom whispered back.

"Then don't."

Tom closed his eyes briefly, clearly envisioning spending the entire day like this with great pleasure.

"Just tell me I'm not dreaming," he said.

"I will if you will," B'Elanna replied drowsily.

Tom opened his eyes and a wide smile spread across his face.

"I still can't believe you're both here. I honestly never thought this day would come."

"I knew it would," B'Elanna said. "That's the only thing that kept me going."

Tom's smile faded.

"Are you sure we're doing the right thing by staying here? If you still want to go, you know I'm with you."

"All I want is for the three of us to be together," B'Elanna assured him. "And I'm starting to think that you're happier here than even you know."

Tom seemed to consider her point.

"It's different," he conceded. "But it's good. And last night was amazing."

B'Elanna lifted her head and rested it on her hand.

"I assume you're referring to what happened after our guests left, but dinner was nice too," she replied, feigning dismay. "Part of me still doesn't believe that we're all together again in the Delta quadrant. But it's strange without . . ."

Tom picked up her thought, "Admiral Janeway."

B'Elanna nodded somberly. "I still miss her. Telling Neelix was awful."

"I know. Just as awful as when I had to tell you."

"What do you think of Eden?" B'Elanna asked.

"She's fair. She's a good captain. And she's going to have my ass if I'm late for duty this morning," Tom suddenly realized.

B'Elanna reached for him as he started to disentangle himself from Miral and pulled his lips to hers.

"And I'll have your ass if you're not back here the moment your shift is over," she assured him.

"Yes, ma'am," Tom said.

As he stumbled toward the 'fresher, he tossed over his shoulder, "How are you going to keep yourself busy today?"

B'Elanna gently shifted Miral, who rolled over onto her side with a faint snort of protest.

"Probably in sickbay at least part of the time," B'Elanna

replied. "Beyond that, I don't really know. I don't suppose they added a preschool during the last refit," she suggested idly.

"Nope," Tom replied through the open door.

"I'll probably start going through the ship's database for educational materials. I might see if I can download Kula's program to our quarters, or maybe to the *Galen*."

"Talk to the Doc. I'm sure he'll help you any way he can. He's still as full of himself as ever."

"I noticed that," B'Elanna chuckled.

She was about to share with Tom her silent disappointment that Harry hadn't joined them last night when the door chimed. Pulling on her robe, B'Elanna crossed into the living area and releasing the lock manually found Nancy Conlon standing before her.

"You're up early, Lieutenant," B'Elanna said in surprise. "Tom's in the shower but he'll be on duty in a few minutes."

"I'm sorry to disturb you," Conlon said, clearly ill at ease. "But I didn't stop by to see Commander Paris."

"Oh," B'Elanna replied. "Okay." After an uncertain pause she added, "Do you want to come in?"

"Thank you," Conlon said, stepping just inside the doors.

"I was just going to replicate some *raktajino*," B'Elanna said kindly. "Would you like something?"

"That sounds good," Conlon said.

B'Elanna quickly retrieved their beverages and set both of them down on the low table in their seating area. She didn't understand why Conlon remained standing almost at attention since she'd walked in.

"You can sit down, if you like," B'Elanna offered. "I don't bite."

"Of course. Thank you, ma'am."

"And seriously, when you say ma'am, I look behind me for the captain. It's 'B'Elanna.'"

"Okay, B'Elanna," Conlon said with a hint of a smile. "You can call me Nancy."

"Great, Nancy." B'Elanna smiled. "What can I do for you?"

"Last night Harry, I mean, Lieutenant Kim, showed me the benamite recrystallization matrix you designed. Our supply is already showing signs of microfractures and I was wondering if you thought the system you developed could be adapted to a larger scale."

B'Elanna smiled inwardly at the slip between "Harry" and "Lieutenant Kim." It simultaneously piqued her interest and filled her with a mischievous desire she hadn't felt in years.

"I'm sure it could," she replied. "I can show you the specs, if you like."

"Oh . . . okay, thank you." Conlon nodded.

"Or I could come down to engineering and take a look at your new drive and make sure there won't be any compatibility issues. Then I could probably take a stab at the designs myself. I mean, if that's what you want," she added hastily.

"Only if that's what you want," Conlon said defensively.

"Nancy?"

"Yes?"

"I think we need to get something straight."

"What's that?"

"I'm a guest on this ship. And I consider myself lucky to be that. I haven't been regular Starfleet for years. Actually, I was never 'regular,' even when I was *Voyager*'s chief engineer. You probably know as much about engineering as I do, and you certainly know more about this ship now than I do. I'm happy to pitch in under your direction. Feel free to ask anytime. But I'm not interested in getting in your way or stepping on your toes. I know how hard your job is. And the last thing you should be doing right now is second-guessing yourself, or worrying that I'm interested in taking something that's not mine. I've had a crazy couple of years. I need some time to readjust to something resembling normal life. And I have a daughter who needs me and will always come first."

Conlon sighed in visible relief. "How is Miral?" she asked.

"She's getting better, thanks for asking."

"People around me have been singing your praises for weeks," Conlon confessed. "You're a legend in that engine room."

"That's the most ridiculous thing I've ever heard," B'Elanna assured her.

"I don't think so," Conlon said. "It took you two minutes to make me feel better."

"I have my moments." B'Elanna smiled, embarrassed.

Tom interrupted them, entering with a sleepy Miral clutched tightly to his neck.

"I think you're going to need a hydrospanner to remove her," he began, but as soon as he saw Conlon his face fell to a more neutral arrangement. "Good morning, Lieutenant."

Conlon immediately rose from her seat and replied, "Commander."

"Everything okay?" he asked dubiously.

"We were just having a little chat," B'Elanna said as she rose and went to work disentangling Miral from her father's arms. After giving him a quick kiss she said, "Now get out of here."

"What happened to *don't move*?" he teased under his breath.

"Times change," she shot back. "Go."

"Aye, aye, sir," he said, scooting out the door.

"I should really go, too," Conlon said. "Thanks for the *raktajino*."

"Anytime," B'Elanna said. "And I'll try to stop by later today to take a look at those microfractures."

Conlon nodded appreciatively but before she reached the door, B'Elanna called after her.

"Just out of curiosity, what were you doing with Harry last night?"

"I just ran into him in the mess."

"Oh, okay," B'Elanna replied, dying to know if that had been an accident, or intention on Nancy's part. "You know, he's a great guy," she added, worrying she might be laying it on a little thick. Those worries faded when she saw a distinct light come to Nancy's eye.

"He's very helpful," Nancy acknowledged. "Oh, speaking of problems I'm having a hard time solving, did your shuttle's slipstream drive ever have any interface issues with your deflector? Processing delays, specifically?"

"No," B'Elanna said, her curiosity instantly tweaked. "But my deflectors were designed specifically to integrate with the slipstream drive."

"Lucky you," Nancy replied.

"Why don't you forward me your most recent deflector control parameters and schematics and let me take a look," B'Elanna suggested.

"I suppose fresh eyes can't hurt." Nancy smiled. "See you later, B'Elanna."

B'Elanna busied herself getting Miral ready for the day. It was a luxurious undertaking now that it could be performed in roughly three times the space they had enjoyed on the *Home Free.*

Just as she was ready to take Miral to sickbay for her

morning checkup, Nancy's data transmission arrived. B'Elanna spent the hour and a half while she was waiting for the doctor to complete his exam engrossed in a thorough evaluation. It was a journey down the engineering road not traveled. But it didn't take long for B'Elanna to discover what she believed was the source of Conlon's interface problem, and once she'd settled Miral in for her afternoon nap, she transferred Kula's program to her quarters.

In main engineering, B'Elanna unobtrusively made herself comfortable at a diagnostic station and began running simulations that would test her theory. Confident she was right, she still wanted to confirm her suspicions. Halfway through her analysis of *Voyager*'s deflector protocols, B'Elanna found something unusual. It was not the subtle misalignment she had expected, but it would certainly account for the interface issues Conlon had described.

What the hell are those doing here? she wondered to herself.

Her next step was to send a message to Vorik.

Counselor Cambridge and the doctor had filed detailed reports with Captain Eden on Seven, confirming that she was capable of performing regular duties and that it was in her best interest to do so. Eden trusted both of these officers implicitly, but she wanted to make her own assessment. The captain entered astrometrics where Seven and Lieutenant Devi Patel—*Voyager*'s senior science officer—were conducting a scan of the system they were approaching.

The two women were working together at the central panel. Patel was a petite, dark-skinned woman whose shiny, straight black hair had an almost Vulcan appearance since she kept it styled in a short, severe cut. Patel barely reached Seven's shoulder. A formidable biologist, she'd proved her worth time and again in the three years she had served aboard *Voyager*.

"Report," Eden ordered as she stepped forward, taking in the vast display on the screen before her. *Voyager*'s astrometrics lab had been an inspired addition, and one that Eden had every intention of making the most of. Seven—quite rightly—deferred to Patel to begin the presentation.

The lieutenant began in her crisp, high-pitched voice, "As you can see, Captain, the *Hawking*'s initial assessment— indicating that the third, fourth, seventh, and tenth planets within the system are inhabited—was correct. With more accurate scans, we have discovered that sentient life-forms inhabiting the third planet appear to fall into six discrete species.

"Six different sentient species inhabiting the same planet, let alone system?" Eden asked.

"Yes, Captain."

"If I may, Captain?" Seven interjected.

"Go on."

"The Borg did encounter and catalog four of the six species in question."

"Really?"

Patel continued, "The least prolific of the six species is humanoid."

"Species 6649," Seven added. "They call themselves the Neyser and are indigenous to a system more than four hundred light-years away."

"How did they get here?" Eden asked.

"Unknown," Patel replied. "On the third planet they live in intimate proximity to the other five sentient species. However, they also appear to have successfully colonized the fourth planet several thousand years ago. The fourth planet is exclusively inhabited by the Neyser."

"Interesting," Eden noted.

"The second species we can easily identify is a cytoplasmic life-form," Patel continued.

"Species 433," Seven added. "The Greech. Native to a binary system a hundred light-years away."

"*Voyager*'s database contains a record of an encounter with a similar life-form," Patel went on, "an insectoid creature that was rescued by the ship and sustained itself by attacking B'Elanna Torres and feeding off her neural energy until its own people arrived to claim it. *Voyager* was unable to establish communication with this species, but that they were capable of interstellar travel suggests that they were highly intelligent."

"Do you remember these cytoplasmic life-forms, Seven?" Eden asked.

"Very well," Seven replied. "The Doctor had a most difficult time attempting to separate the alien from Lieutenant Commander Torres without killing it. Since the alien was sentient, this was not an option. It is worth noting that while the cytoplasmic life-forms we are detecting here do bear a resemblance to that species, there are significant differences, particularly in size."

"Larger or smaller?" Eden asked.

"Smaller," Seven replied.

"Continue," Eden said with a nod.

"The third sentient species is silicon-based," Patel reported.

"Species 912, the Dulaph, can be found on dozens of planets scattered across the quadrant," Seven said.

"In its natural state its body is spherical and it is propelled on many fine cilia. However, on the third planet, it is found only in combination with another life-form Seven is also familiar with."

"The Irsk, species 1629, a bio-mimetic life-form indigenous to the Class-Y planet in this system."

"What does *in combination* mean?" Eden asked.

"All six species appear to live and work in proximity to one another, but the Irsk and Dulaph actually occupy the same space, suggesting that one, most likely the Irsk, actually lives on the body of the Dulaph."

"And is the Irsk the only species we can confirm is native to this system?"

"No, Captain," Patel replied. "The final two species, which the Borg apparently never encountered," she added, shooting a glance at Seven for confirmation, "are likely indigenous. Both are plentiful on the third planet, and I believe one of them, a rather large, moth-like creature, is native to it. The other is a noncorporeal life-form, indigenous to the gas giant, but somehow also able to survive on the third world."

Eden wanted to make sure she had this straight. "So, we have six sentient species living in close proximity on one planet. Three of them are indigenous to this system, and three aren't."

"Yes, Captain." Patel nodded.

"And somehow the bio-mimetic life-form . . ."

"The Irsk," Patel reminded her.

"And the noncorporeal life-form, which are indigenous to planets in this system with very different temperatures and atmospheres, have adapted to survive on a Class-M world as well."

"This is not unusual in a bio-mimetic life-form," Seven replied. "But it is most unusual in the noncorporeal form."

"Agreed," Patel said. "The species that originated on the gas giant should not be able to survive on the Class-M planet."

"So how do we think they managed it?" Eden asked.

"It's too soon to hypothesize," Patel replied.

"Okay," Eden said evenly, "what else do we know?"

"Uninhabited areas of the fourth planet show high concentrations of benamite," Seven replied.

"In crystalline form?" Eden asked.

"No."

Patel went on, "The third and fourth planets are the only ones that contain visible structures. The architecture of the third world, like the ship we encountered, is quite plain and tends to favor cubical and spherical designs."

"Does that suggest anything significant to you, Seven?" Eden asked.

"Beyond a lack of imagination, nothing at this time," Seven replied.

"Let's not judge them too harshly until we've had a chance to get to know them," Eden chided her gently. She then called out, "Eden to the bridge."

"*Go ahead, Captain,*" Ensign Lasren replied.

"Have we received any response yet to our friendship messages or hails?"

"*No, Captain,*" Lasren replied. "*We have been transmitting continuously, per your orders, for the past hour.*"

"Thank you, Ensign. You'll let me know if that changes. Eden out." Turning to Patel she asked, "So how many life-forms are we talking about, total?"

"More than forty billion, ma'am."

"Forty," Eden said aloud, troubled.

"Captain?" Patel asked.

"That's a lot of people who could, it seems, easily answer our hails. You have to wonder why no one is willing to do that."

"Indeed," Seven said ominously.

Eden had only one question left. Addressing Seven she asked, "So were the Neyser, Greech, Irsk, or Dulaph assimilated by the Borg?"

"No," Seven replied.

"No?"

"They were considered unworthy of assimilation. Their biological and technological distinctiveness would have added nothing to the Collective's perfection."

"I see," Eden replied, suddenly relieved for the four species in question. "Carry on," she ordered. As the captian left the lab, her thoughts immediately turned to the away team she would assemble to investigate the aliens should they still get no response.

The *Hawking*'s bridge was small compared with *Voyager*'s, but nowhere near as claustrophobic as Admiral Batiste found the *Galen*'s. The captain and executive officer's seats were located in a sunken, circular area in the bridge's center, separated by a control panel. A few steps forward and down was the conn, occupied by a single flight controller. The elevated rear bank of science stations completed the configuration, with a single station accessible as needed for tactical or engineering personnel located on the starboard side, nearest the viewscreen.

Captain Itak had insisted that the admiral take his seat while on the bridge, and now sat beside him in the XO's spot. Despite the courtesy, Batiste was growing impatient. He had always admired Vulcans' attention to detail, but listening to Lieutenant Vorik and Captain Itak debate, ad nauseam, the probable origins of the subspace instabilities they had been analyzing made him long for the nearest airlock.

Vorik was convinced, given the marginal difference in their current scans and those taken by *Voyager* years earlier, that the instabilities were remnants of the transwarp tunnels the Borg had carved out of the area surrounding their trans-warp hub. Itak countered that they were ancient transwarp tunnels. He suggested they were either naturally occurring, or early efforts by the Borg that were ultimately abandoned.

"Gentlemen," Batiste interrupted, "is it fair to say, at this point, that without further data, it is impossible to determine to any degree of certainty exactly where these instabilities came from?"

"Define *degree of certainty*, Admiral," Itak requested.

Batiste was spared the need to kill one of his captains by Ensign Bloom at ops.

"Captain, scanners have detected a cube-shaped vessel point two six four one light-years from our present position."

"Are our scanners malfunctioning?" Itak asked.

"No, sir."

"By my calculations," Itak said, confirming his words simultaneously by running a quick algorithm on a padd, "we should have detected that vessel thirteen point six minutes ago."

Batiste couldn't have cared less. If the vessel in question was constructed by the same hands that had built the first one they encountered, things were about to get interesting.

"The vessel is floating free in space," Bloom replied, clearly attempting to justify his perceived inadequacy. "Long-range scans cataloged it as debris."

"Life signs?" Itak demanded evenly.

"None, sir."

"Adjust course and speed to intercept," Batiste ordered.

"Admiral, do you believe that is a wise course at this juncture?" Itak asked.

"If I didn't, I wouldn't have given the order, Captain."

"Captain," Vorik began tonelessly from the forward starboard station, "the cube is of identical design and configuration as the vessel previously encountered, with one considerable exception."

Itak turned his chair to face Vorik's station.

"It is twice the size of the previous vessel."

Batiste smiled to himself.

Things are definitely about to get interesting.

The *Hawking* reduced speed as the cube came into view.

Vorik made a point of noting that the cube's current location was in close proximity to the endpoints of four collapsed transwarp corridors.

"Sir," Bloom said, "there appears to be only one power system operable aboard the cube. A weak subspace transmission is being sent out on an extremely narrow frequency."

"I would like to hear that transmission, Ensign Bloom," Itak ordered.

Moments later, a low buzz, spiced with an occasional burst of static, came through the comm system. Then, countless voices joined as one said, *Please accept the offering of the Indign.*

There was a brief pause and the message repeated as Itak's eyes found Batiste's.

"Lieutenant Vorik, do *Voyager*'s logs contain any record of a race known as the Indign?" Batiste asked.

"No, Admiral."

"Are the cube's shields up?"

"No, Admiral."

"Does the cube contain breathable atmosphere?"

"No, Admiral."

"I'm going over there to take a look," Batiste said, rising to his feet.

"Admiral, I must advise against that action," Itak replied, clearly as alarmed as it was possible for a Vulcan to be at the suggestion.

"Your advice is noted," Willem replied perfunctorily. "*Hawking* is to hold position here and maintain transporter locks. Lieutenant Vorik, Lieutenant Lern, and Security Chief Griggs, suit up. You're with me."

The transporter beam released Vorik in the center of a ten-square-meter room shrouded in darkness. Hand beacons were immediately activated revealing stark, unadorned walls and a single opening leading from the chamber.

"I thought this was supposed to be the ship's bridge," Batiste said, his gruff tone evident even through the tinny quality created by the environmental suits the team wore.

"We are in the precise center of the vessel, Admiral," Vorik advised. "The vessel's power systems have either been damaged or inoperable for some time, and as this is the source of the transmission, I believe that assumption was logical."

"Spread out and let's see if we can find the source," Batiste replied.

The admiral played his wrist beacon over the walls and eventually discovered above the opening's upper-right corner a small comm station. After disabling it, he signaled for the team to follow him through the opening.

Before them was a metal-framed catwalk with few visible support struts and wires but no guardrails. After fifteen ginger steps, the team's footfalls creating disconcerting echoes all around them, Batiste made a fist, motioning for the others to halt. Vorik stepped closer and peering over the admiral's shoulder saw a steep metal staircase that descended too far into the darkness for their light to penetrate. Vorik played his light above, and saw nothing as the blackness swallowed up his beam. The ship was vast.

Batiste lowered his hand, and the group began down the staircase.

"Steady as we go," Batiste said. "There's nothing to hold on to."

Vorik wished to pull out his tricorder for a more definitive scan, but given the sharpness of the angle and the obvious safety risks he opted to refrain.

At junctures spaced approximately ten meters apart, narrow catwalks would extend from small landings to the left and right. Batiste paused at the first one, but after searching the gloom to find only more darkness, pressed forward. It seemed likely to Vorik that he intended to reach bottom before beginning a more thorough examination.

After passing seventeen landings, the team finally reached the end of the staircase. Vorik was unable to shake the sense that they were in an incredibly large, empty space. He heard Lieutenant Lern activate his tricorder and immediately did the same.

"Admiral, I am detecting organic remains," Lern advised.

"Where?"

Lern paused to confirm the reading that Vorik was also attempting to analyze and replied, "All around us, sir. The nearest ones are one hundred fifty meters ahead."

Batiste nodded and led the team forward. When they had closed the distance before them to fewer than twenty meters, vague shapes began to emerge from the darkness.

Vorik saw a structure reminiscent of a Borg alcove. It was just large enough to hold an average-size humanoid. However, the figure occupying that alcove was obviously not there by choice, restrained at the neck, waist, wrists, and ankles by heavy metallic bands. The horror of its last moments of life was plain in its wide-eyed and openmouthed terror. Vorik recognized the species.

"Admiral, this is a member of the Ventu tribe, native to Ledos."

Batiste stepped closer to the tortured figure. Its once bronze skin had a grayish sheen in death. Long, black hair was matted to its neck and shoulders. Chafing at the wrists suggested that it had struggled, probably until its strength had gone, against its restraints.

"How did this man die?" Batiste asked.

"Oxygen deprivation," Lern replied. "By my calculations, this vessel has been without life support for approximately three years."

"Why hasn't the corpse deteriorated more in that time?" Batiste asked.

"The ambient temperature, which is below freezing, prevented decomposition," Lern said dispassionately.

Vorik moved his light to the left of the Ventu and discovered similar alcoves as far as he could see. Griggs did the same while Lern continued to scan with his tricorder. A brief visual inspection confirmed that the entire chamber was filled, floor to ceiling, with thousands of dead.

Vorik was able to identify many of the dead: Dinaali, Kraylor, Nygean, Bosaal, Ledosian, even the short, rotund natives of the Hegemony. There were hundreds more who defied categorization.

Finally, Griggs broke the dismal silence. "How did they all get here? Who are these Indign that they would do such a thing?"

"I think the real question, Mister Griggs, is for whom, or what, the Indign intended this offering," Batiste replied coldly.

CHAPTER TWELVE

The third planet contained ten continent-sized landmasses, leaving the remaining eighty-five percent of the surface covered in water. Nearly every square meter was in use, from agricultural to industrial purposes, including starship construction. The cities were filled with masses of the six distinct species living and working in close proximity to one another.

Four hours of constant hails had gone unanswered. *Voyager* and *Galen* were now in orbit around the third planet and were being roundly ignored by the dozens of cubes traveling throughout the system. Captain Eden had substituted the standard friendship greetings for a more detailed description of their encounter with the alien cube, an apology for the cube's destruction, and an offer of establishing friendly relations with the system's inhabitants. *Voyager*'s sensors detected the presence of communications relays aboard the cubes and in their shipyards. However, there were no advanced communications systems. Patel suggested that the varied species might facilitate their communication through nontechnological means. Telepathy was likely. However, most species that possessed highly developed telepathic and empathic abilities also had comm systems.

When *Voyager*'s second message was met with the same resounding silence, Captain Eden authorized Paris to lead an away team there. He immediately assigned Kim to provide security, and chose Lieutenant Patel, Doctor Sharak, and Seven to join him. Captain Eden added Counselor Cambridge to the team.

Paris transported to what appeared to be a large agricultural processing plant several kilometers from one of the smaller cities. The first sight that met the away team's eyes were acres of lush, verdant fields planted in perfect lines. Small clusters of the aliens were tending the crops. Patel reported that the leafy, green sprouts were a nonedible product most likely for use as a fuel source.

"Where are the fences?" Kim asked.

"Let's ask, shall we?" Paris said, gesturing to a group in the nearest field that were scanning the crops using a small, handheld device. The team observed them in silence, one a Neyser, a little more than two meters, the other, a humanoid under a meter. They worked quietly, diligently intent upon their task. Concerned for the team's safety, Paris ordered Patel and Seven to scan the creatures covertly.

The Neyser wore a simple brown tunic over a flowing green skirt. It had short, sandy-brown hair and its skin was either deeply tanned or a natural bronze. Its appearance did not immediately suggest its gender.

The smaller humanoid looked like an offspring of its counterpart. Patel stepped up to Paris, informing him that they were actually two distinct alien life-forms: one a silicon-based Dulaph, and the other a bio-mimetic Irsk, who coated the surface of the Dulaph and gave it its humanoid shape. Paris wondered if this might account for the faint silver sheen of the alien's skin that glinted in the sun.

A faint haze surrounded the body of the Neyser and flitting around within the haze was a tiny, winged creature. Patel identified the haze as the noncorporeal life-form indigenous to the system's tenth planet. The winged creature's DNA confirmed it was native to the third planet, as Patel had suspected.

The Neyser's right arm was covered by what looked like a long insect, which was actually a Greech. Its body was divided into sections with its head resting on the back of the humanoid's hand. Two long antennae sprung from its head, just above two large, orange eyes. Its body got smaller as it curved up its host's arm with the long tail wrapped around the back of the Neyser's waist.

A loud, discordant shriek broke the serenity of the field once Paris and the away team got within ten meters of the aliens. Kim's hand went to his weapon, but Tom held out a firm hand, ordering Kim to stand down. Paris signaled the others to stay put as he stepped closer to the aliens.

"Good afternoon," Paris said cheerfully. "I am Lieutenant Commander Tom Paris, of the Federation *Starship Voyager*. I'd like to speak with you if you have a moment." He got no visible response.

Paris took two more steps toward the group but was brought up short as the Irsk/Dulaph's arm suddenly extended to more than two meters in length as it delicately plucked an insect from a leaf. The arm retreated to its normal size as quickly as it had morphed and the insect was deposited into the alien's mouth and chewed vigorously.

Maybe we're disturbing lunch, Paris thought.

He then repeated his greeting but the aliens continued to ignore him. Reluctantly, he retreated back to the away team's position.

"Maybe they don't understand us," he said, scratching his head.

"It's possible," Kim conceded.

"But unlikely," Seven added.

"Why do you say that?" Cambridge asked.

"They show no curiosity about us whatsoever," Seven replied. "If they did not understand us, but were interested in communicating with us, they would most likely at least look at us."

"They're ignoring us completely," Patel finished.

"Like the Borg used to do," Kim observed.

"There's a less than charming thought," Cambridge said softly.

"Which one made the screaming sound we just heard?" Sharak asked.

"The Greech," Seven replied.

"How onomatopoetic," Cambridge noted. When Sharak tossed him a curious glance, Cambridge explained, "The sound they make . . . it sounds like the name."

"Oh," Sharak said, smiling sincerely.

"They appear to function collectively," Paris said.

"Without further observation, it is unwise to leap to that conclusion," Seven replied.

"They don't seem frightened of us in the least," Cambridge added.

"Why is that a problem?" Patel asked.

"Because they should be," Kim replied. "We outnumber them, and we're armed. Their lack of curiosity, going about what looks like their normal routine, despite our presence suggests that whatever their defenses are, they are formidable."

"Or this particular group is expendable," Sharak suggested.

Paris said, "Let's move on to that larger facility half a klick to the north of our position." In the distance a large perfectly square building could be seen at the edge of the field. Tricorders indicated that seventy-two life-forms were present within.

Paris began to sweat uncomfortably as the away team walked through the field, careful not to disturb any of the well-tended crops. His step lightened once they reached the cool enclosed space.

A large depository of harvested crops was moving through a processing machine. At each of a dozen stations, a collective—identical to the first group they had encountered—worked silently, methodically, and harmoniously.

"Did you say that the Borg assimilated four of these species?" Cambridge asked Seven quietly.

"I did not," Seven replied evenly. "The Neyser, Greech, Dulaph, and Irsk were discovered and categorized by the Borg but were considered unworthy of assimilation."

Shaking her head, Patel said tersely, "It's hard to imagine more industrious folks. If you ask me, it was the Collective's loss."

B'Elanna found Chakotay in the mess hall, chatting amiably with a petite ensign with short, spiked blue hair. Tom had told her about the pilot, but the woman's name escaped B'Elanna at the moment. She quickly replicated a bowl of *plomeek* soup and crossed the busy room to join them.

"It was actually able to survive while attached to the hull?" the woman asked. Chakotay looked up to see B'Elanna and with obvious relief said, "It was. Ensign Gwyn, have you met B'Elanna Torres?"

She turned sharply, studying B'Elanna intently in a way that seemed offensive until Gwyn's face relaxed and she smiled. "You're Commander Paris's wife, aren't you?"

"I am," B'Elanna replied cordially.

Gwyn shot a hungry glance back at Chakotay, then rose, taking her half-eaten salad with her. "Thanks for lunch, Chakotay," she said enthusiastically. "I'd love to hear more about the Hirogen and Species 8472 and anything else you can tell me about the Delta quadrant whenever you have a chance."

"I look forward to it, Ensign," Chakotay said congenially, but B'Elanna could tell he was anxious to end the conversation.

"B'Elanna," Gwyn finished with a curt nod as she left, recycling what remained of her lunch.

B'Elanna studied her perky, bouncy walk and took the seat opposite Chakotay. With a wicked smile she asked, "What was that all about?"

Chakotay shrugged. "I don't know. I stopped by to grab a plate of steamed vegetables and an apple and before I knew it she was . . ."

". . . flirting shamelessly with you?" B'Elanna finished for him.

Chakotay's tattooed brow wrinkled. After a moment he said, "I guess."

"Chakotay!" B'Elanna said in mock indignation.

"Stand down Red Alert," he chided her. "She's half my age and I don't think I was ever *that* young."

"You were," B'Elanna teased. "I remember." Then, batting her eyes in pronounced mockery, she said, "Oh, Chakotay, tell me more about the Hirogen."

He chuckled good-naturedly, shaking his head. "Those are problems I hope I never have again."

"And don't you forget it," B'Elanna insisted. "I'll be keeping an eye on her, just the same."

"Not on my account."

"No, but for the sake of every other man on this ship."

Concern flashed briefly in Chakotay's eyes. "Are you and Tom off to a rocky start?"

"Oh, no," B'Elanna assured him. "Tom, I'm not worried about. *She's* another story. She actually reminds me a little of . . ."

"Seska," they finished in unison.

Chakotay nodded. "I caught that vibe, too."

"It's interesting," B'Elanna said, sipping a spoonful of her soup. "The more things change, the more they stay the same."

"True."

"Speaking of which . . ." B'Elanna slid a padd across the table to Chakotay.

"What's this?"

"Read it."

Chakotay finally said, "These are deflector control protocols."

"Yes, they are," B'Elanna replied tensely.

"So, why am I looking at them?"

"Because they shouldn't be there."

"I'm sorry, B'Elanna, I'm not following."

"During *Voyager's* re-fit—when we returned from the Delta quadrant—all our protocols should have been downloaded and added to the permanent logs, then removed from the active control systems."

"Right."

"Did you restore any of those protocols?"

"Why would I?"

"Oh, I don't know. Did you need to emit a Dekyon beam,

or project any nonexistent starships into space, or maybe open any rifts into fluidic space?"

"No," Chakotay said, clearly growing more puzzled by her questions.

"Of course you didn't," B'Elanna assured him. "And even if you had, those protocols would have been purged again with the redesign Starfleet did to get the ship ready for this mission."

"What's your point, B'Elanna?"

"These protocols shouldn't be here. They're compromising deflector control, which endangers the entire fleet during slipstream flight. What's more, I don't think this was an oversight. I think they were intentionally restored."

Chakotay sat back and studied B'Elanna appraisingly. "By whom?" he asked warily.

"I don't know," she replied with a shrug.

"Where did you get this?"

"Nancy Conlon sent it to me. She didn't know what she was looking at—only that there was an interface bug."

"And you have no idea who put it in the system?"

"There are only three people who could have done it, Chakotay," B'Elanna said with muted intensity, "me, Vorik, and Seven. Vorik was just as surprised as I was to discover that they had been restored."

"And Seven had no access during the last re-fit," Chakotay said a little too defensively. "Since we arrived, her only concern has been finding the Caeliar."

B'Elanna's eyes narrowed as she considered his assumption.

"Then who?" she asked.

"I don't know. You should suggest that Lieutenant Conlon take it up with the captain."

"You could do that," B'Elanna suggested.

"No."

"Why not?"

"She doesn't trust me," Chakotay replied flatly.

B'Elanna started to shake her head, but Chakotay raised a hand to forestall further objection.

"For all she knows I came here under the pretense of helping Seven, but actually determined to somehow get my command back."

"But you didn't."

"You know that because you know me," he replied. "Captain Eden and I met only a handful of times before this mission. She watches me like a pet that isn't quite housebroken, wondering which moment I might choose to soil the carpet. If I go to her with something like this, she'll never believe my intentions are pure. Besides, Conlon found it, so Conlon should report it. That's the chain of command."

B'Elanna pushed the bowl away.

"Do you think Captain Eden feels the same way about me?"

"I doubt it. But I'm surprised Conlon doesn't."

"She did," B'Elanna replied, "until I set her straight."

"Then you've made more progress than I have."

B'Elanna nodded and rose. "I have to get back to the *Galen* to pick up Miral. The Doctor insisted on a full-body scan, but I think he just wanted to spend time with her. His new favorite thing is to tell her stories about me and Tom before she was born. He gets so involved, Miral just loves it. It's kind of cute."

"Mind if I join you?"

"Not at all."

As they headed for the recycler, B'Elanna asked, "Have you met his new assistant?"

"Meegan?"

"Yeah. What's her story?"

"I don't know, but if Ensign Gwyn ever decided to set her sights on a certain hologram, I have a feeling Meegan would object quite strenuously," he replied with a smile.

"Does the Doctor know that?"

"I can't tell."

"Geez," B'Elanna said with a sigh, "I don't remember *Voyager* ever sounding so much like a bad Klingon romance novel."

"That's because the last time you were here, you had more important things to pay attention to."

"I guess you're right." After a moment, she added, "And I'm pretty sure Nancy has a little crush on Harry, which I have every intention of nurturing."

"B'Elanna, let it be," Chakotay pleaded.

"Why?"

"You are many things, my dear, but matchmaker is never going to be one of them."

Eden settled on one side of the conference room table as Paris, Kim, Patel, Cambridge, Seven, and Doctor Sharak were just arriving. Commander Glenn and the Doctor had already reported from the *Galen* and were chatting quietly. Conlon hurried in and took a seat next to them just as Captain Itak, Lieutenant Vorik, and Admiral Batiste entered. Batiste assumed the table's head opposite Eden, and his presence brought the room to abrupt silence.

Captain Itak took the lead in explaining their discovery of the Indign offering. Paris provided a briefing on his team's attempt to communicate with the inhabitants of the third planet. Patel reported on the new data they had acquired about the aliens.

Once these reports were complete, Eden asked, "Are we certain that the Indign vessel *Hawking* discovered can also be traced to this system?"

Captain Itak replied, "Slight variances in the ship's composition and size are attributable to its age—relative to the first cube *Voyager* encountered—but it undoubtedly was constructed by the same hands. Its power systems, though offline, were an exact match, as were its minimal shields and armaments."

"The inhabitants of this system are most definitely the *Indign*," Batiste said briskly, cutting to the chase. He then turned to Seven and asked, "Were the Borg aware of the Indign as we now know them, separate from the four species cataloged individually?"

Seven cocked her head slightly to the right, clearly searching her memory. "On sixteen different occasions, prior to my departure from the Collective, Indign vessels were assimilated. The Borg had already scanned this system, however, and found nothing worth assimilating. Because the vessels identified as Indign offerings contained hundreds of different life-forms, most of which had already been identified by the Borg, no connection was ever made between them and the cooperative species we observed on the third planet."

"The Borg weren't even curious to know who was leaving these gift-wrapped offerings?" Batiste demanded.

"The Borg reserved curiosity for mysteries that might have added to the Collective. The Indign ships were used as raw materials," Seven replied coldly.

"I think the point worth noting is, despite the fact that the

Borg couldn't have cared less about the Indign, the Indign did not feel the same," Eden interjected.

"You think the Indign left those people out there just for the Borg?" Paris asked.

"This system lies just at the edge of what was once Borg space, a mere stone's throw from one of their transwarp hubs," Eden replied. "The offering vessel was discovered at a terminus of several collapsed transwarp conduits. Who else would it have been for?"

"The captain might be correct," Patel said, nodding. "In many ways, the organization of the Indign mimics that of the Borg Collective. Six disparate species work together essentially as one individual."

"Not to mention the architecture on the planet, and the design of their ships," Paris added. "You've never seen so many cubes and spheres."

"Are you saying that the Indign idolized the Borg?" Kim asked.

"Imitation is the sincerest form of flattery," the Doctor observed.

"What sentient species could ever idolize anything as destructive as the Borg?" Batiste asked. "They were monsters."

"Perhaps *idolized* isn't the right word," Cambridge noted.

"Feared," Doctor Sharak observed.

"Exactly," Cambridge said. "Think about it. Your civilization exists right next door to the most powerful force imaginable. There is no reasoning, no negotiation, and no conquering that force. Perhaps by emulating the Borg, they were attempting to accommodate them. Perhaps the Indign believed that these offerings were all that stood between themselves and assimilation."

"Then they didn't understand the Borg," Seven noted.

"What if they understood them better than you think?" Eden said a little sadly.

"Captain?"

"To many less advanced species, dominant ones can appear almost god-like. But the Borg wanted nothing to do with the Indign. What if they were trying to make themselves worthy of the Borg?"

"If, as Seven indicated, at least four of the six Indign species once existed separately, it would have taken thousands of years for them to learn to exist as they do now, in their collective state," Patel chimed in.

"You don't think this behavior evolved naturally?" Captain Itak inquired.

"Yes and no," Patel replied. "There is more to it than simple agreement between the various species. There are evolutionary links between them. Our universal translators can't parse the Greech language, but somehow the Neyser and Irsk/Dulaph understand them perfectly. Nothing in my readings suggests that the Greech are telepathic, though the Neyser do show faint psionic abilities, but it seems clear that one or more of the other species is necessary for them to communicate with one another."

Doctor Sharak went on, "The Greech do, however, secrete a substance that is absorbed into the Neyser bloodstream through the pores on their arms. That substance nourishes the Neyser and might have enabled them to survive in the past without the various food sources the third planet now produces. The small, moth-like creature we observed appears to release a substance, perhaps as waste, which the Neyser regularly inhale and that is absorbed in the lungs but seems to stimulate certain segments of their brains. Additionally, it does not venture beyond the boundaries of the gaseous life-form. Although its DNA profile indicates it is indigenous to the third world, I believe it has been genetically modified to function only in concert with its noncorporeal counterpart."

"And it seems that the Dulaph are able to contribute largely through the aid of the Irsk, which allows it to change shape as required," Patel added. "The genetic modifications we see in the winged alien are also present in the Dulaph. Whether these two were coerced into joining the others, or did so willingly, we cannot say."

"Still, it would be inappropriate to call any discrete group of these six species a *collective*," Seven insisted. "The Borg were more than a cooperative species. Their thoughts were one, directed only by the Queen. There is nothing in the Indign that suggests this level of joining."

"Perhaps *cooperative* is a better word," Eden offered. "Whether by need or by choice, these species have developed relationships that allow them to function as one. It's actually quite a unique and miraculous thing. They might have been inspired by their admiration for the Borg, or simply hoped that there would be strength in their numbers if they hoped to resist them. Either way, it seems certain that the Borg had a hand in influencing the development of the Indign, whether they intended to or not," Eden concluded.

After a brief pause as everyone considered her reasoning, Paris asked softly, "You really think anyone out there would have ever *wanted* to be assimilated?"

Cambridge quickly replied, "Don't judge them too harshly. It must have been clear to any resident of this part of space that the Borg were the master race." With a quick glance to Seven, he added, "Who wouldn't want to be part of perfection?"

"The Borg were far from perfect," Batiste said abruptly and Eden noted Seven's cheeks redden slightly, though she remained silent.

"By our standards, certainly," Commander Glenn piped up for the first time since the meeting had begun. "But we live as individuals. We value our autonomy. It's possible that the Indign didn't have that luxury. I find it hard to believe that if they could have survived as separate individuals, they wouldn't have made that choice. The biological synthesis we've detected might have been discovered quite by accident, but if there was a pre-existing cultural bias in all of these creatures that placed a higher value on *collective* organization, given the success of the Borg as a species, they might have naturally gravitated toward one another."

"Their individuality became irrelevant," Harry said somberly.

"All good theories," Eden said appreciatively, searching the faces of all assembled, "but I still want to know why they won't communicate with us. Their ship fired on ours. We unintentionally destroyed their ship. You'd think they'd at least want an explanation."

"They do possess scanning technology," Vorik said. "It is possible that they have decided, based on our previous encounter, that we possess more advanced offensive capabilities and are simply unwilling to risk the loss of more vessels in a fight they could not hope to win."

"Or possibly, they are simply imitating the Borg," Cambridge suggested.

"We've indicated repeatedly in our hails that we are not a threat, we come in peace, and we want to establish communication with them," Paris said. "Maybe this is their way of saying *no*."

As Eden considered the possibility, Ensign Lasren's voice came over the comm. *"Captain, we are receiving an incoming transmission from the third planet."*

"Put it through to the conference room."

"It's not an audio message, Captain. It's a set of transport coordinates."

"Coordinates?" Batiste asked.

"Six life-forms are at the coordinates. I believe they intend for us to transport them aboard Voyager."

"Any sign of weapons?" Eden asked.

"No, Captain."

"Stand by to transport them aboard."

"Captain?" Batiste asked.

"Weren't you the one who said we needed to do a better job establishing diplomatic relations with the species we encountered in the Delta quadrant?" Eden said evenly.

Batiste could clearly see that she wasn't going to let this go, and he wasn't going to challenge her openly in front of the crew. He had promised Eden that she would have his full support, and it was gratifying to see that he planned to live up to his word.

"Batiste to the bridge."

"Go ahead, sir."

"Drop shields and transport our guests aboard." Turning to Eden, he said, "Assemble your team to meet them."

"Would you care to join us, Admiral?"

He surprised her by replying, "I'll await your report in my office, Captain."

CHAPTER THIRTEEN

The Indign who appeared on the transporter platform was virtually indistinguishable from the ones they'd seen on the third planet. Kim didn't know what he was expecting—perhaps some insignia or more formal dress that might indicate a higher ranking. The simple ecru tunic and light brown pants, accompanied by rough, worn boots, suggested that this cooperative could have just dropped their work in the fields before transporting aboard.

The Greech coiled about the Neyser's right arm emitted a characteristic ear-shredding shriek as soon as the transporter effect faded. Captain Eden didn't flinch, but the same could not be said for Ensign Donner at transporter controls.

The Irsk/Dulaph stood patiently at the Neyser's side, cloaked only from the waist down in a pair of loose hanging, roughly woven trousers. Its bare feet, like the rest of its exposed flesh, glistened in the overhead lights.

Captain Eden stepped forward as their guests stood on the platform, looking about the room with placid curiosity.

"Welcome aboard the Federation *Starship Voyager*. We are honored by your visit."

When the Indign did not respond, Eden continued, "We are explorers from a distant part of the galaxy. We have come hoping to better acquaint ourselves with other species. We regret the results of our first encounter with one of your vessels. Our sensors indicated that it was uninhabited. I offer you our deepest apologies."

The Neyser met Eden's expectant gaze briefly as the Greech undulated on its arm while making a shrill, whining sound. The Indign then stepped down from the platform and moved toward the transporter room door. The pair of security guards standing there looked to Kim to confirm their next move and Harry automatically looked to Eden.

"It's all right," she said. "Give our guests some room." She followed the Indign out the door into the hallway, Patel, Sharak, and Cambridge right behind her. Harry motioned for the guards—Maplethorpe and Gaston—to fall in with him and the party began their tour of the ship.

The Neyser seemed content to make its way regally through the halls while the Irsk/Dulaph capered about. It ran its stubby hands along the hull and when it reached an operation panel, its legs extended themselves to better examine the display. Captain Eden attempted to engage it by giving a brief description of the unit's function, but the Irsk/Dulaph ignored her, apparently content to gather its own intelligence.

When they reached the astrometrics lab, Eden asked Patel to bring up a display of the current system. As the multi-hued planets danced in their orbit of the system's single star, the Indign simply walked gracefully over the platform, ignoring the show.

"Lieutenant Patel, bring up a display of the Sol system," Captain Eden ordered, hoping to find a way to crack the Indign's silence.

Eden attempted to direct the Indign's attention to the home of Starfleet.

The Irsk/Dulaph hesitated once the brilliant blue and

green world awash in fine filaments of white clouds appeared. It then turned back to Eden and suddenly its body began to lose its shape. After a vaguely disturbing display of what appeared to be melting flesh, the creature resolved itself into the form of a human man of medium height with unkempt white hair pulled back into an unruly ponytail. He wore dark pants and a ragged leather vest over a simply patterned flannel shirt. More interesting than its form was the captain's reaction.

She stared in wonder at the figure before saying softly, "That's not possible."

"Who is that, Captain?" Cambridge asked softly.

"My uncle, Jobin," Eden replied.

"Is he still on Earth, Captain?" Harry asked.

"No," Eden said, still awestruck. "But that's exactly how he appeared the last time I saw him, just before I entered the Academy."

"Were you just thinking of him?" Cambridge inquired.

"No."

With halting steps, Eden crossed to the platform and moved gingerly toward the apparition. "The form you have taken is of one very dear to me," she said sincerely. "Thank you for the kindness you have shown in re-creating this form."

Before she had finished the sentiment, however, the figure began to glimmer and lose cohesion. Seconds later, the Irsk/Dulaph had resumed its normal appearance.

The tour continued through the mess hall where the Irsk/Dulaph again did its magic, pulling images from several of the crew members in the midst of their dinners. A parrot, a butterfly, and a friendly yellow Labrador capered about the room to the delight of the crew.

Eden did not allow the Indign onto the bridge—an appropriate precautionary measure of which Kim heartily approved—nor was it allowed to venture into engineering.

The tour was completed with a brief visit to one of the cargo holds, after which the Indign led the way back to the transporter room.

Eden tried at every turn to engage the creatures, yet apart from the whimsical behavior of the Irsk/Dulaph, and the occasional, disquieting sounds from the Greech, the visit ended as curiously as it had begun.

Before ordering Donner to activate the transporter, Captain Eden took one last stab at moving their relationship forward.

"The Federation we represent does not interfere in the lives of those we encounter on our explorations. If it is your wish that we leave your system without further contact, we will honor your wishes. It is difficult, however, to know how best to proceed without some sign from you of your intentions."

The Indign maintained its stubborn silence and with obvious regret, Eden nodded to Donner.

Once their guest had been safely returned to the planet's surface, Eden turned on her staff.

"Impressions?" she asked immediately.

"Fascinating" was Patel's first response.

"Rude," Doctor Sharak observed.

"To me they seem curious," Kim said. "It would be helpful if they'd speak to us, but I think the fact that they decided to transport aboard at all should be seen as a step in the right direction."

Eden favored him with a rare smile.

"I like the way you think, Lieutenant," she said. "And I hope you're right."

"But it's curious," Cambridge finally said.

"Counselor?" Eden asked.

"They could have been attempting to get to know us better. The display of the shape-shifter was entertaining. But they could also have been measuring the drapes."

"Sir?" Sharak asked, truly puzzled.

"You think they were examining our ship because they intend to attempt to take it from us?" Kim asked.

"Ah," Sharak said, his eyes widening with comprehension. "And when it is theirs, they will improve upon the decoration. Yes."

"Did you really sense that their intentions were hostile?" Eden demanded of Cambridge.

"I'm not an empath, Captain. I didn't *sense* anything. I'm merely suggesting that it is too soon to conclude anything about their intentions, as their actions to this point are open to a varied range of interpretations."

At that, Eden turned to Kim and said, "We'll keep an open mind, but we'll also keep our guard up."

"Captain," Donner interrupted.

"What is it, Ensign?"

"We have received another transmission. The same transport coordinates."

"Is it another Indign?" Eden asked.

"No, Captain," Donner confirmed. "It's a small object."

"Does that object have a power signature?" Harry asked.

"Or a lit fuse at one end?" Cambridge quipped.

"It is approximately half a meter in length, and thirteen centimeters in diameter. It is inert and contains no detectable technology," Donner reported.

With a sigh, Eden ordered, "Bring it aboard, Ensign."

A metallic canister roughly the size of a test canister used by Starfleet when checking the transporters shimmered into existence before them.

Eden turned to Donner and said, "Send it to the *Hawking*. Advise Captain Itak to assign a team to analyze it. I'd like to know what it is, and if there's any way to open it."

"Aye, Captain."

Cambridge assumed a posture of mock chagrin, saying, "With your permission, I'd like to revise my earlier assessment."

"How so?"

"Although the Indign appear to be inscrutable I believe we can safely acknowledge one thing about them."

"And what's that?"

"They like to give gifts."

Chakotay walked swiftly across the bridge on his way to Eden's ready room. He had been summoned. Still, his quickness of step was evidence that he might never again feel truly comfortable in the heart of *Voyager*.

You're being ridiculous, part of his mind argued. He had lived most of the last ten years aboard *Voyager* and spent the vast majority of his waking hours on the bridge. But that fact didn't slow his steps.

Commander Paris occupied the captain's chair and he offered Chakotay a pleasant nod the moment he stepped off the turbolift, as Lasren stumbled over a faint, "Hello, Captain . . . I mean . . . Chakotay." These simple gestures only tightened the knot in his stomach.

He paused to collect himself at the door to the ready room and heard the door chime. After hearing a muted "Enter," he stepped inside.

Captain Eden was seated at her desk, poring over a stack of padds. The room had changed quite a bit since it had belonged to him. Apart from the absence of scorch marks, crumpled wall plates, and hanging conduits he vaguely remembered following the battle at the Azure Nebula, the walls behind and adjacent to Eden's desk were now decorated with large expressionistic paintings done in vivid reds, blues, and greens. A medium-sized bronze statue of a cat balancing on its forepaws atop a ball rested on one end of her credenza. Personal photos and mementos were arranged throughout and gave the space an unusually homey feel. The carpet and upholstery retained a subtle new smell he hadn't associated with the room since the first days he'd been on board in the Delta quadrant.

The captain dropped the padd she was studying as he crossed to stand before her desk.

"Thank you for reporting so promptly." She gestured for him to take a seat in one of two streamlined and from the looks of it, rather uncomfortable armless chairs opposite the desk.

"Not at all, Captain," he replied.

Jumping right in, Eden said, "According to Counselor Cambridge and the Doctor, Seven of Nine seems to adjusting well to her duties. Is that your impression as well?"

"It is."

There was a pause as Eden waited to see if he would expand on that thought and when he didn't she went on, "And you've seen nothing in her behavior off-duty to suggest that the voice she reported hearing is inhibiting her abilities?"

"No," Chakotay replied succinctly. Briefly he wondered if his reticence was motivated by pettiness. Once he acknowledged that that might be the case he added, "The neural inhibitor has completely muted the voice. Counselor Cambridge has asked her to disengage the inhibitor briefly in their sessions, hoping that she will be able to control the voice."

Something in his remarks disquieted Eden. She rose and went to the large windows that offered a view of the Indign planet they were orbiting. Eden paused and set her back against the rail that separated the desk area from the seating area. Crossing her arms she said, "I've just received a rather troubling report from Lieutenant Conlon."

"B'Elanna speaks very highly of her," Chakotay offered.

"Yes, apparently Commander Torres is quite generous with her expertise."

"That sounds like her," Chakotay agreed.

"Lieutenant Conlon has discovered a series of unauthorized protocols that has been added to the deflector controls."

Chakotay nodded for her to continue, suddenly realizing that he probably wasn't here to offer his expertise, but quite possibly to defend himself.

"Conlon tells me that the protocols in question have quite specific functions, including one that is capable of opening a rift to fluidic space."

"A system error, perhaps," Chakotay suggested.

"That was my first thought as well," Eden conceded, "but closer examination has determined that it was installed shortly before the fleet entered the Delta quadrant. In fact, just after you and Seven came aboard."

Chakotay considered his next words carefully. "Is there an accusation coming at some point here, Captain?" Chakotay heard more defensiveness in his tone than he had intended.

"Not yet," Eden replied, uncrossing her arms. "But I do think it's curious."

"It's Seven you're concerned about," Chakotay realized.

"Seven has been under emotional stress since the Caeliar transformation. She's desperately searching for answers. Maybe she thinks Species 8472 has them."

Chakotay stood and moved to stand opposite Eden. "The peace accord we reached with Species 8472 was contingent upon never again corrupting their realm. Seven was there. She knows what's at stake. And she would *never* risk the safety of those aboard *Voyager*, even for the sake of her own curiosity."

"I know you believe that," Eden replied. "And I *want* to. But the fact is that Seven is one of only a few people who could have written and installed that program."

"Apparently not."

"I beg your pardon," Eden said, clearly taken aback.

"Someone else clearly did, and you need to find out who and why. I could save you some time, if you were willing to trust my judgment. If not, I really can't help you," Chakotay said with a shrug.

"Thank you for your time, Chakotay," Eden replied evenly.

"I'm assuming you've purged the program, just to be safe?" he asked.

Eden paused before replying, "We can't."

"Why not?"

"It seems the only way to get rid of it would be to completely reinstall the deflector control program. We've already made hundreds of adjustments to the program to facilitate our slipstream travel and to purge it now would leave us vulnerable."

"Is Lieutenant Conlon your best programmer?" Chakotay asked.

"Yes."

"I'd have B'Elanna take a look at it again. She might be

able to find a way around that problem. Creative solutions have always been a specialty of hers."

"I will bear that in mind."

Chakotay nodded and moved quickly to the exit, wondering how long it was going to take for him to dig himself out of the piles of suspicion that he had heaped upon himself in the past three years.

Paris entered his cabin more than two hours after his shift ended. As *Voyager's* first officer, Tom found off-duty to be a much more malleable term than it had been when he'd served as a helmsman. Today it had been Ensign Lasren who'd required a little extra time and attention. Tom had been tempted to suggest that he take his concerns about Ensign B'kar—the gamma shift ops officer's tendency to leave his station configured to accommodate his three-fingered hands rather than Lasren's five—up with Counselor Cambridge. Unfortunately Lasren, like many aboard *Voyager,* had a hard time relating to Cambridge. Tom suggested a few strategies to the young Betazoid over a couple of drinks in the mess. Then he remembered that B'Elanna and Miral were waiting for him.

He fully expected to face B'Elanna's wrath. Instead, he entered their quarters to find the small dinner table set with everything he would have required for a romantic evening, including two tapered candles, and low jazz playing in the background.

The only thing that puzzled him was that the table appeared to be set for four instead of two.

B'Elanna hurried in from the bedroom. At some point during the day she'd obviously replicated the fitted, midnight-blue dress she was wearing. It accentuated her perfectly proportioned neck and toned shoulders, as well as her tiny waist, then flowed softly into a wide skirt, which ended just below her knees.

The "Hi, honey" and tender kiss with which she greeted him made him wonder if he had somehow entered a temporal anomaly wherein his passionate Klingon wife had been replaced by the equally voluptuous and vapid housewives who populated the television serials from Earth's mid–twentieth century.

"You look stunning," he said sincerely. "Now what have you done with my wife?"

B'Elanna smiled. "I hope you don't mind, but I invited a couple of friends to join us for dinner."

He understood that after more than a year spent in the solitude of her shuttle, B'Elanna probably craved social activities. But part of Tom couldn't help wondering how quickly they could finish dinner so he could enjoy helping her out of that dress.

"Where's Miral?" he asked.

"She's already asleep. The anti-viral makes her really sleepy. She had a long nap this afternoon and then went down again right after dinner and her bath."

"But she's better?"

"Oh, yes. The Doc assures me she'll be running both of us ragged again in a couple of days."

"I can't wait," Tom said with a smile.

"That's because you've never actually experienced it," B'Elanna reminded him gently. "Kula's watching over her, but you could take a peek and give her a kiss before our guests arrive."

"Didn't we just do this last night?" Tom demanded with mock annoyance.

B'Elanna turned on him with a withering glance, hands planted on her hips. "And you've been where for the last two hours?"

Tom took her hands in his and replied, "Missing you desperately."

"Oh, good answer, fly-boy," B'Elanna said, stepping close enough for him to begin nuzzling her neck.

At which point, of course, the door chime sounded.

"Make them go away," he whispered.

"Soon, I promise," she replied as she pulled away and crossed to the door.

Tom turned to see Nancy Conlon enter, she and B'Elanna falling effortlessly into shop talk. He stepped into the bedroom and spent a few moments gazing at his sleeping daughter in what had once been the suite's private office. Kneeling down he lovingly caressed her forehead, pleased to find it neither too hot nor too cold. After pulling her blanket up he noted the holographic nanny standing guard in the shadows of the room.

"Hi, there," he said amiably.

"Good evening, Commander," Kula said gruffly.

Tom shed his uniform jacket in favor of a soft, turquoise tunic and returned to the living area to find B'Elanna pouring red wine for both Nancy and Harry.

Tom paused, the muscles in his neck tensing. He and Harry hadn't exchanged a word off-duty since B'Elanna had arrived. They kept their on-duty conversations to a minimum as the ice that had formed between them had yet to begin to thaw. Obviously B'Elanna had sensed this. Still, Tom wished she'd mentioned her plan to him before inviting Harry over. They needed to talk but it wasn't going to happen this way.

He allowed himself to hope that his best friend might be coming around until Harry looked up sharply and met his gaze with hard eyes.

"Nancy," Tom said as he moved toward the table, "it's good to see you."

"Thank you, sir," she replied. "It's very nice of you to invite me to dinner."

"Not at all," Tom assured her. He actually liked Conlon and appreciated how she was warming to B'Elanna.

"Harry," he then said with a nod.

"Tom."

B'Elanna's eyes darted quickly between them before she said, a little too brightly, "Why don't we all take our seats?"

"Sounds good," Nancy said, seemingly unaware of the tension around her. "I'm starved."

Harry took the seat opposite her in silence as B'Elanna retrieved four bowls of a hearty beef stew from the replicator, along with a loaf of warm bread.

"So, Starfleet," B'Elanna teased Harry, once everyone had begun to dig in, "what's it like being chief of security now?"

"It's fine."

"Do you ever miss your old job?" B'Elanna asked.

"Didn't you start at ops?" Nancy added, clearly sharing B'Elanna's desire to draw Harry out a bit.

Harry nodded, continuing to shovel stew too quickly into his mouth to speak.

"Harry was the best ops officer I've ever seen," Tom told Conlon. "If there was an anomalous reading or systems glitch, he'd track it down in a heartbeat. He was so by-the-book he used to have Chakotay and Captain Janeway looking up regulations nobody else ever bothered to memorize."

Harry dropped his spoon and stared at Tom.

"What's that supposed to mean?" he demanded.

"Nothing," Tom said.

"Nothing," Harry repeated. "Maybe if you had bothered to actually learn those regulations you wouldn't have ended up in prison."

Tom felt his face flush.

"Harry," B'Elanna chided him softly.

Nancy turned to Tom, her eyes wide, then tossed a plaintive glance toward B'Elanna.

"It was a long time ago," B'Elanna assured her.

"Thanks, Harry," Tom said, his voice heavy with sarcasm. "I'd almost forgotten that there are people aboard this ship now who don't know every detail of my sordid past."

"Oh, that's just the tip of the iceberg, believe me," Harry told Conlon.

The sadness on Nancy's face clearly expressed her heartfelt desire not to wade any further into these troubled waters.

"I imagine if you go back far enough, we've all done things we wished we could change," she suggested kindly.

"Oh, you don't have to go back too far with Tom," Harry corrected her.

Tom pushed his bowl away and rose from his seat. "I told you I was sorry, Harry. I really don't know what else to say."

Harry stood to face him. "Of course you don't."

"Sit down, both of you," B'Elanna ordered.

"Maybe I should . . ." Nancy began.

"No, please stay," B'Elanna cut her off. "We've all been through too much together to let anything, least of all a misunderstanding, come between our friendship."

When Harry reluctantly took his seat, B'Elanna placed her hand on his and said, "Harry, if you want to be angry at someone, it should be me. I didn't give Tom a choice. I was too frightened of what might happen and I swore him to secrecy."

"I'm not angry at you, Maquis," Harry said, softening a bit in his use of an old endearment between them. "I really am glad that you and Miral are okay. I just . . ."

"What?" B'Elanna urged him gently.

After a long pause, Harry said, "I just can't pretend that everything is like it used to be. Too much has happened. I thought we were a family."

"We are," B'Elanna assured him.

"No," Harry said, shaking his head. "And now I'm not sure if we ever were."

"Harry, don't you think I wanted to tell you? Don't you think that if my daughter's life hadn't been at stake you'd have been the first person I confided in?" Tom said.

"You didn't trust me," Harry replied. "That's the bottom line. Even after everything we've all been through together, you still didn't trust me. The Warriors of Gre'thor could have captured me and tortured me and I would never have given them B'Elanna or Miral. I would have died for them. But you didn't know that about me—which means that even after ten years, you really don't know me at all."

Shaking his head sadly, he pulled his hand away from B'Elanna's and said, "Thanks for dinner. Good night, Lieutenant," he added with a nod at Conlon.

"Harry, don't go," B'Elanna began, as Harry hurried toward the door.

"Let him," Tom said coldly. Once Harry was gone he turned to Conlon and said, "I'm really sorry you had to see that."

"It's complicated," she said. "I get that."

CHAPTER FOURTEEN

Ensign Meegan McDonnell sat unobtrusively in the main sickbay of the *Galen,* reviewing the ship's inventory of stored medical supplies. They hadn't been in space long enough for anything to have expired, but there was little else she was permitted to do when the Doctor wasn't busy with a patient. When she was done with the hypos Meegan moved on to the diagnostic and surgical equipment. Routine, but it allowed her to direct most of her attention to the conversation going on between the Doctor and Lieutenant Barclay.

"Just let it go," Reg insisted.

"I don't believe you want me to do that, or you wouldn't have brought it up," the Doctor replied.

"It's a waste of your memory buffers."

"Reg, I consider you to be a friend. Nothing that affects you is a waste."

Barclay appeared to be genuinely moved by this remark. Meegan certainly would have been in his place.

Placing a hand on Reg's shoulder, the Doctor continued, "If your feelings are genuine, and I have no reason to doubt that they are, you should do something about them. Three years may seem like a long time, but believe you me, it will fly by in the Delta quadrant."

"She would never think of me that way. And why should she? She's beautiful. She's accomplished. She's not at all the type of woman I do well with, unless they're trying to steal Federation secrets from me."

"Commander Glenn is beautiful and accomplished," the Doctor agreed. "But she is also a human being. She has her own set of strengths and weaknesses, her own doubts and insecurities. No one sees themselves the way others do, Reg. You just need to gather your courage, and ask her to join you for a recreational activity. Choose something that will permit both of you the time to talk and get to know each other. The rest will come naturally."

Reg's shoulders lifted as he inhaled and began to imagine the scenario the Doctor had just described. Soon enough, however, he crumpled.

"What if she says no?"

"She won't."

"She could."

"She won't."

"She will," Reg finally decided. "And then I'll have to spend the next three years avoiding her, which on a ship this size won't be easy. We'll constantly be running into each other in the halls—"

"Reg," the Doctor interrupted, ending one of Barclay's meandering, stream-of-consciousness rambles before he could really get going. "You are a Starfleet officer held in high regard by your peers. You served aboard the Federation flagship, you were personally responsible for establishing communications between *Voyager* and the Alpha quadrant, and you are one of the most respected designers and developers of holographic technology currently alive. You are fascinating, and I'm sure that in time, she will come to see that. *But only if you give her the chance*. If you decide now that it will never work, it won't. Decide that it will, and it might."

"*Won't* I can live with. I'm not sure about *might*," Reg said, sighing.

The Doctor shook his head in frustration, grabbed a padd and downloaded selected files from his personal database onto it before presenting it to Barclay.

"What's this?" he asked.

"Social lesson number four—Collegial Conversation. I created it for Seven of Nine, but I think it would serve you well to practice a little. You know, get your confidence up."

Reg dutifully read from the padd.

"Good morning, insert name of officer here. How are you today?"

"I'm very well," the Doctor replied by rote. "How are you?"

"I am excellent. I have been working on, insert name of current project here, and, oh, I don't know."

Meegan jumped up from her stool and crossed to join them.

"I'll help you practice if you like," she offered.

"Oh, that's not necessary, Ensign McDonnell," Reg began.

"That's a wonderful suggestion," the Doctor said buoyantly. "We'll demonstrate." Turning to Meegan, he said, "Good morning, Ensign McDonnell. How are you today?"

"I am excellent," she responded with sincere enthusiasm. "I've just finished going over our inventory and replenished our stocks where required. How is your study of the Caeliar catoms coming along?"

"Incredibly challenging," the Doctor said, "but I'm confident that in time, I'll begin to make sense of them."

"I'm certain you will. You are an extraordinary researcher

and physician. If there is anything I can do to help, I'd be more than happy to assist you."

"That's very kind of you, Meegan."

"Not at all. I noticed that you've been learning a new opera. How's it coming?"

"Very well. Mozart is difficult, but that's what I like about it."

"I'd love to hear you practice some time."

Barclay had been following along in the Doctor's script from the start but soon realized that he wasn't really witnessing an instruction meant only for his benefit. With a faint smile it dawned on him that Meegan's interest in the Doctor was more than professional. Her eyes never left his, and her slightly flushed cheeks were a definite sign of attraction. He assumed he looked much the same way any time he was in the presence of Commander Glenn.

As soon as Seven entered the sickbay she noted that the effervescent cheer with which the Doctor greeted her was diametrically opposed to the reception she received from his assistant, Meegan.

"Am I interrupting something?" Seven asked simply.

Meegan's petulant grimace was only intensified when the Doctor replied, "Of course not. I've been expecting you."

Seven decided to dismiss Meegan's less than professional demeanor as evidence of both her youth and inexperience. Surely anyone with an ounce of maturity would realize that Seven's friendship with the Doctor was purely platonic and would provide no barrier to anyone else with Meegan's obvious intentions. In time, perhaps, she would take Meegan aside and assure her that her obvious jealousy was neither warranted nor necessary.

"Hello, Seven," Barclay greeted her warmly. She felt the corners of her mouth tip upward automatically as she returned the salutation. Reg was as sweet and genuine a person as she had encountered in the Alpha quadrant.

"Have the *Galen*'s unique systems performed up to your expectations so far?" she asked, well aware that he was intensely shy.

"Oh, yes," Reg said, his head bobbing up and down with obvious enthusiasm. "All our preliminary tests of the emergency medical and security holograms have been unqualified successes. All that remains is to test the command holograms, though Commander Glenn has been reluctant to authorize those diagnostics."

"Perhaps the events of the past few days have forced her to adopt a more conservative posture. I would assume that once we conclude matters in this system, she will be more receptive to your requests."

"That's my thought as well, Seven," Barclay replied, "although I did wonder if perhaps she might be a little threatened by the idea of the ECHs."

"I doubt Commander Glenn would have been selected to lead the *Galen* should that be the case," Seven assured him. "But you should not hesitate to voice your concerns. She may not be aware of her own biases, should they exist."

"I quite agree," the Doctor added, with a meaningful nod at Reg.

"I don't want to intrude," Barclay said, suddenly more ill at ease. "Good to see you again, Seven."

"And you, Lieutenant."

Seven then allowed the Doctor to direct her to a private examination room, a thoughtful addition, in Seven's view, to the design of the sickbay. She had grown accustomed aboard

Voyager to limited privacy during medical procedures, but now more than ever, appreciated this unique attribute in the design of the *Galen*.

"And how is your inhibitor functioning?" the Doctor asked as he began to scan her with his medical tricorder.

"It appears to be working properly. As long as it is engaged, I am not aware of the voice at all. It has been refreshing to work without its constant interference."

"Counselor Cambridge has advised me that he has begun testing your ability to control the voice without the inhibitor."

"So far, my efforts in that regard have been less than satisfactory," Seven replied honestly.

"Don't be too hard on yourself," the Doctor encouraged her. "This is uncharted territory. I think you're bearing up extremely well."

"Have you made any progress in your analysis of the catoms?" Seven asked.

The Doctor sighed. "Some, though my efforts in that regard have been less than stellar. I've analyzed the molecules using every diagnostic at our disposal, but I still understand almost nothing about how they do what they do. Clearly they are effective. If they weren't you'd have died."

This was news to Seven, though once she had considered it, she realized it made sense.

"Borg implants contained self-regenerating power sources."

"Yes," the Doctor said with a nod, "and I expected to find something similar in the catoms. But it appears that they rely entirely on external power sources."

"For the Caeliar living in one of their cities, that power source was their omega molecule generators."

"Your biological processes now seem to be powering yours," the Doctor added.

"Then it is likely that the catoms that replaced my implants would be more limited in their scope and potential uses than those used by the Caeliar," Seven reasoned.

"Agreed," the Doctor said. "They are integrated into your body seamlessly, more so than your Borg implants. This integration suggests to me that in time, you should be able to control them."

"That does not necessarily follow," Seven argued. "I realize that you and Counselor Cambridge are both intrigued by this possibility, but it is equally likely that the catoms were placed in my body with severely limited programming. Their only purpose might be to sustain the systems that once required nanoprobes. There might be no neural connection, apart from the catoms that replaced my cortical node, or that connection might be one-way."

"You think they placed that voice in your head and denied you the ability to answer it?"

"It is possible."

"It's also barbaric, and not at all consistent with what little else we know of the Caeliar. I don't believe they intended the voice to torment you."

"Then they failed."

"Or perhaps, we just haven't figured out how to make appropriate use of the gift they have given you."

Seven bristled at the thought of the transformation as a gift. However, it was possible that the Caeliar had unintentionally created her current dilemma.

"I need to disengage the inhibitor to run a diagnostic on it and to download the data it has collected about your neural processes," the Doctor said. "Would you like me to sedate you while I do so?"

"I survived for months with the voice," Seven replied.

"Although I would not consider myself able to perform my duties without the inhibitor at this time, I believe I possess sufficient control to manage for a few minutes while you perform your tests."

"Very good," the Doctor said, and smiled. "Are you ready?"

Seven acquiesced with a nod.

The Doctor gently removed the inhibitor and Seven forced herself to take deep, regular breaths as she awaited the resurgence of the unwelcome presence in her mind.

You are Annika Hansen.

Seven ignored the voice and attempted to focus her thoughts on the most recent scans she had completed of the Indign system. Unfortunately, this led her to thoughts of the reverence the Indign seemed to have for the Borg too quickly. The notion that she and the Indign might share anything in common was decidedly troubling.

You are Annika Hansen.

Seven stole a glance at the Doctor, who hummed softly to himself as he performed the diagnostic. Her heartbeat began to accelerate as she attempted to calculate the length of time it would take for him to complete his work.

You are Annika Hansen.

I am Seven of Nine. I am a unique individual. Your interference is neither helpful nor appropriate. I am Seven of Nine.

Hello, Seven of Nine.

Seven's eyes widened instantly at this abrupt change to the voice's routine. Her breath came in quick, short spasms as she waited to see if it would return to normal, or if, somehow, she might have just discovered some of the control she had been seeking.

Seven of Nine?

"I am here," she said aloud.

Seven of Nine, help me.

"Where are you?"

"Seven?" the Doctor said, puzzled.

"Something has changed," she advised him.

He quickly returned to her side and began to scan her.

"Your heart rate and respiration have increased," he noted. "What's wrong?"

"The voice . . . it has changed."

Seven of Nine, hurry.

Seven quickly pushed herself off the biobed and moved to the door of the examination room.

Seven of Nine.

The voice seemed louder in her head, as if somehow she had stepped closer to it.

"But that's impossible," Seven murmured.

"Seven, tell me what's happening," the Doctor requested more urgently.

"I don't know," Seven heard herself reply.

The Doctor's concern for Seven was heightened as she moved quickly from the exam room and returned to the main medical bay. There, he was surprised to find Lieutenant Vorik consulting with Meegan. Atop the large diagnostic station, a solid metal canister was bathed in a soft, blue light, clearly undergoing analysis.

Seven was drawn to it, her eyes wide as she slowly approached it. She continued to mutter softly under her breath. At first the Doctor assumed that she was carrying on a conversation with the voice, but he couldn't imagine what she had meant when she said that something had changed.

As Seven was engrossed with the canister, the Doctor readied a quick hypospray in the event this troubling situation grew dangerous to her. He had left the inhibitor in the examination room but didn't dare go to retrieve it.

"Lieutenant Vorik, what is that canister?" the Doctor demanded.

Unperturbed, Vorik replied, "It was sent to *Voyager* by the Indign. I have been searching for a way to open it. My scans have revealed a hollow core and a locking mechanism that I cannot access."

"Why have you brought it here?" the Doctor asked, not tearing his eyes away from Seven.

"I have detected faint neural energy within. *Galen*'s bioscanners are the most advanced in the fleet and they should provide me with a more definitive analysis."

The Doctor couldn't fault Vorik's logic.

Seven did not seem to have heard their exchange. She remained focused exclusively on the canister. Suddenly, she disengaged the diagnostic. Vorik began to protest.

The Doctor stopped him. Moving to Seven's side he asked, "What are you doing?"

Seven didn't answer. Instead, she picked up the canister by its ends and slowly began to turn those ends in opposite directions. There was clearly purpose to her actions, yet she gave the impression of a sleepwalker.

"I have already made numerous attempts to open it in that manner," Vorik pointed out. "It is not possible."

With a click and a hiss, one end popped open.

"Apparently it is," the Doctor corrected him as a blinding white light enveloped the medical bay.

─────

According to his internal self-diagnostic subroutines, two point one six minutes had elapsed since the Doctor had recorded his impressions of the light. He had not been offline during that time. All indications were that his program had been functioning normally.

It was impossible to understand, then, why he had absolutely no memory of those two point one six minutes.

Much as he wished to further analyze this mysterious turn of events, the scene that met his eyes demanded his immediate attention. Seven and Vorik lay unmoving on the floor, clearly unconscious. Meegan stood at the far side of the room, studying the main control panel.

"Meegan," he said quickly, "this is an emergency. Why aren't you tending to our patients?"

Meegan made no move to turn or answer him.

"Meegan!" he called again as he grabbed the nearest tricorder and quickly scanned both Seven and Vorik. To his relief, both showed strong life signs and normal neural activity. They would awaken on their own shortly. As he debated formulating a light stimulant to speed this process along, Meegan finally turned and stared at him with cold, merciless eyes.

"I have come," she said imperiously.

"Yes, you reported for duty several hours ago," he chided her. "And since your shift hasn't ended, I'd appreciate your help."

"I have come," Meegan repeated.

The Doctor suddenly realized that nothing in his memory files for Meegan could account for her present, odd behavior. He stepped gingerly toward her, raising his tricorder as he went.

"Meegan, are you feeling all right?" he asked.

"Meegan is gone," she replied. "I have come to speak for the Indign."

Admiral Batiste felt his shoulders stiffen as "Meegan" was escorted into *Voyager*'s conference room, flanked by two security officers. She had been entirely cooperative during her transport from the *Galen*. Upon entering the room she paused and inspected the officers present: Captain Eden, Commander Paris, Lieutenant Kim, and Counselor Cambridge. Trailing behind "Meegan" were the Doctor and Seven of Nine.

"Meegan" certainly looked harmless. Slight of frame with an open, heart-shaped face and wide brown eyes, she looked lost. In Batiste's experience, anything that could possess the body and mind of another sentient creature was both dangerous and unpredictable. The fleet had been at Yellow Alert since the Doctor notified Commander Glenn of the Indign's arrival.

"Meegan" was offered the seat between him and Eden. She accepted it with a gracious, almost regal nod, and sat with her back ramrod straight and her hands clasped in her lap. The admiral had already instructed Lieutenant Lasren at Ops to monitor the meeting from the bridge and use the internal sensors to gather as much information about "Meegan" as possible. Grateful that the Indign's long silence was about to be broken, Batiste firmly believed the best course would be trust, but verification.

Setting his misgivings aside, Batiste began as amiably as possible, "Welcome aboard the Federation *Starship Voyager*. I am Admiral Willem Batiste. I appreciate your willingness to speak with us. However, I am concerned about the officer you have compromised to facilitate this communication."

"Meegan" replied in a flat, unaffected tone. "The organism currently serving as a conduit for our communication is unharmed. When our communication has ceased, she will be restored to you."

Batiste said with a hint of warning in his voice, "Our people place great value on the life of each individual, and her loss would pain us greatly."

"There is no cause for concern in that regard, Admiral Willem Batiste."

Eden was favoring him with a look he knew all too well. A stranger might have interpreted it as intense curiosity. He understood it as an instruction: *Get on with it already*.

"We are curious to understand anything you can tell us of your people. Our observations have been limited, but we gather that you live as a cooperative species."

"The relationship that has developed among the Indign began thousands of years ago, when the Neyser first entered this system. They discovered the healing properties of the Greech and sought their assistance, but this process was complicated by their inability to communicate with one another. The darkness between them ended, however, when two species native to this system, the Imalak and the Neela, became curious about the Neyser and Greech. The Imalak were able to understand the Greech, and the Neyser modified the Neela to translate for them. Eventually, the Irsk and Dulaph sought to join our collective and were also modified to do so. We are now as we have been for a hundred generations. Together we have built a society worthy of the respect of our betters and terrifying to our inferiors. We exist in peace and will resist anything that seeks to disturb that peace."

"You paint a remarkable picture," Batiste said sincerely. "The Federation has found that when disparate species encounter one another, the road to peaceful coexistence is filled with conflict as one species seeks to assert dominance over the others. I am glad to hear that you have avoided this, though I am curious about one thing."

"Ask your question," Meegan replied.

"When you say that the Neela, the Irsk, and the Dulaph were modified, were they given a choice in the matter?"

"Of course. They submitted themselves to the Neyser, who long ago mastered the science of genetic manipulation. It was their desire to join with us. As you value the life of the individual, we value the spirit of cooperation. It has served us well, and allowed us evolve. We have learned that this is the only path to greatness, as shown by those who have become the essence of cooperation and the dominant species of our galaxy."

Batiste felt his cheeks growing hot.

"You are referring to the Borg."

"The Borg *Collective*," Meegan replied, adding emphasis.

"Have you had significant contact with the Borg?"

"They are our betters in every way. We hope one day to be worthy of their attention. Until then, we will strive to emulate and please them in all that we do."

"We discovered a ship not far from here. Was that intended as an offering for the Borg?"

"On their behalf, we have cleansed the surrounding sectors of all life-forms that are hostile to the Indign and inferior to the Borg. They accept our offerings. They have never attempted to conquer us. It is a mutually beneficial relationship and proper between two species when one can only aspire to the greatness already achieved by the other."

"When we neared your system, we encountered one of your vessels firing upon a shuttle," Eden interjected.

"A drone ship, designed to scan for life-forms and disable and capture them. This encounter and subsequent passive scans have led us to conclude that your vessels are tactically superior to ours and we understand that you did not destroy the drone intentionally. We invite you to submit yourselves to the Borg and join in the Collective. If you are judged worthy, it will be cause for celebration among your people. We believe that though your social development is obviously lacking, your technological achievements might make the Borg willing to overlook your other shortcomings."

"We would *never* consider such a thing," Batiste replied sharply.

"That is unfortunate for you," Meegan replied sadly. "But each species develops at its own pace, and perhaps, despite your reluctance, the Borg will take pity on you, nonetheless. If not, we simply ask that you depart this system in peace."

"May I ask how long it has been since you last detected any Borg activity in this area?" Eden asked.

"It can be many years between detection of their vessels. The last occurred more than four years ago."

Batiste shot Eden a harsh glance, but she pressed on, "The Federation does share one characteristic with the Indign. It is a community of hundreds of species who have learned to live in peace and to work together for our mutual benefit."

"I see," Meegan replied with a faint smile. "Like us, you work diligently to demonstrate your readiness for Collective existence."

"No," Eden corrected her gently. "Once one has joined the Borg, all traces of one's individuality are lost."

"A small sacrifice to make," Meegan noted.

"But one that is too great for us. Do the individual members of an Indign cooperative submit their individuality to a collective will?"

"The Indign function as a cooperative. Although there is mutual benefit and some necessity in our existence, each

Neyser, Greech, Imalak, Neela, Irsk, and Dulaph who joins a cooperative does so of their own volition. After many years, a cooperative may disassemble and those who were once joined are free to live out their lives as individuals. We have not yet mastered the seamless harmony of the Borg, though we do aspire to it."

"You've said that you wish for us to depart the system," Batiste said, reasserting his control of the meeting. "Before we do so, would you be willing to discuss the possibility of a trade agreement? The third planet of your system contains a natural resource we call benamite. Would you consider sharing some of this benamite with us, in exchange for something we might be able to offer you?"

"No exchange will be possible," Meegan retorted sharply. "We are self-sufficient and produce all that we require to live. There is nothing you could offer us that would be of equal value."

Eden said, "I am sorry to hear that. We will, of course, respect your wishes. Even so, if, in the future, you should encounter another Federation ship, we hope you would consider them a friend. We would appreciate the opportunity to speak further with you at any time."

"That will not be possible. We do not make a habit of establishing communications with species that are not Indign. All communication from this point forward is terminated."

With that, Meegan's head fell forward. The Doctor hurried to her side and scanned her. After a few moments, the girl lifted her head and her eyes widened in shock at finding herself the center of attention among the senior officers.

"What happened?" she asked, puzzled.

"It will require some explanation," the Doctor assured her. "Admiral, with your permission, I would like to take her to sickbay for a thorough examination."

"Of course," Batiste said with a nod before turning to the others to add, "Return to your posts. Captain Eden, please remain."

CHAPTER FIFTEEN

Seven found herself automatically directing her steps toward Chakotay's cabin after the meeting. As soon as the door had shut behind her, Chakotay immediately moved toward the replicator and ordered a pot of hot tea that he then dispensed for both of them.

"Are you all right, Seven?" Chakotay asked as soon as they were both settled.

"In what respect?" she asked.

"I understand you lost consciousness after you somehow managed to open the Indign canister."

"How could you possibly know that?" Seven demanded.

"The Doctor. He was on his way to check on his medical assistant, who I understand also had quite an interesting afternoon."

Chakotay paused for a moment but when she remained silent, prodded gently, "The Doctor said there was some confusion before you opened the canister."

Seven nodded slowly. "An adequate characterization. He had briefly removed my neural inhibitor to adjust it and at first, as usual, I heard the voice." She faltered a little but continued, "But then I heard something else."

"What did you hear?" Chakotay asked delicately.

"It called to me."

"The canister?"

"The consciousness within," Seven replied. "It called me by name."

"Just out of curiosity, which name?" Chakotay asked.

"It called me Seven."

"Did it say anything else?"

"Not that I recall. There was urgency in it, unlike the voice. It demanded my attention, if that makes sense."

"Did it tell you how to open the canister?"

"One moment I had no idea what was happening, only that I *must* go to it. And the next, I knew exactly what to do to free it."

"It wanted freedom?" Chakotay inquired warily.

"Yes," Seven decided. "It demanded freedom. I don't think I could have refused, even if I'd wanted to."

"That's some communications array the Indign have devised," he observed.

"Indeed," Seven agreed.

Chakotay made his next point as gently as possible. "You've never been even a little telepathic, apart from your time with the Borg?"

"No."

"So I guess what we need to figure out is if this was a result of the Caeliar transformation, or something that was forced upon you by the Indign?"

"They didn't hesitate to force that consciousness on Ensign McDonnell," Seven replied.

"It's obvious they don't share our respect for personal space, and given the way they live, why would they? Maybe they didn't realize how rude they were being," Chakotay suggested.

"I think it is far more likely that the consciousness

contained within the canister was searching for an appropriate host and must have initially found a way to interface with my catoms."

"If that's true, we're going to need to redouble our efforts to help you control them. We can't have you taken unawares like this by hostile creatures on a regular basis," Chakotay insisted.

"They are more than hostile. They are monsters," Seven replied flatly.

Chakotay's eyes widened. "That's a bit harsh, don't you think?"

"They revere the Borg, while understanding nothing of the Borg's nature. They actually desire assimilation, and have sentenced countless thousands to that fate by offering them to the Borg. At the very least, Captain Eden should destroy their ability to continue to do so."

"How would that make her different from the Borg?" Chakotay asked softly. Before Seven could answer, Chakotay went on, "I've never heard you speak about the Borg this way. Why is it so upsetting to find a culture that honors the Borg, when you seem reluctant as well to part with your Borg nature as the voice seems to insist?"

Seven stared at him, defiantly. "I am nothing like the Indign. I was Borg. I see them for what they were. I comprehend the magnitude of their wrongs. I do not honor them. I would never seek to emulate their behavior. What I find it difficult to disregard is the knowledge I attained through the Collective. Who would benefit were I to choose ignorance? Were I to become Annika Hansen, simply because the Caeliar seem to demand it . . . while offering me nothing but a glimpse of how much I have yet to learn. What hope would I ever have of . . ." she trailed off.

"Of what?" Chakotay asked, placing a gentle hand on her knee.

Seven's eyes began to glisten and her chin quivered as she struggled to hold back her emotions.

"Of being worthy of the gestalt?" Chakotay asked kindly. "It is possible you share more with the Indign than you are willing to accept, Seven. Perhaps that is what the Indign consciousness sensed when it first contacted you."

"Doubtful," Seven insisted.

"Maybe we don't know enough about the Indign yet to make that leap. Either way, I think it is more important than ever that you learn to control your catoms."

"How?" Seven demanded.

"Practice," Chakotay suggested.

Eden couldn't believe what she was hearing.

"We're not going anywhere," Batiste repeated when she questioned it the first time.

"They've made contact, and they've asked us to leave," Eden said. "Have I missed anything important?"

"They're capturing and killing innocent humanoids and offering them for assimilation to a race that no longer exists."

Eden took a moment to collect her thoughts, crossing to the bay of windows that offered a more serene picture of the Indign system than Willem had just painted.

"We could set up buoys just outside the system, warning passing ships," she suggested.

"Or we could remain in the system until the Indign are willing to speak with us again, at which point we tell them the truth," Willem countered.

"The truth?"

"That the Borg no longer exist. Their master race was conquered by an even greater species and no longer occupies this area of space. Their offerings are no longer necessary."

"You and I both know that in a situation as delicate as this, sharing that information could prove disastrous."

"So we simply lie to them by omission? And allow them to go on victimizing other sentient creatures in a cause that has gone from irrationally motivated to absurd? That's the Starfleet way?" he demanded.

"We have to respect their cultural norms, Admiral. They *worship* the Borg, the same way humans worshipped gods in any number of forms for thousands of years. It doesn't matter that those gods are intemperate and ultimately unknowable. That's part of the allure for those who are so inclined. It's evidence only of their shortcomings, not those of their gods. It's the basis for faith."

"Their faith is based on gross misunderstanding and lies."

"That's not for you to judge, and you know it," Eden countered.

Batiste crossed to face her, fierce and unyielding determination shining from his eyes. It had been such a long time since Eden had seen such intensity radiating from him, she took an involuntary step back. What she remembered of his passions was their deep and tempestuous nature. Once upon a time, she had met him there, and truly enjoyed wading into those dicey waters. Now, they frightened her.

"What's the point of gathering all our knowledge if others can't benefit from it as well?" he asked.

"*We* benefit from it. But knowledge can't be forced upon others. They have to want it. They have to find it for themselves. And I believe that in time, the Indign will. It's only been a few years. Who's to say that after fifty or a hundred more, when the Borg haven't been seen or heard from by several generations of cooperatives, they won't reevaluate their beliefs and pin their hopes on their own goals, rather than those they once perceived as the accomplishments of another race?"

"If they are anything like humans, it will take a lot longer than that," Willem noted.

"Granted," Eden said with a nod. "But isn't this the point of the Prime Directive? We don't interfere with the natural development of other races because we're not in the god business. You're seeing only the horror of the Borg's influence here. I recognize that, too, but I can also see the positive side. Look at what their example inspired in the Indign, misunderstood though it might have been. More important, there really isn't a decision to be made here. We've followed protocol. We've established first contact. And they've asked us to leave. That's pretty much the end of the story the way I read our regulations."

"Damn the regulations," Batiste scoffed.

"I beg your pardon, Admiral?"

"You heard me. These people will, in time, through contact with vessels like ours, enhance their technological capabilities and they will do so in the name of finishing the work the Borg began. We have an opportunity right here and right now to nip that in the bud."

"And how do you think they'll respond?" Eden asked. "You really want to tell these people we killed their gods?"

"We didn't," Batiste argued. "Not really."

"Yes, I'm sure they'll grasp the distinction. We were *there*, Willem. Our people witnessed the transformation firsthand and we're still trying to figure out exactly what happened. Do you think the Indign are just going to take our word for it? They don't know us. They have no reason to trust us. And all we'd be doing is handing them a reason to make war on us. What's that going to solve, other than making you feel better about this?"

Batiste's breath was quick. Beads of sweat had broken out on his forehead and she guessed that if she had a tricorder right now, it would have shown his heart racing in his chest.

"For the time being, *Voyager*, *Hawking*, and *Galen* will remain in orbit," he ordered.

"I think that's a mistake, Admiral," she replied.

"That much I gathered. For what it's worth, I think you were mistaken to allow Chakotay, Seven of Nine, and B'Elanna Torres to join your crew."

"It's my ship, Admiral. *My crew*."

"That's right. And you get to make mistakes. My ordering you otherwise isn't going to change your nature, nor will it help you learn from these mistakes."

Eden felt her own heart beginning to run its own quick race. "I appreciate your concern, Admiral, but I don't need it. I understand my nature better than you ever could. I recognize my weaknesses and play to my strengths, just as you do. Please don't assume that simply because you have formed an opinion, it's the only viable one to be had. B'Elanna Torres has freely offered her expertise to Lieutenant Conlon. Seven has acquitted herself admirably and hasn't failed once to honor the terms she agreed to when she boarded."

"What about Chakotay? You honestly believe he's only here to help a friend?"

"At this point, yes," Eden replied, conscious of the hesitation in her voice. "But I'm not an idiot. If he has other intentions, they will become clear soon enough."

"You already suspect him of planting those deflector protocols you reported."

"He and I have discussed it and for the time being, I am satisfied with his answers. If that changes, I won't hesitate to throw him or any other responsible party into the brig, pending transport back to the Alpha quadrant."

"Afsarah," Willem said, shaking his head morosely. "You've always been too quick to see the potential in everyone, and you possess a huge soft spot for strays."

"You didn't used to mind."

"No, because when we were together, I knew I could protect you from those who would take advantage of your naïveté."

"You abandoned your post as my *protector* a long time ago," she replied heatedly. "Not that I ever wanted that from you anyway. And I certainly didn't mean to burden you with my propensity for rash Pollyanna-esque lapses."

"That's not what I—" he began.

"You want to know what I think?" she hammered on without waiting for a response. "I think the only thing you hate more than being wrong is when I'm right. You constantly look for the monsters in the darkness. You're terrified of them. Frankly, I don't know how you rose through the ranks of an organization like Starfleet so quickly given your pessimism."

"A lot of people are still alive today because of that pessimism," he countered.

"There's living and breathing, and there's *alive*. One of these days, you're going to learn the difference."

After a short, silent pause, the admiral's breath calmed. "I will note your objections in my logs," he said evenly. "In the meantime, I expect you to carry out my orders. It's your ship, but I'm the senior officer."

"Of course, Admiral," Eden managed with a deferential nod before he turned crisply and left the room.

The moment he was gone, she began to circle the large conference table.

What the hell just happened?

She and Batiste had had their fair share of differences throughout the years, and sometimes they devolved from professional to personal.

But this was different.

She couldn't shake the feeling that he had launched his personal attack on her command choices to deflect her attention.

There was nothing to argue when it came to the Indign. Like it or not, the Prime Directive made this situation nonnegotiable.

So why is he doing this?

Eden replayed the conversation in her head a few times before she realized that she was asking herself the wrong question, as was usually the case with any question that began with the word "why." The right question stopped her in her tracks.

What the hell is he really up to?

Despite Chakotay's suggestion, Seven decided that what she really needed was some rest. She was still uncomfortable sleeping, primarily because until a few months ago, she had never associated rest with anything other than standing upright in a Borg regeneration chamber.

The Doctor had suggested playing soft music in her quarters. He had even provided her with a few works that she found dull and uninspired, but that did have a soothing effect when she focused her attention on them.

She lay with the lights off, as a variety of stringed instruments did little to quiet her thoughts. As the violins whined, she found herself wondering how much practice would really do to help her begin to master her catoms—if in fact they were the true source of the voice in her mind.

Alone in the darkness Seven began to fear another potential cause. It was possible she was suffering from some sort of mental deterioration. She had witnessed years of her aunt's illness, and though she knew that she did not have Irumodic syndrome, there were dozens of other neurological conditions which could produce her symptoms.

Once this thought took hold, she felt compelled to test it. Seven lifted herself on her elbows and swung her legs over the side of her bed. She took a few deep breaths, and did what she could to clear her mind.

Suddenly "Meegan's" face as she described the respect the Indign felt for the Borg floated into her mind. She tried to release the anger that accompanied this image and found it replaced by the face of the young, half-Caeliar Annika Hansen she, Chakotay, and Icheb had confronted in her mental Erigol. Like "Meegan," the face of Annika disturbed her deeply. A childish laugh echoed throughout the caverns of her mind, which tempted her to call for the computer to illuminate her cabin—a temptation she forced herself to conquer.

Searching for a more peaceful thought, she settled on her aunt Irene's face, seated before her at her kitchen table, her chin resting in her hand and her eyes twinkling as she listened to Seven tell story after story about her friends and her students.

Though there was sadness to accompany this image, there was also something in it that both strengthened and calmed her. She allowed it to linger briefly, mentally watching it fade slowly into the distance until it was undistinguishable from a field of stars she imagined floating before her. Each star became an association with someone she knew cared for her: Kathryn, Chakotay, the Doctor, Icheb, Naomi, Neelix, and Tuvok. The list went on as Seven imagined herself bathed in the comfort and care of so many, near and far, who wished her peace.

Buoyed by a newfound sense of strength, Seven slowly raised her hand and shut off the neural inhibitor. The voice returned and as soon as she heard it, she tried to place it among the stars gleaming in her mind. Rather than fight it, she accepted that it was there and tried to imagine that it desired good for her. To her surprise, its volume diminished until it was a faint buzz, part of a sum of galactic white noise, nothing more than one element of a wider tapestry of concerned voices.

Seven felt weariness descending upon her. She realized that intense mental effort was required on her part to sustain this faint control, but now that she had found a path, she knew she could locate it again. Chakotay had been right. All it would take was more practice.

She raised her hand to once again engage the inhibitor and felt a sharp pain streak through her head as a blinding white light flashed before her eyes. Instead of touching the inhibitor, Seven grabbed the sides of her head with both hands, attempting to hold back the searing heat in her mind.

Her stomach began to turn as images cascaded frenetically into her mind: humanoids blown to bits by crude energy weapons, screeching bugs scrambling over rocks as explosions erupted all around them, pools of silver fluid cascading over small scampering creatures, desperate to evade them, and through it all a sense that she was drowning, suffocating in a gaseous haze.

As Seven was bombarded by these sights, she fell to the floor and curled into a whimpering, shuddering ball. Shaking, frantic hands searched the back of her neck until her fingers found the inhibitor and after frustrating, painful seconds, she finally reengaged it.

Lying in the darkness, her heart racing and her breath coming in gasps as her mind grew mercifully blank, Seven tried her best to find the starfield again, but failed to, as faint red and blue flashes streaked across the darkness.

A few hours later, she awakened in the same position, curled uncomfortably on the floor of her cabin beside her bed. A distant shriek echoed in her mind.

Her first thought was to wonder what she had witnessed before losing consciousness. In the absence of their visceral assault, the images were easier to analyze and quickly identify as belonging to the various Indign species. But they had not come from her research or observations. They had not come from anything the Indign had shared with the crew about themselves or their history.

Seven broke out into a cold sweat as she wondered if she might not somehow have witnessed the future of the Indign, should *Voyager* simply leave the system as they had requested. As she weighed the possibility, the consistent shrieking grew louder. Still groggy, she pulled herself up and was almost overwhelmed by the need to retch.

Finally part of her mind understood the loud, repetitive sound. Now that she was fully awake, she realized that it must have been this sound that had pulled her back to consciousness.

Klaxons were wailing throughout *Voyager*.

CHAPTER SIXTEEN

den entered the bridge less than a minute after the alarm had sounded, calling "Report!" She was surprised to note that the viewscreen was blank. The bridge was awash in pulsing crimson light and it seemed that the periods of darkness between pulses was growing longer with each iteration.

"Restore normal lighting," she called.

Commander Paris was already on the bridge, standing over Ensign B'Kar at ops.

"We are experiencing multiple simultaneous systems failures, Captain," Paris advised her evenly.

"Are we under attack?"

"No, Captain. We are trying to get the sensors back up. Our last reading showed no hostile vessels approaching. As best we can tell, this is an internal problem."

Best to be grateful for the little things, she reminded herself, though she immediately wondered how long it might take the Indign to realize that their ship was not operating at full capacity and whether or not that would encourage them to make the most of an opportunity to rid themselves of their unwelcome Federation guests.

"What's the status of *Hawking* and *Galen*?"

"Our comm system is down," Tom reported.

"Their last report indicated that all systems were functioning normally, Captain," Kim added from tactical.

"How many systems are we talking about?" Eden asked, as she moved to stand beside Tom, probably adding to B'Kar's angst.

"Communications, sensors, weapons, navigation, and the list keeps growing," Paris replied.

"Engineering, report," Eden called out.

After a moment of silence, B'Kar said, "I'll add internal communications to the list, Captain."

Eden stepped quickly toward the turbolift, but pulled herself up just short of running into the doors when they failed to open automatically.

"Turbolifts." She turned back to the command well.

"Aye," B'Kar assured her.

Eden had to assume that Conlon was doing all she could from her end to remedy the situation. They'd spent so much time and energy focusing on the slipstream drives and coordinating fleet movement that something smaller but equally disabling could have been missed. Unfortunately, *now* wasn't exactly the optimal time for it to make its presence known.

It was also possible that this might not be an accident.

"Computer," B'Elanna called, "mute alarm." She couldn't believe Miral was sleeping through the ruckus, and was certain that if it didn't end soon, she would awaken just as cranky and edgy as her mother was at the moment.

Her concern began to grow when the computer did not reply to her command.

Tom had been giving her a quick kiss before she had even realized something was wrong. The familiar Klaxons had quickly brought her to full consciousness. The nauseating fear that had been her constant companion for the last three years reawakened. She reminded herself that whatever was happening, the crew would certainly have it under control in no time. It was impossible to even consider that *Voyager* might already have come under attack because of her or Miral.

Finally the alarm system wound down, though it was clear from the slow drop in pitch that it hadn't been shut off. The system was malfunctioning. As the dim cabin lights began to flicker, B'Elanna began to calculate how many systems had to be damaged to affect emergency alerts: the main computer, environmental controls . . .

Her gut tightened as the list grew.

B'Elanna began to pace the cabin, her anxiety mounting with each step.

It's not your problem.

She believed it less every time she thought it.

Hurrying to Miral's bedside, she was gratified to see that Kula was standing his permanent vigil. Holographic systems had always run independently on *Voyager*. Had Kula been offline, B'Elanna couldn't even have entertained the notion she had settled upon.

It's not your problem, Chakotay reminded himself.

Now he just needed to make himself believe it.

He had jumped from his bed and almost reached the door to his cabin before he realized that the alarm was not meant to summon him. His natural response to the sound of a ship-wide alert was so deeply ingrained that pulling himself up short was painful. He told himself over and over again that those in command would certainly resolve the crisis quickly. He reminded himself that he was where he was at this moment because of a conscious choice on his part. He tried to calm his breathing and simply block the sound from his mind. He visualized himself standing at Kathryn's memorial, and tried to recapture the certainty he had felt when he had finally made peace with his choice to abandon Starfleet.

Nothing worked.

Adrenaline poured through his body but without the release that came from focusing that energy on a specific task, he was left in an unbearably anxious state.

He paced his cabin in darkness. The computer wasn't responding to vocal commands. Turning to the personal display station in his cabin, he attempted to pull up a status report. The display seemed to be malfunctioning. It fluctuated between a black screen and a static-filled Starfleet insignia.

He tried to contact Seven. He was debating simply heading for her cabin when his display screen went completely black for ten full seconds and a message finally appeared.

"Meet in astrometrics."

The littlest bit relieved, Chakotay hurried to do so.

Nancy Conlon had enjoyed more than her fair share of bad days in engineering. Compared with her days on the *da Vinci*, *Voyager*'s engine room had started to seem absolutely subdued since they'd managed to conquer the slipstream issues that had plagued them in the early days of the mission. She'd been free to focus her attention on longer-term issues like the benamite problem and deflector controls.

Then all hell broke loose. She'd seen power disruptions,

computer viruses, computer failures, and just about every conceivable system running amok, but she'd never experienced so many happening at the same time. Conlon was pleased that her staff were keeping their heads, working out one problem at a time, but she couldn't shake the feeling that this wasn't simply a random cascade failure.

Teams of engineers were already in the bowels of every major system, running diagnostics and visually inspecting every centimeter. Nothing. Apart from life support and inertial dampers, the only other unaffected systems, at least for now, appeared to be deflector controls and their drives. Her first suspect was the deflector control interfaces, but like the engines, they were running five-five-five.

"Neol, what's the status of the comm system?" she shouted through the controlled chaos all around her.

"I'm working on it," the harried ensign replied.

"Work faster," she instructed.

Turning to cross to the main display panel near the core, she ran into someone else.

"Watch where you're going," she said as calmly as she could.

"I'm sorry," B'Elanna replied. "Can you use a pair of extra hands?"

Part of her wanted to say no. The rest of her grudgingly told her self-esteem to button it and nodded. "Everything points to a problem with the main computer. Nothing else could disrupt so many systems at the same time."

"Did you try to shut it down and reinitialize?"

"We can't with these power spikes. I'm afraid to even try and access the central processor. If we suddenly lose what systems we still have . . ."

"Okay, what's working?" B'Elanna asked.

"Propulsion," Nancy replied.

"What about navigation?"

"Offline."

"That's odd, isn't it?"

"I think so, too," Nancy agreed.

Together they turned to the main console and brought up the current status of the main engine systems.

"Oh, hell," Nancy said softly.

"Am I reading this right?" B'Elanna asked, her voice growing tense.

"Neol!" Nancy shouted. "I need to speak to the bridge right now!"

Ensign Gwyn stifled a yawn. With the ship hanging in orbit and helm controls inaccessible, there was little for a pilot to do at the moment. She almost regretted pulling an extra shift tonight. Despite the zeal with which her crewmates were working to diagnose the current array of problems, she was finding it hard to get too excited. She knew that everything had been normal the last time she'd been able to look, and partial sensors now indicated that there was no sign of an attack coming from the Indign. Every time she glanced at the pitch black viewscreen, she was overwhelmed with a desire to grab a nap.

I'm sure somebody will wake me when it's over, she decided, allowing her eyelids to lower.

She was startled back to alertness by a sudden illumination of the conn. "I didn't touch anything," she said softly as a series of bleeps and control sequences began to coalesce into a serious problem.

"Captain," she called immediately.

"What is it, Ensign?"

"The slipstream drive is powering up," Gwyn reported.

"Shut it down," Eden ordered immediately.

Gwyn was already making the attempt and finding it impossible to do so.

"I don't have control, Captain," she replied.

"B'Kar, take the helm offline," Eden said.

After a moment of silence, B'Kar reported, "The helm is not responding, Captain. I'm locked out too."

"Captain, we can't go to slipstream velocity from orbit," Gwyn advised. "In fact, we shouldn't go to slipstream velocity from within this system, or any system come to think of it."

Eden crossed to her station.

"Do we have terminal coordinates?"

Gwyn was relieved to be able to answer that question.

"Yes, approximately four light-years from our current position."

"Is there anything interesting about that location?" Eden asked.

"It was charted by the *Hawking* during their analysis of the area's subspace tunnels, but otherwise, no," Gwyn replied.

Eden turned to Paris. "Commander, override the doors to that turbolift and get to engineering. I need to know what's happening down there."

"Yes, Captain," Paris replied and Kim immediately moved to assist him in accessing the manual override.

"Captain, I have partial helm controls restored," B'Kar announced.

"Shut down the slipstream drive," Eden ordered again.

"I can't do that," B'Kar replied, "but I can confirm that we are moving out of orbit at one quarter impulse and are on a trajectory to exit the system."

"Are we going to do that before the slipstream drive reaches full power?" Eden demanded of Gwyn.

She studied the display closely before answering, "It's going to be close."

"Captain, *Hawking* and *Galen* are breaking orbit with us, matching course and speed," B'Kar advised.

"Can we talk to them yet?"

"No."

"Of course not," Eden said, shaking her head.

"This isn't happening," Conlon said.

"No, this *shouldn't* be happening," B'Elanna added. They both watched helplessly while the slipstream drive continued to power up as if it had a mind of its own.

"When did you bring the slipstream drive back online?" B'Elanna asked.

"Yesterday," Conlon replied. "I was able to quarantine the errant protocols that were disrupting the interface between the drive and deflector. They're not responsible for this."

Together they studied the engineering code as it ran across the display screen, looking for something to indicate how and why it had suddenly come online.

"Look at the central processor," Conlon instructed B'Elanna. "It's running through every nonessential program in its files and finding so many failures it won't accept our overrides on the primaries."

"A virus?" B'Elanna asked.

"But why isn't it affecting propulsion?"

"Maybe it hasn't gotten there yet."

"This is intentional, B'Elanna."

"Possibly," B'Elanna said, "but first things first. We don't want to risk going to slipstream velocity right now."

"How do we stop it?"

"If it were me?"

"Yeah."

"Break it," B'Elanna suggested grimly.

It was an extreme option, but Conlon had to agree that it might also be their only option. "Break it how badly?"

"Just enough to make it impossible to open a slipstream corridor."

Conlon turned to look at the brightly churning amber glow of the slipstream core. "So we evacuate engineering and throw a wrench at it?" *What the hell, it's worked before,* she thought ruefully.

"No," B'Elanna said, her eyes suddenly filled with light. "Not the drive, just the deflector dish."

Nancy felt her eyes catch B'Elanna's fire. "Vorik could do it."

"The comm is still down," B'Elanna reminded her.

"Just *Voyager*'s."

"We have another comm system handy?"

"Yeah," Nancy replied with a smile.

Captain Itak watched as *Voyager* moved gracefully toward open space. His ship's sensors had detected multiple power fluctuations in the flagship. He was unperturbed by the lack of response to their repeated hails. He trusted that Captain Eden had the situation under control. For the time being Itak had agreed with Commander Glenn that they move into position to flank *Voyager* should the situation devolve into anything more troublesome. The Indign seemed to be taking no notice of the fleet's activities.

"Captain," Vorik's voice called softly from the bridge's engineering station.

"Yes, Lieutenant?"

"I am receiving a transmission from *Voyager*."

"On-screen."

"It has no audio or visual component. It is text only."

"What does it say?"

"It is requesting that we fire upon *Voyager*'s deflector array with minimal phasers."

"To what end?"

"It does not say," Vorik replied evenly, "though the target and phase intensity are precisely spelled out."

"Is the message from Captain Eden?"

"No. And it is not being routed through the central communications array."

"That array is still malfunctioning," Bloom advised them from ops.

"What is the source of the transmission?"

"It is coming from B'Elanna Torres's ship."

"But there is no command code authorization present?"

"No, Captain."

Itak considered the situation and quickly reached a decision. Given what little he could assess of *Voyager*'s present circumstances, it was an unconventional request; however, there was a certain logic to it.

"Move into position and fire when ready," he replied.

"Captain, I've restored power to the viewscreen," B'Kar said triumphantly.

Eden automatically lifted her head from the unresponsive ops controls where she caught sight of the *Hawking* moving into attack position from *Voyager*'s port side.

What the hell? she wondered, just as a bright blue beam erupted from its forward phaser array.

"Brace for impact!" she shouted as the beam struck, rattling the deck and everyone's nerves, but doing no significant damage.

As she waited breathlessly for another volley, having all but concluded that Captain Itak's systems must be malfunctioning as badly as hers, her combadge crackled to life.

"Conlon to the bridge."

"Go ahead," the captain replied.

"Was that the Hawking?*"*

"They just opened fire on us," Eden confirmed. In the background someone on Conlon's end had just let out a cheer.

"Captain," Gwyn interrupted, "the slipstream drive is powering down."

Eden struggled for a moment to put the pieces together. "*Hawking* fired on our deflector dish, and it shut down the slipstream drive," she said, smiling in faint relief.

"Just as we requested," Conlon confirmed.

"*We*, Lieutenant?"

There was a slight pause before Conlon admitted, *"B'Elanna and I. I contacted* Hawking *using her ship's comm system. Since it's not linked to* Voyager, *it's not experiencing the same issues we are at the moment. I've routed this comm signal into our combadges. I'm returning to engineering now. I'll be in touch as soon as I can."*

"Thank you," Eden replied. "Bridge out."

Eden was pleased, of course, that the immediate problem had been solved. The next order of business would be to determine whether or not the multiple failures were accidental or intentional.

A heavy thump sounded behind her. After a moment, a breathless and angry Admiral Batiste crawled out of a Jefferies tube.

"What is going on?" he demanded.

Eden moved to his side and gave him a brief explanation of the last few minutes. His eyes blazed with barely repressed fury as she completed her report.

"You know what this means, don't you, Captain?"

Eden did, but hesitated to give voice to it while in earshot of the rest of her bridge officers. "Yes, Admiral. Unfortunately, I do."

───────

Chakotay was surprised when the doors to the astrometrics lab opened automatically. Most of the others between his quarters and this deck had required manual override. He'd felt the ship shudder beneath what he assumed was weapons fire.

The lab was dark. A small circle of light coming from an auxiliary panel immediately caught his eye, as it was the room's only illumination. Seven's face was a crescent moon, glowing in the panel's uneven light. She did not look up as he entered.

"Is everything okay, Seven?"

"No."

He stepped closer to peer over her shoulder. She was studying scans of the Indign system and seemed to be focusing her attention on the fourth planet.

"Do you have any idea what the emergency is?"

"The ship is experiencing widespread systems failures. When I arrived I found that the lab's power supply had been cut. I only just retrieved the data I require."

"If the power is down, how did you do that?" he asked.

She raised an eyebrow slightly as she glanced in his direction. The look said clearly "I am Borg," though he suddenly realized how long it had been since she had used that particular phrase in his presence.

"I experienced something several hours ago, which I am attempting to understand. Initially I believed it was another product of my catoms and their unruly nature. Upon reflection, however, I have formulated another theory."

"I'm listening," he replied, wondering why her tone filled him with a sense of impending doom.

"I believe someone is using my catoms to try to communicate with me."

"The Caeliar?" was his automatic assumption.

"No," she replied wearily.

"Then who?"

"Someone located on the fourth planet of the Indign system, the one populated exclusively by the Neyser," Seven said, a hint of anger in her voice.

CHAPTER SEVENTEEN

Just as alpha shift was ending, Captain Eden asked Commander Paris and Lieutenant Kim to report to her ready room. She had already reviewed Conlon's most recent report. Most of the affected systems had been restored. Multiple viruses responsible for the failures had been found and eliminated. Conlon was now in the process of reviewing the logs of anyone with command clearance as only someone with that authorization could have accessed that many systems. Eden sensed that Nancy was taking it personally that someone was messing with her engines.

Eden was troubled by the *why* as much as with the *whom*. In the captain's opinion, the most relevant clue might be the coordinates to which the saboteur had intended to direct *Voyager*. The area contained a high concentration of subspace instabilities that suggested a motive to Eden that was most disturbing.

There was a brief, uncomfortable skirmish when Paris and Kim entered, over who should precede whom through the door, that gave the captain pause.

As Kim was mock bowing and gesturing for Paris to enter ahead of him, her patience snapped and she said, "Let's go, gentlemen. None of us has time for this right now."

Appropriately chastened, they hurried inside.

"Take a seat," she ordered, nodding to the chairs opposite her desk. Once they'd settled, she said, "It's going to be
several days before we have a full report on what happened
today, but one interpretation of the information we do have
at hand has disturbed me greatly and I'd like your input."

"Of course, Captain," Harry said immediately.

"We might have a saboteur onboard."

Both looked appropriately stunned.

"Conlon thinks someone damaged the power systems intentionally?" Paris asked, aghast.

"Shortly before we made the journey from the terminus
of the Beta and Delta quadrants to the nebula, Lieutenant
Conlon discovered a series of strange deflector protocols
that had been recently restored to our active systems. Among
them was one whose only purpose is to open a rift to fluidic
space. Conlon has found it impossible to purge this protocol
thus far, though she did successfully quarantine it. I don't
have to tell either one of you how troubling it is to imagine that someone on board might wish to make contact with
Species 8472."

"No, you don't," Kim agreed.

"Today, we suffered massive failures to dozens of systems,
but strangely, propulsion was unaffected, though naviga-
tional control was disrupted. The slipstream drive came online of its own accord and was about to take us to a set of
coordinates where opening a rift to fluidic space might have
been possible."

"Can't we open a rift anywhere?" Paris asked.

"Theoretically, yes," Eden answered. "Practically speaking, you need a naturally occurring quantum singular-
ity, or you have to create an artificial one. That's easier to
do in areas where subspace has already been altered by the

presence of, among other things, transwarp tunnels. Our researchers have found it all but impossible to open even a tiny rift in the Alpha quadrant. That didn't make sense until the destabilizing factors of regular subspace travel, which are readily found here in the Delta quadrant thanks to the Borg's preferential form of FTL flight, were taken into account."

"Captain, you think that someone onboard is interested in picking a fight with Species 8472?" Paris asked.

"I think it's possible, and I want to know who you think might be most likely to harbor such an agenda," Eden replied.

"No one," Paris said immediately.

"Really?" Kim asked dismissively.

"Come on, Harry," Paris went on, "anyone who's ever met those guys wouldn't willingly come within a light-year of them. They're not exactly known for their hospitality."

"Obviously not," Kim said, directing himself toward Eden.

"What about Seven?" the captain asked evenly.

Both paused to consider it.

"I ask, not because I doubt her intentions, but given that she has been under such tremendous stress of late," Eden added quickly.

"No way," Paris insisted.

After a moment, Kim said, "I'd have to agree. Of everyone that comes to mind, she'd be the least likely to underestimate the risks involved in contacting Species 8472 again."

Eden nodded, then asked, "And Chakotay?"

Tense silence descended between them.

Paris was the first to break it. "Absolutely not."

Kim refused to meet Eden's eyes and suddenly looked like he wished he'd never been called into the meeting.

"Lieutenant?" Eden asked.

"I don't know," Kim finally admitted.

"What are you talking about?" Paris demanded, his voice rising.

"I'm saying I don't know," Kim replied forcefully. "I mean, the last time we served with him, he was in pretty bad shape. Then he resigns his commission."

"To help Seven," Paris interjected.

"Maybe," Kim said. "But I can understand why Captain Eden might not be as quick as you are to dismiss him as a suspect."

"Now he's a suspect?" Paris was very close to shouting.

"Look, I'm in charge of security and I'd be remiss in my duties if I didn't consider every possibility, even the ones I don't like," Kim argued.

Paris rose from his chair, his face flushed. "I know Chakotay. I've been through good and bad with him and there is no way the man who helped lead us home and who had our backs for years after that would ever intentionally do anything to put this crew at risk. He has my full confidence, Captain," Paris insisted. "If he says he came here to help Seven, then that's why he's here."

"Maybe he's trying to help Seven," Kim suggested. "Maybe he thinks that Species 8472 has an answer we don't. He did get pretty close to some of them when we discovered that simulation of Starfleet Command."

"That was his job," Paris fired back. "He was an undercover operative. And he worked as hard as any of us to create the peace accord we established then. He's not going to break it, not when it would run the risk of war between the Federation and Species 8472."

"Calm down, both of you," Eden snapped. After a subdued pause she went on, "I want you to work together to review the personnel roster of *Voyager, Hawking,* and *Galen,* and bring me a list of anyone present who might have reason and opportunity to sabotage this ship. I'll expect your report by the end of the day, tomorrow."

Kim rose to stand at attention beside Paris.

"Aye, Captain," he said with a nod.

They both turned briskly to exit. Before they reached the door, Eden added, "Gentlemen, I don't know what personal difficulties you might be experiencing right now, but I need you to set them aside and get this done. You know this ship and crew better than most, and your insight is absolutely required. That said, I'll buck you both back to crewmen and you can spend the next few years scrubbing waste reclamation conduits if you don't find a way to pull yourselves together. Frankly, I'm surprised at both of you right now." She paused to allow her words to sink in. "Solve this," she finished. "Or I will."

"Yes, Captain," they replied in near unison.

B'Elanna was elbow-deep replicating the section of the deflector dish that would replace the portion *Hawking* had destroyed. Having been the one to suggest firing, she felt honor-bound to provide Nancy with a replacement as soon as possible. She'd already spoken with Tom and he had agreed to look in on Miral while working on his own project. B'Elanna didn't know the details—only that he didn't sound happy.

She stood back, pleased to see that those who she had once commanded were performing their repairs both diligently and cheerfully. For them, a crisis in the Delta quadrant was nothing new. Warmed by the fact that many of the engineers had taken a moment to greet her, B'Elanna realized how right it felt. She hadn't expected this.

Nancy Conlon ran her engine room with a quiet resolve. She was tough when she needed to be, generous with praise, and always ready with healthy doses of gallows humor. More important, she was decisive. Many engineers tended to get lost in the details. Nancy was as practical as B'Elanna had always prided herself in being. If B'Elanna had ever wondered if *Voyager* was in good hands, those doubts vanished in an afternoon of hard, but purposeful, work.

These thoughts were momentarily disturbed by the sound of raised voices coming from Conlon's office on the second level. Glancing up, B'Elanna caught sight of the engineer arguing with Admiral Batiste. Her stomach tightened further when Batiste looked down toward her and then continued his rant. Moments later he strode briskly from Conlon's office, descended the utility ladder, and moved straight toward her with Nancy in tow.

She straightened her posture as she said, "Good evening, Admiral."

"You are relieved, Ms. Torres," he advised her coldly.

Taken aback by his tone, she stammered, "May I ask why, Admiral?"

"Lieutenant Conlon has just informed me that you were responsible for the damage to our deflector dish."

"No, sir," Conlon interrupted calmly. "I told you that it was B'Elanna's idea, but that I agreed with it fully. *I gave the order,*" she said with emphasis.

"Be that as it may, your solution was ill-considered, and I do not believe that without Ms. Torres's instigation, it would have occurred to you. This is a Starfleet vessel and we don't damage it intentionally."

"It was a last resort," Conlon argued.

"No," B'Elanna said firmly. "He's right. It was my idea and I take full responsibility for it."

"You are not to report to engineering unless I authorize it," Admiral Batiste went on. "Understood?"

"Of course, Admiral."

With a grim nod he stalked off.

"I'm sorry," Conlon said immediately.

"Don't worry about it," B'Elanna replied, her heart sinking. "I had no business being here in the first place."

"If I don't have a problem with it, I can't understand why he does."

"It doesn't matter," B'Elanna said, attempting to summon a smile. "The new section is almost done. I'll just go back to working on those matrix designs. I'll forward them to you for review when they're ready."

"Thank you," Conlon said sadly.

"No, thank you," B'Elanna replied. "You should be proud of your team. I was proud to be a part of it. And I'll continue to help in any way I can."

"I'll be in touch," Conlon promised.

"Anytime," B'Elanna said with a nod.

She took a moment to wipe her hands, slick with lubricant, and cast a long, last look around. Refusing to give in to regret, B'Elanna departed, anxious to see Miral and Tom, and saddened only by the thought that she wouldn't be allowed to be of further use to *Voyager*.

Meegan sat complacently on the edge of the biobed. The Doctor had completed his examination and she had suffered no serious damage from the Indign possession. She remembered nothing of the event. An engrammatic scan had revealed several alterations to her prior brain patterns and those alterations had yet to return to normal. Privately the Doctor had hoped that Meegan might have been able to access some clue to the Indign during the incident. He supposed he should just be grateful that Meegan had been physically unharmed.

She had always struck the Doctor as enthusiastic. He had ordered forty-eight-hour bedrest but this morning Meegan had begged to be allowed to resume her duties. He had observed her carefully since then, and though she seemed pensive, she did her work with ease. However, Meegan had made errors she never would have made in the past.

The Doctor knew well the pain of feeling useless and would not willingly inflict it on anyone else.

"Your electrolyte levels remain a little low," he said, scanning her test results. "Has your appetite returned to normal?"

"For the most part," Meegan replied, a little evasively.

"Meegan?" the Doctor prodded gently.

Sighing, she said, "It's not that I'm not hungry. It's that nothing really tastes good to me once I've replicated it."

"Hm," the Doctor said. "If you'd like I could provide you with a list of appropriately balanced meals which should restore your normal chemical balance."

"Don't we have anything fresh onboard?" Meegan asked.

The Doctor studied her briefly.

"Or perhaps we picked up something from the Indign homeworld? They produce vast quantities of delicious fruits and vegetables, don't they?"

"As far as I know, our efforts to establish trade with the Indign have failed. But take heart. We'll be regrouping with the *Demeter* in a few weeks, and I'm sure we can find you something from their airponics bay when we do. Meantime, I must insist that you overcome your disdain for replicated fare and nourish your body appropriately. You've been through a trying ordeal and you will need fuel if you are to regain your full strength."

"I promise," Meegan said with a demure smile.

"Any other complaints?" the Doctor asked.

She paused and the Doctor could tell she was debating mentioning whatever was on her mind.

"Come now," he encouraged her. "I'm your doctor. You can tell me anything."

"I don't know," she said softly, refusing to meet his eyes.

Sensing her reluctance, the Doctor set aside his tricorder and stepped closer to give her his full attention.

"What is it?" he asked kindly.

Her large blue eyes met and held his. Quite suddenly he detected increased blood flow to her facial capillaries. Even without his scanner he could easily see that her heart rate was accelerating.

"Meegan?"

Without warning she placed her hands on either side of his face and pulled his lips to hers.

The sensation was sweet, and it sent his memory buffers spinning with many pleasurable recollections, but he was too shocked to return the gesture.

After a moment, the Doctor gently extricated himself and took an involuntary step back.

"Meegan . . . I . . ." he stammered.

"I'm sorry," she said in anxious embarrassment. She quickly jumped down from the biobed and stepped toward the exam room door.

He moved to block her path and replied, "Please, don't

go. You have nothing to apologize for. I was just taken by surprise."

Soft, lambent eyes held his. "I have offended you."

"No," he quickly corrected her. "You absolutely have not."

"You encouraged Reg to act on his feelings, no matter what happened. I just felt like I had to do the same."

The Doctor was stunned. "You have . . . *feelings* for me?" he asked.

"Since the first day I met you," she admitted. "You are an amazing man. I know I'm not halfway good enough for you. Of course you prefer more worldly and experienced women. But that doesn't make these feelings any less real or any easier for me to ignore. I understand if you can't return them. You barely know me. But I spent months preparing for this mission, immersing myself in studies of your experience and your scholarly articles. I felt like I knew you before we'd ever met. And once we did, you were so much more than I even imagined."

To his surprise, the Doctor was genuinely touched by her confession. Of course he'd never given her a second thought as a potential romantic partner. But as he quickly reviewed Meegan's behavior in light of this stunning admission, he suddenly realized that he'd been as blind to her intentions as Commander Glenn was to Reg's.

Even more surprising was the fact that though there was nothing resembling a relationship yet to speak of between them, he could not deny the potential for one. He had wisdom and experience where she had youth and passion. They shared a love of medicine, and she had already expressed an interest in music and art.

Finding himself suddenly unsure, the Doctor reached

tentatively for her hand. She responded eagerly, squeezing his tenderly as her smile brightened.

"I'm glad you told me," he said sincerely. "And I would definitely enjoy the opportunity to get to know you as well as you think you know me. Perhaps tonight we could . . ."

Meegan lifted her free hand to silence his lips. She then rose up and stood on tiptoes to embrace him in a hug and a soft kiss.

This time, the Doctor found himself responding in earnest as he released himself to possibility.

"Computer, where is the Doctor?" Barclay asked as he entered the sickbay to find it empty.

"The Doctor is in exam room one."

Reg hesitated briefly. He hadn't slept since he'd learned that Meegan had been temporarily possessed by an alien consciousness. He'd studied the problem using every tool at his disposal but one and still found no suitable explanation. He could no longer avoid his last option, but didn't want to alarm the Doctor. He had to proceed carefully.

Anxious and irritated with himself, Barclay stepped around the corner to the hall that led to the exam rooms and noted that the door to room one was open. Reg caught a brief glimpse of the Doctor engaged in a passionate embrace with Meegan. Flushing in embarrassment, he quickly stepped back into the main sickbay.

A moment later, the Doctor emerged, followed by Meegan. The ensign refused to look at Barclay as she hurried from the room. The Doctor seemed less flustered.

"I'm sorry, Reg, was there something you needed?"

"I . . . uh . . . I . . ."

"Reg . . ."

"I didn't mean to see," he began. "I just wanted to show you . . ."

"Reg, it's all right," the Doctor said, approaching his stricken friend sympathetically.

"No it isn't!" Reg shocked both of them by shouting.

"I beg your pardon?"

Barclay struggled to get a hold of himself, his mind humming with chaotic thoughts.

This should be happening. But not yet. It's too soon. He doesn't even know her. And it's not as if she could . . .

"Reg, I don't understand your reaction to this. I have a personal life. I follow where my heart leads. It's much too soon to say where it will take me and Ensign McDonnell, but I would have hoped that at least you might be happy for me."

"No, you misunderstand," Reg spluttered, finally reining in his horses a little tighter. "I am happy for you. I'm just surprised. I didn't even think you knew Meegan that well."

"I didn't. I don't. But I think it's time to take the advice I keep giving you and seize the moment. I tend to think of myself as immortal, but the truth is, I face the same hazards we all do in service to Starfleet. This ship could be blown into oblivion at a moment's notice and all that isn't stored in Doctor Zimmerman's backup modules would be gone." His face fell at this realization. "It's actually very unpleasant to contemplate."

As the Doctor continued his existential struggle, Barclay's thoughts returned to the only important matter at hand. He had come here with a job to do and now, more than ever, he needed to focus. Steadying himself, he said, "Doctor, you have been running without interruption for the last several weeks. I've had to make a few alterations to the ship's power systems and I'd like to take you offline briefly and run a simple diagnostic."

"Reg, I hardly think . . ." the Doctor began.

"Please," Barclay said. "This has absolutely nothing to do with the gross invasion of your privacy in which I was just discovered. I apologize profusely for interrupting you and Meegan. It will not happen again."

"Oh," the Doctor replied, seemingly mollified. "Well, if you really believe it is important . . ."

"It is. I do."

"Very well. We are scheduled for a briefing with Commander Glenn at eighteen hundred hours. Will the diagnostic be complete by then?"

"You have my word," Reg promised.

With a faint nod, the Doctor called out, "Computer, deactivate Chief Medical Officer."

As soon as he had vanished, Barclay went immediately to the main data interface and instead of initiating the diagnostic he had promised—a diagnostic he had no intention of running—he opened Meegan's medical file and within minutes had thoroughly digested them. He then programmed the computer to reinitialize the Doctor at seventeen hundred and ten hours. Barclay then hurried to his cabin where he composed and dispatched an urgent message to Doctor Zimmerman.

Given the fact that the relay network was not complete, it would be at least a week before he could expect a reply from the EMH's creator.

And Meegan's.

CHAPTER EIGHTEEN

Seven of Nine was quickly losing patience with Captain Eden. She wanted the captain to accept her recommendation. She forced herself not to fidget as Eden continued to review her presentation. She and Chakotay had requested this meeting with the captain. They had patiently explained their desire to visit the fourth planet of the Indign system to trace the mysterious communication. Seven's interaction with her catoms was barely understood, so she could forgive Eden's wariness.

Almost.

"I'm sorry, Seven," Eden said, "but it's hard for me to believe that what you're suggesting is even possible."

"I've experienced stranger things, Captain," Chakotay interjected. "And I'm willing to bet you have, too."

Eden cast a troubled glance outside the windows of her ready room. Sighing deeply, she chose her words carefully. "The Indign sent a messenger to us. You were there, Seven. If your assumption is true, couldn't they just have used you to facilitate communication?"

Seven paused to formulate her response. She realized she was running the risk of appearing dismissive and irrational and tempered her words accordingly. "I do not believe that the same individuals responsible for sending the consciousness that briefly assumed Ensign McDonnell's body to us are the ones who are trying to communicate directly with me."

"But you said that the consciousness that instructed you to open the canister also used your catoms."

"Yes, I did," Seven agreed.

"Why do you assume that you are now dealing with a different individual or group of individuals?"

Seven replied evenly. "The consciousness within the canister spoke directly in my mind. I heard its words and felt its need. The knowledge required to free it came to me directly, almost as if it were controlling my actions. The second communication was free of an emotional connection. There were no words, but rather just images. Those images were distressing. It was like sharing a memory—not at all like the violating presence I experienced in sickbay."

"And how can you be certain that this second communication originated on the fourth planet?"

"The most distinct image that I remember was of a village. Crude tents and small stone structures were organized around a central clearing containing a well and communal fire pits. There is nothing like this to be found on the third planet. The fourth one—the one we believe to be the Neyser breeding and retirement ground—contains a number of these settlements. Many of the Neyser on the fourth planet live in cities, but a few live on a remote continent and have maintained a rustic existence. I cannot tell you to a certainty that this was the origin of the communication, but it is an educated guess."

Eden ran her hand over her short, black hair, massaging her scalp as she considered Seven's words.

"A guess, Seven? They *asked us* to leave their system. You

want me to violate the Prime Directive on a guess? First the admiral, now this," she mused, shaking her head.

"Excuse me, Captain," Chakotay said. "The admiral?"

The look on the captain's face suggested she wished she hadn't let that particular fact slip.

"He believes that unless we provide the Indign with further information about the Borg, including their transformation by the Caeliar, we are damning other sentient beings to being captured and killed for Indign offerings."

"Admiral Batiste is correct, Captain," Seven was quick to note.

Eden's eyes flared. "In what respect?"

"We should reveal to the Indign the true nature of the Borg."

"I understand why you feel that way, but it's also a Prime Directive issue, Seven," Chakotay advised her.

Seven noted the surprise on Eden's face at Chakotay's words.

"It is," Eden agreed. "I hope the Indign will realize in their own time that there is no need to make further offerings to the Borg. But we cannot corrupt their cultural development by—"

"By telling them the truth?" Seven said with obvious heat.

"It's not that simple," Chakotay said in a clear attempt to mollify her. "We could share with them the fact that the Borg no longer exist. But once you pull that tiny thread, the rest of the fabric begins to unravel. We cannot provide them with proof of our assertions. We cannot give them classified details about the Federation's role in the matter. It's not really a question of telling them the truth. It's *how much* truth should we tell, and guessing what their likely responses will be."

"The Indign pose no tactical threat to our vessels."

"Not one at a time," Eden agreed, "but their fleet is quite large and I really don't want them chasing us all over the Delta quadrant seeking revenge."

Seven swallowed her frustration.

The door chimed.

"Enter," Eden commanded.

Counselor Cambridge crossed in a few long, loping strides to stand at the railing that separated Eden's desk from her more casual conference area.

"Sorry to be late," he said. "Either Conlon's got it in for me, or the turbolifts on my deck are lower on her priority list than they should be. It doesn't matter. How soon before we depart on our little mission to the fourth planet?" he asked cheerfully.

"You've already been briefed on Seven's request?" Eden asked.

"I have." Cambridge nodded. "Seven, Chakotay, and the Doctor have concluded that this matter should be investigated further. I was with another patient, or I would have been here sooner to add my support. I assumed you would have granted your blessing long before now, Captain."

"Then you assumed wrong," Eden replied.

Cambridge raised a quizzical eyebrow, but said nothing further.

"The Indign have asked us to leave their system," Eden said.

Cambridge looked puzzled.

"*That's* the problem?" he finally asked.

"Yes, Hugh," Eden replied. "That's the problem."

"But that's ridiculous," he said with a shrug.

Chakotay dropped his head forward to hide his smirk.

"Counselor . . ."

"No," Cambridge said firmly. "Never in all of my years of anthropological, sociological, and psychological study have I come across anything like the Indign. We're supposed to be damned explorers. Why are we here if not to explore this exact sort of culture?"

"Were you absent the day at the Academy when they explained the Prime Directive?" Eden countered.

"No. The vision provided to Seven could easily be construed as an invitation, which makes the Prime Directive irrelevant. We leave the third planet alone. But a call for help from the fourth planet? A planet we know to be inhabited by a warp-capable species? How can we ignore that?"

"I do not believe we can," Seven said with a nod.

Eden turned to Chakotay, obviously hoping to find backup. His face was calm and his thoughts were his own.

"That's quite an assumption, Hugh," Eden finally said.

"Not necessarily," Chakotay said, before Cambridge could respond.

"*Et tu?*" Eden asked in mock annoyance.

"We have to consider the possibility that the Indign who was sent to speak to us did not necessarily represent the wishes of all Indign," Chakotay offered.

"You think they lied to us?" Eden demanded.

"Wouldn't you in their place?" Cambridge shot back. "A heavily armed group of ships arrives in your space, you tell them whatever you must to make them go away. Fortunately for them, we are respectful and accommodating enough to take them at face value."

The look on Eden's face said clearly that she hadn't considered this possibility.

"Damn," she finally said softly.

There was a tense pause as everyone waited for the captain to render final judgment.

"All right," she finally said. "We're going to do this. But we're going to do it quietly. Under no circumstances, Seven—should you succeed in making contact with those on the fourth planet who initiated communication—are you allowed to disclose what we know about the Borg or Caeliar."

"Aye, Captain."

As Seven and Chakotay rose to leave, Eden said, "Counselor, a word."

"Something on your mind, Captain?" he asked immediately.

Years ago Eden had learned to rely on Cambridge's frank and uncensored opinions. "I want you to keep a close eye on Seven and Chakotay during the mission. At no time are you to leave either of them alone."

Hugh seemed equal parts intrigued and surprised. "Do you have a specific concern, Afsarah?"

"None that I'm going to share with you right now. Suffice it to say that I am concerned, especially in light of recent events."

"You're talking about the series of ship malfunctions?" he surmised.

Eden nodded.

"I will, of course, do as you have asked," Cambridge replied, with a deep sigh. "It is my belief that your suspicions are unwarranted. If I've misjudged their actions, motivations, or general character . . . well, all I can say is, it's probably time for you to find a new counselor."

"Be that as it may . . ."

Cambridge raised his right hand in a mock salute. "Aye, aye, Captain."

As he left, Eden returned to her desk to reread Paris's and Kim's reports. The list of those who possessed the skills necessary to have sabotaged the power distribution system was lengthy. It included all of her senior staff, and Seven, B'Elanna, and Chakotay. Every crew member who had been aboard *Voyager* during its time in the Delta quadrant was listed as having substantive connections to Species 8472— although Chakotay's name was at the top.

You accepted the big chair, Afsarah, she reminded herself.

She would wait. She would thoroughly review all the information again once she had received Conlon's final report. Eden knew having Chakotay aboard *Voyager* was a questionable call. Throwing him in the brig without proof . . .

Let me be wrong.

"Computer, raise lights," Batiste called as he entered his cabin.

Two things registered simultaneously as he walked gingerly toward his desk, allowing his eyes time to adapt to the change in illumination: the hiss of his cabin doors closing behind him, and a cool tingling sensation on his neck.

Before he had time to connect these sensations, he found himself unable to move. He was stuck mid-stride as the coolness on his neck immediately spread throughout his body, rendering his trunk and limbs frozen chunks of lead.

"Computer, dim lights," a voice Batiste did not recognize said softly.

He attempted to shout for security, but he could not make a sound and his lips remained still despite vigorous efforts to free them from the paralysis engulfing his body.

"We need to talk, Admiral," the voice went on.

About what? Willem thought.

"About our mutual problem," the voice replied.

Willem suddenly realized that this situation had just become significantly more dangerous than he had yet imagined. If whomever had attacked him could also read his thoughts . . .

"Of course I can," the voice replied with a tinge of amusement. "Now calm down, and listen. I know who you are and I know what you want. The good news is, I want the same thing, in a manner of speaking. I believe that if we work together we can solve two problems at once."

Rot in hell, Willem thought angrily.

A light, tinkling laughter chilled him further.

"I already have, for thousands of years. I don't recommend it." After a short pause, the voice went on, "But if that's your preference, it can surely be arranged."

It was nearly noon, local time, when Seven, Chakotay, and Cambridge transported to the outskirts of one of the larger Neyser settlements on the fourth planet.

Time was of the essence. They had made the trip in one of *Voyager*'s shuttles which was now parked in orbit over the north polar region, its transporter locked on their combadges. Their entry and exit strategy was designed to bring as little attention as possible to the away team.

Not daring to use sensors, and knowing that the clock was ticking, they began their search of the colony. Several hundred elderly Neyser were clustered in a small encampment. Some were roasting animal flesh over communal fires. Others were beating dust from densely woven fabrics hung between posts near the central well. A neatly tended herb garden was planted nearby. Several of the humanoids strolled lazily down dirt paths.

Apart from the crackle of the fires and the scuffle of feet across the dirt, the settlement was shrouded in silence. Seven and Cambridge noted the strangeness of seeing individual Neyser. They appeared diminished, almost naked, without their fellow species, and their movements and behavior lacked the streamlined precision of the cooperative Indign. The community appeared both peaceful and prosperous. The silence confirmed that the Neyser were either stubbornly silent, or communicating telepathically.

The team collected themselves on a small, rocky ridge that formed the southern boundary of the colony. Seven disengaged her neural inhibitor and waited for another communication.

Nothing.

Frustrated, she finally reengaged the device.

Undeterred, the group had remotely triggered the shuttle's transporter and moved on to their next target. They also studied three smaller communities without finding any substantive revelations.

Finally, they reached their last stop—the smallest and oldest Neyser colony. Here, only a dozen small, well-worn stone huts were in evidence. Unlike the other communities, this one featured an intricately paved central square and hand-painted carvings adorned the stone well.

It was twilight. The huts lay in darkness, and the tricorders detected no life signs. Previous scans had indicated that this colony was inhabited by at least two dozen Neyser. Chakotay led them forward quietly to the central square and studied his readings in dismay.

"This colony has been here for at least two thousand

years," Cambridge reported softly. "The others we observed today were between five and seven hundred years old."

There was something about this place that set Chakotay's nerves on edge. He reset his tricorder to scan for organic remains and found that the ground beneath their feet was rich with them.

"I'm not sure that anyone has lived here for a long time," he observed. "I believe this is a burial ground of some kind."

Seven had begun to wander through the cluster of small buildings. Her tricorder sounded with a loud chirp that shot up Chakotay's spine as it broke the stillness around them.

"Why do I feel like we shouldn't be here?" he asked Cambridge.

"Because you believe that spirits don't like to have their resting places disturbed," the counselor replied as he continued to scan the carved stones. "It's quaint, though terribly unlikely."

"You don't believe in spirits?"

"I don't believe they give a damn what we do with their bodies once they no longer have a use for them."

"Remind me to tell you one of these days—" Chakotay began, but was distracted by an urgent whisper from Seven.

She stood at the entrance of one of the huts and was gesturing for them to join her.

"What is it?" Chakotay asked softly as they approached.

"Look," Seven said, directing their eyes to the darkness within where her palm beacon revealed the body of a Neyser crumpled unceremoniously on the dirt floor.

These were definitely remains, but they were much fresher than any Chakotay had believed they would find.

Cambridge hurried to the body and gently turned it onto its back. His tricorder revealed what his eyes could barely see.

"This woman was murdered, in the last several hours if I'm not mistaken."

"How did she die?" Chakotay asked.

"Compression rifle, Starfleet issue."

Together, they examined the rest of the buildings. Twelve more bodies were found. All of them had been advanced in age, and most were asleep on mounds of animal skins when they were killed.

"What the hell happened here?" Cambridge demanded as they returned to the center square.

"I don't know, yet, but we're not going anywhere until we find out," Chakotay replied.

"Chakotay," Seven said, passing her tricorder to him to examine.

"Life signs, faint," Chakotay replied. "This way."

They headed down a cobbled path that appeared to end at a mound of stones arranged atop a low hill. Several of the stones showed signs of recent collapse.

"Help me," Chakotay urged, as he knelt and gently began to move the stones. Soon enough, a small opening was revealed and a flight of dirt stairs led into the darkness below.

"Not exactly inviting," Cambridge mused as he played his palm beacon into the abyss.

"We have to check it out," Chakotay advised him.

"Of course we do. We're Starfleet. Never a dark, spooky cavern left unexplored, right?"

Seven began to descend into the darkness. Chakotay and Cambridge followed. Fifteen meters in they came to an open space.

"Catacombs," Chakotay said softly as he studied the small alcoves littered with bones and decomposed cloth.

"This way," Seven commanded, heading farther into the

bowels of the graveyard. "The life signs are growing stronger."

The single path sloped gently downward and as they went deeper they discovered hundreds of remains entombed in the walls. The deeper they went, the colder it became, and the skeletal debris was little more than dust when they finally reached a small chamber.

There they discovered a single Neyser, its back against a small wall, struggling for breath as it clutched a gaping wound in its abdomen. Cambridge was instantly by its side, and after a quick scan said compassionately, "There, there. Let's make you a little more comfortable."

Placing his hand around the being's neck he gently lowered it into a recumbent position. As he did so, the creature let out a plaintive shriek.

Cambridge then tapped his combadge but received no response from the shuttle's transporter.

"Damn it," he cursed.

"The signal won't reach through the rocks," Chakotay advised. "We need to move her to the surface. We can transport her from there."

"She'll never survive the trip," Cambridge warned.

"So we do nothing?" Chakotay demanded in frustration.

"No," Seven said as she knelt beside the figure and took a deep breath. "We do what we came here to do," she added as she disengaged her inhibitor. She immediately grabbed the sides of her face in pain, and Chakotay hurried to Seven's side. She turned wide, terrified eyes on him, but as he reached for her neck to reengage the device she stopped him, clasping his hands tightly in hers.

For the next few seconds, she rocked back and forth, holding on to Chakotay for dear life. Cambridge turned his tricorder on her and his fearful eyes met Chakotay's.

"Her heart rate has increased and her neurological activity is off the charts, particularly where her cortical node used to be."

"Seven," Chakotay said insistently, "can you hear me?"

She squeezed his hands in response, but made no move to terminate the communication.

After a moment, she released him and turned to the darkness, searching the ground on hands and knees.

As her arms buckled, Cambridge said, "We have to put a stop to this."

Seven lowered herself to the ground and raised a hand to slap at the back of her neck. Chakotay immediately intuited her purpose and quickly moved to activate the inhibitor.

The tension slowly left Seven's body and her breath came in gasps. On shaking hands she pulled herself toward the Neyser who stared at her with pain-filled eyes.

"I understand," Seven barely whispered.

"What do you understand?" Cambridge asked impatiently.

"She is dying."

"That much we knew," Cambridge said. "There's nothing we can do to help her now."

"The holes . . ." Seven began.

Cambridge and Chakotay shared a confused glance.

Seven pointed into the darkness she had explored only moments earlier. Chakotay illuminated the area and revealed what appeared to be eight freshly dug holes.

"Are these graves?" Chakotay asked.

"No," Seven replied, her breath coming easier now. "They were secrets. They were hidden here for protection."

"That's intriguing," Cambridge noted.

Finally Seven struggled to rise to her feet with Chakotay's assistance.

"Her people are coming. They can't find us here. They'll think we took them."

"Took what?" Chakotay asked.

"We have to move!" Seven insisted as she lurched forward unsteadily.

Chakotay and Cambridge moved to either side of her and clasping her under her shoulders began their ascent as rapidly as they could.

As they neared the first level of the catacomb Chakotay activated his combadge. "Emergency transport. Three to beam up."

They materialized in the shuttle. "What happened?" Cambridge asked.

"I'm not entirely sure," Chakotay answered.

Breathless and frantic, Seven demanded, "We need to contact *Voyager* immediately. You must tell Captain Eden. The canister the Indign transported to *Voyager* . . . it wasn't an offering. It was a weapon . . . the most destructive they possess. There were eight and now all are missing. They were weapons of last resort. You have to tell . . ." Seven said, her head lolling forward as she lost consciousness.

CHAPTER NINETEEN

B'Elanna stumbled through the darkness of the cabin toward the door. Tom had barely opened his eyes when the door to their cabin had chimed. B'Elanna had told him to go back to sleep while she went to see who thought it was necessary to disturb them.

"Sorry to wake you," Nancy offered.

"It's okay," B'Elanna mumbled, rubbing some of the grogginess from her eyes. "Come in."

Once she had entered, Nancy moved immediately to the desk and computer panel stationed just to the right of the cabin door. She quickly uploaded the contents of a padd she had brought with her, and gestured for B'Elanna to take a look at it.

Turning her attention to the screen, B'Elanna discovered a long string of encrypted programming code. "Okay, I'll bite," she said. "What have we got, Conlon?"

"What you are looking at is the command code override that allowed our saboteur to insert the virus into the power distribution hub," Nancy replied.

"You had to rebuild these logs by hand, didn't you," B'Elanna observed, her estimation of Conlon's abilities rising accordingly.

"Yep," Nancy said, stifling a yawn. "The code deleted itself as soon as the interface was terminated. I just had to look through about a billion places to find it."

"And it was encrypted when you found it?" B'Elanna asked.

Nancy nodded. "That's kind of what made it stand out. It also made it easier to find the other instance in which this override code was recently used."

"Let me guess," B'Elanna said. "The same code was used to restore those old deflector protocols, wasn't it?"

"It was," Nancy replied. "And to bring the slipstream drive online during the general system power failure."

"Have you traced the user?" was B'Elanna's next question.

"I have," Nancy said, "which is why I'm here."

"What do you mean?"

"The encryption . . . you don't happen to recognize it, do you?"

B'Elanna felt a sudden chill. Dutifully she turned back to the screen and gave the code a closer look.

Kahless, no, she suddenly thought as her heart began to pound.

"It wasn't even hard to break. It's been stored in Federation databases for more than a decade," Nancy mused.

"It probably hasn't been used much in that time," B'Elanna conceded.

"You're right. The Maquis were pretty good at altering their encryptions as soon as they were intercepted."

I remember, B'Elanna thought sadly. Soon enough, however, that sadness was transmuted to anger.

He wouldn't, part of her heart insisted.

But her head and the evidence before her told her unequivocally that Chakotay obviously had, most likely with Seven's help.

"I wanted to tell you before I told the captain," Nancy said, her voice trembling with regret. "I know how much Chakotay means to you and Commander Paris."

B'Elanna wasn't sure she could find it in herself to be grateful for Nancy's obvious attempt at kindness.

Barclay knew it was too soon to expect a response from Doctor Zimmerman. Four hours earlier, he had reactivated the Doctor, informing him that the diagnostic—that he had not run—had revealed no new information but that he would continue to study the problem. He then spent the intervening hours in the holographic research lab examining Meegan's files in minute detail.

Everything he had found was in perfect order.

Which was troubling because that meant it should have been impossible for the Indign consciousness to assume control of her body.

Meegan didn't have a body.

Meegan was a hologram—the most advanced hologram ever to spring from the minds of Lewis Zimmerman and Reginald Endicott Barclay. The lieutenant no longer remembered whose idea it had been to construct her. He only knew that he and Zimmerman had come to the conclusion that the Doctor needed a companion.

They knew neither of them would be able to provide long-term, emotional support for the Doctor. He needed a companion, one of his own kind. Zimmerman and Reg started designing one. Her personal holographic emitter—based on the Doctor's—was embedded in the center of her matrix, not far from where her heart would have been. The emitter could operate independently. She could assume a solid or permeable form, and could also alter her appearance at will. Meegan had been created with interests and pursuits the Doctor shared, but not a complete working knowledge of those pursuits. For her to become sentient—like the Doctor—they believed she would need to grow as an individual.

However, she was not programmed to fall in love with the Doctor. Meegan was designed to be the type of woman the Doctor would grow to respect and, it was hoped, she would also grow to respect and admire the Doctor. It was intended that their relationship would take years to evolve. That's why Barclay had been so surprised to see them in a passionate embrace.

The Doctor was not aware that Meegan was a hologram. A subroutine had been added to her systems that required her to speak to Reg or Zimmerman before telling anyone. Both felt that if either she—or the Doctor—were aware that she had been created for him, both would reject the notion out of hand. Reg had hoped that over time, nature would take its course. Then, he would counsel Meegan to tell the Doctor that she was not organic. It was hoped that by then, the Doctor would not see this as a hindrance.

Barclay was the only member of the fleet who was aware that Meegan was a hologram. He had not, until this moment, confronted the possibility that he might actually need to tell someone.

He proceeded to review the personal logs of the officers who had been present when Meegan had been used to speak for the Indign. Reg belived that the consciousness was a program. Only a program should have had the ability to assume control of her matrix and overwrite her subroutines. Why would the Indign create such a program? It was not necessary to facilitate their cooperative lives. It certainly had no practical application to their spacefaring vessels. The program would have been unique and extraordinary; why wasn't it further integrated into Indign society?

Barclay knew the time had come to contact Captain Glenn and Admiral Batiste and advise them of the situation, but he remained hesitant.

Reg didn't mind working on complicated problems. But he hated not being able to present the solutions to his superiors. Convinced that he could solve this on his own and preserve a future between the Doctor and Meegan, Reg summoned Meegan to his quarters. The moment she entered, he said simply, "Computer, freeze program Meegan McDonnell. Authorization Barclay, delta, four, seven."

Barclay was relieved that she froze instantly at his command. He had fretted for the last several hours that the alien incursion might have done some permanent damage to her matrix. Naturally, he did not doubt his ability to discover how she had been possessed, but he worried that if he did not do it quickly, he would be forced to reveal Meegan's true nature.

Turning to his workstation, Reg began a level-ten diagnostic of Meegan's program, beginning with an analysis of her memory buffers. He ignored the physical readings she was designed to emit.

Instantly, he realized that her memory files had been compromised. Though most of them were still intact, the vast majority of her extra memory space, designed for hundreds of years of experiences to be stored, had been filled almost to capacity by what appeared to be a large block of data.

His initial attempts to access this data were fruitless. Intrigued, he began the painstaking process of purging the data.

"Don't worry, my dear," Reg said softly. "I'll get to the bottom of this in no time and have you back in . . ."

Reg paused as a chill shot down his spine.

Meegan had frozen in a neutral pose after greeting Reg cordially.

Why is she smiling now? Reg silently began to fret as he slowly turned his face to look at her again.

That was the last thought he was conscious of for some time.

At Conlon's request, Eden, Batiste, Paris, and Kim had convened in *Voyager*'s conference room. She had already advised the captain of the sensitive nature of her discovery.

"Go ahead, Lieutenant," Batiste ordered.

"We have completed our repairs. The deflector dish has been fully restored and all other systems are functioning normally," Conlon began.

"Good work," Eden was quick to interject.

"Thank you, Captain." Conlon took a deep breath before distributing a small stack of padds to each of the officers. "I believe I have also discovered the cause of the multiple system failures. It was centered in the power distribution hub. It was not, as I had hoped, random, or simply a new bug we didn't discover during our shakedown."

"What was it?" Batiste asked.

"If you'll direct your attention to the program string I've provided, you'll clearly see that the power distribution hub was intentionally damaged by an implanted virus designed to cause numerous simultaneous power disruptions without actually destroying anything. The programming code used was encrypted and was also designed to eliminate all traces of itself once it was initiated. It took a long time to find. By analyzing our backup logs line by line, I tracked it down. The encryption code is identical to that used to disrupt the deflector control and to activate the slipstream drive."

"It was the work of one person," Batiste said.

"Yes, Admiral," the chief engineer admitted, dejectedly.

"And can you identify that person?" Eden asked.

"It was Chakotay," Conlon said, though it obviously pained her.

"I don't believe it," Paris asserted.

"I didn't want to either," Conlon replied, turning to him with a sympathetic glance. "But access to the central power distribution hub is command clearance only. Chakotay's codes were eliminated the minute his command was transferred to Captain Eden. At some point, shortly after he boarded, his command codes were reactivated, briefly. Just long enough to allow him to access the systems he needed to. Further, I have confirmed that the encryption protocol was Maquis in origin."

Eden bowed her head and briefly read through the report. It was nothing more than a tactic to buy her the time she needed to compose herself. She had allowed Chakotay to join her ship based on Seven's request and her trust in anyone who had ever worn a Starfleet uniform. Eden struggled to grasp Chakotay's possible motives.

He wants his command back, her heart warned. *And he'll do anything to get it, short of destroying the ship. A series of malfunctions, followed by an incursion into fluidic space . . . Command will have me back in the Alpha quadrant quicker than you can say quantum slipstream drive.* Batiste had accused her more than once of being naïve. She hated that he had been proved right.

To his credit, when Eden looked up to meet the admiral's eyes she saw only sadness. They had all been deceived.

Everyone wore the same despondent expressions, with the exception of Commander Paris.

His face reddening and his eyes blazing he said, "I don't believe it."

"No, you just don't *want* to believe it," Kim chided him softly.

"*No*," Paris insisted. "*I don't believe it.*"

"Based upon this report, can either of you think of another likely suspect?" Eden asked softly.

"No," Kim said, and Paris did not correct him.

"There's no evidence that any of the new crewmen has ties to any individuals who might wish to confront Species 8472," Kim continued. "And none of those who was aboard during *Voyager*'s original seven-year journey have either motive or access. If we broaden our scope to consider anyone who simply might want to damage the ship or shorten our current mission, the list gets too long to be useful."

"What do you mean?" Batiste demanded.

"We're all Starfleet officers. We go where Command sends us. But a lot of us devoted years to trying to return to the Alpha quadrant and perhaps some were not thrilled about returning to the Delta quadrant," Kim replied evenly.

"Every officer assigned to this mission was advised that it was a deep-space, long-term assignment and all willingly accepted those terms."

"With due respect, sir, deep space is one thing," Kim countered. "The Delta quadrant is something entirely different." He paused before adding, "The vast majority of the fleet's current staff, apart from senior officers and engineering specialists, had only days to wrap their brains around our new assignment. I'm sure it took many of them by surprise."

"Does that include you, Lieutenant Kim?" Batiste asked pointedly.

"Yes, sir," Kim admitted without reservation. "But that doesn't mean I wasn't ready to accept Command's decision. I believe this mission is necessary and am happy to do my part. But I can't speak for everyone."

"This is ridiculous," Paris said angrily. "No one who served under Captain Janeway and Commander Chakotay would endanger this ship. We're more than comrades in arms. We're a family. We risked our lives for one another day in and day out for seven years and that doesn't change just because we might have reservations about our new assignment. If anything, we're all more determined than ever to prove our worth to Command, who frankly didn't seem to have much use for us in the Alpha quadrant."

"Tom, facts are facts," Eden said flatly. "For what it's worth, I, too, find it very hard to believe that anyone, least of all Chakotay, would do this. I agree with your characterization of your old crew. But we can't simply ignore the evidence."

"Will Chakotay get a chance to defend himself against these accusations?" Paris demanded.

"Chakotay will be confined to the brig until a hearing can be scheduled," Batiste said in a tone that brooked no argument. "He will be assigned counsel and will have every opportunity to make a case for his innocence." Turning to Eden he said, "Where is Chakotay now?"

"He, Seven, and Counselor Cambridge were dispatched to the fourth planet of the Indign system to investigate a potential communication Seven believed she had received."

"May I say one more thing?" Paris asked.

"Of course," Eden replied.

"Apart from the fact that Chakotay just wouldn't do this, I think you also have to consider the reality that I'm not sure he *could*."

"Commander?" Conlon asked.

"This is high-level programming. Seven of Nine, B'Elanna, Vorik, even you, Lieutenant," Paris went on, with a nod to Conlon, "have the appropriate skill-set. But this just strikes me as too subtle an attack for Chakotay. Which is not to suggest," he added hastily, "that I'm accusing anyone else I just named. If Chakotay were trying to sabotage us, this isn't how he'd do it."

Eden surprised herself by agreeing with her first officer. Chakotay was certainly capable of subterfuge, but she wasn't sure that he was capable of such a technologically advanced attack.

"A point I'm certain you'll have the opportunity to make once his hearing is convened," Batiste replied briskly, his right eyebrow twitching with annoyance. "However, bearing that in mind, Captain Eden, I would also suggest that Seven be detained as well."

Eden nodded, as a cold sweat broke out on her forehead.

Batiste went on, "Once they're aboard, have Chakotay and Seven confined to the brig. I'll begin questioning them as soon as they arrive."

"You will?" Eden asked incredulously.

"Absolutely," Batiste replied firmly. "I hardly think any of their former crewmates should have a duty such as this imposed upon them."

"As chief of security . . ." Kim began to object.

"You report to me, Lieutenant," Batiste barked. "End of discussion."

CHAPTER TWENTY

Commander Glenn didn't have to think twice when she received word that Counselor Cambridge was requesting emergency transport for himself, Chakotay, and Seven to *Galen*'s sickbay. She immediately approved the request and sent word to *Voyager*, assuming that one or more of them had been injured during their away mission.

She reached the sickbay to find Chakotay and Cambridge conferring quietly while the Doctor treated an unconscious Seven on one of the main biobeds.

"Report," Glenn ordered as soon as she entered.

The Doctor did a quick scan of his most recent diagnostic results before crossing to join the small group and said quietly, "She has suffered mild neurological inflammation, undoubtedly brought about by the communication she received from the Neyser. It appears to have overwhelmed her catoms."

"I realize we're talking mostly hypothetically when we're discussing catoms at all," Cambridge said, "but should that really have happened? We know they've done significantly more extraordinary things."

"Yes, but Seven's seem to have been specifically designed to have a very limited capacity. Without an external power source, their transformational ability could not compare with those that made up an entire organism like a Caeliar. I'm also beginning to believe that in addition to comparatively minimal power, they might have minimal intended use."

"You think they were meant to keep her alive and nothing else?" Chakotay inferred.

The Doctor nodded. "Yes. And, quite possibly, to ease her transition from Borg to human."

"'You are Annika Hansen,'" Cambridge mused softly.

"Correct," the Doctor replied. "The Caeliar might have assumed that anyone in Seven's position would have been comforted by this reassuring voice during and just after the transition."

"Pity they don't really know our Seven," Cambridge noted.

"Indeed," the Doctor concurred. "Because Seven could not or would not accept the message, the voice has grown stronger."

"But if she had accepted it long ago, it might have disappeared altogether?" Chakotay asked.

"I think so," the Doctor said. "Since she was unwilling to do that, however, we've asked her to try to control them—to force the issue, so to speak—"

"And her catoms are responding as best they can," Cambridge agreed. "She is learning to control them, but by expanding their uses beyond what was intended, she's also made herself vulnerable to them. They will do whatever her mind can clearly instruct them to do, including facilitate this telepathic link with the Indign species, but at great cost to her."

"This last effort left her physically exhausted. I have already begun liquid nutrient infusions, but I don't want to wake her until I can be sure that the neurological inflammation has diminished."

Glenn followed their exchange carefully. "Thank you, Doctor," she finally said. Turning to Cambridge, she asked, "How exactly were these injuries sustained?"

"Seven was able to make telepathic contact with one of the Neyser on the fourth planet," he replied.

"The Neyser in question had been seriously injured by a Starfleet-issue weapon. A dozen others in its village were dead when we arrived," Chakotay added somberly.

"Who could have . . . ?" Glenn began.

"There's more," Cambridge cut her off.

"More?"

"Before she lost consciousness, Seven said that the canister the Indign sent to *Voyager* was not intended to be a method of communication."

"What was it?"

"A weapon."

Glenn turned to the Doctor, who immediately said, "I have thoroughly evaluated Ensign McDonnell's physical condition and I can assure you that she was not harmed during the—"

Suddenly the sickbay was awash in flashing red lights. Alarm Klaxons blared harshly.

Glenn's gut tightened as she tapped her combadge. "Glenn to the bridge."

"*Lawry here,*" the terrified ensign's voice replied.

"Who ordered Red Alert?" Glenn asked, conscious of the brittle edge in her voice.

"*I did, Captain. I'm locked out of helm controls. The warp drive has come online but the helm is not responding.*"

"Glenn to Lieutenant Benoit," she called.

"*Go ahead, Captain,*" the harried chief engineer responded.

"I want the warp drive shut down immediately," Glenn ordered.

"*We're trying,*" Benoit assured her. "*We're locked out of the system and I'm trying to find a way through but the code is pretty dense and the system is not responding to my overrides. I could use some help.*"

"I'll see to that. Keep me advised," Glenn replied. "Glenn to Lieutenant Barclay." When there was no immediate response, she called, "Computer, locate Lieutenant Barclay."

"*Lieutenant Barclay is in the holographic research lab.*"

"Barclay, this is Commander Glenn," she attempted again. "Please respond."

He didn't.

"Computer, dispatch a team of security holograms to the lab and have them bring Lieutenant Barclay to me on the bridge. And bring the Emergency Engineering Holograms online to assist Lieutenant Benoit," she said as she turned toward the door. "This is getting out of hand," she added, frustrated.

"Don't you mean *more* out of hand?" Cambridge asked too cheerily to be taken seriously. "Captain, is the *Galen* equipped with emergency escape pods?"

"Of course, Counselor. Why?"

"Just asking."

Eden sat in her ready room, waiting for further word from Commander Glenn. She trusted Glenn's assumption that if Seven had been injured on the away mission, Chakotay would have wanted her evaluated by the Doctor. It would explain the team's request to transport to the *Galen*. Of course, it was also possible that Chakotay might know that his time was running short and intended to use the *Galen* to further his own ends.

"*Bridge to the captain.*"

"Go ahead, Ensign Lasren," Eden replied.

"Galen *has broken formation and is headed toward unknown coordinates at high warp.*"

Eden instantly came to her feet and hurried to the bridge. As soon as she arrived, Eden ordered, "Hail the *Galen.*"

After a moment, Commander Glenn's tense face appeared on the viewscreen.

"What's happening, Clarissa?"

"*We've lost control of the helm. Our engineering specialists are working on it, but for now, we're at the mercy of whatever or whomever is controlling our ship.*"

"Do you know where you're headed?"

"*Lawry has plotted several possible destinations, all of which are deep in the heart of what used to be Borg space.*"

"Helm, lay in pursuit course," Eden said. "Lasren, advise Captain Itak to hold position here until we make further contact." Turning again to Glenn, she said, "Captain, at Admiral Batiste's request, I am ordering you to take Chakotay into custody."

"*I don't understand . . .*"

"Confine Chakotay to secure quarters," Eden cut her off.

"*Aye,*" Glenn agreed.

"*Voyager* out," Eden said, closing the transmission. "Ensign Gwyn, stay with them."

"Yes, Captain," the helmsman replied crisply.

As she took her seat, Eden found her thoughts turning inexplicably to the first day of her honeymoon. At the time, she had pretended to enjoy herself. Years later, she realized that it had been an exercise in lowering expectations. The very first day, when she had planned a tour of Delgara's botanical gardens, Batiste had insisted on remaining in their suite, working.

Analyzing encrypted Cardassian intercepts.

Perhaps these memories pestered her now because it had been the first in what would become a long line of disappointing days with Willem. It was during that lonely week that Eden had first confronted the reality that Willem was a very good liar.

It was there, right in front of her. In one version, Chakotay had worked daily to undermine her position since he had come onboard. Their report of the Indign threat was one of many red herrings meant to throw Eden off. He had to be responsible for whatever was now going wrong on the *Galen*. In a few short hours, Eden knew she would be proven right. Her only concern now was making sure her ship and her crew survived what was coming.

The Doctor checked Seven's vital signs and found to his great relief that she seemed to be stabilizing. The inflammation of the tissue surrounding what had once been her cortical node had subsided and her electrolyte levels, organ functions, and blood count were all, once again, within normal ranges. He considered injecting her with a stimulant to wake her, but decided against it. Commander Glenn had ordered the Doctor to report on Seven's communication with the Neyser as soon as possible. He thought it best that she continue to rest until she regained consciousness. His attention was diverted from her by the entrance of two security holograms, a Klingon and a Gorn. They were carrying the unconscious form of Reg Barclay.

"Report," the Doctor ordered as they placed Reg's body on the nearest biobed. The Gorn hologram responded in perfect Standard, "He was found in the holographic research lab. His body had been hidden beneath the deck plating, which had been forcibly dislodged. Our scans suggest mild concussion of his occipital lobe."

"Thank you, gentlemen," the Doctor replied curtly. "That will be all."

The holograms nodded in unison and left him to his patient. He quickly confirmed their initial assessment and then injected him with a hypospray.

Reg's eyes opened wide and immediately found the Doctor's.

"Where is she?" were Reg's first, disquieting words.

"Where is who?" the Doctor replied gently.

Barclay immediately pushed himself up on his elbows but was thwarted by a wave of nausea and pain. He winced, bringing his hand to his forehead as he murmured, "Ouch."

"I've provided you with an analgesic that should ease your discomfort, but you need to rest," the Doctor advised him.

"There's no time," Barclay replied, steeling himself to endure the throbbing in his head as he pulled himself into a seated position and then lowered his feet to the floor. He stumbled a little, obviously dizzy.

"Reg, I really must insist that you—"

"Doctor, I'd like you to route your program through your mobile emitter and come with me."

"You're not going anywhere."

"We have to find Meegan," Reg insisted. "She's been compromised by the Indign. The consciousness never left her. It's still in control."

"How do you know that?" the Doctor demanded.

"I'll explain later."

"Reg, really," the Doctor said in his most soothing voice. "Why don't you lie down again, and—"

"No," Barclay said, holding his head between both hands as he shook it. "I know what to look for. You have to come with me. In case she tries to stop me again."

"Reg, I have another patient to attend to."

Reg saw Seven's still form.

"Did Meegan do this too?" he asked with obvious concern.

"Of course not," the Doctor replied. "Seven's injuries were sustained on an away mission."

Reg immediately went to the nearest control console and activated a holographic nurse to attend to Seven.

"Once the Doctor and I have departed, you are to seal the sickbay and under no circumstances are you to open those doors to anyone without the Doctor's order or mine," Reg instructed.

"Yes, sir," the EMH responded, unperturbed.

He then hurried to the Doctor's office and retrieved his mobile emitter, affixing it unceremoniously to the Doctor's sleeve.

"Let's go."

"Reg, I don't understand."

"I know," Reg replied. "But I promise, I'll explain when all this is done."

Despite his odd behavior, the Doctor had no reason to mistrust his friend or the urgency of his intentions. Satisfied that Seven would be well cared for in his absence, he followed Barclay from sickbay.

"Captain, the *Galen* has dropped out of warp."

"Stay with them, Ensign," Eden ordered Gwyn. "Where are we, Lieutenant Lasren?"

"We have traveled more than four light-years from the Indign system," Lasren reported.

"Are there any nearby star systems or inhabited planets?" Eden asked evenly.

"No, Captain," Lasren said. "This area was previously charted by *Hawking*. It contains a high concentration of subspace instabilities. It is likely that dozens of transwarp tunnels once intersected this sector."

Paris shot a knowing glance at Eden who only nodded stoically.

"Hail the *Galen*," Eden requested. Commander Glenn's face filled the viewscreen. Her sea green eyes were stormy, but filled with resolve.

"What's your status?" Eden inquired.

"*We appear to have arrived,*" Glenn noted, "*but we're still locked out of helm controls.*"

"I could transport Conlon and one of her teams over to provide assistance," Eden offered. Both women knew that *Galen*'s engineering staff was the least experienced in the fleet. The *Galen* and *Demeter* hadn't been intended for deployment in combat areas.

Circumstances change, Eden thought grimly.

"*I'd appreciate that,*" Glenn replied.

"Expect them momentarily," Eden confirmed.

"*Chakotay is in custody as ordered,*" Glenn added.

"Acknowledged," Eden replied, then nodded to Lasren to close the channel.

"Bridge to Conlon."

"*Go ahead, Captain,*" Nancy's voice replied. The trepidation it held was impossible to miss.

"Assemble a team for transport to *Galen*. They are still locked out of their helm controls."

After a brief pause, Conlon replied, "*I'm sorry, Captain, but I can't spare anyone at the moment. We have a little problem of our— Damn it, Neol, I told you to shut it down!*"

Eden rose automatically from her chair. Her instincts already told her what was coming.

"Nancy, what's happening?" Eden demanded.

"*We've lost control of the deflector,*" Conlon replied. "*The protocol for opening a rift to fluidic space is overriding every other system. Give us a minute.*"

"Belay that," Eden ordered calmly.

"*Captain?*"

"I doubt you'll be able to disengage the system in time anyway," Eden added. Turning to Paris she said, "Computer, locate Admiral Batiste."

"*Admiral Batiste is in the main shuttlebay.*"

"Lock it down," Eden instructed Kim. "Commander Paris, the bridge is yours." As she hurried toward the turbolift she added, "Lieutenant Kim, dispatch a security team to meet me at the shuttlebay. They are not to enter until I arrive."

"Understood, Captain."

"Captain?" Paris said. "You might want to see this."

A bright beam shot forth from *Voyager*'s deflector dish. Where its energy dispersed, a roiling greenish-white miasma churned before them. Eden's stomach fell at her first actual glimpse of fluidic space.

"Red Alert," she ordered immediately. "Lieutenant Kim, can you close that rift?" she demanded.

"Yes, Captain," Kim replied confidently, "but it may take a few minutes."

"Best possible speed, Lieutenant," Eden requested.

Paris crossed to stand at Eden's side, watching expectantly.

"Get to the shuttlebay," he said softly. "I've got this."

Eden met his eyes and nodded briskly.

"Anything comes through that rift—"

"I'll take care of it," he assured her.

Without another word, Eden left the bridge. She now knew to a certainty who. She was finally going to learn why.

Captain Itak was meditating in his quarters, as was his custom at the end of a duty shift. His breath was slow and regular. His limbs were light as feathers. He floated in a sea of tranquillity, at one with the universe in its vast, mysterious harmony.

"*Ops to Captain Itak.*"

"Go ahead, Ensign," Itak responded as he gingerly shifted his weight and rose from a kneeling position.

"*Long-range scans are detecting two dozen Indign vessels moving in formation away from their planetary system.*"

"Heading?" Itak asked, moving intently but unhurriedly to the door of his cabin. From there he was mere meters to the bridge.

"*They're headed straight for us!*" Bloom announced with less restraint than Itak would have wished.

"How soon will they intercept our vessel?" Itak said evenly as he entered the bridge and moved gracefully to his chair.

"*Nineteen minutes, sir,*" Bloom replied.

"Red Alert," Itak ordered. "Send a priority message to Admiral Batiste, advising him of our position, and request instruction."

After a brief moment, Bloom confirmed, "Message sent, sir."

Lieutenant T'Pena arrived moments later and assumed the bridge tactical station.

"Analysis, Lieutenant T'Pena?" Itak requested.

"Twenty-four vessels, moving at high warp. Their shields are raised and their weapons are online."

"Are their offensive systems similar to those of the first Indign vessel we encountered?"

"No, sir," T'Pena replied. "The energy signatures suggest significantly more intense firepower. I am also detecting additional phaser banks. If we maintain our position and engage, the odds are eighty-nine point seven nine percent that we will be destroyed. It appears they have learned from our first encounter," he suggested.

"They have done more than that, Lieutenant," Itak corrected him. "They have adapted."

"Sir, *Voyager* has received our message but there is no response from Admiral Batiste," Bloom reported.

Itak did not require a response to come to the only logical conclusion.

"Set course for *Voyager*, maximum warp," he ordered.

Recalculating the odds, Itak determined that even with the flagship's assistance, the likelihood that any of the Federation vessels would survive the coming encounter was less than thirty-five percent.

CHAPTER TWENTY-ONE

Barclay led the Doctor systematically throughout the *Galen,* one section and room at a time. As they searched each location, Reg deactivated all security holograms in the area and locked out the holographic generators. The Doctor searched in vain for a method to Reg's madness.

"Are you certain that Meegan is still onboard?" he asked as the second of *Galen's* small cargo holds was cleared. "If she injured you intentionally, perhaps she . . ."

"There's only one way to be certain," Reg replied.

"But you are disabling the only systems that will protect us against her," the Doctor pointed out as they entered engineering.

There, a dozen emergency holographic engineers were working under the direction of Lieutenant Benoit.

"At this point I'm tempted to shut the entire propulsion system down and reinitialize," Benoit said, clearly frustrated. "Reg?" he greeted them. "Where the hell have you been? We've got a real mess down here."

Reg didn't hesitate. "Computer, deactivate all holographic personnel and disable all holographic emitters. Lock out changes unless rescinded by Lieutenant Reginald Barclay. Clearance code beta pi delta six one."

Benoit's mouth fell open as his assistants dematerialized. "What the hell do you think you're doing? We've got an emergency and I don't have the staff to—"

"I'm sorry, Lieutenant," Reg said more authoritatively than the Doctor ever remembered. Scanning the area visually and with the aid of his tricorder he gave a satisfied nod and continued, "Do the best you can."

"But—"

The Doctor found himself hurrying to keep up the pace with Reg as he quickly departed engineering.

"Computer, how many holographic personnel are still online?" Reg asked, apparently oblivious of the havoc he was wreaking in his path.

"*Seventeen,*" the computer replied.

"What is the location of any near our current position?" Reg asked.

"*One currently located in transporter room one,*" the computer advised. "*Two located in section five corridor, deck three.*"

"This way," Reg said, quickening his pace.

"*Commander Glenn to Lieutenant Barclay.*"

"I'm a little busy right now, Captain," Reg replied, not breaking stride.

"*Benoit just advised me that you've disabled the Emergency Engineering Holograms—without my authorization,*" Glenn said with emphasis.

"I'll explain later," Reg said.

"*You'll explain now,*" Glenn demanded. "*We're hanging dead in space until we regain helm control and* Voyager *has just opened a rift to fluidic space.*"

"Why would they do that?" the Doctor said, his voice rising in distress.

"*Report to the bridge immediately,*" Glenn ordered.

"I'm on my way," Barclay replied as he entered the transporter room. "Barclay out," he added, closing the comm.

"You heard Commander Glenn," the Doctor said nervously as he caught sight of two security officers guarding the transporter controls—a human male and a Hirogen hunter who looked up in alarm.

"Computer, deactivate all holographic personnel and disable all holographic emitters. Lock out changes unless rescinded by Lieutenant Reginald Barclay. Clearance code beta pi delta six one," Reg said as he raised his phaser toward the holograms.

The Doctor was about to physically restrain Reg if that was what it took to get some answers when it dawned on him that the computer had indicated that only *one* holographic officer was located in the transporter room.

The human man vanished. The Hirogen hunter remained in place, staring coldly at Reg.

Barclay redirected his weapon to point directly at it.

"Hello, Meegan," he said.

A faint smile flickered around the hunter's lips. The Doctor suddenly realized that the hunter had a loose bag. The hunter then leapt in two short strides to the transporter padd and disappeared in a shimmer of cascading light.

Barclay moved to the control panel immediately, presumably to reverse the transport. Shaking his head in frustration, he slammed his fists down on the interface.

"Where did she go?" the Doctor asked.

"I don't know," Reg replied. "The console deleted her coordinates as soon as the transfer was complete."

"What does that mean?" the Doctor demanded.

"It means we're not done searching," Reg said grimly.

Paris wished that Kim would hurry up and seal the interdimensional rift. He knew it was a delicate procedure and one not best performed under duress, but right now he needed Harry at the top of his game.

The organic ships used by Species 8472 had populated Tom's nightmares for years after *Voyager*'s first encounter with them. The ship had just reached the borders of Borg space. Their best hope of surviving transit through Borg territory had been a small passage completely devoid of cubes. The crew soon discovered that the absence of Borg vessels was due to the fact that it was controlled by hundreds of single-pilot ships. The unique biology of Species 8472 allowed them to link their pilot to the ship and to control the ship telepathically. Their shields and weapons far outstripped *Voyager*'s and the Borg's. The Doctor had devised a nanoprobe-based warhead that infected the organic mass of the Species 8472 vessels and literally ate them alive.

It had been more than seven years since Paris had laid eyes on the vessels, but he had never forgotten the elegant sleekness of their design, a cylindrical body with a forward array of extended prongs from which concentrated energy could strike with devastating force. Several ships could converge in an attack, joining their weapons' energy beams and then focusing them into a single strike that had the ability to destroy a Borg cube in one shot.

Captain Janeway had formed an uneasy alliance with the Borg by offering to share the nanoprobe-based torpedoes. All Janeway had demanded in return for sharing this technology was safe passage. It had been an uneasy alliance. Janeway had been forced to confront the unpleasant reality that the Borg had begun the conflict. Still, *Voyager* had emerged relatively unscathed. Species 8472 had been driven back to their home in fluidic space.

A little more than a year later, *Voyager* once again encountered Species 8472. This time, Janeway's diplomatic aplomb had resulted in a peaceful resolution.

A single vessel, its forward array locked on *Voyager,* emerged from the rift. Paris found himself wondering if *Voyager*'s winning streak with Species 8472 was about to come to an end.

"Mister Kim, never mind closing the rift now," Paris said sharply. "Prepare to engage."

"Shields are up and weapons are armed," Kim replied.

"Gwyn, move us into position to defend the *Galen,*" Paris added.

"Aye, sir."

"Ensign Lasren, open a channel."

"Channel open, sir," Lasren replied as the small but deadly craft made a beeline for *Voyager.*

"Organic ship, this is Commander Tom Paris of the Federation *Starship Voyager.* We mean you no harm."

The image on the main viewscreen was replaced by a familiar face. Paris almost smiled in relief until he realized that the alien genetically altered to look like a human female didn't look happy to see him.

"*I should hope not, Commander,*" the woman replied.

"If you'd give me the chance, I'll be happy to explain," Paris offered.

"*I have been authorized to negotiate only with Captain Janeway,*" the woman said. "*Please contact her immediately.*"

Tom's shoulders slumped involuntarily.

"Captain Janeway is no longer aboard *Voyager,*" Tom replied. "She was killed in the line of duty more than a year ago."

The woman's face softened. "*I am sorry to hear that. She was a unique individual and exceedingly competent for a human.*"

"We all miss her," Tom agreed.

"*In her absence, I will speak with Commander Chakotay,*" the woman said obligingly.

Tom didn't even blink.

"I will contact him immediately," Paris replied. "A moment, please."

The woman nodded warily. "*I assume you know better than to play games with us, Commander Paris.*"

You bet I do, Tom thought.

Turning to Lasren he said softly, "Drop shields, lock on to Chakotay's signal aboard the *Galen,* and transport him directly to the bridge."

"Commander Paris," Kim interjected from tactical, in two words and five syllables communicating his forceful disapproval of the course the first officer had settled on.

"Later, Mister Kim," Paris said grimly, "assuming any of us live through this."

Paris counted every pounding beat of his heart between the moment he gave the order and the moment a confused Chakotay materialized by his side.

"Commander?" Chakotay immediately asked.

Tom didn't say a word, but simply directed Chakotay's eyes toward the main viewscreen. Tom was relieved to immediately see a wide grin break open on Chakotay's concerned face.

"Hello, Valerie," Chakotay said warmly.

Eden led the security team into the shuttlebay, her phaser at the ready. It had been a long time since she had engaged

286 ■ KIRSTEN BEYER

in a combat scenario that wasn't a simulation, but her body remembered what her mind would have preferred to forget.

She directed the eight officers with her to fan out, surrounding the shuttle in which Batiste was waiting. Then, in a loud, steady voice, she commanded the shuttle's occupant to open the aft hatch and surrender.

After a tense minute, during which she debated forcing Batiste's hand, a hiss and a clank signaled the shuttle occupant's intention to comply. The rear door of the small vessel swung gracefully up and Eden watched in horror as Admiral Batiste strode gracefully down the short ramp.

Batiste's face retained its haughty, rugged charm. But his eyes did something Eden could never remember seeing before. They *pleaded* with her. Whether it was for mercy or understanding, was hard to tell.

"You've locked out my command codes," Batiste said as he approached her position casually.

"Stop right there," she ordered.

He paused.

"If I may ask, how long have you known?"

"Not long," Eden confirmed.

"And what gave me away?"

"The Maquis encryption was laying it on a little thick, I thought," Eden replied.

"Hm."

"It might have been a little less obvious if you hadn't spent the better part of our honeymoon locked in the hotel suite analyzing Cardassian and Maquis intercepts." Cryptography had been a specialty in Willem's early years, and a hobby in his latter ones.

"And I should have realized the moment you refused

to leave the Indign system that something more than out-
rage was keeping you here."

"I did worry you might," he agreed.

"The last straw was your willingness to wait until *you*
could interrogate Chakotay and Seven."

"Really?"

"Part of me understood your concern that their old
friends weren't the best interrogators. But your willingness
to give it four or five hours before they were even questioned? You should have ordered *Voyager* to intercept them.
But you weren't in any hurry because there was nothing to
learn.

"Plus, your right eye twitches when you lie."

Batiste spread his arms wide. "Well done."

Damn you, Willem, Eden swore to herself as pain she
thought she was long past feeling welled in her chest.

This time she was the one with the power. She was going
to get answers.

"I can explain, Afsarah," Willem offered.

"Do so, quickly," she said in a voice near freezing.

Batiste cast a troubled glance at the other officers who
were still leveling their weapons in his direction, despite the
disbelief on their faces.

Eden knew what he wanted, and she was tempted to give
it to him. He clearly read her hesitation and shook his head,
almost sadly.

"Are you sure this is what you want?" he asked.

"*Now* you care about what I want?" Eden replied, aston-
ished. "I don't think so."

Batiste took a deep breath, then turned briefly back toward the interior of the shuttle. Eden's arm automatically
tensed but she was unprepared for the suddenness of his next

move. In an instant he bounded from the ramp toward her, forcing her to the deck as a high-pitched whine filled the bay. She struggled beneath him as he wrestled her weapon from her hands and once it was secured, he helped her up from the floor, pinning her arms to her sides with a strength she had never before felt from him. Eden instantly looked to her security team and saw all of them lying motionless on the floor.

"They're only stunned," he assured her.

"Let go of me!" she shouted, still struggling against his iron grip.

He did so, only to pluck her combadge from her chest and toss it to the floor.

"Listen to me," he demanded. "We don't have time for this."

Furious with herself, Eden ceased her struggle and glared at Batiste with eyes that would have immolated him on the spot were such things possible.

"I promise you, Afsarah, I had my reasons."

Eden felt her strength fleeing, replaced by shock. She tried to imagine what those reasons could possibly be, tried to remember the last time she had seen him so filled with purpose and so certain of himself. She was surprised by the memory that came immediately to mind—Willem seated in his apartment almost three years ago, arguing the necessity of sending *Voyager* back to the Delta quadrant.

But that makes no sense. Why would he fight so long and hard to bring us here, only to scuttle the mission after just a few weeks?

His eyes followed the working of her mind and a soft crease formed at the edge of his lips.

"You had to get to the Delta quadrant, to an area where subspace was destabilized by the Borg's use of transwarp to easily access fluidic space," Eden said as the truth began to coalesce in her mind. "Your command codes are the only ones that could have compromised so many of *Voyager*'s and *Galen*'s systems. You set all of this in motion and made it look like Chakotay was to blame. But if you thought the Borg were dangerous, you know they're nothing compared with Species 8472. Why antagonize them intentionally? You don't seek out conflict any more than I do. That's not your nature. You can't want another war."

"Of course not," he replied gently. "I only want to go home."

Chakotay had believed he was ready for anything. His years of service to Starfleet had taught him how quickly things could change. He was reeling from the disquieting shock of being accused of sabotage, confined, and wondering what he would have to do to convince Captain Eden that he was not responsible. Then a transporter beam had taken ahold of him.

He sensed the tension on *Voyager*'s bridge the moment he materialized. He turned to see the beautiful, aqua blue eyes and loosely upswept auburn hair of the creature he had known as Valerie Archer.

The first time they'd met, she had been his assignment. *Voyager* had discovered that Species 8472 had constructed an exact duplicate of Starfleet Headquarters. They didn't know why. As the aliens had perfected a means of genetically altering their bodies to appear human, Chakotay was able to pass among them undetected. He found that despite their obvious differences, there was much that he and Valerie shared in common, not the least of which was genuine curiosity about each other.

She had kissed him once, to test him. A bond had formed between them, and he found that it had not diminished over the years.

"*To what do we owe the pleasure of this unexpected visit?*" Valerie asked, clearly responding to his obvious warmth.

"I'm not certain," he replied sincerely. "What I can tell you is that we've been experiencing a number of technological failures. We suspect that someone onboard might be attempting to reach fluidic space, though we cannot guess why."

Confused consternation spread over Valerie's face. She closed her eyes briefly, then opened them in alarmed discovery.

"What is it?" Chakotay asked immediately.

"*I believe you have a stowaway onboard, Commander,*" Valerie replied.

"What kind of stowaway?" he asked.

"*It's surprising,*" she went on, "*because we did not detect his presence the first time we encountered your vessel.*"

"A lot has happened since then," Chakotay admitted, well aware of how greatly he was understating the case.

"*You made it home, didn't you?*" she asked, smiling in realization. "*How did you manage it?*"

"We had help," Chakotay admitted. "We actually made it back to the Alpha quadrant almost three years ago. We've returned to continue our exploration and diplomatic efforts."

"*Then this makes a great deal more sense,*" she replied.

"Not to me," he said.

Valerie paused. He knew her well enough to understand that she was struggling against her desire to trust him and distrust the Federation.

"*The last time we met, we advised you that we were able*

to construct our simulations using only information we retrieved from your databases," Valerie began.

"I remember it well."

"That was partly true."

Chakotay felt his face hardening. "Which part did you leave out?" he asked, careful to keep his tone neutral.

"Just after the Borg compromised our realm and you came to their aid, we sent agents to the Alpha quadrant for reconnaissance purposes," she said with emphasis. *"There were a number of uncharted anomalies that allowed us to create small interdimensional rifts. Those anomalies were collapsed after our agents used them to infiltrate your space. They were advised that their mission was one-way. They gathered the information we required to supplement your databases and began to assess the threat you posed. They were provided with only enough isomorphic compound to maintain their human forms for a few years. We believed that all of them had followed their orders to terminate themselves. It appears that one of those agents is now onboard your vessel."*

Chakotay always wondered at the amount of detail Species 8472 had acquired about the Federation. The possibility that one or more of their agents might still exist in the upper echelons of Starfleet was terrifying to imagine.

"I thought we agreed to stop spying on each other," Chakotay finally said, dismay clear in his voice.

"We did. And we intended to honor our side of that bargain," Valerie replied quickly. *"As I said, we believed those agents to be long dead."*

Chakotay paused. He didn't really have the authority to authorize the next logical course of action, but he wasn't sure if it was a good idea right now to make Valerie aware of that fact. Tom immediately stepped toward him and said softly,

"I think we should authorize her to transport the long-lost agent onboard her vessel."

Chakotay turned back to the viewscreen and said, "I'm not sure how best to proceed from here, but if you're willing to transport our stowaway to your vessel . . ."

"*I'm sorry, Chakotay,*" Valerie replied. "*That won't be possible.*"

"Why not?"

"*He has maintained his human form long past the time it should have been possible. His return would corrupt our realm. We will not allow it.*"

Oh, and this reunion was going so well, Chakotay thought sadly.

Eden had listened as Willem had explained to her his predicament. He had come to the Alpha quadrant years ago to spy on the Federation. He had utilized his position to gain access to the medical facilities required to extend the life and effectiveness of the isomorphic compound he'd brought with him. Once *Voyager* had returned to the Alpha quadrant, he had recognized the futility of his mission, but found suicide unacceptable. He knew that in time, Starfleet would once again set their sights on the Delta quadrant. His only goal was to accompany them and find his way back to fluidic space.

Eden had wasted too many years wondering what she had done wrong when it came to Willem. Standing in the cold, gray shuttlebay, learning that her struggle had been in vain and that the life they had been living was a lie, she was overwhelmed by regret and anger.

"Was our marriage part of your mission?"

Willem had the grace to appear stung by her words.

"Yes," he replied. "Most of my counterparts had families and often questioned my insistence that domesticity never appealed to me. I got tired of their questions, but ultimately found living constantly with a human more trouble than it was worth."

Tears welled up in Eden's eyes, but she refused to allow them to fall.

"You never loved me at all."

"I tried," Willem insisted. "I tried to accept the fact that I might never return home, and wanted to be a good companion to you. But humans are so frail and weak. Your doubts are crippling. You reject the simplest course of action in favor of endless debate and high-minded principles that reality has shown time and again are untenable. Unless you accept your place as masters of what little space you have managed to explore and colonize, you will never survive." After a short pause in which he searched her eyes for understanding, he realized that they'd been having this conversation for years, and it was unlikely they were going to resolve it. "I fear for you, Afsarah—for you and for all your people. But I cannot help you. You will succumb to the forces around you that do not share your ideals, and your precious Federation will one day be nothing more than a memory."

"The weak will perish," Eden said softly, remembering the first words ever communicated by Species 8472.

"As they should," Willem agreed.

After a moment Eden said, "You don't understand us."

Willem appeared to be taken aback.

"You didn't have to lie to get what you wanted. You didn't have to put this ship or the fleet in danger. You could have simply asked."

Willem actually chuckled. "You think I should have put it to a vote? Can you imagine what Command would have done if they'd learned what I really was? There are dark holes in the Federation that most of you refuse to acknowledge. The secrets buried and studied there would turn your blood cold. I had no intention of becoming lost in one of them."

"I mean," Eden said, swallowing hard, "you could have asked *me.*"

For the first time Eden could ever remember, Willem appeared stunned at the notion.

"I betrayed you. You would have been honor bound to betray me in return."

"Or maybe I would have found a way to help you. We may be weak, but we're also consistent," she added.

Willem eyed her warily. "Are you saying you're willing to let me go?"

"You could have stunned me along with the security team. You didn't. I think you wanted me to know the truth and you need me to let you go. I could destroy the shuttle you're about to take through that rift with one shot."

"And will you?"

"Of course not." Taking a deep breath, she said, "Now get on that shuttle and get the hell off my ship."

Willem reached for her hand but she automatically flinched, pulling it away.

"Thank you, Afsarah."

"Good-bye, Willem."

CHAPTER TWENTY-TWO

Willem was elated to learn that Afsarah wasn't going to make his final step in a journey it had taken him years to plan and bring to fruition any harder. His gratitude was appropriate. The fact that he was incapable of regretting the loss of her was something he hoped she would come to accept in time.

It wasn't that he hadn't loved her. Willem was incapable of *loving* anything. The bonds that joined his people to each other surpassed this fragile human feeling. Constant access to one another's thoughts, heightened by the connection every individual member of Species 8472 felt to their universe of fluidic space, made the distances that separated the life-forms of Afsarah's galaxy seem impassable. His time as a human had been lonelier than he had ever imagined or feared. An individual, encased in delicate flesh and bone, unable to do more than guess at another's motives or feelings, was ultimately an inferior and weak creature. The achievements of the Federation that had overcome these obvious limitations were noteworthy, and had earned Batiste's grudging respect, but he saw nothing promising in their future until the species that made up this alliance had evolved past the need to communicate with one another so clumsily.

As he still understood too little about his unexpected and undesired companion, he gave Meegan as wide a berth as possible. He reentered the shuttle, sealed the hatch behind him, and moved to the helm.

"You weren't planning to leave without me, were you, Willem?" she asked in a tone that was somewhere between mocking and flirting. "Meegan" had subdued him in his cabin and explained her intentions and the ways in which his plans, which she had discovered—*probably by violating his mind telepathically and simply taking the knowledge she required*—would correspond with hers. Since then, he had been her prisoner. Any attempt to thwart her goals would have resulted in his exposure. Providing her with a Starfleet shuttle with which to return briefly to the Indign system and, now, to make her escape seemed to Willem a small price to pay to secure her freedom and his own.

"Of course I wasn't," Willem said gruffly as he brought the shuttle's power systems online and prepared for launch. "How did you manage—"

"I was waiting in *Galen*'s transporter room and noted that she and *Voyager* simultaneously dropped their shields. I took the opportunity when I saw it."

Batiste observed in the seat next to him a soft, mesh bag filled with what appeared to be metallic canisters.

"What are those?" he demanded. If they were other captured consciousnesses, his former comrades might one day have to reckon with more than one "Meegan," and as far as he was concerned, one was one too many.

"They are none of your concern," she replied in a voice that left no room for further inquiries.

Nodding, Batiste slipped the shuttle gracefully from the shuttlebay and set course to the rift that promised peace, sanctuary, and the only existence he had ever known worth experiencing.

———

Eden was halfway across the bridge before she realized that Chakotay was standing before her chair. She pulled herself up short and was about to take Paris to task when Lasren called out, "Admiral Batiste's shuttle has cleared *Voyager*, Captain."

"Let him go," she replied.

The woman on the viewscreen was familiar. Suddenly, Eden realized why Chakotay was aboard. She approved of Tom's swift action.

Stepping between them she said, "I'm Captain Afsarah Eden. It is a pleasure to meet you. As you have chosen to assume human form for this contact, may I call you Miss Archer?"

Valerie's face expressed surprise and puzzlement as her eyes met Chakotay's. He offered a subtle nod and she turned haughtily back to address the captain.

"*You may,*" she replied.

"Captain," Kim called softly from the tactical station, "our shuttle has been captured by a tractor beam emanating from Miss Archer's vessel."

"Split the screen. Give me a visual," Eden replied.

Kim did so, and in an instant, the right half of the viewscreen showed the shuttle hanging dead in space, engulfed in a bright green web of energy. The other half retained Valerie's composed countenance.

"The shuttle you have captured contains one of your people," Eden offered. "He has gone to great lengths to return home. It is our fervent hope that you will allow him to do so."

"*As I have already explained to Chakotay, that will not be possible,*" Valerie replied.

"Why not?" Eden asked, surprised by her anger.

"*He accepted his mission long ago, knowing it was a one-way trip. His inability to accept that now is of no importance. It took us years to purge our space of the contamination brought about by Borg and Federation incursions. We will not intentionally pollute it further now for one who is unwilling to do his duty.*"

"What will you do with him?" Eden asked, fear creeping into her voice.

"*I will gladly destroy his vessel if you are not up to the task,*" Valerie replied.

"No," Chakotay interjected before Eden had the chance.

"I thought you said these were your people," Meegan said, glaring at Batiste, incensed.

"They are," he replied, his jaw set firmly.

"Then why have they trapped us in this tractor beam?" she demanded. "Shouldn't they be overjoyed at your return?"

Batiste understood the corruption his human form would bring to their realm. The perfect balance between organic and fluidic matter was essential to the health of both and it would take considerable time to be fully restored to where his presence would not affect the delicate harmony.

"I will make them understand," he assured her. "Can you take the helm?"

"Of course."

"Then do it," he said, brushing past her.

He had waited so long for what must come next, and anticipated it with such relish, it was almost anticlimactic to remove the hypo spray from the med-kit he carried with him at all times. A quick injection into the flesh of his thigh, and the isomorphic compound that had allowed him to maintain his human form was rendered inert.

With unrestrained joy he felt his uniform ripping to shreds as his true limbs were freed from years of confinement.

After a brief, disorienting moment as he steadied himself on shaking legs, he heard in his mind, for the first time in years, the sounds of home.

It was close enough to taste.

And then . . . *she* was there.

"You know this cannot be allowed. You have come all this way for nothing. Your cowardice does you no credit."

Willem could only find one word in response.

"Please," he begged.

Meegan stared in wonder at the creature Admiral Batiste had become. The "human" part of her programming, all that remained of the true Meegan McDonnell, which had become little more than an annoying gnat to be swatted down whenever it appeared, roared forth in terror at the sight. "Meegan," however, saw only the grace, the majesty, and the raw power of Species 8472.

It was beautiful to behold.

Meegan briefly considered releasing one of her fellow prisoners to this magnificent form. She dismissed the idea, uncomfortable with the thought that one of them could enjoy something she was denied by settling upon the frail hologram as her host.

Glorious as he was, she must be rid of him.

She quickly located the shuttle's hatch controls and with

only a moment's regret, activated them. The change in pressure as the hatch opened to the vacuum of space immediately sucked the creature from the shuttle. She was unaffected by the shock, or the pressure, and calmly sealed the hatch, wondering how long it would take for the organic ship to lose interest in the shuttle and turn its attention to the creature now at the mercy of open space.

It took longer than she'd hoped, almost thirty seconds, before she felt the shuttle lurch beneath her as the tractor beam dispersed.

She immediately plotted her new course and brought the shuttle's warp engines online. Meegan allowed the shuttle to drift clear of the immediate vicinity of the organic ship, primarily to avoid arousing undue suspicion. As far as anyone on *Voyager* or *Galen* knew, the shuttle was now empty. She knew she could not wait too long. Eventually they'd get around to attempting to retrieve the shuttle.

Finally, at a critical point in the conversation between the aliens and *Voyager*'s command crew, she discreetly maneuvered the shuttle beyond *Voyager*'s visual range and engaged the warp drive. Finally, she and the rest of The Eight were free.

A collective gasp sounded on the bridge as the crew watched the shuttle's hatch blow and send a singular form tumbling into space. It struggled for a few moments to right itself and once it had attained a floundering sort of equilibrium, literally began to claw its way toward the rift like a drowning man trying desperately to gain a distant shore.

"No . . . ," Eden said softly.

"It's all right," Chakotay said, trying to reassure her. "He can survive indefinitely in open space."

Eden should have remembered that. But watching Batiste struggle so pathetically made her breath come in short gasps.

"Valerie, listen to me," Chakotay said. "You spent months outside your realm doing what you thought you must for the security of your people. Obviously they welcomed you back. Why is he any different?"

Valerie was not oblivious to his plight. She quickly transferred the tractor beam from the shuttle to Batiste's form. His ungainly motion was instantly stilled, which was somehow more horrifying to witness than his earlier, flailing efforts.

"*Thousands of us returned to fluidic space at once,*" she replied. "*It was disruptive, but necessary. His form has been altered, however, for long-term exposure to your dimension. He can never be fully restored like those of us who had only been separated briefly from fluidic space.*"

"There must be a way," Chakotay insisted.

Eden turned to him, amazed that, given Willem's treatment of him, Chakotay would now take on Willem's cause as passionately as if it were his own.

"*I'm sorry, Chakotay.*"

"Valerie, you know us. You know the lengths to which we were willing to go to return home. Everything said it was impossible. Time and again we should have turned back and given up. But that's not who we are. And perhaps by sending him to live among us for so long, we have corrupted more than his physical form. It's possible we have infected him with our determination to do what we must, despite the odds, because we refuse to accept the limitations others would impose upon us."

"*I would be lying if I didn't tell you that this is one way in which our species have always been more alike than my people would ever willingly acknowledge.*"

"Are you still reading your Shaw?" Chakotay asked.

"*It's been a while,*" Valerie admitted.

"'The reasonable man adapts himself to the world; the unreasonable one persists in trying to adapt the world to himself. Therefore, all progress depends upon the unreasonable man.'"

Valerie paused.

"*Progress, eh?*"

"In its absence, it's often hard to see the point of existence, isn't it?"

Valerie nodded.

Eden had watched their exchange with her heart in her throat. She wanted to add her pleas to Chakotay's, but knew that if he could not reach Valerie, no one could.

Moments later, Willem's form was released from the tractor beam and disappeared in a cascade of glowing molecules.

"*Despite my better judgment, I have transported him aboard my ship,*" Valerie said. "*Delightful as it has been to see you again, Chakotay, we can't make a habit of this. My people are still a long way away from trusting yours. Perhaps he will bring us evidence that our fears are groundless. That alone would justify his return to us and would definitely count as progress. In the meantime, I caution you not to trouble us further. If we are to meet again, it must be by our doing. Do you understand?*"

"I do. And I am most grateful for your choices here today. Be well," Chakotay said, smiling wistfully.

The mingled sadness and regret clear on her face matched his as she terminated the connection. After a few moments, her ship reversed course and headed back into the rift, which sealed itself behind her in a blinding white flash.

For the first time in what felt like hours, Eden could once again breathe. Turning to Chakotay, her eyes glistening, she said, "Thank you."

"My pleasure, Captain," he replied.

"Captain," Lasren's voice said, cutting through the tension suspended around them, "the *Hawking* is approaching our position at high warp, along with several Indign vessels."

Eden turned abruptly toward him.

"How soon will they arrive?"

"Three minutes, Captain."

Eden glanced at Chakotay and gestured toward the empty seat to her right. "Take a seat," she said. "It looks like we're not out of the woods yet, and I could use your help."

Chakotay inclined his head in obvious surprise, and did as she requested as Paris failed to hide a smirk, moving to take his chair at her left.

Eden lowered herself between them and in a cool, commanding voice said, "Mister Kim, do we have time to retrieve our shuttle?"

"The shuttle's gone, Captain."

"*Barclay, where are you?*" Commander Glenn's voice called.

At the moment he was reconstructing transporter logs, trying to figure out where Meegan had gone. He was certain that wasn't the answer Glenn wanted to hear.

"I'll be with you in just a moment, Captain," Reg replied, too focused to remember to be nervous.

"Reg," the Doctor hissed. "What did the Indign do to Meegan? How did they alter her appearance?"

Just a few more seconds, Reg thought, as the data recompiled itself before his eyes.

"Reg?"

"There it is," he said, breathing a triumphant sigh of relief.

His next step was to open a comm channel to *Voyager*'s bridge.

"*Galen* to Lieutenant Kim."

"*Go ahead,*" Kim's strained voice replied.

"Several minutes ago Meegan transported directly to one of *Voyager*'s shuttles. Lock down your shuttlebay and send a security team to intercept her."

Kim replied, "*All our remaining shuttles are empty, Reg. One launched a few minutes ago.*"

"Well, go after it!" Reg shouted.

"*It's gone, Reg. We have a warp trail but we're about to intercept the* Hawking *and about twenty Indign vessels. We're not going anywhere right now.*"

Reg's mind whirred. "Did you record any passive scans of the shuttle once it left *Voyager*?"

"*I'm sure we did.*"

"Forward them to me at once," Reg replied.

"*Transmitting now.*"

"*All hands, this is Commander Glenn. Red Alert. Prepare to coordinate transfers of incoming wounded. Doctor, have your staff stand ready. Lieutenant Barclay, report to the bridge.*"

"Reg," the Doctor interrupted his thoughts as he studied the transmission he had just received from *Voyager*. His heart began to pound furiously when he realized that not one, but eight anomalous signals had been present aboard the shuttle when *Voyager*'s sensors lost track of it. "You've locked out all of the emergency holographic personnel. I need them brought back online at once."

"Of course," Reg replied, unable to accept the magnitude of the mistake he had just made. He rescinded his lockout authorization and barely noted the huff of frustration as the Doctor left.

They'll never understand, Barclay thought sadly. *And it's all my fault.*

With leaden feet he departed the transporter room to report to Commander Glenn. The peril in which *Galen, Voyager,* and *Hawking* now found themselves barely registered. He was now certain that whatever the Indign were about to throw at them, it could not compare with the fury he had just unleashed upon the Delta quadrant.

"Ensign Lawry?"

"Helm control has been fully restored," Lawry replied, though his voice held a tinge of uncertainty, considering what was bearing down upon all of them.

"Extrapolate probable intercept and move us clear. One-quarter impulse," Glenn ordered. "Ensign Drur, prepare to coordinate with Doctor Sharak on *Voyager* and Doctor Lamar aboard *Hawking.* Advise them that we stand ready to receive incoming wounded as necessary."

As these maneuvers were flawlessly executed, Glenn felt herself relaxing. The last few hours had been hell, wondering if she'd regain control of her ship. Now that she had, her job became a little simpler.

The fleet had rehearsed a number of combat scenarios that would make the most effective use of the *Galen's* unique abilities. Their armaments and defenses were sufficient to aid other fleet vessels, but only as a last resort. Their primary function was to remain out of the fray. Dozens of flight patterns had been created that would allow the *Galen* to execute sharp flybys. Shield frequencies were designated that would drop at five-second intervals to transport wounded.

The bridge turbolift opened, and Glenn turned to see Lieutenant Barclay enter as if in a stupor. "Lieutenant," she said firmly, "when I order you to report to the bridge, I expect to see you here as soon as possible."

"I'm . . . I'm sorry, Captain," Barclay stammered.

Clearly he was upset. Now wasn't the time to dress him down.

"Meegan is no longer aboard," he offered with obvious regret.

"Where did she go?"

"She transported to *Voyager* and departed in one of their shuttles. It's too late to track her now."

Glenn nodded. She knew what Meegan was now, a weapon set loose on the quadrant.

One disaster at a time, she told herself.

"It's likely that in the next few minutes, we're going to need to access all of our supplemental holographic personnel," Glenn said. "I'd like you to coordinate with Velth, Benoit, and the Doctor from the bridge."

"Aye, Captain." Barclay nodded curtly.

"And Reg?"

"Yes, sir?"

"Don't worry. When all this is done, we'll find Meegan."

He didn't look like he believed her, but managed a faint smile nonetheless before moving to the rear interface beside tactical controls. From here he could easily access transport protocols.

Raising her voice, Glenn said, "All right, folks. This isn't a drill. Everybody take a deep breath, and stand ready."

CHAPTER TWENTY-THREE

Cambridge stared at the sleeping form of Seven of Nine. He knew that the feelings that accompanied this lovely vision were inappropriate to the doctor-patient relationship. He promised himself that he would bury them as soon as she awoke. In the meantime, however, a little fantasizing never hurt anyone.

It had been a long time since Hugh had found a woman fascinating. He'd met many who were intelligent, attractive, and quite successful in their professional pursuits. He'd made it a habit of sharing his private time with those who were none of those things, but gifted in the only things that he required in a lover: discretion and disinterest in any long-term attachment. Frankly, he had long ago abandoned the notion that he would ever succumb to anyone's charms. He'd lost something of himself in loving once before, and found the entire process of attempting to sustain a meaningful relationship messy in the extreme. He had concluded it was not worth the effort.

And then he had met Seven.

She had been resting comfortably for the last several hours and her medical scans confirmed that she was now out of danger. He did not doubt that the moment she awoke, she would be able to share more of her amazing communication with the Neyser. What he had observed of the connection between them had clearly touched Seven deeply, though it had come at too high a cost. Hugh was not anxious to see her push herself like that again, but he couldn't decide if it was his personal or professional feelings talking.

He reached for her forehead and gently brushed away a few loose strands of hair which had pulled free. He allowed himself to imagine what this gesture might feel like if she was awake. In the midst of this he realized that her eyes were open, and meeting his in wide consternation.

"Counselor?"

Hugh immediately dropped his hand back to his side and attempted to mask what he hoped she hadn't read on his face.

"How are you feeling, Seven?" he asked softly.

Seven paused, reflecting on her physical status, and replied, "I am undamaged."

"That's only because the Doctor is a brilliant physician," Cambridge replied. "You were injured in your contact with the Neyser. It took an incredible toll on your body and we were all concerned that its effects might have caused permanent damage."

Seven sat up in a swift, fluid motion. "I did not intend to cause you alarm."

Hugh smiled, shaking his head. "That's hardly the point."

"Have we located the weapons that were stolen from the Neyser colony?" Seven asked.

"Not to my knowledge," he replied. "But that's not to say that the last several hours haven't been exciting."

"Explain."

"It now appears that our illustrious Admiral Batiste was

not human. He was apparently a member of Species 8472, genetically modified to pass as a human."

Seven's eyes widened as he continued.

"By overriding our control systems he brought *Galen* and *Voyager* to an area of Borg space filled with subspace instabilities and succeeded in opening a rift to fluidic space. After a tense but effective conversation between Species 8472 he was granted permission to return home. I observed the exchange from *Galen*'s bridge. After that, I excused myself to check on you."

Seven accepted this with her trademark stoicism. "If the crisis has passed, why are we at Red Alert?"

"Apparently the Indign aren't through with us," Cambridge replied. "Last I heard, a few dozen ships were converging on our position. Unless I am much mistaken, in the next few minutes, they will engage *Voyager* and *Hawking*."

Seven pushed herself off the bed to stand before him.

"I must return to *Voyager*."

"Why?"

"They will require my assistance."

"Seven, you've done your job. Now it's time to let everyone else do theirs."

"Conlon reports that all systems are nominal, as does *Galen*," Paris noted as the Indign armada grew closer. "We could bring the slipstream online and make a run for it."

"Too dangerous," Eden replied. "It's unclear if we've purged all systems of Batiste's sabotage."

"Your plan, Captain?" Chakotay asked.

"We'll start with diplomacy," Eden went on. "They've made no aggressive actions toward us so far. They sent a representative to make contact, frustratingly one-sided though it may have been."

"And immediately following that they sent us a Trojan Horse," Paris reminded her mirthlessly. Tom was still stunned by Chakotay's report of Seven's discoveries at the Neyser settlement and the idea that the "consciousness" had somehow been a weapon.

"We've assessed their tactical capabilities," Eden continued, unruffled, "and they don't compare with ours. They're not stupid. They know that, which is why they were willing to take the extreme measure of unleashing what they believe to be their most destructive weapon upon us."

"It's likely that when 'Meegan' didn't succeed in destroying us, they realized that the only other viable option was an all-out assault," Chakotay observed. "One mosquito is a nuisance. A swarm of them is a legitimate problem."

"We'll destroy them all if we have to," Eden replied. "But I don't want it to come to that."

Paris was comforted by her decisiveness.

"Two minutes to intercept, Captain," Kim advised.

"Ensign Lasren, open a channel to the approaching vessels," Eden ordered.

"Channel open."

"Indign vessels, this is Captain Afsarah Eden of the Federation Starship Voyager. We have honored your request to depart your system. We have no intention of troubling you further. If there is something else you require of us, please advise us and we will do whatever we can to accommodate you. There is no need to resort to armed conflict. We bear you no ill will."

In response, the Indign began to break their approach formation and move to positions to surround *Hawking* and *Voyager*. For now, they seemed content to ignore *Galen*, whose position several hundred kilometers from her sister ship's was precarious.

"Indign vessels," Eden began again, but was cut short by a crisp, monotone response.

"Return what you have stolen," the Indign demanded.

Eden's brow knitted itself into hard lines as she considered their demand.

"That's going to be a problem," she observed. Once Chakotay had briefed her, Eden had realized that Willem must have aided Meegan both in her attack on the Neyser colony and her escape. Clearly, she had stolen what the Indign were now seeking to retrieve.

"We would do so most willingly," Eden replied. "The canisters that were stolen from your fourth planet have never been in our possession. The consciousness you sent to us took possession of a member of my crew, then destroyed your colony and collected the remaining canisters. She escaped before we were able to apprehend her. We do possess her last known coordinates and heading and would gladly join with you to capture and subdue her. If you scan our vessels you will be able to assess the veracity of my words."

After a brief pause during which Paris entertained the hope that the captian might have gotten through to them, the three vessels nearest *Voyager* unleashed a salvo of phaser fire, rattling the decks.

"Shields are holding," Kim advised. "Shall I return fire?"

Tom threw a quick glance in Chakotay's direction and was met with his former captain's unperturbed eyes. He seemed more curious than concerned.

Eden shook her head, rising from her chair and stepping toward the helm. "Evasive actions only," she replied. "Indign vessels, this attack is unprovoked and unnecessary. Please disengage at once and let's work together to solve what is now our *collective* problem."

Paris watched Chakotay nod slightly in approval at her choice of adjectives.

After a moment, the three vessels that had opened fire adjusted their targeting solutions and fired as one at *Voyager*'s port nacelle. Gwyn immediately dropped the bow, offering only the mid-decks.

"Shields at ninety percent," Harry called out.

"Damn it," Eden hissed under her breath. "Ensign Lasren, are these ships unmanned drones or are there life-forms aboard?"

Paris understood the captain's reluctance. B'Elanna's shuttle was able to disable the Indign ship. *Voyager*'s weapons— even on a lower setting—would easily destroy them.

"I'm detecting hundreds of Indign cooperatives present," Lasren replied. "Approximately seventy-five cooperatives per vessel."

With obvious regret the captain turned to Kim and said, "Target the lead vessel's weapons and fire when ready."

A series of rapid, pinpoint bursts flew from *Voyager*'s phaser arrays, and multiple destructive explosions burst into bloom. The damaged vessel moved in ungainly fits and starts to clear as another cube dropped into its place.

"Indign vessels," Eden attempted again, but was cut off by an abrupt discharge from every cube in sight. The majority of their fire was concentrated upon *Voyager*, though the *Hawking* was also taking a beating.

Shaking her head, Eden ordered, "Mister Kim, arm photon torpedoes and target the vessel directly ahead. We have to get clear of the net they've thrown up around us. Gwyn, advise *Hawking*'s helm to be ready to follow our lead."

"Aye, Captain," Gwyn replied.

"Lieutenant Kim?"

"Making a hole, Captain," Harry replied and fired.

———

Seven had been willing to accept the notion that from *Galen*'s sickbay there was little she could do to assist the fleet in this battle. She had immediately commandeered the nearest data interface and rerouted *Galen*'s visual display of the battle and the comm chatter that accompanied the conflict.

Voyager and *Hawking* weaved and darted through the Indign vessels. Though they greatly outnumbered their Federation foes, clearly their prowess in battle was not on par with *Voyager*'s. Their responses were too slow and their ships, once damaged, did not recover quickly. Twice as Seven watched, *Galen* was able to dash quickly through their lines and maneuver swiftly past *Voyager* and *Hawking*, no doubt retrieving overflow wounded who were, even now, being treated by the Doctor and his staff in the triage area.

The advantage of the Indign numbers, however, could not be denied.

Part of her analyzed the battle, regularly revising her estimations of the potential for success. A calm, clear space in her mind fretted over the single communication that had originated from the Indign: *Return what you have stolen.*

The Neyser Seven had contacted was panicked that the essences contained in the canisters could be unleashed. It was further pained at having failed to protect the remaining canisters from Meegan's attack. The canisters contained the highly destructive engrammatic essences of Neyser who were deemed incapable of existing in civilized society. Seven thought back to their first communication with "Meegan." She was inclined to dismiss her story as a tale spun to placate the fleet's crew and buy herself the time required to make her escape.

One persistent memory of the meeting troubled her.

The Borg are our betters in every way. We hope one day to be worthy of their attention. Until then, we will strive to emulate and please them in all that we do.

It was possible that this statement in no way reflected the beliefs of the Indign, but the structure of Indign society. Their obvious, deliberate choice to refrain from communicating with other sentient life-forms suggested that "Meegan" was probably speaking a version of the truth. They had broken their silence only to secure the return of a weapon they could not re-create.

When the Borg had faced war with Species 8472, they had agreed to an atypical compromise because Janeway possessed a weapon that could destroy their enemy. The Indign had no way of knowing that the Borg had seen the tactical necessity of such an alliance. Seven found herself wondering if this piece of the Federation's history with the Borg might be worth sharing.

The communication between herself and the consciousness that had possessed "Meegan," as well as the individual Neyser, had been forced upon her. In the cavern she had opened herself up to the Neyser, but had not been in control of the situation.

Seven knew what she must do. Every moment she hesitated, however, the battle grew more desperate. She realized that one thing neither her human, Borg, nor Caeliar nature could countenance was succumbing to fear.

Turning to Counselor Cambridge, she said, "I believe I can assist the fleet from here."

"How?" he asked.

"I intend to speak with the Indign."

His eyebrows shot up in surprise. "What are you going to tell them?"

Seven paused for a moment before she settled on her response.

"Whatever it takes."

Cambridge inhaled sharply, but maintained his composure. "I'm not sure that's a good idea. Your last contact with the Neyser didn't go all that well."

"You would ask me to risk less than my friends to secure our safety?" Seven demanded imperiously.

Cambridge's shoulders dropped. Finally he asked, "Is there any way I can help?"

"Contact Commander Glenn and advise her of my intentions," Seven replied with a nod. "And no matter what happens, do not attempt to terminate whatever connection I may establish with the Indign."

The doubt in his eyes reflected her own trepidation, but he nodded firmly and offered her a friendly smirk. "Once more unto the breach, my dear."

Between *Voyager* and *Hawking*, eight Indign cubes had been destroyed and six disabled in the first five minutes of the battle. While this left only ten to continue their assault, *Voyager*'s shields were at thirty-six percent, significant damage was done to several decks, and there were dozens of wounded personnel.

Hawking's shields were below twenty percent and one of

her phaser arrays was fried. In his last communication, Captain Itak had direly reduced their potential odds of success to less than ten percent.

Eden was forced to agree with his assessment. It seemed her options had gone from severely limited to none. *Voyager* and *Hawking* would have to destroy every Indign vessel or be destroyed.

Eden had dreamed of years spent in peaceful exploration, unlocking mysteries barely imagined, and productive contact with dozens of unknown species. In none of her dreams had she presided over the crippling of her ship in a single battle, never mind the destruction of another race's fleet.

She cursed Willem for leaving *Voyager* vulnerable. He had compromised their systems thoroughly. She could have ordered her three vessels to engage their slipstream drives and eluded the Indign before the attack began. Unfortunately now, it was a little late.

But not necessarily for Galen.

"Eden to Itak," she called, as Gwyn executed a near flyby of a cube and Kim unleashed a barrage of phaser fire upon its weapons array.

"*Go ahead, Voyager,*" Itak's maddeningly calm voice replied.

"Are you still capable of slipstream flight?" Eden asked, attempting to match his tone.

After a short pause, Itak replied, "*Lieutenant Vorik assures me that we are.*"

"Very well. Break off your attack and regroup with *Galen*. I'm going to order Commander Glenn to engage her slipstream drive. *Hawking* should enter into the corridor *Galen* forms and rendezvous with the rest of the fleet as planned."

"Voyager *will not survive this battle alone,*" Itak offered.

"You let me worry about *Voyager*," Eden replied. "Stand by."

"*Acknowledged.*"

Eden then keyed her comm panel to hail Commander Glenn and quickly repeated the orders she had just given Captain Itak.

"*I understand, Captain,*" Glenn replied. "*However, Counselor Cambridge has just advised me that Seven of Nine is attempting to speak directly with the Indign. I don't believe we should leave the area if there's a chance she might succeed.*"

Eden looked to Chakotay. "What the hell is she doing?"

Chakotay shrugged. "I don't know. But I'll tell you this: if Seven thinks she can get through to them, I wouldn't bet against her."

Eden found herself hoping he was right.

"I can give her three more minutes. Advise Counselor Cambridge to let her know. If she doesn't get anywhere in that time, you are to coordinate your escape with *Hawking* as directed."

"*Understood. Glenn out.*"

Eden looked again at Chakotay, amazed at his resolve in the face of the odds arrayed against them. She only wished she could share some of his confidence. Wordlessly he offered her a tight smile and for just a moment, she did.

"Commander Paris?"

"Yes, Captain."

"Can we keep this up for another three minutes?"

"Let's find out." Paris smiled grimly.

———

Seven began by seating herself on the edge of the biobed and bringing the face of Irene clearly into her mind's eye. Irene was soon joined by Kathryn, Chakotay, Icheb, Naomi

Wildman, and for good measure, Commander Tuvok. Seven allowed herself to imagine strength and support radiating from each of them into her. She met the eyes of each of them, drawing upon her memories of their love and steady resolve before arraying them behind her in an ordered formation, her own imaginary battle line.

Studying the battle proceeding on the viewscreen before her, Seven selected a single Indign vessel that seemed to be holding position and allowed it to grow larger in her mind.

Finally, she took a deep breath, and disengaged her neural inhibitor.

There was a moment of confusion as she floated in blackness. Bright flashes of orange and red assaulted the periphery of her awareness but Seven ignored them, willing the Indign vessel to her consciousness.

She found herself standing in a cold, gray room surrounded by four Indign cooperatives. Seven knew she was not physically present among them, but was pleased that she had managed to come this far.

Hear me, she thought.

A tinny buzz began to suffuse her consciousness. At first it sounded like distant static, a distortion to be cleared from the signal she was attempting to transmit. As it grew louder, however, she realized it was the frequency that the various Indign species used to communicate with one another. Individual thoughts buzzed between the Neyser, Greech, and Irsk-Dulaph, all of whom were studying the battle as intently as she had. Concern, alarm, and pain wove their way through the miasma as their companion vessels suffered, and resounding cries of happiness corresponded with direct hits upon the Starfleet ships. Through it all Seven sensed the intensity of their purpose and the absolute unwillingness to accept anything less than the annihilation of their enemies.

Focusing her attention on an individual cooperative, Seven attempted to discern the particular harmony that separated it from the other cooperatives collected in the room.

Evade.

Fire.

Reconfigure shield parameters.

Adjust course.

The cooperative was commenting upon the battle, anxiously awaiting their chance to join the fray.

The simplicity of communication between the creatures reminded Seven of the Borg. The lack of extraneous description, uncolored by emotion, was cold but somehow comforting.

Hear me! Seven demanded, distorting briefly the unity of the cooperative, but not getting their attention.

Who are you?

Seven drew herself up to her full height before she realized that the question had not come from the Indign.

Standing before Seven was the half-human, half-Caeliar child Seven had confronted in Erigol.

You know who I am, Seven replied. *Now get out of my way.*

You are Annika Hansen, the girl said. *You are not wanted here.*

Perhaps not, Seven said, raising her chin defiantly. *But I am needed.*

The girl's knowing laughter broke through the buzzing of the Indign, distracting Seven's focus.

You are Annika. Nothing more. You need nothing beyond that to live peacefully among all life-forms. Be at peace, Annika. That is all we require of you.

Your requirements are irrelevant, Seven replied. *You abandoned me. You deemed me unworthy of your collective gestalt. I owe you nothing.*

The girl's face fell into unbearable sadness.

Why do you resist? It is unnecessary.

Seven bent at the knee to meet the girl's eyes.

If you truly wish to help me, she countered, *cease your interference. I am Annika, but I am also Seven of Nine. I cannot be less than that for you or anyone. I am more than you can possibly imagine or contain. Accept me as I am, and I will do the same for you.*

The girl smiled shyly, then threw herself into Seven's arms. Where she touched Seven's body, she dissolved into it.

Seven rose unsteadily to her feet. The strength tingling through her was something she had never felt before. She was once again embraced by the countless billions of the gestalt and she tasted their power, but she also felt their compassion. In a flash she remembered the last time she had stood before them and remembered with stark clarity the truth that had eluded and haunted her every moment since that time: the truth that had made the voice the Caeliar had encoded into her catoms both necessary and no longer relevant.

The moment was as fleeting. This time, as it dissipated, Seven found that she was able to keep a firm hold on all that she was.

Seven turned again to the Indign.

Focusing on one cooperative was no longer necessary. She expanded herself to include all the Indign around her and said, *I am Seven of Nine, Tertiary Adjunct of Unimatrix Zero One.*

Hundreds of voices ceased their internecine dialogues and focused a single thought upon her.

You are Borg?

I was, Seven corrected them. *I come bearing the collective wisdom of billions. Hear me.*

As the Indign hung breathless upon her next words, Seven opened her mind to them, showing them *Voyager*'s initial confrontation with the cube on which Seven had been stationed when she was assigned to act as an intermediary between the Borg and humanity. She shared with them Kathryn Janeway's unfathomable request for alliance, and the Borg's acceptance of her offer. She showed them the results of that alliance, the defeat of their mutual enemies. She showed them Janeway severing Seven from the Collective.

The Indign began to lose their cohesive quality. Each co-operative had its own questions. Soon hundreds of voices were peppering her mercilessly with individual requests for guidance and information. They stood face-to-face with their god, having tasted of the fruit of knowledge, and hungrily began grappling among themselves for the rest of the apple.

Seven had intended to use her memories as a means to convince the Indign that they should ally themselves with *Voyager* as the Borg had. Amid the chaos she realized that this would be too complicated for the Indign to accept.

Cease your hostilities against the Federation vessels, Seven ordered, cutting sharply through the chorus of frightened and shrill voices bombarding her.

Why?

Why?

Why? Why? Why?

Part of Seven hated to answer their question in the only way she knew they would understand. But she also recognized that this was probably the first of many such discussions she would inevitably have with the Indign and her only goal now was to end the fighting so that the more productive work could actually begin.

The Borg are pleased with your offerings, Seven replied. *They have sent me to assure you of this. If you would be worthy of our continued attention, you would do well to heed my words. Cease your attack and return to your homeworld. I will find you there.*

Seven knew the power of a superior voice, but the infinitely greater power of that voice's silence.

She imagined herself seated once again in the *Galen's* sickbay. As she opened her eyes to find Counselor Cambridge, the Doctor, and Commander Glenn staring at her with wide-eyed wonder, she terminated her connection with the Indign.

The Doctor immediately moved forward and began to scan her with a medical tricorder as Cambridge offered her the inhibitor.

"What did you do?" Glenn asked.

A dull throbbing in the front of Seven's skull quickly sharpened its assault until it felt as if someone were pounding upon it with a hammer.

"Have the Indign retreated?" Seven asked as the strength that had briefly sustained her limbs dissipated and her arms and legs became heavy as tritanium weights.

Glenn advised her gently. "Eden's last report just came in. They broke off the attack and set course for their system."

"And not a moment too soon." Cambridge smiled even as he studied Seven's face intently.

"What did you do?" Glenn asked again.

Seven didn't know if her reluctance to answer was the result of the many levels of physical discomfort now washing through her, or the reality that though she had succeeded, she had failed to uphold Starfleet ideals.

"I lied to them," Seven finally replied.

Glenn appeared to be puzzled, the Doctor shocked, but Cambridge nodded almost gleefully.

"Well done," he said, and smiled.

CHAPTER TWENTY-FOUR

"You did *what?*" the Doctor shouted, dropping the padd he'd been using to update Ensign Sanchez's chart with a clatter onto a tray of surgical tools.

Galen's triage center had gone from chaotic to controlled insanity over the last several hours as the wounded from *Voyager* and *Hawking* had been prioritized and treated both during and in the immediate aftermath of the battle. Doctor Sharak and Doctor Lamar had tended to as many critical patients as possible on their respective vessels, but the *Galen*'s ability to absorb the overflow had been an undeniable asset, despite the toll it had obviously taken on her medical staff, including the Doctor. Naturally the Doctor wasn't at risk of exhaustion, but that didn't mean that hours of performing continuous, high-stress procedures wouldn't make him a little more testy than usual.

Supplemental medical holograms continued to work diligently around them, cleaning up the area as they went. One was good enough to collect the instruments the Doctor had disturbed in his outburst and whisk them unobtrusively toward the medical replicator for recycling.

Barclay had waited to deliver what he knew would be troubling news about Meegan. Actually, had it been up to him, he might have waited longer. But he was due to debrief the senior fleet staff in less than half an hour and his report would contain Meegan's true nature, as well as his disconcerting conclusions. Reg couldn't bear the thought of the Doctor first hearing what he had to say in a public forum. He suddenly wished desperately for another shipwide crisis that would require his immediate attention, ending this conversation. However, the lieutenant reminded himself that what he and Doctor Zimmerman had done in creating Meegan was out of concern.

Somehow this didn't make Barclay feel any better.

"We were worried about you," Reg asserted, attempting to convey in only a few words the care they had taken in their plans.

The Doctor's scowl sharpened and his eyes glistened with brittle anger.

"*You,*" the Doctor said with emphasis, "were worried about *me*?"

"Well, both Doctor Z and I thought that . . ."

The Doctor seemed to sense the number of eyes and ears now focused upon them. Quickly and a little painfully, he grabbed Reg's forearm and directed him to an unoccupied hallway that separated the recovery area from the main sickbay.

"You didn't think!" the Doctor insisted. "If you had, you might have realized that in the years I have been active, I've had no difficulty whatsoever of engaging in normal romantic relations with a wide variety of women." He stepped back, shaking his head in disbelief. "Honestly, the two of you. Just because you're flesh and blood you think you understand my feelings, my needs, better than I do? You thought I needed your help? Reg, you can't put three words together in the presence of a woman you find attractive and your last liaison was with a woman who only bedded you to steal Starfleet secrets for the Ferengi!"

Barclay blushed at the unpleasant memory, but maintained his composure. "Doctor Z rightly pointed out . . ."

"Doctor Z? You think I need to be taking romantic advice from a man who hasn't so much as touched a member of the opposite sex since before the founding of the Federation?"

"That's not true."

"I was exaggerating for effect," the Doctor huffed. "But my point still stands."

"I realize you may not have shared our concerns," Reg said as evenly as possible. "We never doubted your ability to find and maintain lasting relationships. *You* weren't the problem. The issue at hand was a partner who could actually share a life as long and diverse as that which is ahead of you."

The Doctor softened at this.

Sensing the subtle shift, Reg continued, "Neither of us could bear the thought that one day, you were going to fall in love with a woman who would age and die while you remained essentially unchanged. How many times would that process repeat itself before you decided it was no longer worth the pain? Ultimately, you might grow less human than you've already become . . . less compassionate, less . . . *feeling*. The only solution was to create an appropriate counterpart for you. We designed Meegan in the hope that one day, she, like you, would attain sentience. She was the most extraordinary piece of engineering Doctor Z had ever conceived of. She wasn't programmed to fall in love with you. Meegan was given interests and skills that complemented yours but we both believed it would take years before nature would, hopefully, take its course."

The Doctor eyed Barclay warily. "Did she know she was a hologram?"

"Of course. But she also knew that she was a unique hologram." Reg admitted, "And her programming did not allow her, at least for now, to reveal to anyone that she was not human."

"So she had limited free will?" the Doctor said with a hint of accusation.

"We didn't want you to know," Reg admitted.

"Why not? If she was meant to be my perfect mate, why not include me in her design?"

"You would have rejected her," Reg replied flatly.

"You don't know that!"

Barclay returned the Doctor's loaded stare with one of his own.

"All right," the Doctor allowed. "I *probably* would have."

"I'm sorry this didn't work out the way we planned. Like I said, we shouldn't have had to cross this bridge for years. If Meegan hadn't been attacked . . ."

The Doctor's gaze shifted past Reg as he suddenly began to process the ramifications of Barclay and Zimmerman's foolhardy choice.

"The Indign consciousness that possessed her . . . it never left, did it?"

"No," Reg confirmed.

"So when she kissed me, that wasn't really her?"

"No."

"Why do you think she did it?"

"I have no idea," Reg admitted. "My guess is, she was

looking to cover her tracks, diverting our attention from her true plans. Or maybe she just found you irresistible."

"Sex as misdirection," the Doctor said, nodding sagely. "A tried and true tactic, I'm afraid."

"Yes," Reg agreed. "And now, that consciousness is in possession of a matrix it can alter at will with a mobile holographic emitter at its heart."

"She will live forever, in any form she chooses to take," the Doctor realized.

"And with a Starfleet shuttle at her disposal."

The Doctor paused, as the destructive potential that had unwittingly been unleashed upon the galaxy took vivid and terrifying form in his processors.

"What have we done?" the Doctor all but whispered.

"No," Reg corrected him sadly. "What have *I* done."

Barclay had already grasped the seriousness of the situation but seeing the Doctor's response as prelude to the reception he would undoubtedly get from the senior fleet staff, his worry intensified.

Lieutenant Barclay, who had thoroughly briefed Captains Eden, Itak, and Glenn about Meegan's true nature, sat stony and silent, like a condemned man waiting to learn whether his punishment was life in prison or swift, merciful death.

Eden would leave it to Glenn to mete out disciplinary measures should she deem them appropriate, but silently added Barclay's actions to the growing list of matters requiring review.

"Thank you for your report, Lieutenant," Eden said. "We will take your recommendations regarding Meegan under advisement."

Barclay nodded and Eden turned her attention to Seven.

Seven sat at Eden's right. She appeared wan and her voice was weary, yet she seemed anxious to recount what she had learned in the days since the battle with the Indign armada. Chakotay, Cambridge, Sharak, Patel, and Paris appeared as interested as Eden was to hear what Seven had to say.

"I first attempted to speak with the Indign again four days ago. My initial communication with them was difficult and subsequent efforts, more so."

"How?" Doctor Sharak inquired respectfully.

"The Indign retain their individuality, even in the co-operative state. The harmony that exists between these individual members of a cooperative is facilitated by the Neela and Imalak. A cooperative functions as one, but each cooperative maintains a singular "frequency" for communication that is distinct. Initially, I was able to address hundreds of cooperatives at one time."

"They possess no organizational hierarchy?" Patel asked.

"No," Seven replied. "Each cooperative assumes a distinct task, but there is no centralized authority that directs their efforts. Just as the members of a cooperative function as one, groups of cooperatives interact with little difficulty and are free to contribute to their society in whatever way they desire. Great emphasis is placed on maintaining the social order. Differences of opinion are quickly resolved, not by an outside party, but by their inherent desire to avoid conflict.

"Our appearance in their system was met with silence until a single cooperative expressed curiosity in studying us further in an effort to assess any threat we might pose. We were understood to be sufficiently advanced to warrant attempted destruction by the most efficient means they possessed."

"Meegan?" Eden asked.

Seven nodded. "Yes, Captain. However, given the difficulty of trying to speak with the Indign, most of what I have learned about their society and history, I was able to glean while in conversation with the Old One we first discovered in the catacombs beneath the ancient Neyser colony."

"How did she survive?" Cambridge interjected.

"The Greech were able to repair the damage. She has been moved to another colony on the fourth world and the site of the ancient city has been eradicated.

"I attempted to explain our actions to the Indign, but found the effort more disruptive than productive. When I learned that the Old One had survived, I was brought to her, and found her anxious to continue our communication.

"The Neyser have the longest life span of any Indign species. Consequently, it falls to them to retain both the cultural history of the Indign, and to transmit their knowledge through to successive generations.

"The Old One has lived for more than six hundred of our years, and is the oldest living Neyser. As such, she is accorded a certain amount of honor among all Indign, and she was tasked with the duty of protecting The Eight."

"And Meegan was one of these Eight?" Barclay asked for clarification.

"Yes. Though Meegan's description of the history of the Indign was clearly lacking in a number of important details, it was not completely fabricated. The Imalak, Irsk, and Neela were all indigenous to this system. The Greech came to the third planet longer ago than the Neyser can remember, but it is unlikely that they originated in this system.

"The Neyser originated in a system tens of thousands of light-years deeper into the Delta quadrant. Apparently, roughly five thousand years ago, they began to experiment with genetic alterations that would allow them to expand their already considerable life span."

"They wanted to live forever?" Cambridge asked.

"Apparently. The result was a group of Neyser now known as The Eight. They were effectively immortal. In time, through violent means, they ascended to the leadership among the Neyser and immediately set about expanding their territories in the most brutal ways possible. Eventually, disagreements drove The Eight to make war upon one another. This fragmentation allowed the remaining Neyser to rise up and defeat them. Because The Eight could not be killed, their engrammatic essences were separated from their bodies and contained in the canisters we were accused of stealing. A group of Neyser volunteered to take the canisters to a distant world and bury them. They made it as far as the Indign system before they crashed on the third planet."

"Once again proving that no good deed goes unpunished," Cambridge remarked.

"Counselor," Eden chided him.

"Did this Old One describe the nature of these engrammatic essences in detailed terms?" Barclay asked hopefully.

Seven said, "All I can confirm is that organic material was enhanced through genetic programming and the resulting mutation was The Eight."

"What details about the development of the Indign did Meegan refrain from sharing?" Eden asked, bringing them back on track.

"After the Neyser crashed, there was bloody and brutal conflict between the Greech and Neyser because they lacked the ability to communicate with one another. Peace was finally achieved once the Neyser realized that the Neela and

Imalak could be modified to serve their needs. Once communication was established, their conflict diminished."

"So Meegan was only interested in painting a pretty picture of the Indign's past?" Eden noted.

"She told us what we wanted to hear," Cambridge added. "And what was most likely to limit our continued interaction with the Indign."

"Where do the Borg fit in?" Patel asked.

"The Neyser had never seen the Borg until they reached this system; however, the first steps toward their cooperative existence had already been taken by then. Initially, it was the Neela and Imalak who saw the Borg's structure as an example of perfect cooperation. They transmitted to the other Indign species the necessity of pleasing the Borg in hopes that they might work together for their mutual benefit. The Borg had no interest in the Indign. Eventually, the offerings began in hope that this might change the Borg's mind."

"Unbelievable," Cambridge said, shaking his head.

"While I could not make the Indign understand the true nature of the Borg, I did explain as much as I could to the Old One. She has assured me that she will pass the information along to the Indign and will do all she can to bring an end to the offerings."

"That's good to hear," Eden said sincerely.

"The Old One was surprised to learn that the Borg were conquered by the Caeliar, and asked if there was any way to contact them. I assured her that there is not, and she seemed to accept that for now. I further assured her that we will continue to pursue Meegan and the rest of The Eight. I advised her that we accept responsibility for her actions, which included the destruction of the Old One's colony with our weapons, and that should we find them, we will see that they are returned to Neyser custody."

"If Lieutenant Barclay is right, that's going to be a pretty tall order," Paris observed.

"But still, a task worth completing," Eden added.

"The Old One did ask if there was anything the Indign could offer us to compensate us for any losses we sustained. I suggested that a small supply of benamite would be greatly appreciated. The benamite extruded as a waste product by the Irsk-Dulaph is of no intrinsic value to the Indign, and in its present form is not compatible with our systems. However, I believe that the recrystallization technology developed by Commander Torres might be adapted to convert it to crystalline form. They have provided me with transport coordinates and I would suggest we retrieve it as soon as possible."

Eden said, "I'm sure I speak for all of us when I say, thank you, Seven. I know this mission was difficult for you and you've done more toward normalizing our relations with the Indign throughout the last few days than I would have thought possible. Job very well done."

"You're welcome, Captain."

As she rose to return to her quarters for a period of required rest—ordered by the Doctor—Seven was halted by a soft, "A moment, Seven."

She turned to see Captain Eden crossing to speak with her. Counselor Cambridge moved quietly to the door to wait for her.

"I noticed that you are no longer wearing your neural inhibitor," Eden said.

"I no longer require it."

The captain perched herself on the edge of the conference table as she said, "Then I take it the voice no longer troubles you?"

Seven had not yet had enough time to confirm her suspicion that the voice would actually *never* trouble her again, but she had not used her inhibitor for days.

"Before I was able to assume the control of my catoms required to facilitate communication with the Indign, I was forced to confront the voice."

Eden's dark brow furrowed. "Do you mind telling me exactly how you managed that?"

Seven considered her words carefully before answering. "The Doctor, Chakotay, and the counselor have been working to assist me in controlling the voice. One of the tactics I employed was visualization. I found that in a relaxed, almost meditative state, I was able to interact with the voice and to diminish its power over me."

"So you've essentially learned to ignore it?" Eden asked.

"Not exactly," Seven replied. "At one point while I was reaching out to the Indign, a manifestation of the voice appeared in my mind: a little girl I have seen before."

Eden nodded solemnly for her to continue.

"I instructed the girl to allow me to complete my task and, as always, she attempted to persuade me that my actions were unnecessary. Rather than argue the point, I simply realized that she represented only one part of my nature. In accepting this, I accepted her and when I did so, I remembered something about my transformation that I had forgotten until now."

"What was that?"

Seven felt her cheeks begin to burn, though she felt no

shame in revisiting the memory now, only sadness and regret. "When the Caeliar transformed the Borg, I was invited to join the gestalt, but the final choice was mine."

Eden's posture stiffened at this rather alarming disclosure.

Seven went on. "The Caeliar represented the fulfillment of the Borg's deepest needs and the vast majority of drones would have entered the gestalt quite willingly."

Eden paused as she took this in. "You were given a choice to join the Caeliar?" she asked.

"I was."

"And you turned them down?" Eden said, clearly surprised.

"I did."

"May I ask why?"

Seven shook her head. "I cannot yet provide you with a definitive answer, as I myself do not completely understand. I do know, however, that the voice was meant to comfort me. Having accepted that, I no longer feel the same anxiety and confusion I once did. The voice has vanished because it became irrelevant."

"Do you believe you have learned all there is to know about your catoms?" Eden inquired.

"No," Seven replied. "The Doctor believes any potential use will be extremely limited because they were designed to sustain my physical systems once supplemented by nanoprobes. He has also discovered that they are powered by my own biological processes, which also limits their abilities. Using them toward any other end—communicating with the Indign, for example—is very draining. I will continue to test their limits under controlled conditions, but do not believe they will augment my current capabilities in any significant way."

"I'd say they already have, Seven," Eden said with a faint smile. "You don't give yourself nearly enough credit." The captain stood and placed a compassionate hand on Seven's shoulder. "You have done a remarkable job and you have my gratitude for that."

Seven hadn't given much thought to her future with the fleet, but the captain's words felt like a farewell. "Is it your intention, then, to return me to the Alpha quadrant?"

Eden was clearly shocked at the suggestion.

"You want to go home already?"

"Now that I understand the nature of the voice, I find I must reassess the likelihood that we will find evidence of the Caeliar in the Delta quadrant. I will, most certainly, not be able to provide you with any particular expertise in searching for them, and I am inclined to take them at their word."

"You think they're really gone?"

Seven nodded.

"And you believe that's the only reason I wanted you to join the fleet?"

Seven could not find an immediate reply.

"Wow," Eden said, disbelief plain on her face, "for an individual who has single-handedly saved herself, her friends, her ship, and from time to time, the galaxy, you measure your ability to offer meaningful contributions too cheaply. You are an asset of incalculable value, Seven. I will always welcome your services and I very much hope you will be willing to stay and continue to provide them."

Seven felt her cheeks flush again, this time with happiness.

"That would be acceptable."

Eden smiled brightly.

"Good."

Seven turned to see Counselor Cambridge staring at them both.

"This was meant to be a private conversation, Counselor," Eden said semi-seriously.

"Then you should have held it somewhere else," he tossed back. Crossing to Seven he extended his hand. "Glad you've decided to stay, Seven."

"Thank you, Counselor," Seven replied. "Your assistance has been most instructive."

"You say that like our work has come to an end," he said quizzically.

"Hasn't it?" Seven asked.

"On the contrary, our work has barely begun. I'll see you in my office, eight hundred."

"I don't understand."

"The voice may be gone, but the conditions that allowed it to create such distress within you have hardly been addressed, let alone resolved. And I'm positively dying to hear more about that little girl."

"You intend to continue our sessions to satisfy your own curiosity?" Seven asked, displeased at the thought.

"Don't be ridiculous. No one is that interesting," he insisted. "I intend to continue our sessions until I am satisfied that you have fully integrated these experiences into a more complete sense of self."

"I believe I have already made significant progress in that regard," Seven said a little defiantly.

"Did I miss the part in your service record where you achieved advanced degrees in psychology?" When Seven didn't immediately answer he continued, "As I told you several weeks ago, I can only be as helpful to you as you are willing to allow. I still do not believe that you have really made peace with the circumstances that led to your assimilation, or your subsequent transition from Borg to human. At the very least, you have to grant me this much. You were offered perfection. You turned it down and even now, you can't tell me why."

"I had my reasons," Seven stated.

"I don't doubt it," Cambridge concurred. "I think we should go looking for them together."

"I'll see you in the morning."

CHAPTER TWENTY-FIVE

"Yucky, yuck, yuck," Miral said, shoving the last of her string beans to the edge of her plate.

"Miral, you used to love string beans," B'Elanna said, finishing her last bite with a flourish to encourage the little girl. "Mmmm," she continued, overdoing her enjoyment a little just for effect. "If you want to grow up big and strong like your mommy and daddy, you have to eat your vegetables."

Miral's bottom lip poked out and she glared at B'Elanna defiantly. "Ganana," she requested as the glare transitioned to pleading.

"When you finish your string beans," B'Elanna insisted.

The little girl's eyes flashed back and forth as she considered her mother's proposal.

Tom, who had hurried to their quarters to enjoy lunch with his two favorite women, winked at B'Elanna mischievously and picked up one of Miral's unwanted beans. "Shuttlebay Miral, this is Shuttle String Bean One requesting clearance to dock." Tom held the bean high between his thumb and forefinger, bringing it in on a wobbly trajectory toward Miral's mouth. "Shuttle String Bean One," he continued, altering his voice to a higher pitch and creating fake static to blur the transmission, "the shuttlebay doors are malfunctioning. Do not approach! Repeat, do not approach!"

Miral's face broke into a delighted smile but that smile left no room to insert the bean.

"Shuttlebay Miral, we have taken heavy fire," Tom went on, allowing the bean to sputter along on its course. "We must land now. Please, Shuttlebay Miral!"

"Miral, open the bay doors!" B'Elanna encouraged her. "You don't want that shuttle to crash."

Tom brought the bean to a stop just a few inches from Miral's mouth. "Can't . . . maintain . . . position . . . all hands will be . . . lost. Please, save us . . ." he said, taking the bean into a nosedive toward Miral's chin.

Fascinated, Miral watched the bean's progress and just before it "crashed" opened her mouth wide to eat it. Once it was inside she chewed hungrily.

"Whew, that was close," Tom said. "Shuttle String Bean One is in your debt, Miral Paris."

Miral clapped her hands together and commanded, "Do it again, Daddy."

"Shuttle String Bean Two," Tom began obligingly as the door to their quarters chimed. B'Elanna planted a quick, congratulatory kiss on his cheek before crossing to the door to greet their visitor. She was surprised to see Captain Eden waiting.

"Good afternoon, Commander Torres," she said congenially. "May I come in?"

"Of course," B'Elanna replied, stepping aside.

Tom quickly came to his feet, saying, "Captain."

"Please, as you were," Eden said with a smile. She hesitated only a moment before crossing a little closer to Miral and staring at her affectionately. "Our littlest crew member appears to be fully recovered."

"She's doing very well. Thank you, Captain," Tom said.

"We were just finishing lunch, but if you'd care to join us," B'Elanna offered.

"Thank you, but no. I actually stopped by hoping to speak to you, Commander," Eden said, addressing herself to B'Elanna.

B'Elanna shot a curious glance in Tom's direction. His eyes widened as his brows collected themselves near the bridge of his nose in obvious curiosity, suggesting this visit was as mysterious to him as it was to his wife.

Pulling herself up and squaring her shoulders a bit, B'Elanna gestured for Eden to join her in their small living area. Eden selected the single chair and B'Elanna settled herself on the sofa as Tom announced that it was time to swab the shuttlebay decks and carried Miral toward their bedroom and the suite's 'fresher.

"What can I do for you, Captain?" B'Elanna asked.

"It's my understanding that several days ago, Admiral Batiste effectively restricted you from engineering."

"That's right."

"I'm officially rescinding that order."

B'Elanna smiled with relief. "Thank you, Captain."

"As I'm sure you know by now, Admiral Batiste," Eden said, clearly struggling a bit with her own troubling thoughts, "had his own agenda for this fleet which had nothing to do with our mission."

"Tom told me what happened," B'Elanna admitted. "You and the admiral were married, weren't you?"

"We divorced almost five years ago."

"Still, it was probably quite a shock," B'Elanna went on, treading carefully.

"It was. A betrayal of this magnitude is difficult to comprehend and even harder to accept. However, that's not what

I came here to discuss," Eden said, settling her face into firmer lines.

"Of course not. I didn't mean to . . ."

"I appreciate your concern, B'Elanna," Eden said kindly. "However, we have a lot of work to do," she went on. "Conlon has provided me with a report on your designs for a ben-amite recrystallization matrix. We've just received a rather large supply from the Indign and I'd like to begin processing it as soon as possible."

"I'd be happy to report to Lieutenant Conlon and provide whatever assistance I can," B'Elanna assured her, warming at the thought of once again having a meaningful task to perform for the ship's benefit.

"I'm glad to hear that. But I was actually thinking a little bigger."

"Bigger?"

"You ran your own engine room for seven years. I think your expertise will be invaluable to *Voyager* but I don't think we should define your role quite so narrowly."

"What did you have in mind, Captain?"

"Just as the fleet is commanded by a single officer, I'd like to create a position of Fleet Chief Engineer for you."

B'Elanna's jaw dropped.

"The matrix you design should be installed on every fleet vessel. Our slipstream flights are also closely coordinated and adjustments will continually have to be made fleet-wide as we perfect this means of travel. The last few weeks have shown me in no uncertain terms that Lieutenant Conlon and all of her counterparts will no doubt have their hands full. Your job will be to think on a broader scope. And all of the fleet's chief engineers would report to you in this position."

B'Elanna's mind began to spin as she contemplated the possibilities.

"I realize it's a lot to ask," Eden went on. "Obviously your daughter will also require your attention and your husband's responsibilities are also very demanding."

B'Elanna nodded slowly. She had enjoyed her time with Conlon, and yet she spent the last few days focused completely on her daughter. She had resigned herself to a quiet life. She had begun to replicate early child development materials and planned to request the Doctor's input in developing a curriculum. She had also gone through the fleet's crew manifest and found two other officers—one on board the *Quirinal* and one on the *Demeter*—who also had young children. When the fleet regrouped, B'Elanna planned to contact them to see if play dates might be arranged to begin to broaden her daughter's social horizons. Adding a full-time fleet position to these tasks was daunting, but also filled B'Elanna with an inordinate sense of purpose and pride.

The truth was, she had decided when she was pregnant with Miral that she would do whatever she must to balance her personal and professional life. She would sacrifice professionally what she must, but also knew there were creative ways to arrange Miral's schedule, and Tom's, that might make accepting this proposal possible.

"I'd like to discuss it with my husband," B'Elanna finally said.

"Of course," Eden replied. "I'll await your answer."

"Thank you so much, Captain," B'Elanna said sincerely. "The idea that you would consider this is gratifying."

"I didn't know Kathryn Janeway as well as you did," Eden said. "But I have studied her logs. I believe that journey's success was due to her ability to find unconventional solutions to complicated problems. The people she chose to fill her critical staff positions were an integral part of that success. I feel lucky to have so many of her officers serving under me now. I think it would be wrong not to take advantage of them."

"She was an extraordinary person," B'Elanna agreed. "She taught me so much. Under her command I became someone I never knew I could be. I think the only way I can ever repay her faith and generosity would be to pass those lessons along."

The captain rose and extended her hand. "As I said, talk to Tom and let me know what you decide."

B'Elanna took Eden's hand and shook it firmly. "I will," she said, but she already knew what her answer had to be.

As soon as she'd seen the captain to the door, she turned to see Tom standing in the bedroom doorway holding Miral's hand as she teetered forward. His huge smile indicated clearly that he'd overheard their exchange.

"Fleet Chief, huh?" He grinned.

"Maybe," B'Elanna said, bending her knees and opening her arms to Miral. "What do you think?"

"I think I might just be the luckiest man who has ever lived," Tom said gleefully.

"It's going to be a lot of work, and a lot of schedule juggling. You're first officer. That's not something you can drop for a scraped knee or a runny nose."

"You're right," Tom said. "But I don't think that's the question on the table."

"What is?"

"What do *you* want?" Tom asked. "Whatever it is, we'll make it happen."

B'Elanna felt a chill of delight course up her spine.

"I want to do it," B'Elanna whispered.

Tom crossed to take his wife and daughter into a warm embrace.

"Then let's do it," he said.

Chakotay was still sweating when he entered his quarters to find Counselor Cambridge standing before his replicator.

"Hello, Hugh," Chakotay greeted him cheerily. An hour of hoverball had left him feeling pleasantly refreshed. He hadn't taken the time in the last several weeks to take care of himself. But Seven seemed to be managing and the ship's current crisis had passed. The time had come to begin thinking about his future. He'd agreed to meet Hugh for lunch to discuss it, but hadn't expected to find the counselor waiting in his quarters. "Am I late?" Chakotay asked.

"No, I'm early," Cambridge replied. "I hope you don't mind that I let myself in. The medical override of security systems is such a handy little tool."

Chakotay no longer found the counselor's abrupt and condescending style as unnerving as he once had. And he still wasn't sure he knew Cambridge well enough to trust what he was sensing. Nonetheless, he couldn't shake the feeling that Hugh was a tad more surly than usual.

"I was going to grab a shower before lunch. I can meet you in the mess hall in fifteen minutes," Chakotay offered.

"Go ahead," Hugh replied as he instructed the replicator to produce a glass of synthehol scotch.

"It's a little early in the day, isn't it, Counselor?"

"It's cocktail hour somewhere," he replied as he took a generous sip.

"Something bothering you?" Chakotay asked.

"Of course not," Cambridge replied. "I'm generally unpleasant."

Chakotay couldn't argue with that, but he also no longer believed it to be true.

"I understand Seven's report went well this morning," Chakotay said, deciding to do a little fishing.

"Oh, yes," Cambridge agreed, taking a seat at Chakotay's desk and continuing to nurse his drink.

"She seems greatly improved."

"She is."

"Are you concerned about her progress? Are you worried that she's taking too much on, or maybe putting too much faith in her ability to control her catoms?"

"At the moment, I'm more worried about you," Cambridge said.

Chakotay sensed deflection more than consideration on the counselor's part but decided to play along. "I'm fine," he said sincerely.

"You're a man without a country and a job," Cambridge retorted. "Surely you've realized that by now and no amount of exercise-induced endorphins changes that fact."

"It's true that my original purpose in accompanying Seven to *Voyager* appears to have run its course," Chakotay allowed, "but I'd hardly consider that cause for concern."

"What are you going to do now?" Cambridge asked.

Chakotay shrugged. "We'll be regrouping with the fleet in a couple of days. Depending on their status, I imagine Captain Eden will dispatch a vessel back to the Alpha quadrant for wounded and personnel transfers. I'll go with them and from there . . . I really don't know."

"That's ridiculous," Cambridge said testily.

"I made my choice, Hugh," Chakotay reminded him.

"Every single person in the universe you care about is a member of this fleet."

"Not true. My sister is still in the Alpha quadrant along with a number of old friends."

Hugh gave him a withering glance.

Chakotay offered, "I have to find my own path now. It's going to be a challenge, but I'm optimistic about the possibilities."

"You're an idiot."

"What is your sage advice?" Chakotay demanded.

"If I had an answer, do you think I'd be drinking this early in the day?" Cambridge quipped. "I assumed it would be years before we'd be having this conversation."

"Captain Eden to Chakotay," Eden's voice rang out over the comm.

"Chakotay here, Captain."

"Please report to my ready room."

Chakotay hated to do so without sprucing up, but saw little choice.

"I'm on my way," he replied. Settling a firm gaze on the counselor, he went on, "I'll meet you in the mess hall when I'm done, but only if you promise to stop trying to cheer me up."

"No worries there," Cambridge assured him.

Eden stood in her ready room, staring out at the vast starscape. When she was a child and had trouble sleeping, her uncle Jobin had told her to count the stars visible from the portal over her cot on their exploratory vessel. Though she never told him, she had changed the game a little after her first few years of failing to drift off even as her count reached the mid two hundreds. Instead of counting them, she had begun to name them. By forcing herself to repeat the list over from the beginning as each new star was added, the vast list had impressed itself indelibly upon her memory. Once this task had been completed, she had begun to imagine the planets surrounding those stars and populated them with a wide variety of species pulled from Jobin's and Tallar's stories and databases, as well as a number of which she created from whole cloth. Over time this game had become less the soothing and relaxing exercise Jobin had intended to lull her to sleep, and more an endlessly fascinating mental landscape where an entire universe was ordered according to Eden's childish whims.

Instead of creating a fantasy version of her home star with loving parents and fascinating friends, she had always believed that her home lay just beyond the visible stars. It comforted her to think it was out there, and one day she would return to it. Eden hesitated to speculate about its inhabitants. Even as a child she understood disappointment. Lately, however, a tense knot of anxiety formed in the pit of her stomach whenever she thought even briefly of that unnamed place.

She was no longer a child. As her eyes drifted over the countless stars, Eden found herself wondering if it was possible that right now, she was staring at the star that warmed the planet of her birth. The thought filled her with a longing she had never before known. She had grown complacent during years of believing that she would probably never find the place where she had come from. But now that there was actually a chance, the need she had buried and assumed long-dead reasserted itself.

The captain decided that this feeling was not something she could casually indulge. As much as she had once shied away from naming her home, she now feared *wanting* it too much. She'd seen the lengths to which Willem had gone and absolutely refused to acknowledge any similar tendency in herself.

Should she dedicate herself, as Willem had, to the selfish desire to recover her lost past? Could she abandon all that she had become as a citizen of the Federation and a Starfleet officer? Circumstances might yet prove her to be as frail and despicable as her husband had been. But Eden had to believe that was her choice and not a foregone conclusion. And she would, from this day forward, sift her intentions carefully for any sign that she was treading too close to the dark path he had forged before her.

The chime at her door sounded, pulling her from these troubling waters. Straightening her shoulders, she turned and called, "Enter."

Chakotay ambled in. The gray tank top he wore beneath a loose-fitting black jacket clung to his chest, damp with perspiration, and his cheeks were still flushed with recent exertion.

"Were you in the middle of a workout?" Eden asked as she descended the two steps which led to the seating area and moved toward her desk.

"I just finished," he said with a smile.

The most puzzling about Chakotay was the ease with which he seemed to put the recent past behind him. He had offered his assistance to her and her crew at every turn, despite being met with Eden's caution and suspicion. He seemed disinclined to hold a grudge, but the captain didn't believe that if their situations were reversed, she would have found within her the ability to do the same.

Eden considered taking the seat behind her desk to put

a little professional distance between them but in an instant realized that this was part of her problem. She had been intentionally keeping him at arm's length, concerned that he had come to regain his command and if she were completely honest, worried that he was right to do so. But if there was any chance that they would be able to move beyond these last few weeks, she needed to lower her shields.

She knew it was the right course and casually settled herself in one of the two chairs which faced her desk while gesturing for Chakotay to join her in the other.

As he did so, she said, "I owe you my thanks."

"For what?"

"For speaking to Species 8472 on Willem's behalf."

Chakotay's eyes clouded over as if the memory was somehow unpleasant. This surprised Eden as at the time he had appeared to act with casual ease.

"Was it difficult for you to do so?" she asked.

"No," he assured her, shaking his head slowly. "My past experiences with the woman we call Valerie Archer were, on the whole, fascinating and productive. I believe to this day that we share much more in common with Species 8472 than they will ever willingly acknowledge. And seeing Willem struggle in open space, so desperate to reach his home . . . I felt nothing but compassion. There were days when we were first thrown into the Delta quadrant where it seemed we were floundering just as hopelessly and I would have been grateful to find aid from any friendly quarter. I didn't know for certain that I could make Valerie understand, but I didn't doubt for a moment that it was the right thing to do." After a moment he added, "But I can only imagine how painful it was for you to watch."

Meeting his eyes with as much openness as she could

muster she replied, "It was, though probably not in the way you might imagine."

"How so?"

Eden shrugged beneath the complicated emotions still unsettled within her. "He betrayed all of us, but I must admit, I took his actions a little more personally than I imagine the rest of you did."

"Of course you did," Chakotay said.

"Even though my heart felt the same compassion yours did, my head wasn't as easy to convince," Eden said. "Part of me wasn't sure he deserved our sympathy."

"I know what that's like," Chakotay agreed. "Once Seska revealed her true nature and joined the Kazon, I suffered the tortures of the damned wondering how I could have been so stupid as to believe in her. But that didn't mean I was happy to see her die, even after she assaulted me, lied to me, and left me and my crew for dead on the barren wasteland of a planet."

"And now that we know he conspired with Meegan to make his escape, I'm willing to grant him even less," Eden added.

"We'll probably never know the circumstances of that ill-fated alliance," Chakotay conceded. "But I'm inclined to believe that he might not have had much choice in the matter."

"I'll guess we'll have to ask Meegan when we find her."

"Most definitely," Chakotay agreed.

"Willem played all of us against each other to cover his tracks, and succeeded in making me believe, at least for a little while, that you were the real threat. I should have known better."

"No, you shouldn't have," Chakotay countered.

"I . . ."

"Captain, you knew him for years. You've known me almost no time at all. He'd already earned your trust. Though I'm assuming you no longer think the worst of me, I don't blame you for taking your time. All you had to go on was my word."

"And an outstanding Starfleet record and the faith of your former crew which they were quick to voice as often as doubts about your intentions were raised," Eden said.

Chakotay smiled faintly.

"That record has seen better days," Chakotay acknowledged. "And, my recent resignation probably didn't make it any easier for you to determine exactly where my loyalties lay."

Eden pulled herself forward. "Why did you resign?" she asked.

"Starfleet and I have always had a challenging relationship," he said, smiling. "It was easy to forget that serving with Kathryn. She always represented what was best in the organization—its passionate ideals, its curiosity and determination. Once we returned and she was promoted, I started to see that those were *her* attributes and I suppose I took Command's ability to settle time and again in the name of political expediency a little harder than I should have. When she died, I lost sight of those ideals completely until I remembered that being a leader was never about Starfleet for Kathryn; it was always about the people she led. I could accept Starfleet's decision to take *Voyager* from me. It was predictable. But that didn't mean I could abandon my people. Seven's circumstances were unique. To have assumed command of another vessel and left her to fend for herself was not an option. I did the only thing I could do at the time."

"Do you regret it?" Eden asked.

"Not a bit."

Eden rose from her chair and moved behind her desk to retrieve a padd. "I'm sorry to hear that," she replied enigmatically.

Chakotay stared at her, puzzled.

"We made contact with the *Esquiline* three days ago. Along with *Achilles* and *Curie,* they have successfully established our communications link to the Alpha quadrant. Using the relays they dropped, we are able to maintain contact with the Alpha quadrant and even in the deepest reaches of the Delta quadrant we should suffer nothing more than a seventy-two-hour delay."

"That's quite an accomplishment," Chakotay said, though his consternation remained clear.

"I took the opportunity to make a full report of our first mission to Admiral Montgomery, including the loss of Admiral Batiste, and have just received our new orders."

Chakotay nodded for her to continue.

"Before you left Earth to rendezvous with us, did you receive confirmation from Starfleet Command that your resignation had been accepted?"

Chakotay considered the question. "No," he finally replied.

"Why not?"

"I guess I assumed it was a mere formality, and I was a little busy at the time."

A slight smile teased Eden's lips. "It wasn't."

"Well, surely by now . . ." Chakotay began.

"At this moment Starfleet is short capable officers in all areas," Eden cut him off. Offering him the padd she continued, "I was asked to advise you that your resignation was not, in fact, accepted."

A number of emotions tumbled across Chakotay's bemused face as he scanned the padd's contents.

"In Batiste's absence, I have been given a field commission of fleet commander, though I still retain the rank of captain. That leaves *Voyager* without a captain. I have been authorized to offer you that command once again and I do so with every hope that you will reconsider your decision and accept the position." Dropping the formal tone, Eden crossed back to stand before him and he rose automatically to face her.

"You said you could never abandon your people," she continued cautiously. "I hope that's still the case because they need you on this mission. What's more, *I* need you, Captain."

Eden searched his eyes for an affirmative response as the silence between them stretched out over too many tense seconds.

CHAPTER TWENTY-SIX

Chakotay paused for a moment before entering the mess hall. He knew well what awaited him on the other side of the doors and, as always, found it difficult to imagine enjoying any celebration convened specifically in his honor.

Memories of previous parties held in this room drifted through his mind's eye, particularly those that had taken place when Kathryn had commanded *Voyager*. At the time, those celebrations had felt a little like whistling in the dark. Everyone had grown accustomed to the cloud hanging over them—their return to the Alpha quadrant was probably going to take a lot longer than any of them hoped. And as each new danger was met and conquered, as comrades were lost and new faces added, it was easy to imagine that they were making the most of the hand they had all been dealt. Neelix had been an amazing host, almost assaulting his guests with food and drinks meant to banish for a few hours the often more grim reality that awaited them when they returned to duty. But once *Voyager* had made it home and so many of her crew had scattered, it had somehow become impossible to recapture the camaraderie that had sustained them during those seven years together.

Standing just outside the range of the door's sensors, Chakotay decided that the time had come, once and for all, to put the past behind them. There was important work to be done. Though he had willingly accepted his need to leave Starfleet to do what he thought he must, part of him was grateful that he had not been forced to wander too deeply into the wilderness alone. There would most certainly be new trials to face in the coming weeks and months, but he would face them with his friends—*his family*—by his side.

The uniform he had abandoned felt a little more restrictive than he remembered. The pips gleaming on his collar seemed a little heavier than they once had. But his heart was full and his step was light as he entered the mess to find dozens of happy faces turning toward him and a raucous cheer raised along with many glasses lifted in his direction.

Tom and B'Elanna were the first to hurry toward him, their smiles beaming. He immediately extended his arms to take Miral from B'Elanna. As the child began to tug at his shiny pips Tom said, "It's good to have you back, Captain."

"Is it possible I'm holding my future captain's assistant in my arms?" Chakotay asked as he grinned at B'Elanna.

"She's yours if you want her," B'Elanna replied, "but I'm telling you now, she's more trouble than she's worth."

"*P'tak!*" Miral cried out gleefully.

"Miral!" B'Elanna shushed her in wide-eyed horror.

"Just like her mother," Chakotay teased. As Miral began to squirm and Tom relieved Chakotay of his burden whispering softly to his daughter about words we don't use around company, Chakotay said, "I understand you've decided to go back to work, Commander Torres."

B'Elanna blushed slightly as she nodded.

"I guess I'm not the only one onboard who's not really ready for retirement," she replied as Lieutenant Conlon approached their group.

She immediately extended her hand and said, "Congratulations, Captain Chakotay. I look forward to serving with you."

"As do I, Lieutenant," Chakotay replied, shaking her hand lightly. "B'Elanna has been singing your praises for weeks, as has Captain Eden."

"Thank you, sir," Conlon replied.

"He's lying about one thing," B'Elanna quickly interjected.

Conlon's face fell into curious lines as she turned to B'Elanna.

"I *never* sing," B'Elanna explained, which brought an amused chuckle from Conlon.

"With good reason," Paris added.

"Hey!" B'Elanna said, feigning offense and smacking Tom lightly on the back of his head.

"Are you still excited about having her as your fleet chief?" Tom quizzed Conlon.

"Do you think I'm dumb enough to say otherwise right now?" Conlon shot right back.

Chakotay was pleased to see their easy banter. It suggested that only after a few tumultuous weeks, the staff had begun to bond. From the corner of his eye, however, he noted Harry, standing well apart from the group and casting only quick glances in his direction.

"Excuse me, won't you?" he asked and casually wove his way through the throng toward Harry.

Chakotay found him engaged in conversation with Ensign Gwyn. The last words he heard were, ". . . telling you, you really have to try it. I'd be happy to set up the holodeck program for . . ."

"Sounds like fun," Harry tossed back without serious commitment as he turned to greet Chakotay. "Captain," he said, sounding more than a little strained.

"Ensign, would you give us a moment?" Chakotay inquired of Gwyn in a tone that clearly left no room for refusal.

"Of course, Captain," Gwyn said dutifully, and thankfully without her normal flirtatious undertones.

Once she was out of earshot, Chakotay said, "Are you all right, Harry?"

Kim immediately straightened his shoulders and replied, "Of course, sir. It's good to . . . uh . . . I mean I'm glad . . ."

"Harry, at ease," Chakotay ordered.

Harry deflated a little, though his face remained a mask of concern.

Chakotay was struck by a sense of unusual sadness. He suddenly wondered if everyone was truly as happy as he was that he was once again in command of *Voyager*.

"I know that the last several months we served together weren't my best days," Chakotay said sincerely. "And I'm probably a little late in offering my apologies directly to you. I know you suffered terribly after the battle at the Azure Nebula, and I was as relieved as anyone to hear that you pulled through. I don't know what else I can say, but if you ever want to talk about it, I'm here."

"Thank you, sir," Harry said a little more warmly.

A heavy pause hung between them. Finally Chakotay placed a hand on Kim's shoulder and added, "You've never failed in your duty to me or this ship and I want you to know how much I appreciate that and will continue to count on it in the days to come."

"Then Tom didn't tell you?" Harry asked out of the blue.

"Tell me what?"

"I'm putting in for a transfer to the *Esquiline*."

Chakotay's heart sank.

"May I ask why?"

"I'm surprised you have to," Harry replied.

"Harry, it's me," Chakotay said, searching the young man's dark eyes. "Whatever is bothering you, I'm sure we can work it out."

"After I told Captain Eden that I agreed you were most likely the one sabotaging the ship, I'm surprised you think there's anything to discuss," Kim said.

This revelation hit Chakotay like a blast of cold water to the face. "You had good reason to think so," he finally replied. "Trust isn't something I take for granted. I know it has to be earned, and I hope you'll give me the opportunity to regain yours."

"I appreciate that, sir," Kim said, obviously taken aback, "but I still think it would be best for everyone involved if I went ahead and transferred now."

Chakotay truly couldn't imagine what would have led Harry to this place. For ten years, his had been such a positive and reassuring presence on the bridge. Chakotay doubted he understood the depth of the loss Harry was asking him to contemplate.

"What does Tom say?" Chakotay asked.

"I haven't discussed it with Commander Paris," Harry replied icily.

A light went on in Chakotay's head. B'Elanna had mentioned the tension between Tom and Harry since her return, but it seemed beyond comprehension that these two old friends hadn't come to terms by now.

"Very well," Chakotay replied. "I will take it under advisement, but I'm not promising you anything right now."

"Sir?" Kim asked. It was true that Chakotay had the right to refuse the transfer, but it was usually not done except under extreme circumstances.

"We won't be meeting up with *Esquiline* for a few more days. In the meantime, I want you to give it some more thought. I don't want you to go, Harry."

"I understand, sir, but I . . ." Harry began. Under Chakotay's hard stare, however, he backtracked and finished, "Thank you, sir."

"Thank you," Chakotay replied, then turned and made a beeline toward Counselor Cambridge, who was chatting amiably with Captain Eden.

Seven and the Doctor were enjoying a fascinating conversation with Doctor Sharak. Perhaps it was his relative newness to Starfleet service, but the novelty of exploration, and the discovery of the Indign in particular, had whetted the Tamarian's appetite for more. His golden eyes were lively as the Doctor shared Seven's most recent developments and he turned them on her regularly with penetrating intensity.

The Doctor had conferred with Sharak about Seven's catoms, in hopes that together they would be able to test the limits of one another's thought processes and push each other toward new developments. Seven decided that working in conference with other experts was a skill the Doctor had not mastered until he had worked with the Federation Institute.

Sharak had taken to the research readily and was amazed at how far Seven had come. She understood his curiosity and had answered his rapid-fired questions as patiently as she could.

"Then you have resolved not to change your designation to Annika, though you do reject your Borg identity of Seven of Nine as insufficient?" Sharak asked.

"I do," Seven replied. "The truth is, neither 'Annika' nor 'Seven' is an appropriate designation, but both are equally insufficient. I am a human, who was once Borg, and now also am part Caeliar. Only time will tell which, if any, of these pieces of my heritage will prove dominant. It is my intention, however, to focus my continued efforts on exploring the area which I have always found most challenging."

"Which is that?" the Doctor asked.

"My humanity," Seven replied.

After a moment, Sharak asked, "Do you believe the Indign will be able to abandon their admiration for the Borg?"

"Initially I was horrified at the thought of any sentient beings admiring the Borg. But the Indign were not malicious. They were simply naïve. In some ways, their fascination with the Borg was more like my inappropriate adulation of the Caeliar."

"That's news to me, Seven," the Doctor noted.

"I have discussed it at some length with Counselor Cambridge, and I'm sure our future discussions will add to my insight. The Caeliar are a powerful race. However, the perfection I once attributed to them does not exist and would be, I believe, a rather boring way to spend eternity."

"Alra and Hevra and the well of Irin," Sharak said, nodding as if he understood completely.

"I beg your pardon," the Doctor said.

"Apologies," Sharak said, realizing he had lapsed into his native tongue.

As he began to explain the Tamarian reference, Seven glanced toward Counselor Cambridge, who was staring appraisingly at her. There was something so intent in the look, she was momentarily disarmed. The feeling passed quickly, however, as he returned his attention to Chakotay and Eden.

Seven felt her heart flutter in her chest. Chiding herself internally, she wondered why a simple look had the ability to elicit such a visceral response. She set the question aside. It was irrelevant to their continued working relationship and might, in fact, hinder her ongoing psychological exploration.

Peeking toward him again, however, Seven found his eyes searching for hers. Returning her full attention to Doctor Sharak, she found herself smiling faintly.

The following morning, Tom was the first to arrive on the holodeck. Captain Chakotay—he smiled every time he thought about it—had given him the next three days off. Ostensibly it was to devise a schedule to accommodate the requirements of B'Elanna's new position and Miral's needs.

B'Elanna had surprised him when they awoke by insisting that he give her an hour and then meet her in holodeck three. He assumed she was going to show him some of the rough work she had been doing on holographic educational scenarios for Miral and was looking forward to it. His heart sank appreciably when the holodeck doors slid open and Harry entered.

Harry appeared as dumbfounded as Tom was to see him there.

"I'm sorry," Harry said immediately, turning toward the door.

"Harry . . ." Tom attempted, hoping to try and bridge at

least some of the palpable distance present whenever they were in the same room anymore.

"No, I must have misheard Nancy," Harry cut him off.

"Oh," Tom said, smiling sincerely. "You've got a date with *Nancy*?"

Harry rolled his eyes. "Lieutenant Conlon and I are working out," he corrected him a little too forcefully. "Excuse me, Commander," he added for good measure. When he reached the holodeck doors, they remained shut.

"Computer, unlock the door," Harry commanded.

"*Unable to comply.*"

Tom's concern level shot up a notch and he crossed to the holodeck control panel beside the door.

"Computer, on whose authority was this door locked?" Tom demanded.

"*Overrides established by the supreme leader of the universe, the majestic and all-powerful Chaotica.*"

Harry and Tom turned to one another, their faces mirroring each other's confusion.

"Computer, Commander Thomas Paris orders you to override Chaotica's orders," Tom attempted. "Authorization epsilon beta nine six."

"*That security authorization has been disabled.*"

"I bet they still haven't got all of Admiral Batiste's encrypted files out of the system," Harry suggested, tapping the manual override on the control panel.

He was stilled in his work by a tap on his shoulder. Turning, he saw a monochromatic and inhospitable wasteland stretching over kilometers. In the distance, one of Chaotica's many castles rose on a ridgeline.

"I don't think that's it," Tom said.

"Greetings, mongrels," the unmistakable voice of Chaotica boomed all around them.

Tom scanned the desert as the winds began to pick up around him and Harry.

"There," Harry said, pointing to a train of attendants moving toward them. Soon enough Counselor Cambridge, bedecked in Chaotica's fine, flowing robes and black headpiece, appeared. The counselor was riding a huge and fierce tusked animal that resembled an elephant but probably wasn't anywhere near as docile. The creature came to rest ten meters from them and Cambridge descended from its back, stepping on the shoulders and then prostrate backs of his many armed servants.

"Welcome to the far end of the universe," Cambridge said imperiously.

"Look, Counselor," Tom said, stepping forward, "I don't know what this is . . ."

"This is our first counseling session," Cambridge replied. "For weeks your commanding officers and fellow crewmates have expressed concern about the state of your professional and personal relationship. Having reviewed your files thoroughly, I have selected the most appropriate counseling milieu based upon your respective levels of emotional maturity. This is not a simulation, gentlemen—my garish attire notwithstanding. The holodeck safeties have been turned off and you will not be allowed to leave this room until I am satisfied that you have both managed to resolve your present, petty differences."

"I . . . protest!" Harry stammered.

"You may take that up with the captain when we're done here," Cambridge replied. "You have both been cleared from *Voyager*'s duty rosters until such time as I see fit to reinstate you."

"I . . ." Harry began again.

"Forget it, Buster," Tom replied. "There's only one way out of this."

"You are correct about one thing," Cambridge interjected. "The only way out is through. You are not, however, addressing Buster Kincaid, faithful sidekick of Captain Proton, Mister Paris. For our purposes, you will not have access to any of their tools or equipment." Cambridge waved a regal hand and in an instant, Tom and Harry's uniforms were replaced with the black-and-white equivalent of rags. "You are both maggots ... unnamed slaves ... and like the rest of this world you will bow before Chaotica, or you will die."

"This unnamed slave bows before no one," Tom replied.

"Me either," Harry added.

"Excellent," Cambridge replied with a wide smile. "Then let the games begin."

Tom was momentarily blinded by a whirring of dust erupting at Cambridge's feet. As the storm gathered intensity, Chaotica's forces were concealed within it and when it began to disperse, Tom and Harry found themselves alone.

"Damn," Harry said.

"What?"

"I wish I'd eaten before I came."

Tom slapped him on the back to buck him up. "Don't worry, we'll find you something. I bet that castle is full of food."

Harry began trudging toward it wordlessly, straining with each step as the deep and shifting sands moved beneath their feet.

Tom hurried to keep pace. "You know," he began, "I can't remember the last time you and I had time for this kind of thing."

Harry merely shrugged.

"It could be fun," Tom continued, trying desperately to make the best of it.

"This isn't going to fix anything," Harry muttered. "It's stupid and pointless, just like every Captain Proton program we ever ran together."

"So now you're not even interested in having *fun*?" Tom exclaimed. "You really have changed, Harry."

"No I haven't," he countered hotly. "*You* have."

"Here we go," Tom began.

"Later," Harry said, his eyes looking past Tom's and widening in alarm.

"No, let's talk about it now," Tom insisted. "This is ridiculous. You're my best friend and I'm not going to let this go . . ."

"Later!" Harry screamed, tackling Tom to the ground as an energy bolt flew over their heads.

"What the hell was that?" Tom asked.

"I don't know," Harry said, covering his head as more pulses began to pound the sand around them.

Tom quickly assessed the situation and started to pull Harry to his feet.

"What are you—" Harry demanded.

"Run! Now!" Tom replied, breaking for a low hill of swirling sand, the only nearby cover.

Turning back, they both saw the approaching troops. They weren't human and they were heavily armed.

"I'm with you," Harry agreed.

Crying out in unison, they threw themselves over the crest of the hill.

B'Elanna was tapping her foot nervously and biting fitfully on her thumbnail when Counselor Cambridge emerged from the holodeck, smiling.

"Well?" Nancy demanded.

"Thank you both for agreeing to aid me in getting these two patients to their first session."

"Did you really turn off the safeties?" B'Elanna asked nervously.

"Even if he did, I can override that," Nancy assured her.

"Of course, I didn't," Cambridge replied, clearly offended. "I'm mad, but I'm not *mad,* if you take my meaning."

B'Elanna didn't and from the look on Nancy's face, neither did she. Of course the ridiculous flowing robes and villainous black moustache did little to instill confidence.

"How long do you think this is going to take?" B'Elanna asked.

"As long as it takes," Cambridge replied. "Now if you'll excuse me, I have a planet to destroy." With an evil and joyful "Mwa-ha-ha-ha-ha-ha," Cambridge turned on his heel, his cape swirling around him, punctuating his movement as he reentered the holodeck.

"What have we done?" Nancy asked when they were again alone.

"I don't know," B'Elanna replied. "I just hope it works."

Deep in her heart of hearts, B'Elanna suspected it would.

"Want to grab breakfast?" Nancy asked.

"Are you a fan of banana pancakes?" B'Elanna replied.

"Never tried them."

"Oh, you don't know what you've been missing."

"Really?"

Chakotay decided that the bridge's center seat was a lot more comfortable than he remembered. He knew that the bridge had been completely refitted in his absence, but he hadn't expected the upgrades to include relative luxuries.

He turned to the empty seat to his left. By now, Tom and Harry should both be well into their first counseling session. Chakotay smiled at the thought of both of them at the mercy of Cambridge. He had no doubt that soon enough they'd come to their senses. The counselor was singularly skilled at forcing people to confront their own idiocy—a fact Chakotay could attest to from personal experience.

"Captain?" Lasren asked from ops.

"Yes, Ensign?"

"*Hawking* and *Galen* report ready to depart."

"Very good." Chakotay nodded.

"If I may, sir?"

"Yes, Lasren?"

"Are Commander Paris and Lieutenant Kim unwell?"

Though Lieutenant Maplethorpe had taken Harry's place at tactical for this shift, Chakotay had refrained from assigning another officer to take Tom's place.

"Are you worried I'm going to ask you to take command of the bridge?" Chakotay asked.

"No, sir," Lasren replied, brightening at the thought.

"Both Commander Paris and Lieutenant Kim have been assigned to a special project and will not be needed on the bridge for the next several days."

"I see, sir," Lasren replied.

"Helm?" Chakotay asked, turning back to face the main viewscreen.

"Ready to engage warp engines on your order, sir," Gwyn reported.

It had already been determined that the fleet vessels would clear the area of subspace instabilities between the Indign system and the site of the former Borg transwarp hub before moving into coordinated slipstream flight.

"Captain Eden to the bridge," Chakotay called over the comm.

After a short pause, Eden replied, "*Acknowledged.*"

She exited the turbolift a few moments later and crossed immediately to Chakotay.

"Problem?" she asked.

"We're ready to rejoin the fleet, Captain," Chakotay said simply.

Eden gazed at him curiously. Moving gingerly to take the seat on his right she asked softly, "Didn't I already give you clearance to depart at your discretion?"

"You did."

"Then, what am I doing here?"

Chakotay did his best to hide a smile, though he was sure his eyes were giving him away. "I realize you're terribly busy commanding the fleet and all. I just want to make sure that while you're on *Voyager,* you don't miss any of the fun stuff."

Eden stifled a chuckle. "The *fun* stuff?"

Chakotay sat back and gazed toward the starfield adorning the viewscreen. "We're heading out again into the vast unknown," he replied. "Doesn't that sound like fun?"

Eden matched his posture, settling herself into her chair. "Now that you mention it, it really does," she replied.

"Ensign Gwyn, are you ready to see what else is out there?"

"Yes, sir."

"Bring the warp drive online," Chakotay ordered. "Set course bearing one four six mark two. Warp five."

"Planning on doing some sightseeing?" Eden asked.

"At warp five?" Chakotay asked.

Eden shrugged. "This ship does warp nine point nine without breaking a sweat."

"I remember."

"A slipstream velocity makes that look positively sub-dued."

"I remember that too."

"So?"

"We have two days until we regroup with the rest of the fleet. We could be there in minutes, but I thought the point was to explore. Our sensor readings will be more thorough if we take it a little slower."

"True," Eden agreed.

"Course laid in," Gwyn advised.

"Any objections?" Chakotay asked.

"You're the captain," Eden replied.

Damn right, Chakotay thought, smiling inwardly.

With a wink to Eden, Chakotay ordered the helm to engage.

ACKNOWLEDGMENTS

We're adding some new names to the roundup of usual suspects who help make this work possible. First among them, Margaret Clark, who assumed editing duties halfway through this process under daunting circumstances. I know that in the private sector nobody gets a medal for showing up and doing their job every day but there are times when I think it should be done anyway and this is one of them.

The second is Kevin Dilmore. There are sometimes dark days in the creation of a story when the best of us finds it hard to trust our instincts. He patiently reminded me to do just that and it helped more than he can possibly know.

This novel is the end result of a process that began years ago; a re-imagining of the *Voyager* universe. During that time, my family, friends, and fellow authors have listened patiently as I thought through these stories out loud, and provided many important insights along the way. They also demonstrated admirable patience as I distanced myself from much more pleasant activities to complete this work. They have both my apologies and my gratitude.

Special thanks to my husband, David, who continues to amaze me daily; my mother, Patricia, and my brothers Matt and Paul; to Heather, Samantha, Vanessa, Tara, Chris, Fred, Marianne, Freddie, Vivian, and Ollie Jane; to Maura;

to Lynne; to David Mack, Chris Bennett, Keith DeCandido, William Leisner, and Christie Golden.

Last and most important, however, to Marco Palmieri. He was the first to invite me to this party, and this book began under his watchful eye. His passion and creativity have inspired me and countless other authors to reach deeper and push harder than we thought we could in the name of creating meaningful and exciting Trek fiction. He has left an indelible mark upon my work and deserves every kind word that has ever been said about him. I do wonder if I am truly worthy of the faith he placed in me. I know that he gave more than most readers will ever realize to the world of *Star Trek,* and in honor of that, I dedicate this work to him and to the bright future that no doubt lies ahead of him.

ABOUT THE AUTHOR

Kirsten Beyer, in addition to *Unworthy*, is the author of its immediate predecessor, *Star Trek: Voyager—Full Circle*; the last Buffy book ever, *One Thing or Your Mother*; *Star Trek: Voyager—String Theory: Fusion*; the *Alias* APO novel *Once Lost*; and contributed the short stories "Isabo's Shirt" to the *Distant Shores* anthology and "Widow's Weeds" to the *Space Grunts* anthology.

Kirsten appeared in Los Angeles productions of *Johnson over Jordan*, *This Old Planet*, and Harold Pinter's *The Hothouse*, which the *L.A. Times* called "unmissable." She also appeared in the Geffen Playhouse's world premiere of *Quills* and has been seen on *General Hospital* and *Passions*, among others.

Kirsten has undergraduate degrees in English literature and theater arts, and a master of fine arts from UCLA. She is currently working on her first original novel.

She lives in Los Angeles with her husband, David, and their very fat cat, Owen.